Chad Fury And The Dragon Song

Doug Gorden

ISBN: 1500787655
ISBN-13: 978-1500787653

FOR MY WIFE

What can I say to the person freely and unselfishly gave her life to me? I am ever grateful for your love, prayers, companionship, faithfulness and strength.

I thank God for you, every day.
I love you.

CONTENTS

ACKNOWLEDGMENTS

First, I would like to say thank you to my wife for her assistance editing and helping me take a story that lived solely in my mind and put it into print. Her support in creating a cohesive story was invaluable.

I also need to say thank you to my good friend Corey who posed for the cover picture of this book. I need to make the following confession to his wife, "yes the only payment I agreed to was a signed copy of this book; he really does need help with his negotiating skills."

And lastly, I must say a few words about human trafficking; it is a real and a serious problem. There are voiceless children and adults in this country being bought and sold as modern-day slaves. For more information please check out the following websites.

US Department of Justice:
http://www.justice.gov/crt/about/crm/htpu.php

US Department of Homeland Security:
http://www.dhs.gov/topic/human-trafficking

US Department of Health and Human Services:
http://www.acf.hhs.gov/programs/orr/programs/anti-trafficking.

CHAPTER ONE

I know I could find a more comfortable spot to sit and talk, but I want to be here. I need to be here, on this rooftop, on this abandoned building, overlooking that tattoo parlor across the street. I must be here because this is where I died.

No, I'm not a ghost. I'm still very much flesh and blood, but the man I was died. That man fought tooth and claw to keep living. But, in the end there was no choice; death came as predictably for his life as it comes for each of us mortals.

It seems right, somehow, my talking to you, partly because you've been blamed for changing men into monsters. But we both know the truth about that. Moonlight has nothing to do with changing men into monsters; the Sisterhood is to blame for all of that. I know; I have first-hand experience. It's a long story. So, my dear Mr. Moon, let me get as comfortable as I can here on this roof top and you just keep looking down from above. I don't expect you to reply...please, just let me ramble.

Who am I? I'm glad you asked. The name's Chad, Chad Fury. I'm a twenty-seven year-old pre-med student, or at least I was when all of this started. Before college I spent a little time in the Army. I went into the Army right after high school, mostly because I didn't know what I wanted to do with my life. I figured the Army was a good place to be while I figured out just what I wanted to do with my life. When I got out, I went to Oklahoma University in Norman, Oklahoma. Like I said before, I was pre-med. It was my last semester; all I had left was one month of classes and then finals, graduation, and off to medical school. That's when everything went wrong, badly wrong.

I suppose it all really started with the decision to get a tattoo. When I was in the Army a lot of guys got tattoos for all kinds of reasons. Some got theirs when basic training was over, some when they got their deployment orders, and some just because they wanted to fit in. I decided I would get mine when I graduated college and I was on my way to making something of my life. I was about to graduate, so I determined that it was time for me to mark the occasion with my tattoo.

I had done research on local artists, visited tattoo parlors, looked at thousands of designs on the internet, and had finally chosen Bill Warrant as the man I wanted for the job.

It was two PM on a Friday afternoon when I walked into Imagine Ink to keep my appointment. And there she was, the most striking girl I could have ever pictured. I could not take my eyes off of her. Her green eyes danced and her dark brown hair hung playfully around her shoulders. Her high cheekbones made the corners of her mouth appear broad and innocent. She wore a perfect tan on flawless features. I guessed she was about twenty-five.

The green-eyed girl spoke to me before I even considered speaking to her. She asked me what I was doing, and I told her how getting a tattoo was my graduation gift to me.

The green-eyed girl asked what design I had chosen, and out of my hip pocket I pulled the picture of the dragon I had copied from the internet. I told her it was going on my left arm. She clicked her tongue a couple of times and shook her head in disapproval. She pointed out pictures of bears, wolves, tigers, and lions hanging on the wall. She told me one of those would be much better. She nagged me so much that I finally pretended to agree to the bear just so I could change the subject.

It was at that moment Bill Warrant called me back to his work area. I took off my shirt and settled into the chair. The green-eyed girl followed me in. She handed me a slip of paper with the name "Lisa", and a phone number.

"That's my cell", she said. "Call me."

Bill cleared his throat, shook his head and shot a disapproving look at Lisa. "You might want to find something else to do for a while."

Lisa slid a hand over my right shoulder and across my chest as she spoke in a sultry voice.

"We're friends, aren't we...uhm...what's your name?"

"Uhhh..." I coughed, "Chad. Chad Fury."

"Well, Chad, Chad Fury, we're good friends now."

Lisa slid her hands down both of my arms, lightly drug her fingertips across the back of my hands and squeezed my hands tight. She smiled and kissed the air just an inch from my lips.

"You will call me, tomorrow. It's Saturday, and I want to go out. You will take me out...to dinner."

Lisa turned quickly and left. Bill looked disapprovingly in her direction.

"Keep away from her", he said. "That one's trouble. Trouble like sane men run from."

I just sat there dumbfounded. I'd never been approached like that before. I had a girlfriend, a serious girlfriend. I was even planning on proposing right after graduation. But there was something about this green-eyed girl. It felt like she was deep inside my brain. It was something I could never describe; somehow she was in my head and I knew I wasn't getting her out.

Bill proceeded with the dragon design I wanted. It was four hours later when he sent me on my way with a large piece of gauze covering the work he had done.

When I got back to the dorm room I saw a note from Kevin, my roommate, sitting on the mini refrigerator between our beds. The note said he had a date. I knew that meant he might not be back until morning.

I grabbed a slice of leftover pizza from the refrigerator and plopped down on the side of my bed. I took a couple of bites, and immediately got sick to my stomach. I raced to the toilet but I didn't make it. My shirt and my pants took the full hit. I took off my shirt and pants and hung around the toilet to see if I was through emptying my digestive tract.

After a few minutes the sick feeling let up a little, and I decided a shower might make me feel better. I removed the gauze from my arm. That's when I saw it. I could have sworn the dragon's tail moved. I shook my head and blinked a couple of times while letting out a four letter word. The skin on my arm was puffy, and pink around the fresh design. I touched the dragon's tail. The skin was tender to the touch, about like a sunburn and little like a bee sting.

The shower cleared my head, and I admired the new ink under the cool, running water. The dragon wasn't moving. I stepped out of the shower to dry off. That's when I saw in the mirror that the dragon wasn't on my arm!

I looked over at my arm and just stared in wonder. The skin was pink and puffy where the dragon should be, but the ink was gone! I looked in the mirror and saw the dragon; the dragon was on my chest! It flicked its tail, shook its head, ran across my ribs, and disappeared around my back. I screamed like a little girl. I tried to look at my back, but there was nothing there. I looked at my left arm, and there it was. The dragon was moving and pawing at the air.

The room started to spin; my head felt strange, like it was full of cotton. I could barely think. I stumbled back to the bed and collapsed face down. I mean I collapsed! Everything went dark and I was immediately asleep and dreaming.

CHAPTER TWO

I had slept hard, and I had dreamed. I spent the night dreaming about dragons. I even dreamed that I was a dragon. I ran through green fields on four limbs. I snarled and sniffed and snorted. There were other dragons around me. I fought with the other dragons to win the right to lead my pack.

There were hunters in my dream; men hunting my pack and me. To save my pack I had to hunt the hunters. I destroyed every one of the men hunting my pack.

I slept until I felt something stabbing me in the shoulder blade. I heard a voice.

"Dude! Dude!"

I rolled over to see my dorm mate, Kevin, through the haze of sleep still in my eyes.

"I'm sick."

"Uh huh, well whatever you were doing last night I don't need to know about it. Just put some clothes on, man. I can't un-see this."

I got up and put on a clean pair of pants. Before I grabbed a shirt, I pointed to my left arm.

"Hey Kevin, what do you think of my new ink?"

"That's pretty cool. It's going to be a real chick magnet

as long as you keep the guns beefed up."

"Yeah, right. Whatever. I did it for me, not to get girls."

"Chad, I may be a few years younger than you, but I got this figured out already. Life is all about the three G's; gold, glory, and girls. The first two are nothing more than tools to get girls. What you have on your arm is number two, a little bit of glory. You can spend your time looking at it in the mirror, or you can let the girls see it and touch it. I know what I would do."

"Right. I know what you'd do too. The same thing you were out doing last night. I also know what people end up calling a man like you, a father."

I thought that had pretty well ended our exchange for a little while so I finished dressing and brewed a cup of coffee. While the coffee brewed I started pushing a protein bar down my throat. Suddenly a thought crossed my mind.

"Hey, Kevin, what time is it?"

"It's nearly one-thirty."

"Dear Lord! I was supposed to be at work today!"

I checked my cell phone; there were two missed calls from Mitch Andrews, my boss at Green Wholesale Distributors, where I worked part-time in the warehouse. I thought aloud, "I guess I had better call in sick while I still have a job."

One very awkward phone call later I was still employed, but just barely. Not that the job was that good, but it was at least a regular paycheck, and that was still a priority in my life.

I paced up and down the room a few times before Kevin spoke up.

"Dude, stop wearing a hole in the carpet. Turn out the lights and go somewhere or do something quiet. I need to get some sleep."

"I don't know what to do."

Kevin sat up on the side of his bed. "About what?"

"Chrissy. I need to call her and cancel our date tonight."

"Uh, OK, but why is that a problem?"

"Because, well, I have a date...I think."

"Excuse me, Chad, I lost something there. What are you talking about?"

"I met this girl at the tattoo parlor yesterday, and well, I think I have a date."

"So, you met a girl and you asked her out behind Chrissy's back."

"Not exactly..."

"She asked you out?"

"Well, no. She told me I'm taking her out, and now I don't have a choice; I have to."

"Chad. You're a freaking mess. Take your cell phone and your personal problems outside and deal with it. I honestly don't care!"

I did just that. I grabbed my phone and left. I made my second awkward call for the day. I called Lisa, and tried to cancel the date I never made.

The call was strange. I couldn't get the words out of mouth. Instead of cancelling the date I heard myself saying, "Why don't I come over now, we could get an early start and spend more time together." Lisa said yes, gave me her address, and I headed straight for my car.

The address wasn't far from the dorm and I was there in only a few minutes. I was taken back at how huge the houses in the neighborhood were. I wondered why a girl who lived in a neighborhood like this would hang out around tattoo parlors. I knew something was wrong with the whole situation. I tried to turn the car around, but I couldn't; my arms wouldn't obey me. I had to go on.

When I pulled into the driveway Lisa came out the front door and waved. Her hair and features were just like I remembered. She wore a yellow top and skin tight blue jeans with cowboy boots. I stopped the engine, got out, and walked toward her.

I made it up the walk as far as the second shrub. Something rustled in the bush next to me, then a sharp pain went through my neck. My throat grew hot and my world faded to black.

CHAPTER THREE

The first thing I remember is hearing voices. I couldn't tell what the voices were saying, but I was definitely hearing voices. I could barely force my eyes open. I remember seeing light; a very bright light. Everything was too blurry; I couldn't focus my eyes. All I could make out were brown people-shaped figures. I drifted back into unconsciousness.

When I came to again, I had more of my wits about me. I saw women in brown robes walking around and talking. I tried moving my right arm, but it only moved a few inches before it stopped abruptly. I stared at my arm and saw that I was handcuffed to a metal framed chair. I moved my left arm and found it restrained the same way. I looked down. My shirt and my shoes were missing. My ankles were chained to the chair like my wrists. I tried to move the chair, but it wouldn't budge.

I yelled out.

"Hey, let me go!"

One of the robed women turned and looked at me. It was Lisa. Lisa walked up to me, and put a finger to her lips.

"You just be still now. There's nothing you can do, and

struggling will only make it worse."

"Worse?" I shouted, "What the hell do you think you're doing to me? Let me out of here!" I jerked and strained at my bonds.

Lisa shook her head from side to side, turned away, and walked toward the only door I could see. The rest of the women followed her. I didn't count how many there were, but at least twenty or more of them paraded out the door and left me all alone.

I don't know how much time passed; it seemed like hours. I was feeling sick, probably from whatever they used to knock me out. I continued to struggle; testing my restraints against the arms of the chair. There seemed to be no way to break my bonds.

After a while the women started coming back through the door. At the front of the line was an older woman; she looked to be about seventy. She stood directly in front of me while the others formed a circle around us.

The old woman called out, "Lisa!"

Lisa left her place in the circle and stood next to the woman. She lowered her eyes and replied, "Yes, Matron."

The old woman clenched her teeth and hissed out through them, "What…is…this?" The old woman was pointing at my new tattoo.

"It is a dragon, Matron." Lisa trembled.

The Matron whispered, "We're ruined."

The old woman looked around the room and appeared to study each face for a moment. In full voice she addressed the entire group.

"The totem inscribed on the subject must represent a real animal; one of the four totems. I made that clear in the instructions I gave. Lisa, explain this to your sisters. Tell us how this happened."

"Matron, I beg your forgiveness. I thought he had settled upon the bear. As you instructed, I could not force his choice with my voice, I had to let it be his decision. I waited an entire week, and there were no others choosing one of the four animal totems. This one told me he had chosen the bear."

"We are out of time, Lisa. The Abomination has tracked us to Oklahoma City. They are close to taking us, and they will stop at nothing to get our pages of the book. Tell me, what did you do with the serum?"

"I did exactly as you instructed, Matron. I placed most of it in the ink used by the artist, and the rest I rubbed into his arms and chest."

The old woman turned her attention to me.

"Tell me son, did you dream?"

I stared into her eyes.

"Go to hell!"

The corners of the old woman's mouth turned up slightly in a partial smile.

"Well, at least you have spirit."

From somewhere within her robe she pulled out a small double edged dagger. She brought the tip of the dagger to my chest and drug it across quickly. I let out a yelp.

The old woman put the dagger away, bent down slightly and placed her hand over the fresh, bleeding cut.

"I ask you again, did you dream?"

I didn't answer her. My mind flashed through the contents of my recent dreams.

The Matron smiled.

"I see that you did dream. You dreamed of dragons."

The Matron straightened up, used her robe to wipe the blood from her hand, and addressed the group.

"Sisters. The subject has been prepared. But I put it to you, what should we do? Do we proceed with the song, or do we turn him out in hopes of another, more suitable candidate?"

A voice came from behind me, I couldn't see who was speaking.

"Matron, if I may."

The Matron nodded, and the voice continued.

"We risk very little by attempting the song. It is true that this man may not survive. It is also true that he may not transform because the totem is not a match to the serum. But we don't know what the effects of the song will be. He may become useful to us."

The Matron lowered her head and clasped her hands together beneath her chin. She was clearly thinking it over. Finally she spoke.

"Agreed. We will try. Sisters, prepare to sing the songs of each of the totems. We will begin with the song of the bear."

A voice from my right spoke up.

"Matron, if I may interrupt."

"What is it, Sister Emily?"

"We've not reset the frequencies of our transresinators. Perhaps we should do that now, before we forget."

"Very well."

The Matron reached into her robe and pulled out what looked like a two inch glass cube with silver and gold edges. She held the cube in the palm of her right hand and stretched out the index finger of her left hand over the top of the cube. When her finger rested on the cube it began glowing with a soft orange light. It pulsed like the beating of a heart.

"Ladies, are we ready?"

She looked around the room and I looked too. All of the women I could see were holding similar cubes in the same way. The cubes were all glowing the same pale orange, and pulsing, each one to its own heartbeat. The Matron seemed to be satisfied with what she saw.

"Sisters. First I will reset our pass key."

The old woman sang an unfamiliar melody and the cubes changed to all the colors of the rainbow with the Matron's changing tones.

"Now, I will change our communication frequency."

She sang again, this time it sounded more like someone practicing musical scales. The cube glowed blue, then red, and back to the soft orange.

The ladies put their cubes back into their robes as the old woman took a position directly in front of me within the circle.

"We shall begin the bear song."

The Matron moved her mouth like she was singing, but I heard no sound. Then, suddenly there was a low, bass growl coming from her mouth. Others began joining in. It was a cacophony of growls and shrieks.

After a few more seconds of this, I felt something snap in my head; it was like a chain breaking. My heart pounded in my chest, and I felt my guts twisting.

The singing, if you could call it that, became louder, and higher. My arms twisted. I felt my feet contorting. There was nothing I could do. My body was being molded and twisted and reshaped. The experience was far from pleasant. I screamed in pain, but the sounds of my screams were muffled by the inhuman sounds the women around me were making.

When the song ended, I slumped down in my chair. If it hadn't been for my restraints, I would have slid out of the chair and onto the floor. Two women pulled me back up into the chair.

The Matron called for a break, and said they would sing the song of the lion totem in ten minutes. After the room had emptied, I noticed that I had lost control of my bowels and bladder during the ordeal. I cried. I couldn't help it. I sobbed like a child, and I couldn't stop.

When the women returned, I was still sobbing, sitting in my own urine, feces, and sweat. The women seemed totally unmoved by my plight. They did bring me some water before starting, but soon they were singing again, and I was writhing and contorting like before. I made it through the second song, much like the first, but much weaker and more exhausted than the first time. I may have blacked out briefly during the third and fourth songs, but somehow I made it through.

When the fourth song finished I felt as though I were dead. I had no strength; I couldn't even lift my head. I remember hearing the old woman speaking.

"We have failed in the creation of our protector. None of the totem transformations adhered. The Abomination took Sister Alice three days ago, and now we are at risk of being taken or killed off one by one.

Presently, we are too tired to plan our next course of action. The council will convene tomorrow evening to discuss what will be done. For now, I need volunteers to return this young man. Put him in his car. Drive him back home and leave him. Good night my sisters, get some rest."

My shackles were removed and I was dragged by my wrists outside the building to my black Ford Interceptor parked in an alley. I was placed in the back seat of my car. It was dark, and I was cold. I passed out.

CHAPTER FOUR

I woke to sunlight shining in my eyes. The glare was painful. I rolled over and fell onto something hard. It was a minute or so before I realized where I was. I was in my car…somewhere. I was lying on top of my shirt and cell phone, on the floorboard of the back seat. There was an awful smell, it was me.

I opened the car door and stumbled out. I grabbed my shirt, keys, wallet, and cell phone from off of the floorboards. The disorientation lifted and I saw that I was standing in the dorm parking lot. The sun had just risen to the top of the buildings, and it was too early for hardly anyone to be outdoors. I put on my shirt and hurried toward my dorm.

As I reached the door of the dorm building, I stopped. I wondered if I should call the police. If I did call, what would I tell them? Would I tell them I had been drugged, abducted by a group of women, witches or I don't know what, and tortured for hours on end? Would they believe any of it? How much of my story did I believe?

I unbuttoned my shirt and looked down at my chest. There was a cut across the left side of my chest. I saw that my wrists were badly bruised where the handcuffs had been. My ankles ached and they were bruised too. I smelled like a sewer, and probably looked even worse.

I took my cell phone and started to dial nine-one-one. But then I realized I couldn't even tell anyone where all this had happened; I didn't know where I had been taken. I had passed out on the trip back; I couldn't even guess how far I had been driven. I knew the address of the house where I met Lisa, but that's all. And that probably wasn't even her house.

I redialed the cell phone number Lisa had given me. I swallowed hard and held the phone up to my ear. A second later I heard three ascending tones and an automated voice saying, "The number you have reached is not a working number…" I had nothing.

I went inside the dorm and slipped quietly up the stairs to the second floor and down the hall to my dorm room. I went into my room as quietly as possible. Kevin was asleep and snoring.

I crept into the bathroom. I took off my clothes and put them in the trash. They were so filthy I couldn't imagine trying to wash them. I tied the trash can liner in a knot so I could take my clothes to the trash dumpster later.

I looked at myself in the mirror. There was dried blood under my nose, at the corners of my mouth, and around my ears.

I turned on the shower and stepped inside. I never had a better feeling shower in my life. I allowed the water to beat on my face and nourish my aching skin as it ran down my body and carry the filth down the drain. I opened my mouth and drank the water streaming from the showerhead. The water was tepid, but I didn't care. I was so very thirsty that it just didn't matter. I looked at the dragon tattoo on my arm. It disgusted me.

As I turned off the water and stepped out of the shower I felt hunger and fatigue waging a war inside of me. Hunger was winning the battle.

When I exited the bathroom I saw Kevin sitting up on the edge of his bed. He yawned and spoke.

"Dude, when did you get in? I've never known you to be gone this long."

I put my arms behind my back in an effort to hide the bruises on my wrists; I hoped he wouldn't notice my ankles.

"I just got in and took a shower. It's no big deal, it's just one night."

"Chad, you're messed up. You mean two nights. This is Monday morning, not Sunday."

"Stop fooling around, Kevin; it's Sunday."

Kevin pulled out his smart phone and showed me the date on the display.

"No dude, it's Monday. Do I need to plan an intervention?"

"I'm OK. I don't want to talk. I'm going to the cafeteria; I need breakfast."

Kevin laid back down and rolled over in bed. I grabbed some clean clothes and dressed as quickly as I could.

The walk to the cafeteria did me some good. The fresh air and the sun seemed healing. I needed to be out in the open where I could see everything around me. The trees and the grass somehow seemed more secure than being inside four walls.

All of the sounds were crisp in my ears. I never remembered noticing so many little sounds like the insects and rustling leaves. I heard a dog howling in the distance. I seemed to know what it was saying. It seemed to be a male declaring his territory, stating, "I am here, this area is mine."

When I arrived at the cafeteria I could smell the food before I went inside. The pungent aroma of coffee nearly knocked me over as I swung the door open and stepped inside.

I inhaled and knew immediately what was on the buffet line; scrambled eggs, pork sausage, turkey sausage, bacon, pancakes, syrup, cereal... I stopped and wondered how I could do that. I've never been able to sort out all those smells before.

I inhaled again, and caught the scent of perfumes, cologne, perspiration, and stale cigarette smoke. With a quick scan of the room I could even tell which smell belonged to which person.

It was all just far too strange. I decided the drugs must still be in my system and I was imagining all of this.

I filled my tray from the buffet, and took a seat in the far corner with my back to the wall. I sat facing the door and tried to observe everything in the room. I ate like I hadn't eaten in days, because, well, I hadn't eaten since Saturday.

As I ate, I thought about everything that had happened to me since Friday. The more I thought about it, the less I trusted my memories. My mind had to be playing tricks on me. I must have been drugged from the very start, that's the only explanation. How else could I account for all this; the dragon tattoo moving, the strange sounds the women made, the contortions of my body while I was chained. Maybe none of it happened? Maybe the whole thing was a wild drug induced trip?

I couldn't explain the bruises on my wrists and ankles, but maybe there was a reasonable explanation for that too…if I could just come up with it. I settled that much in my mind. I made a deliberate choice to believe I had been drugged, and nothing I remembered since Friday had actually happened.

I finished breakfast and headed back toward the dorm. My Developmental Biology class would start in a couple hours. I needed my books.

On the walk back the campus was looking more like what I was used to seeing; the grounds were full of people milling about and talking on their way to somewhere.

I found myself going out of my way to stay out of people's paths. I jumped at the sound of footsteps behind me. I looked suspiciously at people headed my direction. I was studying every face for any sign of malevolence.

As I walked I thought about escape routes; which way would I run, where I could duck and hide. My heart raced as my paranoia grew. There was no way I was going to be able to sit confined in a classroom full of people today.

I kept muttering to myself, "You're OK Chad, it never happened. It wasn't real, Chad." But, I couldn't reassure myself. The pounding of my heart in my ears was telling me I had a need to protect myself, to be safe.

The compulsion was overwhelming. I thrust my right hand in my pants pocket and felt for my car keys. "Good", I muttered, and started off in a full run toward my car.

I didn't remember ever running harder. I pumped my legs against the sidewalk as hard as I could. The scenery raced past my peripheral vision.

The concrete ended and my stride changed as my feet connected with the softer earth. I raced on.

A four foot hedge stood between me and the next set of buildings. I pushed on toward it. My brain made all of the necessary calculations unconsciously, and when I reach just the right point in front of the shrubbery my muscles propelled me up and forward. My legs scissored, one in front and one behind as I sailed over the top. My trailing leg pulled forward, bent at the knee, and cleared the obstacle like a professional hurdler.

I didn't stop running. I raced around the trees standing in my path. I dodged people like they were pylons on an obstacle course. Soon, I was at my car. I stopped and thought about what I'd just done. I had just sprinted faster than I ever remembered, and I wasn't winded. That entire run felt like nothing more than a brisk walk in the park.

"OK", I said aloud, "that's not drugs. That was real. So what the freaking hell has happed to me?"

One thing I knew for certain is that I didn't want to be around people. I put the key in the door of my black Ford Interceptor.

The car had been a gift from my father when I entered college. Now that my father was gone, the car meant so much more to me than anything else I owned. That's why my heart sank so deeply when I opened the door and the smell from my last ride hit me in the face. I wasn't sure how I would ever get the stink out of my baby. Using air fresheners would be like throwing flowers on a dead cow.

I got in, started the car and rolled down all of the windows. It was only short drive to the outdoor and hunting store in Oklahoma City's Brick Town shopping center.

When I got to the store it was just opening. I went straight to the gun counter and picked out a Glock G22, .40 caliber pistol and ammo. It took longer for me to pay for it and submit the registration papers than to pick it out. The clerk wouldn't let me have the gun until the background check was completed, which took about an hour with their automated system.

When I got back in the car I took the gun out of the plastic carrying case, loaded it, and tucked it securely between my belt and my spine. I sat there for a while trying to convince myself that I felt better and safer now. But, I didn't. I still felt like I was being followed and that everyone around me was a potential enemy.

I remembered Afghanistan. The Army made me spend a year there. I was in only one fire fight that year. It shook me up a little, but I had been trained for it. Also, I wasn't alone back then. My buddies from the unit were there with me. We had each other's back. If anything happened, I knew we could count on each other.

This was different. I was alone, and I was vulnerable. I finally put my finger on it. I felt violated. Something had been taken from me, by force. Something intimate and personal had been ripped out from deep inside me, and I was different now.

What I needed was a friend. I pulled out my cell phone and found Ronnie Ferguson's number. He was my best friend in the Army. I didn't know what I would say to him, I just wanted to talk.

CHAPTER FIVE

While I was dialing my cell phone to call Ronnie, the phone rang. The display showed Chrissy's name.

"Oh, my God! I never called Chrissy!"

I took a deep breath before answering the phone.

I spoke as cheerfully as I could.

"Hi, Chrissy!"

A very disturbed voice came back through the phone.

"Chad, what's going on? You stood me up on Saturday. I called you a thousand times Saturday and all day Sunday. This morning I saw you tearing out across campus like the devil himself was after you. What's happening?"

"Chrissy, I can explain."

I had lied and I knew it. I didn't have the foggiest idea how I could even begin to explain.

"I had to go somewhere this morning, and I'm there now. Your last class is over at four today. I'll pick you up at your dorm and we'll have a nice dinner while I explain everything to you."

"I don't think I want to go to dinner with you." The words stung in my ears. "Meet me at the student union at four-thirty. We can talk there. Don't be late."

"OK, Chrissy. I'll see you there. I love…"

The call disconnected before I could finish my sentence.

At least I had some time to think of what I was going to say to Chrissy. I drove back slowly. I wandered through the neighborhoods and meandered around the city streets while I thought. I went over the events of the last few days aloud, trying to see what sounded reasonable.

"While I was getting my tattoo, I was drugged…"

How could I have been drugged? I didn't have anything to eat or drink there; was there really something in the ink?

"I met this girl at the tattoo parlor and she told me to take her out…"

I could imagine how well that will go over.

"I was injected with something in my neck. I was abducted by a bunch of women and tortured…"

Who in their right mind would believe any of this? And, how could I tell Chrissy I was meeting another woman for a date when it happened?

"I was sick."

OK, I think I can say that. That's OK, but what do I say next? I hallucinated being abducted?

The bruises. I'll show her the bruises on my wrists and the cut on my chest. I'll start with that. That's something tangible, something that she can't argue against. I was chained up. But do I even really believe all of it?

Before I had my story sorted out I was parked in my usual spot near the dorm. I got out of the car, looked at my watch, and started toward the student union. It was a good five minute walk, and I took advantage of the time to continue to work on my story.

About half way there I felt something rub against my low back. I reached my hand behind me and felt the gun. I panicked. Guns aren't allowed on campus! If I get seen with this I could spend time in jail as well as be expelled!

I adjusted my shirt and continued on, just hoping that the shirt wouldn't gap open.

Chrissy was standing just inside the doors of the

student union. I said "Hello", she returned a very terse "Hello". We took a seat at a free table near the center of the room.

Chrissy looked at me and spoke in measured tones.

"OK, Chad, tell me what's going on. Why did you stand me up, and why did you not call me all weekend? I talked to your roommate, and Kevin said you were out from Saturday afternoon until this morning."

"Chrissy, I love you. You know I do."

Chrissy looked away, took in a deep breath and let it out slowly. She turned back and looked me in the eyes.

"Chad, *darling*."

That was the most sarcastic 'darling' I'd ever heard.

"Let's save talking about how we feel about each other until later. For the moment, let's focus on you. What happened this weekend, and what could have possibly prevented you from calling me?"

"Chrissy."

I swallowed and decided to start with the bruises. While looking her directly in the eyes, I stuck my right arm out in front of her and pulled back the shirt cuff.

"This is why. Take a look at my wrist."

"What about your wrist?"

Chrissy looked briefly at my arm. Her expression never changed.

"The bruises. My wrists are bruised because I was in handcuffs. My legs are bruised too from being chained. I was chained to a chair in some kind of warehouse all weekend."

"Your wrist looks fine to me. Try again."

I looked at my right arm. It was fine. No, marks, no bruises. I checked my left arm, there was a faint red mark near my watch band, but that could have been caused by anything. I pushed my chair away from the table and looked at my legs; they were fine too.

I blurted out, "My chest. They cut my chest!" I unbuttoned the top buttons on my shirt only to reveal normal undamaged skin.

"Please, Chad. Get on with it. I don't want to play games with you."

"No, please. I was handcuffed and chained…"

"By who?" Chrissy interrupted.

"No, it's the truth. I was drugged and I woke up in a warehouse, chained, and surrounded by twenty or more women."

"Well, that must have been *real fun* for you, every man's fantasy…"

"No, it wasn't like that!"

"Just what *was* it like? Do I really want to hear this?"

"They tortured me."

"How? They beat you and cut you and left those invisible bruises and scars?"

"No, they sang. Well, they called it singing. It was more like howling and screeching."

Chrissy stood up.

"Chad, don't call me. Don't call me ever again. You go do whatever it is that you feel you need to do with your life, but do it without me. One piece of advice, though. Get some help. You need professional help!"

I stood up, leaned over, and placed my palms flat on the table top. That's when it happened. My shirt hiked up in the back and gapped open to reveal my new gun.

Before I could implore Chrissy to stay and listen, a female voice shouted from behind me, "GUN!! GUN!! He's got a GUN!!"

Instinctively I straightened up and turned toward the exit. There were already three men I recognized from the football team standing between me and the door.

Out of the corner of my eye I saw a member of OU's finest, the campus police, headed in my direction. I raised my hands as the officer yelled "Freeze!" I felt an overwhelming need for profanity, so I used some.

First came the pat down, and then my arms were pulled behind my back for the application of the silver bracelets. I heard the man say, "You're under arrest for possession of a firearm on State property. You have the right to remain silent…"

Following the reciting of the Miranda rights, the officer made a call on his radio. Based on what I overheard of the conversation, I learned that a car was being brought around for me, and I would soon be taken to the campus police office for questioning.

The room was now filled with the buzzing of conversations and the artificial shutter clicks made by cell phone cameras. All I could think about was how frightening my future appeared. I didn't know how to survive being in jail, and jail seemed to be definitely looming on the horizon.

A campus patrol car arrived pretty quickly. I was led out of the building and maneuvered into the back seat of the car with the officer's palm on the top of my head and a firm grip on my left shoulder.

I was struck by how uncomfortable it is to sit in a car seat with your hands cuffed behind you. I started to ask if the cuffs could be loosened, but then thought it was better if I didn't ask.

From where I was sitting I saw another officer enter the student union. He was probably there to take statements and talk to everyone who was willing to put their two-cents in. And, I was certain he would be talking to Chrissy.

I couldn't imagine what Chrissy would tell the officer. All I had been able to tell her were bits and pieces of a wild sounding tale. There was no telling what story would sound like after she got through retelling it.

We took a very slow ride to the campus police office. I was escorted into the building and into what looked like a makeshift conference room. The room was just big enough for a small table and four chairs.

There were two other men already in the room. The officer who brought me in removed the handcuffs. A large black haired man seated near the door introduced himself and invited me to take a seat on the opposite side of the table.

"I'm Officer Farley. You've met Officer Grant, and this is Officer Turley."

My words hung in my throat. All I could do was nod as I took a seat in a metal folding chair. Officer Grant left the room and closed the door. I felt like a caged animal. I wanted to leave so badly that I sat there with my feet pointed toward the door.

Officer Farley shifted in his chair before speaking again.

"I'm told your name is Chad?"

"Yes sir."

"Chad, we need to understand what's going on here. Why did bring a loaded gun into the student union?"

My mind was racing, and my heart was pounding. I didn't have enough of my wits about me to know how to answer questions put to me.

"I was scared, sir."

"Scared? Scared of what, or who?"

"That's really difficult to say, I'm not sure."

"You don't know what you're afraid of?"

A drop of sweat ran down the end of my nose and I nervously brushed it away.

"I was in a bad situation over the weekend, there were some people who tried to…"

My voice trailed off. I wanted to explain, I just didn't know how.

"Do you want to tell me about it?"

"I can't. I wish I could."

"It's OK. You're safe here, we might be able to help. Go ahead and try. Tell us about the people. What did they try to do?"

"I don't know. They tried to…I don't know what they tried to do. They tried to…"

The words caught in my throat. I was wondering if I

had imagined the whole thing. The bruises were gone, if they were ever really there. I had the tattoo on my arm, but that didn't prove anything, not even to me. It wasn't just these officers who needed an explanation, I needed one too.

I sat there in silence, unable to get a handle on any words. My face grew hot, and the pit of my stomach turned sour. My legs and arms felt like lead. I couldn't move with the weight of what was happening. I sat there, quietly looking at the floor until I heard Officer Farley speaking again.

"Chad. We have another problem. Officer Turley can explain."

Officer Farley turned to the blonde man sitting quietly next to the wall.

Officer Turley spoke.

"Chad, I'm going to show you some emails that I've printed. I want to know what you can tell us about them."

I had not noticed the sheets of paper laying face-down on the table. Officer Turley turned them face-up and pushed them my direction. I picked up the first page. My right hand was trembling and the page shook so much my eyes couldn't focus on the words. I laid the page on the table so I could read it.

I didn't recognize anything there. The text was one long, run-on sentence. The email mentioned holy wars, threats of blowing up buildings, and shooting people.

I put that page aside and looked at the other pages. They were very much like the first one I had read. I looked at Officer Turley and then Officer Farley.

"I've never seen these before."

Officer Turley spoke up.

"There's been some strange activity over the weekend. Someone placed several backpacks in trash cans around the campus. The backpacks were all stuffed with newspaper. Do you know anything about that?"

"No sir, I don't."

"Chad, do you live here, on campus, in the dorms or in a frat house?"

"Yes sir, in the dorms…in Johnson Tower."

"And your roommate is…"

"Kevin Kemp."

"And if we ask Kevin what you were doing this weekend, will he know?"

"No sir."

"Why is that?"

"I wasn't at the dorm most of the weekend."

"Where were you?"

"I can't say."

"You can't or won't?"

"I can't. I don't really know. I was in a warehouse, I think…"

I stopped talking at that point. I began to realize just how deep of a hole I was digging. From Saturday afternoon until Monday morning I didn't have a clue where I was. Any description of what I remembered, or thought I remembered, only made me sound like I was crazy.

Officer Farley took over the conversation.

"Chad, there's too much here that you can't seem to explain. I think it's best if we let some other people talk to you. I'm putting a call into the Sherriff's office."

I don't know how much time passed after that. It could have been more than an hour before the Sherriff's deputy came and put me in one of their cars to take me to the county jail.

I don't think I moved during the entire ride. I just stared at the scenery passing by. I wondered how much of my life was going to be like this. From this point on, just how much was I going to be able to choose what I would do versus having to do what I was told?

My life as I knew it was over. My heart sank even deeper when I realized that eventually I would have to face my mother. At least dad never lived to see this, but mom, how was mom going to take this?

CHAPTER SIX

Processing and booking at the Cleveland County Jail isn't nearly as entertaining as it may sound. I was placed in a room with dirty white walls. Five plastic chairs were lined up against one wall. I still had on the handcuffs; I guess no one but me saw any need to remove them.

I took note of a black plastic bubble in the center of the ceiling. It was obviously hiding the position of a camera. I decided right then and there that I needed to act like my every move and every sound was being recorded.

I sat alone in the room for what seemed like thirty or forty minutes before a deputy came in with a clipboard and a set of bathroom scales. I was instructed to stand on the scales. He said, "one ninety-seven" as he wrote on the paper. He wrote down a few other descriptions like blue eyes, brown hair, and Caucasian.

The deputy then told me to stand with my back against the wall where a tape measure was glued in place. Another officer came in with a digital camera and snapped my picture, I guess to show I was being properly measured. The officer with the clip board wrote "six feet" on the form.

The two officers pulled a couple of plastic chairs out to

the center of the room, and told me to sit back down near the wall where I had been. The officer with the clipboard began reading the form.

"Full name?"

I thought about not answering, but decided that it might make my life easier if I tried to cooperate at least a little. These questions were probably the easy ones and I might as well answer the easy questions. I could save my silence for the hard questions that I knew were coming.

My voice cracked as I answered.

"Chadwick Fenton Fury."

"Address?"

I gave the man my mother's address in Tulsa. I had stored my things at my parents' house while I was in the Army. After I left the Army I went straight to college. I had never bothered to get a real place of my own.

The rest of the questions were pretty mundane. I gave them my Social Security Number, names of relatives and friends, and verified the list of personal effects they had confiscated from me.

The cuffs finally came off when they asked me to sign the intake form.

Immediately after signing the form, two different officers came in and the first two exited. One of the men was carrying an orange jump suit neatly folded into a square with a pair of slip-on shoes resting on top. The other officer carried a brown paper bag and wore blue surgical gloves on his hands. I swallowed hard because I could guess what was coming.

This was the moment when I knew my freedom was truly gone. The first officer removed my handcuffs and the man with the bag said one word, "strip". I removed my clothes. As each item was removed the man with the gloves took it, felt for any hidden objects, and placed it in the brown paper bag.

I was then told to squat in the floor and cough. That was how the infamous body cavity search was initiated.

After being thoroughly examined, I was given the orange uniform and told to put it on.

I suppose my behavior had been acceptable because the handcuffs stayed off.

I was taken from that room to another room for finger printing and mug shots, followed by a short walk to an empty cell.

The cell was a small room with three cinderblock walls, a bed against one corner, and a combination stainless steel sink and toilet against the adjacent wall.

I had not asked for my one phone call; I wasn't ready to talk to anyone. As far as I was concerned, nobody could help me. Honestly, it was a relief to be alone and I chose to imagine that the officers had placed me by myself as a simple act of kindness.

When the cell door clanked shut behind me, I sat down on the bed. It wasn't much different than the bunk I had in basic training. I sat for a minute wondering what I should be doing.

There were no emotions left in me, too much had happened. There were no tears and no fears inside of me. There was only that moment, I had no future and everything leading up to that second was a distorted and disjointed dream.

I tossed the pillow on the floor, and moved to the end of the bed where the pillow had been. I sat on the bed with my back against the wall. I pulled my knees up under my chin and wrapped my arms around my legs.

I decided to pray. I prayed for the first time in years.

"Dear God, it's Chad. I know we don't talk much. Please don't ask me to explain how I got here. If you know that, I'd really appreciate it if you'd explain it to me, 'cause I can't make sense out of most of it. I'm not real sure what it is that you do for people in a mess like this, but I'd be real grateful for anything you can do. Amen".

I sat with my chin resting on my knees as I listened to the bantering of the people in the cells around me. I was amazed by how much the experience was like what I'd seen in movies. Everything I'd seen and heard in theaters and on TV, I was experiencing now. I sat there silent and motionless. I had learned from the movies that chattering with inmates was generally a bad idea. As the cell block grew silent, I drifted off to sleep.

I woke up to a guard rattling the cell door, yelling, "Hey, you. You want to eat?"

I nodded and the guard took a tray off of a rolling cart.

I could smell the food almost before the guard took it off of the cart. The smell made me rethink whether or not I was hungry.

The tray slid easily under a gap at the bottom of the door. I picked up the tray and examined it. I guessed it was supposed to be a hamburger and fries. There was some bread that resembled a bun. I lifted the top of the bun to expose a little piece of meat in the center and a pickle slice. The meat wasn't much larger than the pickle. There were a few white, limp, strips of potato sitting next to it. There was also a drink box of milk and a chocolate chip cookie which actually looked pretty good.

I looked around my quarters and found a tin cup sitting on the combination sink and toilet. I filled the cup from the tap and sat back down on the bed to eat. I ate the cookie. It was the only appetizing thing on the tray. I was just finishing when I heard someone on the other side of my cell door clearing his throat.

A man in a sheriff's uniform stood on the other side of the bars looking very sternly in my general direction. The man's uniform made his five foot eight inch frame look like ten pounds of sausage stuffed in a five pound casing. I didn't have to go through medical school to know that this man was one value meal away from a heart bypass.

"Son, we need to go over some rules. When someone comes to escort you out of your cell, you will stand up and back up against the door with your hands behind your back. Your escort will put a set of cuffs on you through the bars. Then and only then will the door be opened and you will be taken where you need to go. Do you understand?"

I nodded and he said, "Let's go. There's some people here that want to talk to you. It's gonna' be a long night for all of us."

I followed the procedure he'd just described and was soon being walked past groups of sad looking men in cages. I wondered if that was how I looked from the outside.

We arrived at a grey metal door at the end of the cell block. The sheriff waved a plastic card in front of a card reader on the wall and looked up at the camera above the door. A few seconds later a buzzer sounded and we exited through the door.

As we walked I became conscious of the changes in the odors around me. I must have been too distracted and preoccupied to notice earlier, but everything seemed to have its own unique smell; and not all of the smells were pleasant.

The Sheriff smelled of perspiration and something like rancid butter; the only thing I could figure was it was because of his diet. There were so many other unique smells that I wished I was free to investigate and discover their source.

One hallway and two right turns later I was standing in a room that had a central table and four uncomfortable looking chairs. The table was bolted to the floor. A two-inch wide metal pipe was bolted parallel to the long edge of the table top. The sheriff motioned me toward the table. Before I was seated he removed the handcuff from my right arm and fasted my left arm to the pipe.

The room looked like interrogation rooms I had seen on TV shows. The walls were white, the florescent lights were bright, and a mirror covered the upper half of the wall directly in front from me.

The Sheriff pulled up a chair opposite me. He leaned

forward, laid his right palm on the table and looked me in the eyes before speaking.

"Son, I like you. You don't strike me as the kind of young man that ought to be in here. But, here you are.

I probably shouldn't tell you all of this, but I'm going to say it because I like you. Up 'til now, you've not given anyone in here a single problem. You've been respectful, said 'yes sir' and 'no sir'. You've done what you were asked and you've not yelled, cussed, or caused any kind of a ruckus.

But son, you are smack dab in the middle of ground zero of a huge shit-storm!"

The sheriff was grinding his index finger into the table top and moving his hand side to side to emphasize his point.

"I want to help you. I can only help you, if you help me. The more I know about who you are and what you were doing, the easier it will be for me to help you. Refuse to tell me what we need to know and you take away my ability to help you. Do you understand, son?"

I answered back, "Yes sir, I believe I do."

"You're a smart boy. I think you do understand. Here's what's about to happen. You are about to be questioned by a lot of people from agencies that go by three letter abbreviations; FBI, DHS that's the Department of Homeland Security, and the OSBI the Oklahoma State Bureau of Investigation."

I heard a voice behind the glass chuckle and say, "OSBI is four letters."

Another voice said, "I know, but that goombah we've got in there is too scared to notice."

That statement was followed by laughter from what could have come from four different people.

I interrupted the sheriff.

"Excuse me, sir."

"Yes son."

"Well, I was just wondering, is this room sound proof?

I mean just how private is all of this?"

"Oh, OK. I really wasn't going to talk about it, but I don't want you to be self-conscious. We are totally alone in here, and yes, the mirror is a two way mirror. But there's nobody on the other side right now."

When he said there's nobody on the other side, I could have sworn I saw his pupils dilate slightly, and a faint odor a little like onions wafted my way.

I wondered about that. Why would I notice his eyes, and what's with the odor? I looked at the mirror and said, "I'm sorry. I was just being a goombah."

Somebody on the other side of the glass let out a colorful four letter word and I turned my attention back to the sheriff who continued speaking.

"As I was saying son, the people you will be talking to go by first names like 'Special Agent' and 'Agent'. Remember that, and treat them with respect. They will each want your story, and they may want you to tell it in different ways. If at any point you need something, you ask them to call your friend, Sheriff Lawson and I'll see what I can do to help you out. Are we OK with that?"

"Yes sir", I replied.

"Good. Now before the first person comes in, is there anything you'd like to tell me, like why you had a gun?

You've got to realize that if this had happened thirty years ago the gun would have been taken away from you and you would have gotten a stern talking to. But now, there's so many people running around ready to snap, we just can't take chances.

We've had too many terror threats and too many campus shootings in this country to look the other way. That's why so many people are going to be talking to you. So let's start by having you tell me a few things. Why did you bring a gun on campus?"

"It was an accident, sir. I had just bought the gun. It was still in my waist band when Chrissy, my girlfriend called. She wanted to see me at the student union, so I went there and just forgot I had it."

"Son, because of you, Christina Winston, or Chrissy as you call her, has spent a great deal of time telling us about your conversation and why you were meeting her at the student union.

Now, from what she says, there's a whole lot more to this story than what I just heard from you. Why don't you start from a little further back? Tell me about the drugs and the wild sex party."

"Oh, my God! Is that what she…I mean, I never…It never…There was no sex party! I was.... You know what, I don't think I have much more to say. Nobody's going to believe the truth. I want a lawyer."

"Son, I thought we were getting off to a good start, and now you go and pull this. Unless you change your mind about an attorney, I can't continue to help you. I will be forced to stop asking questions, but that won't stop the other people who want to talk you.

There's this thing called the Patriot Act, and it gives my associates the power to continue to talk to you if there is any suspicion of terrorism. And they will get to the truth. So, what do you have to say to me?"

"Respectfully sir, I don't think the truth will be believed. I want a lawyer."

"Do you have a lawyer, son?"

"No sir. I do not."

"That's not good news. That's going to slow things down a lot. I'm not going to be able to help you out."

The sheriff turned and walked out. I sat there, I didn't have a choice. I listened to the voices behind the glass. I heard a door open and close, and then I heard the sheriff's voice on the other side of the glass.

"Well, I tried. I really had hopes of getting somewhere. It looks like I'm done for a while. I'll have to file the paperwork for the judge to appoint an attorney; I can make that take a while. How do you folks want to proceed?"

A female voice answered, "I don't care when I go in. We have two choices, we can throw the gauntlet at him now, or build the pressure little by little."

The sheriff spoke up, "Why don't we let him sweat a little while. Let him sit there and the situation will sink in. Time has a way putting its own pressure on people."

The female voice spoke again. "Send in the FBI next. They can play the terrorist card and make him tell us something."

"OK, I'll go in and get it over with." It was the same voice that called me a goombah. "Maybe I can get finished in time to go home and get some sleep."

I decided that I didn't care anymore. I'd had about all I wanted. My life as I knew it was over, and I saw no reason to play their game by their rules.

The people behind the glass wanted to apply psychological pressure to me and get me to confess to only God knows what. I wanted to tell the truth, but I didn't know enough of the truth to be able to tell it. Not only that, but the truth would not undo the fact that I had indeed brought a gun on campus; that I was guilty of.

I spoke to the mirror in my most authoritative voice.

"Bring it on, this goombah's ready! Maybe you can finish and get some sleep!"

I heard the female voice.

"Damn it, sheriff! Move that man to another room…one where he can't hear us!"

I heard a door open and close, and soon the sheriff was coming into the room followed by two deputies. He unfastened the handcuff from the table, instructed me to stand, and put the cuff back on my right arm very tightly.

The Sherriff had made his point. He was silent as he led me across the hall to another room. The new room looked exactly like the first.

Sherriff Lawson looked me in the eyes as he spoke.

"We're going to try a little experiment. We have some friends on the other side of the glass. I've asked them to talk, and to shout. As soon as I or my deputies hear them, we will wave at them. OK. Start talking."

I listened; I heard the voices behind the glass as they started soft, got louder, and then stopped.

I wondered why the sheriff and the deputies were acting like they couldn't hear the people on the other side the glass. I thought, "What kind of game is this? How does it help them, if they pretend they can't be heard?"

I shook my head, and decided to keep my mouth shut.

The sheriff removed the handcuff from my right arm and hooked me up again, like before. I sat down. The sheriff and the deputies left the room and I waited.

The sheriff returned a few minutes later accompanied by a young man in lab coat, carrying what looked like a black tackle box.

The sheriff looked at me.

"I'd like to introduce you to Sam. Sam's our own version of CSI. He's here to take DNA samples.

You can exercise your right to refuse, which is what most guilty men do, or you can, like most innocent men who have nothing to hide, let him take the samples now.

If you refuse, we will produce a warrant, you will be restrained, and the samples will be taken by force. Which do you prefer?

"Let's get this over with."

I opened my mouth and let Sam swab the inside of my cheek six times.

"Are we done?" I asked.

"Oh no son, there's more. We need hair samples, skin cells, and a urine sample."

The sheriff flashed a toothy grin. "Ain't this just a laugh a minute?"

Sam pulled out some small envelopes measuring a couple of inches wide and about three inches long. The envelopes had the word "EVIDENCE" on one side, and my name on the other.

Sam also produce a pair of tweezers and plucked

twenty hairs from different places around my scalp. He placed each sample in an envelope and wrote down where it came from.

Sam spoke for the first time.

"Undo the top of your jump suit."

I complied, and he plucked hair from my chest, my underarms, and forearms. Sam looked at me and said flatly, "I need pubic hair."

"Well", I said, "When you get a little older, then your body will start to change…"

Sheriff Lawson barked, "Watch it son! Respect! This man has a job to do, and he's trying to do it."

I used my free hand to pull down the waistband of my jumpsuit just low enough to give the needed access. Sam plucked three hairs. When that was done he had me lift a leg onto a chair, and he took samples from there too.

I looked at the sheriff, "Are we done?"

"Almost, son. We just need the urine sample."

The sheriff unfastened me from the table and escorted me across the hall to a bathroom. Sam started to follow me inside.

I looked at the sheriff and he said, "Get used to it, son. There's no privacy here."

After all of that was over I found myself back in the room, attached to the table like one of those ink pens you find in bank lobbies.

I don't know how much time passed with me sitting there alone. While I sat I listened to the idle chatter behind the glass. A voice behind the glass flatly said, "I'm going to get this started." I heard a door open and close, then a few seconds later a new face entered the room. I caught the faint odor of stale cigarette smoke.

This man's appearance was the opposite of the Sheriff's. He was over six feet tall, lean, tanned and somewhat muscular. He was wearing khaki slacks and a light blue dress shirt without a tie. He carried himself like he had been in the military. The way he walked reminded me of the Marines I had met while in Afghanistan. He was carrying a black leather, zippered notebook which proudly bore the seal of the FBI. He sat down in a chair facing me and made a little show out of arranging his toys.

The man unzipped the leather notebook, extracted a file folder and placed it on his left hand side. The folder had my full name printed neatly on the tab. He reached into his shirt pocket and produced a slim digital recorder and placed it between the two of us. He produced a black ink pen from inside the notebook, and laid it in the center of the blank notepad. He adjusted his position in his chair, clasped his hands together and rested them on the table in front of him. He sat there and stared at me, expressionless.

I didn't want to be a smartass, but I couldn't help it. I looked back at him, and said, "Can I get you something, anything? Perhaps a cup of coffee, a magazine, maybe a cigarette? Something to help you pass the time?"

The man replied, "I don't smoke."

The moment he said it, I smelled onions.

"Yes you do. I can smell it."

The man frowned, and after another twenty or thirty seconds, he switched on the recorder and started speaking.

"This is Special Agent August Milton, interviewing the subject, Chadwick Fenton Fury. Refer to this recording's metadata for the appropriate date and time stamp.

Mr. Fury. Do you understand why you are here?"

I looked at him and tried to mimic his dead pan expression.

"Not entirely, no. Any explanation you can provide would be appreciated."

"You brought a concealed weapon onto the grounds of a State University. Until proven otherwise, this act will be treated as an act of terrorism. It will be investigated as a terrorist act until such time it has been determined that it was not a terrorist act, but a lessor criminal offense. As a course of this investigation, several warrants have been issued."

That actually made me relax a little. There was no way to connect me to any terrorist, because I didn't know any terrorists.

Special Agent Milton unclasped his hands and opened the file folder. He continued.

"I have here copies of warrants that have been issued. The warrants give us the right to search your dorm room, your car, your mother's home, and your place of work.

All of the people you know; your friends and your relatives will be interviewed. If there is anything to be found, it will be found. Would you care to save the United States taxpayers a few dollars by making a statement?"

I sat up in my chair, and positioned my feet directly in front of me.

"I can't give any statement, other than I am not a terrorist. I do not know any terrorists. I had no plans of committing any crime, especially crimes of terrorism. My statement will not change because it is the truth."

I leaned back against my chair. Agent Milton reached into a folder and produced a stack of photographs. He sat the pictures on my side of the table.

"I want you to look at these pictures carefully. Please tell me if you recognize any of the faces."

I looked at the pictures. I counted a total of thirty-four. I took my time looking at each photograph, and said I did not recognize anyone. All the while I was aware that my own face was being studied through the glass for signs of recognition.

We then went through a similar process with a list of names, part of which sounded more like someone was trying to read a bowl of alphabet soup rather than pronouncing a person's name.

Those exercises were followed by a series of questions regarding politics, religion, my four years in the Army, and various personal questions that were quite frankly none of anybody's business. When it was over, the others waiting behind the mirror took their turns.

I saw two more people who played out similar games but used different theatrics. There was Special Agent Alecia Munoz from the DHS and finally Officer Frank Kennedy from the OSBI.

When they were all satisfied that I either would not or could not tell them anything, it was over. I was escorted back to what the Sheriff referred to as the presidential suite where I welcomed any rest I might be able to get.

CHAPTER SEVEN

I had slept most of the day, Tuesday. I ate the food they brought, and I slept. There was nothing to do, but, then again, I didn't want to do anything. I was mentally and physically exhausted. What thinking I was doing was limited to Lisa. She seemed to be my only connection to what had happened to me, and I desperately wanted to talk to her more than anyone else.

It was Wednesday, sometime after breakfast, when a deputy showed up at my cell door saying that some people wanted to talk to me. I backed up to the door and let myself be handcuffed.

The deputy walked me down the corridor, through the metal door, and to the interrogation room that the sheriff had first placed me in. The sheriff was waiting there along with Officer Kennedy from the OSBI. Neither of them stood. The deputy cuffed my left hand to the table and exited the room.

Sheriff Lawson spoke first, "Son, do you still want an attorney?"

"Yes sir", I said. "I believe I do."

"Well son, for the first time since we met, I think that may be a good idea. We're working on getting an attorney for you. It will be a little while longer before one is appointed.

In the meantime, I have some news. Some of it's good, some of it's bad, and most of it is worse. Before I give you the news, I have just one question. What kind of crap are you into? Is it a cult?"

"I don't understand."

"OK. Let's come back to that later, possibly with your attorney. Here's the good news. The FBI and DHS have decided you're not a terrorist, or at least you're not connected to any terrorist group. That's the good news."

I let out a sigh of relief.

"Don't get your hopes too high, son. Here's the bad news. As a result of the FBI and the Department of Justice acting on the warrants issued, evidence has been discovered that links you to a recent murder."

"No! Hell, freaking, no!! I never killed anybody, not even while I was in Afghanistan…I don't think I should be talking to you without an attorney."

"Son, let me stop you right there. You've asked for an attorney. Out of courtesy, we're telling you what information we have."

Once more I could smell the onion-like odor; I knew this had nothing to do with courtesy.

Sherriff Lawson continued, "We could keep this information to ourselves now and tell your attorney later, who in turn would tell you. But, it could be another forty-eight hours before you have an attorney, and then it could be a few more days before your attorney visits you. I'm not asking for information. I'm disclosing information we have."

The onion odor got stronger. I didn't know what kind of trick this was, but something wasn't right, I could literally smell it.

I listened for what I might hear behind the glass. "That's good," said a voice I hadn't heard before, "let's watch his reactions. Take note of any signs of schizophrenia or excessive paranoia. We need to determine pretty quickly if he's a psych case."

I almost told the voice behind the mirror that I was not a psych case, but I stopped myself not wanting a repeat of the previous experience.

"Now, son, I'm going to let Officer Kennedy take over. He's going to explain what was found and try to answer your questions as best he can. I'm going to stay right here."

Officer Kennedy opened a large folder with my name on it.

"Mr. Fury, or do you prefer Chad?"

"Chad's fine."

"Alright, Chad. The search of your computer and cell phone showed us nothing significant. There were two calls to an unknown number, one on Saturday, and one on Monday morning. That's going to be something we will want to know more about, later. But, so far, that looks pretty insignificant. What is significant, is your car."

Sheriff Lawson spoke up, "Son, just what is it you do in that car of yours? It smells like a damn sewer! I mean really, that's no way to be treating a fine machine like that!"

Officer Kennedy threw a disapproving look toward the sheriff and continued.

"As I was saying, we found blood in the back seat. The blood samples contain human and animal markers, so during our investigation we will want to know just what kind of animals you've been transporting, and what you've been doing with them."

"I've never had any animals in my car. The only thing that's been in the back seat is me. I must have bleeding when…"

I stopped. I was saying too much.

"Go on, Chad."

Officer Kennedy waited for my response, but I kept silent until he continued.

"Are you trying to tell me that was your blood in the

back of the car?"

"Yes, sir."

"I'll make a note to circle back to that. Another odd thing was what we found in the trash in your dorm room. It looks like you were trying to throw away your shirt and pants, and I can't say I blame you much on that one. Your pants were pretty soiled. You'd crapped and pissed 'em.

The blood samples found on your shirt are consistent with the samples from the car. From the transfer pattern it looks like whatever had been bleeding was laying on the shirt."

Officer Kennedy paused. I said nothing.

"Continuing on, then. There were fingerprints in the front seat of the car, on the driver's side. The prints matched one Emily Smith. A forty-two year-old third grade teacher found murdered in her apartment. The coroner states that she died between midnight and four AM Monday morning. Here's her picture."

Officer Kennedy slid some eight by ten glossy pictures my way. The first picture showed a woman lying on the floor, her throat was slit from ear to ear. The amount of blood was disturbing. I had definitely seen her. The dead woman in the picture was one of the women I saw while I was chained to a chair.

I found a little comfort looking at the picture. This proved at least some of what had happened to me might be real, how else could I have recognized the woman in the picture? I still wasn't sure that my memories weren't more than just a drug induced nightmare, but picture of the woman? Had I actually seen her over the weekend? Was it possible I had seen her somewhere else, or was she just familiar looking?

The other pictures were of the woman's apartment. There was blood everywhere. Bloody prints were clearly visible on the objects in the room. Whoever had killed her had put their hands in her blood before touching things in the room.

My head was spinning. All I could be absolutely certain of was that I woke up in the back seat of my car. Was it was possible that I had something to do with this. Could I have actually killed someone without knowing it?

Officer Kennedy thumped the table top with his index finger to get my attention. "I can see that you do recognize her. What can you tell me about her? How do you know her?"

"I don't *know* her." I heard myself unconsciously emphasizing the word 'know'.

"She was in your car. She may have even driven it. Why are the fingerprints of a murdered school teacher in your car?

If I told them what I remembered, they would put me in the psych ward. If I didn't tell them, I might end up on death row. I slumped in my chair and looked down at the floor.

Officer Kennedy pushed the pictures closer to me and fanned them out.

"Take another look. Tell me you had nothing to do with this. Where were you Sunday night and early Monday morning?"

I couldn't look at the Sherriff or at Officer Kennedy.

"I…I don't know."

"You don't know, what?"

I didn't trust my memories. At that moment I needed something to let me know that at least part of what I remembered was real. I looked at the pictures. I stared at the pictures both hoping and afraid I might remember something.

In the third picture I saw something. I couldn't stop my hand from moving over the object. My index finger stroked the image in the picture. I tried not to speak, but I heard myself saying, "*Trans…res…i…nator.*"

My mind transported me back to the warehouse and the chair. I was seeing the old woman holding the glass cube. I was watching it glow and hearing her singing to it. I was seeing the robed women around me holding their glowing cubes.

Officer Kennedy's voice snapped me back to the present.

"Chad. Chad."

I looked into his face.

"Chad. What is that thing? What can you tell us about it?"

"I don't know."

"The FBI has several unsolved cases like this one, across the country. The most recent case is in Washington, D.C. where two women were bled to death. Those little cubes where at each crime scene. In some cases the victims were clutching a cube in their hands, just like this time. You seem to know about it. Now what is it?"

"I don't know anything."

"You know something, you gave that thing a name."

"I swear, I don't know anything!"

"Chad, you called it a 'trans...' something or other. You know about this object. The FBI's going to want to talk to you some more. Just how many of these murdered women are you connected to?"

The room was spinning. Maybe I could have hurt someone, once, without my knowing it, but there's no way I could have anything to do with other murders in other cities. Still, fact and fiction seemed to be separated by a thin gray line quickly fading away in my mind.

Sheriff Lawson pulled his chair close to the table and used my name.

"Chad, let me sum this up for you.

Monday morning, you bought a gun, and that afternoon you took that gun onto the grounds of Oklahoma University. You were seen with that gun while having an argument with your girlfriend, which is what landed you in here.

Since then we've discovered human and animal blood in the back seat of your vehicle. We've got the same blood on the clothes that you threw away.

There's fingerprints and hair of a murdered woman in your car. And, you haven't told us where you were or what you were doing at the time the woman was murdered.

You obviously know the murdered woman, and you know something about that cube. The cube is connected to several other unsolved murders. And what you know about that cube could very well connect you to one or more murders."

The Sherriff kept talking, but nausea and dizziness prevented me from following what he was saying. Through a disorienting haze I looked at Sheriff Lawson.

"I want an attorney, and I want my phone call."

Sheriff Lawson frowned.

"Alright, son. I understand. You'll get your phone call today.

By the way, once I receive the official statement from the FBI that you're not under suspicion for terrorist activity, I'm going to have to relocate you out of our one bedroom suite. Sometime tomorrow you'll start sharing accommodations with some of our other guests."

I was escorted back to my cell, and later that afternoon I did get my phone call. I called my mother in Tulsa.

The call went about as I expected. There were tears, and she seemed to be as worried as I was. Mom insisted on coming here and staying in a hotel. That actually made me feel a little better. I don't exactly know why, but maybe it was because I knew I had at least one person in my corner.

After the phone call, I was full of nervous energy, and I decided I needed to work it off. Back in my cell, I dropped to the floor for a set of pushups. I didn't bother counting, my goal was to simply wear myself out. After a while I stopped the pushups because I noticed I wasn't struggling and I wasn't tired. That's when it finally hit me. I had changed since the weekend. I remembered how I ran across the campus and wasn't even winded. I was hearing things other people could not hear, I was smelling things better than before and I was even noticing an onion-like smell when people lied to me.

I decided that I would be better off if I did not stay here like a caged animal, just waiting for other people to do something for me.

The legal system wasn't trying to clear me, it wanted to pin something on me. I didn't think I would be able to trust an attorney because my story was too unbelievable; I'd be just as well off blaming everything on Bigfoot.

I had to do something. I thought about it for a while. It was obvious that I needed somebody who would believe my story, or I needed somebody who could fill in the missing pieces about what happed to me and why. Only one name came to mind, Lisa. Lisa could answer my questions. I didn't know how I could convince her to help me, but I had to find her, and I had to try.

Problem number one had become how to get out of the Cleveland County Jail. At this point I had no faith that I would be let out on bail. Even if I was, time was passing. The longer I waited, the less likely it seemed that I would be able to locate Lisa. It felt like my best option was to start thinking like a criminal; criminals try to escape and I needed to escape. I thought about escaping until I drifted off to sleep.

CHAPTER EIGHT

By morning I had convinced myself that the real trick to escaping from anywhere was to be observant; to recognize an opportunity when it presented itself and be ready to take it. From what I had observed, I would need to make my move while I was on the outside of my cell. I wasn't Superman, I wasn't going to pretend that I could bend steel bars in my bare hands. Beyond my cell was a steel door at the end of the cell block. I needed to be on the other side of that door.

So far during my stay food had been brought to me; there had been no trips to the mess hall. I had not been out of my cage except for questioning and to make my one phone call.

The Sheriff had said that I would be moving to another cell. Maybe that's when I could do it? Maybe there would be more opportunities after I was moved?

I waited and I listened to the conversations of the other men in the nearby cells. A couple of men about three cells down, on the opposite side, were talking softly. They were talking about different ways to get out, and about people who had tried escaping. I decided to pay closer attention; not that I believed they had any good ideas, but it might spark something. And, I certainly didn't want to try something that had failed before.

There was one thing I heard in their conversation that sounded promising. According to them, there was a man-sized access port in the ceiling of the shower room. If what I was hearing was right, then it would lead to a crawlspace in the ceiling, and from there a person might be able to get almost anywhere in the entire three story building.

Unlike the free populace, bathing at the Cleveland County Jail was not a daily ritual. Guests were escorted to the 'spa', as the guards called it, once a week. At that time each person was issued a fresh change of clothes and a towel, and given five minutes to complete their ablutions unobserved. I hadn't been privileged to the spa, but I would keep my eyes open when my time came.

Luck was with me. This turned out to be my day for the showers and a fresh change of clothes. A guard escorted me and seven other men from our row through the grey metal door, down several hallways and a stairwell, and into the changing area. Towels and jumpsuits were sitting in stacks on tables against one wall. The center of the room had three wooden benches bolted to the floor. That's one thing I learned, every large object was bolted down in this place.

We were told to strip, place our clothes in a nearby rolling bin, and head to the showers. I grabbed a towel, a folded jumpsuit and my shoes before following the group through the doorway. The shower room was large with three, seven-foot tall metal posts in the center of the room. Each post had four shower heads attached near the top. The men wasted no time cleaning up.

I scanned the room and located the access port in the ceiling at the far corner of the room. I walked over for a better look.

One of the men yelled out, "Don't bother, you can't fly!"

I waved him off; I needed to do this unobserved.

I returned to the shower head and stayed under the running water until I saw the last man leaving. I left the water running and grabbed my towel and jumpsuit. I put on the jumpsuit and shoes as fast as I could. I knew it was a desperate chance, but I had to try.

I ran to the corner beneath the access port and leapt upward. To my surprise, I touched the access port and knocked the latch free in a single motion. The hatch swung open as I landed on my feet.

I didn't want to leave my towel behind. I snatched it up and wrapped it tightly around my waist, over my jumpsuit. I leapt upward with all my strength. My hands cleanly caught the edge of the port and I lifted myself through the hole like a gymnast.

Reaching back through the port to the access door, my fingertips grabbed the screw that held the latch. I pulled the hatch closed. By turning the screw that held the latch, the latch turned and secured the hatch door.

It was dark inside the crawlspace, but my eyes soon adjusted to the small amount of light filtering in through various cracks in my surroundings.

I took a moment to think about my next move. In less than a minute, the guard would know I was gone. He would figure out that I had gone through the access port; it would be the only explanation.

Soon the search would be on throughout the ceilings. I looked for some way to jamb the hatch; to make it so that it couldn't be opened. I figured if it was stuck, then there was a chance they might assume I had slipped out around the guard.

I laid in the crawl space. It was a little over two feet high. I felt around, and found a drywall screw lying next to the hatch. I felt the edges of the hatch door. My heart skipped a beat, as my fingers found a small hole in the lip of the door just above the edge of the mounting plate. The screw barely fit through the hole. I twisted the screw in as far as I could with my bare fingers, moved away from the hatch and waited.

Timing was everything. I knew I could race blindly through the crawl spaces, hoping to stay ahead of my pursuers, or I could find some place to wait, and listen, and make my way out after they thought I was long gone.

I looked around for the darkest corner and made my way silently and carefully across the ceiling joists. I sank into sheltering recesses of the shadows to wait.

I took off my towel from my waist, rolled it, and used it as a pillow. There was nothing comfortable about lying in the dirty crawlspace, but it did feel safe.

Alarms sounded, and soon there were voices filtering up through ceiling. I listened, partly out of amusement, but mostly for information. I wanted to know where the guards would be searching; that's where I wanted to go after the area had been cleared.

I heard some colorful language as perplexed guards tried to figure out just how I had disappeared. I heard the guard who had been my escort to the showers say emphatically, "There's no way he got around me! He must be in the ceiling." Someone called for a ladder.

I started to worry. If the screw didn't hold, somebody would be sticking his head through the hole and shining a flashlight around. I needed to get behind something.

The access port was near two load bearing walls, blocking my path; I didn't have many options. I put my towel back around my waist, and started moving away from the access port, along the nearest wall.

By my estimation I was over the changing area so I stopped to listen. Luck was with me. A couple of men below me were speculating about what I would be doing if I really was crawling around in the ceiling.

A baritone voice full of swagger let me know exactly what to do.

"You know, Carl, if he was smart, he'd head west, over to the offices. They replaced the sheet rock with them acoustic tiles last year. He could drop down through there.

From there he'd walk out of the office and down the hall to the guard's locker room, steal himself some clothes, and walk straight outta here."

Carl had to put his two cents in.

"Nah, John. Ya' see, there's folks in and out of them offices pretty late, and th' doors and windows have alarms. But, you're right. If he could get to the locker room, that'd be the thang to do."

That settled it. I'd head for the locker room, but which way? The guard said west. I didn't have a blueprint, and I didn't have a clue which way was west. I thought for a moment, and something inside my head was telling me that my feet were pointed due north. If that was true, I needed to turn to the right. I decided trusting my instincts seemed as good as any blind guess I might make.

I crawled slowly and carefully keeping what I felt to be north on my right hand side. I soon encountered a load bearing wall taking shape in the shadows. I took a chance and turned left. I followed the wall for about twenty feet, and discovered an opening. It was a square hole. It was probably where some kind of duct work used to be. I crawled through. The cinderblocks and mortar scraped my arms and legs. I was sure I was bleeding.

Once through, I turned right again, and crawled carefully in the dark. Pretty soon, toward my left, I noticed that the crawlspace looked larger, and lighter. I moved closer to discover I was at the edge of a drop ceiling with acoustic tiles. It had to be the office space I'd heard about.

I listened. I heard a phone ring, and an official sounding female voice answered it.

"Yes sir, there's no news yet… Yes, they did get the access door opened in the showers... There seemed to be a screw jamming it.... No, they don't know if he put it there... No, we don't know for sure that he went into the ceiling... The ceiling over the showers is fourteen feet high... Yes, I am aware that he would have to climb the walls to get to it... Yes it has been over two hours since he escaped… Yes, we will call you as soon as we hear anything."

This seemed like a great place for me to be. I could lay here silently and hear the progress of the search. I had time to think again. They'd been searching for at least two hours. The longer I could stay hidden, the more certain they would be that I had gotten away.

But what to do next? I needed street clothes, and there was a jackpot of ordinary clothes just waiting in a locker room. The light filtering through gaps in the acoustic tiles was enough for me to see a cinderblock wall separating me from what I believed must be the locker room.

I could drop down into the office, but if the office door had an alarm, that would be a problem. There had to be some other way.

I wondered about the things I'd suddenly discovered that I could do, and I considered that I might be able to knock a hole in an old cinderblock wall if the mortar happened to be old and brittle.

When I was sure the last person had left the office, I crawled over to the cinderblock wall. I thumped it with my fist. I thought back to the Karate classes I took as a child. I had watched the masters break boards and cinderblocks. It was all about concentration.

I laid on my back and positioned my right foot against a block in the wall. I imagined my foot striking the wall, and the cinderblock giving way. I grabbed the ceiling joists with my hands, counted down from five, and then struck. To my surprise, the block moved. I gave it a second kick and it fell on the other side. I needed to make the hole larger. I tried again. I liberated a total of four cinderblocks and crawled through the hole, feet first.

I dropped to the floor and rolled when I hit, barely missing hitting my head on a block. I didn't know how much time I had; I needed to hurry. One by one, I opened every locker that did not have a lock hanging on it. On the fifth locker, I struck gold. I found blue jeans, a shirt, and tennis shoes. The pants were a little big for me, but the shoes fit. And, thankfully there was a ball cap and an ID badge on the locker shelf.

I picked up the cinderblocks off of the floor, and placed them on top of the lockers. I used my towel and orange jumpsuit to clean up the debris from the floor. I placed the debris, jumpsuit, and towel in a trash can near the sink, and tied off the top of the liner.

I headed to the only door in the locker room. I pulled it open slightly and looked through the crack. The hallway seemed to be empty. The door to the outside was only a few feet away. I swung the door open and walked quickly to the exit.

A man with a mop and a bucket was swabbing the floor at the far end of the hall. He looked up from his work and saw me. I hesitated and waved. The man ignored me and kept working. I took the final few steps toward the exit.

The exit door required a key card. I held my breath as I passed the badge in front of the card reader. The lock on the door clicked. I walked outside to discover I was standing in what must have been the employee parking lot. I breathed in the night air.

I stepped backwards into the shadows by the entrance, and pretended to smoke a cigarette while I scanned my surroundings. The lot was fenced. Razor wire crowned the top of the fence. Climbing the fence was not my first choice.

There was a pickup not far away, but lying in the pickup bed didn't seem like a good idea. If I tested the doors on the few cars sitting there, I might call too much attention to myself, and besides I was a college student, not a car thief. I had no clue how to hotwire a car. But, perhaps I could run through the gated entrance.

I spotted the main gate directly ahead of me. The gate was motorized, and would slide from side to side to open and close. I spotted a little guard house on the outside of the fence. A man inside the little booth was looking at a book or a magazine. I was certain there had to be a pedestrian entrance somewhere close.

I took a drag on my imaginary cigarette and scanned the fence. I had to look up and down the length of the fence three times before I saw the chain link gate about twenty-five feet to the right of the little guardhouse. I focused on it, and it seemed to fill my entire field of vision. The hinges were on the right, and a black card reader panel was on the left. I wondered if it would really be that easy. Would I be able to stroll casually out through the gate and to freedom?

I gathered my courage as I faked one last drag from my pretend cigarette, flicked it to the ground, and crushed it out with my heel. I started toward the fence. As I reached the gate, the man in the guardhouse waved. I returned the wave and placed the badge against the card reader. A second later, the latch clicked, and I pulled the gate open.

I almost ran, but I restrained myself. My heart was pounding in my ears as I crossed the threshold. The gate closed behind me with a 'chink', and tears filled my eyes.

CHAPTER NINE

Every time I looked behind me, the jail looked a little smaller. I was heading toward what I thought was west; eventually I would get my bearings and find someplace to just be for a little while. I kept walking faster and faster, until finally I was jogging. I didn't know what time it was, I just knew it was dark. My eyes had long since adjusted to the moonlight and I was able to navigate the terrain as easily as daylight. I heard the sound of traffic and realized I was approaching the I-35 Highway.

I ran across the highway and continued running. I don't know how long I ran but I finally stopped to get my bearings as I crossed into a park. I slowed to a walk and read the name on the sign, "Ruby Grant Park".

I knew where I was; I turned south and started running again. The entire time as I ran, my mind was racing. I had a new set of priorities now. I needed a couple of changes of clothes, food, money, and rest. I ran on.

Oklahoma City has no shortage of convenience stores along the access roads running parallel to the main highways. I ran south, following the I-35 access road. It wasn't long until I saw a nice large convenience store. I recognized it as part of a chain that boasted about their hotdogs and fountain drinks. I ran to the parking lot and slowed to a walk.

Inside the store I grabbed two large bottles of water, three hot dogs, and a bag of chips. I took my food to the counter and placed it by the register. I made sure to stand within reach of an old milk jug stuffed full with coins and bills. The jug was sitting next to a sign, "Blue Star Mothers, Supporting Our Boys Overseas".

The young man behind the register wearing a red shirt and khaki slacks, rang up and bagged my goods.

"That's fifteen forty-two."

I wanted him to look the other direction, so I said the only thing that came to mind.

"Oh, I need a pack of cigarettes, menthol, one hundreds."

The clerk turned his back to me to get the cigarettes form the center kiosk. While his back was turned, I took the sack, grabbed the plastic jug of cash, and ran as fast as I could out of the store, continuing south.

I had officially committed larceny. But, I reasoned, it was a much lesser charge than breaking out of jail, and the murder that I sincerely hoped I had nothing to do with.

I was sure the store cameras had gotten a pretty good look at me, and in the long run, it might cost me, but if I did this right I just might be able to create a trail that would lead the law away from me.

Anyone looking for me would know that I was on foot. What my pursuers didn't know is how long I could keep running, and quite frankly, neither did I.

I ran for at least another mile, until I saw a three story building that looked like it might be a school. The building seemed as inviting as any other, so I decided to stop there to eat the food I had taken from the convenience store.

I walked the perimeter of the blonde brick building looking for a way inside. Every window and door was locked. The sign on the front read, "Passages Church". Passages seemed somehow appropriate to my situation.

I got to thinking that if the police came, I didn't want to be trapped inside a building with no place to go. I looked up toward the roof. I found a sturdy looking pipe running up the side and decided that would be my way up. I removed my shirt, and placed my food and the jug of money inside and tied the arms around it. I tied my bundle to my belt and began climbing the pipe.

As I made my way over the edge of the roof I was happy to see that there was an access door. I tested the door; it was unlocked. I took my bundle off of my belt and went inside.

The darkness inside was thick, even for my newly improved eyes. On the top floor I found a room with a sign reading "Youth Loft". Inside the room was a sofa and some tables. At the opposite end was a bathroom with a real toilet and a real sink. I considered myself fortunate to have discovered this oasis.

I went to one of the tables and unpacked the food and water. I sat down to eat and rest. As I took a drink of water I saw a clock on the wall; it read two AM. It was now Friday morning.

While I was eating I gave some thought to my situation. There was little doubt that I had been seen on camera stealing food and money. It wouldn't be long before the police saw the tape and recognized me. The police would concentrate their activity on areas where I was likely to be. What I needed now was to figure out how to use this to my advantage.

I asked myself aloud, "Now that I've stolen food and money, what would I be expected to do?" The answer, was run; run fast and run far. So, if that's what they expected that's what I wanted them to believe I was doing. A plan started forming in my mind and I became a little more hopeful.

Before laying down to sleep on the sofa, I had one last task. I found a pair of scissors in the room and cut the plastic jug open. I pulled out the bills and counted them.

There was two hundred thirty-seven dollars in mostly tens, fives, and ones. I picked out handfuls of quarters, which I didn't bother counting, and put them in my pockets. I poured the remaining coins out on the table and left them there, knowing that the money would be put to good use.

I paused for one more prayer, after all, I was taking refuge in a Church. It was my second prayer since this mess started. I cleared my throat and looked up.

"Excuse me Sir, this is Chad again. I don't have to tell you that, and I don't have to tell you what I've done. I'm sure you probably don't approve, and I'm sorry for that. But you do approve of justice, and that's what I want too. If you have a desire to do something for somebody, then I could use some help finding this Lisa person so that I can clear my name and also find out what's happened to me. I'm just asking, no pressure, and by the way, thank you."

I laid down on the sofa, closed my eyes and slept.

CHAPTER TEN

The window was facing east. When I woke up it was still dark outside. I looked at the clock, it was five-forty AM. I walked over to the nearby toilet and sink and turned on the light. Looking in the mirror I saw how filthy I was. The bottom layer was dirt from the crawlspace, on top of that was dirt from my cross country run, and the clothes I was wearing smelled like I had been running. I was ripe.

I wandered through the building and eventually I found the kitchen. The kitchen had some large metal sinks which I used to wash out my clothes and to wash myself.

After washing my clothes I wrung out as much of the water as possible, and laid the wet clothes over the edge of the sink to dry. I found a little plastic bag in a nearby drawer and put my bills in it so that they would stay dry in my pocket.

While my clothes were drying I checked out the refrigerator and pantry. I took advantage of the supply and fixed breakfast for myself. There were plenty of eggs, breakfast meats and even some pre-baked biscuits and orange juice.

After breakfast I cleaned up after myself and dressed myself in my damp clothes. I retraced my trail back through the building to the room where I had spent the night.

I picked up my trash and put it in a sack to take it with me. I saw no reason to leave too many clues that I had slept here. I made my way to the roof and exited the way I came.

I climbed down the pipe to the ground. I put my trash in a nearby dumpster and took a moment to stretch before I started running south again.

I started running slowly and soon I was traveling at full speed. My goal was to find one of those twenty-four-hour super stores. I needed the basics from a toothbrush on up to more clothes. I ran; I guess it was about a three mile run through subdivisions and shopping centers.

When I got to the store, it was nine AM according to a sign at the bank across the street. I made a mental note to look for the security cameras and make certain the cameras saw me. This was step one in creating a trail leading away from Oklahoma City.

For step two, I grabbed a cart and headed off to find all of the things I had decided I needed. My list included:

- A backpack with a bedroll.
- Flashlight.
- Swiss Army style knife with a can opener.
- A lighter.
- A set of camping dishes.
- Travel-sized toiletries & toothbrush.
- A pair of jeans and T Shirts.
- A hooded sweatshirt.
- A pair of athletic shoes.
- Socks and underwear.
- A watch.
- Two pre-paid cell phones.
- Padded Envelopes.
- A note pad.
- Ink pens.
- A package of blank postcards.

• Protein bars and other assorted foods that would not spoil. And,

• Postage stamps.

I took my things to the front of the store and chose a checkout lane with an attractive young girl behind the register.

I wanted to be remembered. I wanted the authorities to know I had shopped here, so I read the clerk's nametag and decided to flirt.

"Hello…Andrea! I'm Chad."

"Hello, did you find everything OK?"

"I need a book of stamps. And now that I've found you, I shouldn't ever need anything else."

Andrea looked at me uncomfortably as she pulled a book of postage stamps from her cash drawer.

I smiled my toothiest grin.

"I just wish I could stay in town, I'd love to get to know you."

"You're headed somewhere?"

"Nowhere special, it's just time for me to leave."

When Andrea told me the total, I was pretty pleased with myself. I had spent one hundred ninety-eight dollars. I still had a little cash plus the quarters bulging in my pockets.

As I left the store, I picked up a bus schedule from a wire rack located near the exit. I studied bus schedule and figured out how close the buses went to Bill Warrant's tattoo studio. I took a seat at the bus stop two blocks away and waited. While I waited I transferred my purchases into my backpack. I almost threw the plastic bags away but instead I put them in my backpack too.

The bus was nearly empty and the ride was uneventful so I used the time to activate one of my new cell phones and dial information for some numbers that I didn't have memorized. There were two numbers I needed, one was for Bill Warrant's studio, Imagine Ink, and the other was for my best friend from the Army, Ronnie Ferguson, who was living in Shreveport, Louisiana.

I needed the number for Bill Warrant because I couldn't show up in person, and I needed to talk to him. I needed Ronnie's number because I wanted to send the authorities on a wild goose chase away from Oklahoma City. It was a gamble, but I hoped I could count on Ronnie.

I moved to the back of the bus and dialed Ronnie's number. The phone rang four times and someone picked up on the fifth ring. A distinctly female voice landed gently in my ear.

"Hello?"

"Hello, Shareese?"

"Yes, who is this?"

I paused. I hadn't thought that far ahead. My name was probably national news, and Ronnie's wife, Shareese, didn't know me as well as Ronnie did.

I lowered my voice a little. "I'm an old Army buddy from Ronnie's unit. Could you tell him Trevor is calling?"

I hadn't exactly lied. I wasn't Trevor, and I didn't actually say I was.

"Sure, just a minute."

I waited with a knot growing in my stomach.

Ronnie answered, "Trevor, what are you up to, you old dog?"

"Ronnie, it's not Trevor. It's Chad..." There was a long silent pause. "Ronnie, are you there?"

"I'm here." Ronnie's voice was flat and lifeless.

"Listen, I think I should explain some things to you first."

"Maybe, Chad, or maybe I shouldn't be hearing any of this."

"Ronnie, you're my best friend. I'm still the man you knew in Afghanistan. Nothing's changed. I'm in trouble, and I need your help."

"OK, man. You played the Afghanistan card, so, yes, I owe you. I will listen, make it good."

"I don't know what you heard on the news, but I can guess. I can also tell you none of what you heard is true. I'm not a terrorist, and I'm not a murderer. I've never killed anybody."

"Go on…"

"This is going to sound wild, but I've been setup. I don't know why they chose me, maybe I was in the wrong place at the wrong time. I don't know, but I need to find out. The only people who can tell me are in Oklahoma City. The problem is, the police are looking for me here. Clearing my name could take a while and I need for the police to think I'm somewhere else."

"Tell me why I should believe you. I've got a family, and I won't risk that. Convince me. You have one shot."

My mind raced. I didn't know what I could say that would make Ronnie trust me.

"Ronnie, listen. I've been nothing but a friend to you. And I'm not going to try to manipulate you.

Just tell me this. You know my character. You know how I've treated people. I stayed with you over Christmas vacation. Just tell me one thing... Is there anything that could change me from what I was in December to what you've heard in the last week?"

"No. You're right. I don't believe you are what I've heard. Tell me what I can do for my best friend."

"Ronnie, I need to be free to find the people who did this to me. I can only think of one way to do that. I need the police to think I'm somewhere else."

"How can you do that?"

"I can't, not by myself. I need your help. And, I promise it won't involve lying to anybody."

"OK, Chad. Tell me what I need to do."

"Ronnie, I'm going to send you an envelope. I don't want you to open it unless you're wearing gloves."

"What's inside?"

"Postcards."

"Why do I need gloves for postcards?"

"Listen carefully, Ronnie, I don't want your fingerprints on those cards. Only mine."

"What's special about the cards?"

"I'm going write out a dozen postcards, address them, and put stamps on them. They'll all be addressed to my mother. I want you to send one every week or two from any city other than Shreveport. If you have to, send a few to friends and have them mail them. If you can, make it look like I'm traveling across country."

"OK, Chad, I get it. Your mom will be questioned and she'll show the postcards to the Feds."

"Right, and as long as we feed them a card here and there, they won't be looking for me in Oklahoma."

"It sounds simple, Chad. And all you want me to do is aid and abet a known felon."

My heart sank into my stomach.

"You're right. I'm asking far too much. But, I'm still asking. If you say no, I'll understand."

"Damn it Chad!! Send your package. But don't you ever do anything like this to me ever again!"

"Thank you, Ronnie. I'll never be able to pay you back for this."

I hung up the phone and sighed as the bus arrived at forty-sixth and Classen Blvd., six blocks away from the tattoo studio. I exited the bus.

I needed a temporary base from which I could start working my plan. I started walking north, hoping to find an abandoned building or an empty storefront near the studio.

As I approached the studio, I saw what I had hoped for. An old abandoned three story brick building was on the east side of the street and it directly faced the studio on the west.

I stared at the building. The first floor windows and door were boarded up. I walked behind the building. The back was covered with gang symbols and graffiti. I looked at the grey metal door in the middle of the back wall. I tried the handle. The knob spun freely in my hand; it was obviously broken. I pushed and the door refused to open.

On the second floor above me was a gaping hole where a window had once been. Back in the jail I had jumped and reached the hatch, but I decided not to try that here. I studied the wall in front of me. I ran my fingers along the recesses between the bricks. I wondered if I could scale the wall like a rock climber.

I reached my right had above my head, securing my fingertips on the edge of a brick. I pulled myself up a few inches and placed my left hand in another recess. My feet found a little traction I could put to use. I started my climb, hand over hand.

Scaling the wall and climbing through the window proved to be easier than I expected. I crawled through the window and surveyed my surroundings. The place had been gutted. The only walls standing were structural, everything else was gone. The old wood floors creaked and gave a little too freely under my weight. I proceeded cautiously.

People had been here recently, I could smell the perspiration. There was more graffiti on the walls. The thought of people made me uncomfortable; I needed to be totally alone and I didn't want to be worrying that some freaked-out tweaker would try to rob me for his next fix. I decided I needed a closer look at the other two floors.

The stairs leading up to the third floor were rotted out. I thought that I might be able to climb the outside wall if I was really curious, but a look at the first floor would be much easier.

I pulled out my new flashlight, and inserted the batteries. I descended the stairs slowly, flashlight in hand. My flashlight showed that the ground floor was empty, but it was a mess. There were old papers scattered around, a couple of old mattresses lying on the bare floor, a small card table and a couple of chairs in the center. On the table were three half-burned candles and some old spoons.

I knew what this place was. At some point there would be people here getting high and then sleeping it off.

I started to leave, but then decided I couldn't give this place up. It was across from the tattoo parlor and this was the best place for me to watch and hide. I almost laughed at myself for thinking that I could share the place with whoever might show up, but even a drug addict would turn me in for the reward as fast as anyone else. If the situation called for it, I might have to fight.

I cleared off the table and moved it and the chairs to the second floor. I took the candles; no use in using my batteries up. I started to take the cleanest looking of the two mattress, but decided I just couldn't lay on it, not even using a bedroll and leaving my clothes on.

I made it my next priority to figure out how people were getting inside this building. I looked at every wall. The boards on the windows were secure. The back door was nailed closed. I took a closer look at the front door. It was a solid wood door, and very sturdy. I turned the handle on the old wooden door. The old door swung freely toward the inside, revealing a wall of plywood.

On closer inspection I saw that the plywood across the door opening was hinged. I hadn't seen it before because I wasn't looking for it. I could have come in through the front door all along.

I set my mind to securing the front door. I didn't have much in the way of tools, so I couldn't do very much. If my visitors were determined, anything I could do would only be a hindrance and not a permanent barrier.

I started digging through my backpack looking for anything I could use. I laughed out loud when I pulled out my new knife and said, "Damn clever of those Swiss!"

The knife had both a Philips and a plain screw driver. I opened the door and used the Phillips bit to remove the doorknob. Next I removed the hinges from the door.

I placed the door back in its position. I took the hinges and mounted them horizontally across the door and door jambs; two hinges on the left and one on the right. The door was now a wall.

With my work complete, I ascended the stairs and sat down at my table. I made my call to "Imagine Ink" across the street. Bill Warrant answered the phone.

"Imagine Ink, Bill speaking."

"This is Glenn, I've made a decision about what I want, and need to make an appointment."

"OK…Glenn, you said?"

"Yes, Glenn Davis. I was in a couple of weeks ago. I spent quite a while talking to your friend, Lisa. Lisa helped me decide what to get."

"I'm sorry I don't remember you, but if you talked to Lisa, then you were definitely here for a very long time."

Bill Laughed, and I laughed at his joke.

"Bill, when can you take me? How about today or tomorrow?"

"Uhm…That's going to be pretty tricky. It depends on how complicated the design is…what are you wanting?"

"I'm wanting the wolf you have on your wall, top row, in the middle. I want it on my chest."

"That will be about a five hour job. I'm booked today and all day tomorrow. I'm closed Sunday and Monday. I can take you on Tuesday. How's one PM work for you?"

"That will be great! By the way, would you let Lisa know that I picked the wolf? I really like her, and I'd like to talk to her again."

"She's not around today. But she'll probably be in tomorrow. I've got a guy coming in at three to get a lion on his shoulder. Lisa likes to watch me do animal tattoos. I'm pretty sure she'll be here then."

"Great. We're set for Tuesday, and I may drop by tomorrow just to see Lisa."

I hung up. I almost shouted. I felt like God was smiling on me. Now I didn't need to be wasting time and energy searching all the tattoo shops in the city. I knew where Lisa was likely to be. I needed to decide what I could do with this new opportunity.

But before I did anything about Lisa, I had one other phone call to make and I couldn't make it sitting in my new loft. This call had to be one that would lead the authorities away from Oklahoma City. For that I would need to use the second phone I had bought.

I needed to call from any location as far away from my new quarters as possible. I put on my back pack and exited through the window the same way I had come. I climbed down the wall, and let myself drop when I was close to the ground. I stretched a couple of times, and looked at my watch. I knew I had been running fast, but I was curious about how fast I could run. I watched the second hand on the watch. As soon as it hit twelve I took off headed to the west.

When I arrived at Pennsylvania Avenue, just about one mile west of Classen Blvd., I looked at my watch. I couldn't believe my eyes. If my watch was right I ran that distance in less than two minutes. I did the math in my head, twice. That was somewhere close to forty miles an hour. I was certain my watch or my math had to be wrong.

I waited until the second hand hit six, and I counted the seconds the way we're all taught, one Mississippi, two Mississippi. The watch seemed perfect. I shook my head and prepared to continue my run.

The next major road was a mile away. I tried timing myself again. When the second hand hit twelve I started running. One and a half minutes later I was at the next major road. I did the math again. I still couldn't quite take it in that I was running at forty miles an hour.

I shook my head, and chose not to try the math another time. I just ran west. I ran until I found myself in Will Rogers Park. I decided this was far enough away from my abandoned building.

I pulled off my backpack and searched for my second cell phone. Television had taught me that cell phones could be traced. Once I made this call, the police would have the phone number and would get a warrant for the cell tower data. It wouldn't be long until they would know where the call came from. I activated my second phone. I was ready to call my mother.

My gut wrenched with guilt. Mom would never deliberately lie to the police. I didn't want to lie to my own mother. But I knew I could never get her to lie for me and I desperately needed the police to believe I had left Oklahoma City. The only thing I could do was to convince my mother that I was on the run. I inhaled and exhaled a couple of times, slowly and began dialing.

My mother's voice come through phone. She sounded both weak and tired.

"Hello."

"Hi, mom." I waited.

"Chad, is it really you? Are you OK?"

"Yes mom, it's me. I'm OK."

"Tell me where you are. I need to understand what's happening."

"I can't explain anything. I am innocent, I didn't kill anybody. But I'm scared. There's no way I can prove I didn't do it. I've got to leave Oklahoma for a while. I'll come see you in Tulsa, when I think I can come back. I'm really sorry. I love you."

"Chad, no. I love you. Please, don't do this. Turn yourself in. Go back. We'll figure all of this out, but running away won't help. You've never run from anything before, don't start now."

"I can't mom. It has to be this way. I'm sorry. I love you. I'll write. I'll call when I can. I love you."

I hung up the phone and returned it to the backpack. I started running west again. This time I stopped at Route 66 Park. I reached into my backpack and withdrew the phone again. I saw that I had missed four calls from my mother. I was both happy and sad. Happy, because now there was a data trail leading west. I was sad; I knew my mother was hurting and I couldn't do anything about it.

I started to call my mother again, but had second thoughts. I decided I didn't need to hurt mom again. Any call I made from this phone would work at this point.

I dialed information and asked for the number of a motel chain in Amarillo, TX. I dialed the motel's number and asked for directions from Oklahoma City. That was all that was needed.

After making the call I pulled the battery from the phone. I dropped the phone on the ground and crushed it with my foot. I put the battery in my backpack to use with my first phone.

It was time to turn around and run back. On the way back I stopped to buy a rope, get some food, and make some plans.

CHAPTER ELEVEN

I woke up almost rested. I would have slept the entire night if it had not been for my visitors. Around ten-thirty that night I'd heard some people at my front door, trying and failing to get in. The whole thing turned out to be pretty boring. I was prepared to exit through the window if they came in, but the door held.

I stood up and stretched. I soon realized that I was going to miss having hot running water. I remembered seeing an old gas station a couple of blocks away, and I decided I could clean up there. It was a simple matter to climb down and then to walk behind the buildings keeping out of sight from the street.

When I got to the station it was closed and the bathroom door behind the building was locked. I gave the doorknob a sharp twist to the right, heard a snap, and the door surrendered to my request.

The bathroom inside was filthy, but fortunately I was even dirtier, which left me with every possibility that I would come out cleaner than when I went in.

On the short walk back I found a quarter. I chose to believe that it was a good omen; that fortune was favoring me and my luck was going to hold out.

I climbed back through my window and set about getting breakfast. Breakfast consisted of a protein bar and bottled water. I was going to miss coffee, especially if this adventure continued on for very long. I daydreamed about coffee as I ate. I decided that coffee was going on my list of things that I would never give up by choice. I made myself a promise to never let a day pass without a cup of coffee, if at all possible.

I finished breakfast and cleared the table. I laid out my postcards and my assortment of ink pens. There were four pens; three black and one blue. I intended to change pens as I wrote the cards. If anyone choose to examine the cards, I didn't want it to look like they were all written at the same time.

I addressed the cards to my mother. I wrote pretty much the same thing on all of the cards; "I love you…", "I'm sorry I can't come home…", "I'll explain everything someday…", "I'll be home when I can."

I debated putting a date on the cards, but I realized it would create a problem. I was relying on somebody else to send the cards. If a card was sent out of order my charade would be over.

Also, there was another problem; birthdays and holidays. If I was actually sending the cards, then I would mention my mother's birthday and I would make references to a holiday here and there.

"Damn it! How do I deal with birthdays and holidays? I can't guarantee that Ronnie or whoever else will send the cards at the right time, or even in the right order. If I mention the Fourth of July or Mom's birthday, and the card arrives in November, that's just no good at all."

I didn't have a choice. I had to keep the cards generic. But not mentioning holidays and special occasions would make the lifespan of this rouse limited. Eventually someone would figure it out. I just hoped that all of this would be over before then.

I completed the cards, put them in the large envelope,

addressed it to Ronnie and added plenty of postage.

I didn't remember seeing a mailbox around, but I decided not to go out searching for one. I needed to stick around and watch the studio across the street. Also, daylight excursions were dangerous. I needed to stay hidden, especially now that I was supposed to be headed out of Oklahoma.

The man getting the lion tattoo would be in the studio at three PM, and I was betting Lisa would be there. I took the rope I had bought the previous day and cut several four foot lengths. I needed the rope to tie Lisa's hands and feet.

I was actually looking forward to tying Lisa to a chair, after what I had been put through. I had to stop and tell myself that this was not about revenge, this was about justice and clearing my name.

I was after information. The murdered woman was part of the group in that warehouse, and I was betting that Lisa knew something about the murder. I was counting on Lisa being able to tell me if I had anything to do with that woman's death. If I was going to sort all of this out then I needed to know what Lisa knew. I also wasn't pretending that Lisa would be letting go of the information easily.

I had some time to kill, so I spent most of my time doing sit-ups and pushups, and thinking. When I wasn't exercising off the nervous energy, I was considering how to interrogate Lisa. Would I be able to intimidate her into letting go of what she knew? Was I capable of inflicting enough discomfort on her that she would believe telling me what she knew was her best option?

I kept aware of the time. I was hoping that Lisa would carry out a similar performance with Bill's three PM client as she had done with me. The day I got my tattoo she was already in the shop when I arrived, so I started watching the street around two-thirty, hoping to spot her. I had a couple of lengths of rope underneath my shirt and tied around my waist. I had a clean sock in my hip pocket. I figured the sock would make for a decent gag if I needed it. Lisa wasn't going to appreciate it, but I had talked myself out of using a dirty sock.

I was watching as two-thirty came and went, and I saw no sign of Lisa. I was getting nervous. To stay calm I had to keep telling myself that if today went badly, there would be other opportunities. The problem was, I didn't believe it. If didn't Lisa show up today, there was every possibility that I would be on the run for the rest of my life.

At ten minutes before three I saw a car pull into a parking space near the studio. A man with full crop of wild, bushy red hair got out of the car and went into the shop. I was amused at how much the hair reminded me of a lion's mane. Still there was no sign of Lisa.

I kept watching, wondering if Lisa was running late. Maybe she was already inside and somehow I had missed her? I clung to those possibilities with as much hope as I could muster. I was wishing I could go inside and take a look, but I didn't dare risk being seen, not yet. It was going to be dangerous enough doing this in broad daylight on the open street.

Shortly before three-thirty the front door of the studio opened, and out stepped Lisa. "Oh, my God", I said aloud, "I've got to hurry!" I ran for the rear window and climbed out quickly. I lowered myself half way down, and pushed off from the wall. I landed on my feet and started running around the building. I spotted Lisa getting into the passenger's side of a car parked just south of the studio. I said a little too loudly, "Crap! I counted on her being alone!"

This was a real fly in my ointment. I slowed my pace, and made a mental note of the license number, just in case it might come in handy. The car pulled away as I stood there not knowing what to do next.

I returned to my perch. I kept watching the studio until it finally sunk into my thick skull that there could be a 'plan B'. I may not have Lisa, but the man in the studio had a way to contact her. That same group of women was planning on abducting him. He was valuable to Lisa and that was something I could use.

I put on my ball cap, pulled the brim down low, and exited my loft. I made my way quickly across the street and into the alley behind the studio. I sat down on the pavement with my back against the building and listened. I could hear the hum of the tattoo needle. I could hear the voices inside. I relaxed a little because I would know when the session was over, and I would be ready.

I heard when the tattoo needle stopped humming. I heard a voice telling Bill that he loved the work. I stood up and walked to the corner of the building nearest the man's car. A bell chimed as the front door opened. My heart began racing.

The red haired man stepped into view. He stood about five feet ten, and was solid; he probably weighed around one hundred eighty pounds. I spoke as I approached him, "Hey, Lisa wanted me to give you a message."

The man stopped and looked at me. "What is it?"

"She wants…" I made a fist with my right hand and swiftly landed it on his jaw. The man flew backwards and landed hard on the asphalt.

I ran over and tied the man's hands and feet. He wasn't moving. I checked his pulse and was relieved to find it strong and steady. I picked him up over my shoulder in a fireman's carry. I trotted across the street and ran behind the building just hoping I hadn't been seen.

I placed my new, unconscious friend on the ground with his back against the wall and told him my dilemma. "Well", I said in disgust, "I certainly didn't' think this through. I need both hands to climb. How do I get you up there?"

My sleeping friend had no suggestions. He simply sat there with his hands tied in front of him and his head lolled to one side. I ended up putting my head between his arms and letting his limp body hang behind me.

The climb was difficult; I nearly lost my grip twice. I made it to the widow and rolled through. I drug the man to the opposite wall near my table and chairs. I rolled up my bed roll and put it under his head for a pillow.

I went through his pockets. I thought that since I've already assaulted the poor guy, I might as well find out who he is before he wakes up.

I got the man's name from his driver's license; Dwayne McFarland. There was two hundred ten dollars in the wallet, and I took it. I considered the money payment for the service I was providing him. He didn't know it, but I might very well be saving his life.

I saw a wedding ring on Dwayne's hand. That was going to be a problem. He was going to be missed. That meant that very soon I would need to move his car away from here. My fingerprints were on file; moving the car was going to be tricky.

I took the following items from Dwayne's pockets and wrote everything down in my notebook next to his name. I didn't want to be a thief. I had every intention of returning his stuff or at least reimbursing him, eventually:

- Car keys
- A folding hunting knife
- Leather billfold with two hundred ten dollars
- Debit and credit cards

A wave of relief swept over me when I searched his left hip pocket. I found a scrap of folded yellow paper with the name "Lisa" and a phone number written in black ink.

Dwayne was starting to come back to the land of the living. He moaned, coughed, and opened his eyes.

"Where…what…what happened?"

Dwayne's eyes scanned his surroundings, trying to make sense of his unfamiliar world.

I squatted down near Dwayne's head.

"You OK, friend? I'm really sorry about this, but I need for you to be unavailable for a while."

Dwayne raised his shoulders trying to sit up. His

shoulders moved a few inches before dropping back to the floor.

"Why can't I get up? What are you talking about?" Dwayne saw his hands and feet in the fleeting light of the sunset coming in through the window. "My God! I'm tied up! Let me go now!! You SOB!!!"

It struck me at that point just how much of a de-motivator profanity can be. I made a conscious decision to stop using it.

I looked Dwayne in the eyes and spoke as calmly as I could.

"Dwayne, you're safe, and you're going to stay that way."

Dwayne's expression was fierce.

"Who are you?!! What are you doing to me! Explain! Now!"

I backed up a little to return some of Dwayne's personal space. I thought for a moment. I hadn't considered what I would say to him.

"My name's Chad. And, we need to talk. You're in for a pretty rough night, but not from anything I'm doing."

Dwayne was sitting up now.

"You've done enough. Untie me!"

"I can't do that." I reached behind me and grabbed a plastic grocery bag.

"Here."

I put the bag in between Dwayne's hands.

"You'll need this; you're going to be getting sick before long."

"No games! Talk straight."

Dwayne was trying to stand up, and failing miserably with his ankles tied together.

"OK. But most of it you're not going to believe."

I told Dwayne the whole story. I thought he might as well hear the whole thing. I knew he wouldn't believe it, at least not yet. Eventually he might…after he got sick, hallucinated his tattoo moving, and had the wild dreams.

Then, he might believe.

I told my story, leaving nothing out. He called me crazy a few times. But, considering his situation, he stayed pretty calm.

I had just finished telling Dwayne my story when we both heard something outside. There was a thud and a crack. I looked out the window and down onto the dimly lighted street. Directly below me were six figures, two looked female.

One of the male figures had a crowbar and was attacking the front door. In that instant I knew the door wasn't going to hold. I broke my promise to myself and used some profanity, very, very loudly. The group below heard me, and the man with the crowbar yelled up to me.

"This is my house! You're a dead man!"

I looked at Dwayne.

"Keep quiet. I'll take care of this. And If I can't, well it's been nice knowing you."

Dwayne looked a little panicked as I exited down the stairs.

On the ground floor I had a decided advantage. I had discovered that my eyes were seeing very well in the darkness. I would see the invaders long before they saw me.

I moved to the far side of the door and waited. A combination of training and instinct started taking over. The Army had taught me some self-defense. Also my Army buddy, Ronnie, is a Krav Maga fanatic and I used to spar with him on a regular basis.

The door gave way, falling to the floor with a thud. As soon as it fell, the first man ran in with the crowbar raised. I took hold of his raised arm and spun one hundred eighty degrees. His forward momentum plus my spin hurled him face first into the brick wall. The next three men came running through the door before I could turn back around. The two women remained outside.

I leapt across the doorway and into the darkness on the

opposite side. The three men were standing in the light from the doorway, scanning the darkness and calling for their friend. "Kyle…Kyle….You OK?" Kyle couldn't answer. Kyle was lying in the little heap on the floor near the door.

One of the men pulled a gun. The other two just stood there behind him. I decided the man with the gun had to go first. I crept quietly around the perimeter of the room, decreasing the distance between me and my target.

The three men were starting to fan out a little. I crouched down on the floor. I made a fist with my right hand and pressed my knuckles firmly against the floor. My knees were bent; I felt my leg muscles swelling and pressing against my jeans.

I leapt and sprang forward like a shot. My right shoulder hit the man with the gun squarely in his mid-section. A primeval growl slipped from my throat. The gun flew from the man's hand. Both he and I hit the floor together in the thick darkness. I heard his gun hit the ground.

I rolled to the side twice and ran quietly for a dark corner of the room.

The man I had just knocked down stood up and groaned. One of his friends had grabbed the gun and started pulling the trigger in the direction of the sound. He didn't stop firing until the gun was only making clicking noises.

The man in the shadows fell back down. I returned to the fallen man. I picked him up with a growl and hurled him at his two standing friends. They fell over like bowling pins.

The two men scrambled to their feet and ran out as fast as they could. I didn't follow. I returned to the unconscious man lying by the wall. I drug his limp body to the center of the room and laid it across the corpse of his friend.

I considered taking both of them somewhere, but

decided against it with Dwayne upstairs. It was better to leave them for now. When the man they called Kyle came to, he might move the corpse for me.

I returned to the second floor and to Dwayne. Dwayne had thrown up in the bag, and was now disoriented and saying things about his lion tattoo moving on his arms. I was very relieved to see that his tattoo wasn't moving even though he was screaming that it was.

Dwayne didn't seem to be aware that I was standing there, so I moved back a few feet and let him hallucinate. He would be passed out soon.

I turned my attention to other matters. My shirt was blood stained. I took it off and placed it in the bag with the vomit. I tied the bag closed so I could dispose of it later. I put on a clean shirt and debated whether I should remain here or find another place to stay.

I didn't know what was about to happen. There were too many variables. Every day was introducing new elements to my situation. Soon there would be too many things for me to control. I needed to not only keep Dwayne away from Lisa and her group, but I felt obligated to keep him safe.

I was still a wanted man and I needed to keep myself hidden. That included doing something with the car belonging to Dwayne. That car was sitting just across the street and I needed to do something with it to draw the authorities away from me.

There was also the corpse downstairs. Even though the dead man had been a drug addict, his death would spark an investigation of this place, and clues of my being here would be too easy to find.

I looked at Dwayne. He had passed out. At least that would make moving him simpler; he wouldn't fight me. But what to do?

Then it hit me. The third floor. The stairway had rotted out, and I had not tried leaping up there because the floor around the opening looked rotted and unsafe. But, I could climb in from the outside.

I grabbed all the small stuff, and put it in my backpack. I took the remaining rope and tied one end to the backpack. I tied the other end under Dwayne's arms. I took Dwayne and the backpack to the stairwell. I threw the backpack upward through the opening, and it landed on the third floor. I exited through my window, and climbed up the wall to the opening directly above.

Looking around I saw that everything looked much the same, except for the gaping hole where the staircase should be. I walked across the floor carefully. It was more solid than it appeared to be.

I went to the hole in the floor where the stairs once stood. I took out the slack in the rope and slowly brought Dwayne up to me. I untied the rope from him and placed Dwayne over by the window facing the studio.

I left one end of the rope on the backpack, and threw the free end back through the hole. After a quick climb down the outside wall and back onto the second floor, I tied the table and chairs to the rope so I could bring them up like I had done with Dwayne.

After moving everything to the third floor, I took Dwayne's keys, wallet, and cell phone and put them in my pockets. I found a clean pair of socks to use as make-shift gloves.

It was a quick climb down; I was getting proficient at scaling the wall. Once on the ground, I went around the building and entered through the front door. Kyle was gone, but his friend's body was still there. I decided I had to move him.

I pulled the corpse to the front door, stuck out my head and scanned my surroundings. The street was empty. I grabbed the body by the shirt collar and drug it across the street to the far side of Dwayne's car.

I took out the car keys and held them between my teeth until I had the socks on my hands. I opened the car and put my John Doe in the passenger seat and buckled him in. I got in the car and started driving north.

At the first bank I saw, I pulled in and stopped the car near an ATM machine. I pulled the brim of my cap down low, and kept my face to the ground. I was going to let the surveillance cameras only see the top of my head. I wanted them to see just enough to know it was not Dwayne using his bank card. I didn't really care whether I got any money out, I just wanted it to look like someone stole Dwayne's card and tried to get cash.

I took the socks off of my hands so I could handle Dwayne's debit card. I noticed that Dwayne had written a four digit number on the back of his card. The number proved to be his pin.

First I checked Dwayne's account balances. There was a little over eight hundred dollars in his checking account, and there was three times that in his savings. I took five hundred from his savings. That's all that the ATM would let me have in a single withdrawal. After putting the money in my pocket, I put the socks back on my hands.

I continued driving north. I found a convenience store. I stopped and filled up the car with gas, using Dwayne's credit card.

After filling up, I pulled the car up to the front door. I pulled his cell phone out of my pocket and wiped it thoroughly with my sock covered hand. I threw the phone and car keys on the driver's seat, got out, locked the door and closed it. I removed my make-shift gloves and threw them in the nearby trash can. I went into the store for a few items. I bought food, trash bags, hand wipes, and other things I wanted. I even bought a newspaper.

Hopefully someone or a security camera somewhere saw me get out of the car with my cap pulled low. Maybe my face was hidden well enough that I would not be recognized.

With any luck the authorities would believe that someone had abducted Dwayne, stolen his car, and left it there with the body. As to where Dwayne was and just who had shot the man in the passenger seat, that would remain a mystery.

I ran back to my building the way I had come. On the way I looked at my watch. It was three AM, Sunday morning. At this time last week, a woman I had seen, but never known, was being murdered. I just hoped I had nothing to do with that. I prayed that whatever had happened to that woman happened while I was passed out in the back seat of my own car.

CHAPTER TWELVE

I slept late that Sunday morning, I didn't wake up until almost ten AM. Dwayne was still sleeping. I decided it was safe to untie him.

It wasn't like Dwayne would be able go anywhere; the only way down was straight down. As I was untying his hands, Dwayne started waking up; he was disoriented. I gave him a bottle of water and then set about untying his feet.

"What's this? All of the sudden you trust me? What's to keep me from knocking you senseless and going to the police?"

Dwayne's face was dead serious. I paused and gave him a serious answer.

"Knocking me senseless wouldn't do you much good. Let me show you a couple of things."

I walked over to the stairwell and motioned for him. He approached cautiously.

"That hole leads straight down, three stories. There used to be a stairway here, but it rotted out a long time ago."

I walked over to the nearest window and Dwayne followed.

"You're on the third floor of an abandoned building. There are no fire escapes and no ladders. You're not getting down without help. Yes, you could stand at the window and yell for help, but I'd prefer you didn't.

We need to talk a little about several other things before we talk about your leaving."

I walked back to my table and pulled out the two chairs.

"Have a seat, Dwayne, I'll fill you in over breakfast."

Dwayne walked over and took a seat while I pulled a box of donuts and two bottles of orange juice out of a plastic sack.

"I apologize that the juice isn't cold. It was cold when I got it at three AM this morning."

Dwayne smirked and grunted before opening his juice.

"Dwayne. Before I tell you what you don't know, I want to tell you what you do know. Last night you saw your new lion tattoo move all around your arms and your body. You felt sick, and you slept very hard.

You dreamed. You dreamed about lions. You dreamed you were a lion. You were running, fighting, and destroying everything in your path. You fought to become the leader of your pack. The pack was hunted, and you started hunting the hunters."

Dwayne blinked, and his expression relaxed.

"How did you know?"

I pointed to my tattoo.

"Remember, I told you. It happened to me. And now you're thinking about Lisa. You're telling yourself that you have to call her."

"OK, you're right. Maybe there is something to the wild story you told. But that didn't give you the right to knock me senseless and tie me up."

"The right? That's true; I was thinking about two things. First, I need to find Lisa so that I can find out what happened to me. I need to find out about a murder and, hopefully, clear my name. I can't do that if Lisa disappears.

If Lisa gets what Lisa wants, if she succeeds in doing to another person what she tried to do to me and wants to do to you, then I may never find her.

Secondly, I was thinking about keeping you safe. If Lisa and her friends get their hands on you, you'll wind up dead or worse."

Dwayne looked puzzled.

"What do you mean by '*dead or worse*'?"

"Well, I would think you know what dead means, it means…dead. Worse, I don't know. I can't explain it. I just know they wanted to…change me somehow, and I wasn't going to like it."

"So what's the plan, Chad?"

That was the first time Dwayne had called me Chad. I took it as a sign that things were becoming a little less adversarial.

"The plan. I don't have much in the way of a plan. I've spent too much time covering my tracks to do much planning.

You might want to know what I've done. Do you remember the fight and the gunshots last night?"

"Not really. I remember some noise, and maybe I heard a gunshot."

I related the story of how four men broke down the door on the first floor and how one of them was shot and killed by one of his friends. I continued telling him that I relocated us to the third floor, adding my thoughts on why it was a good move.

Dwayne had his own thoughts about our little sanctuary; he did not agree with me. He made it obvious that he preferred the comfort and safety of his own home. He added some thoughts about calling his wife because she would be worried sick. I cleared my throat and told him we'd get back to that shortly. He gave me an ugly look.

At this time I chose to tell Dwayne about the cash withdrawal, the car, the corpse I had put in the front seat of his car, and his cell phone.

Dwayne seemed to lack appreciation for what I was doing for him. In hind sight, I probably should have left him tied up before telling him all of that.

Dwayne stood to his feet, enraged. I had no desire to take a beating sitting down. I stood up and attempted to deescalate the situation using both words and body language. I backed toward the center of the room. My hands were down at my sides, palms facing out.

"Dwayne, friend. Try to understand. The police were going to start looking for you. I needed a reason for them to look somewhere other than here, and…"

Dwayne charge toward me. At the last possible moment, I jumped about three feet to the left. If I had stayed in place, my face would have stopped the forward motion of his fist.

Dwayne turned to face me, and threw a second punch with his right arm. I rotated clockwise; his arm extended in front of my face. I reached up and grabbed his forearm with both hands. I used his arm like a lever, pulling it downward toward the floor and then up in a circle behind him. As his arm came up behind him, his shoulder joint locked, he bent at the waist, flipped over, and landed solidly on his back.

I took two steps back, put my hands up level with my ears and displayed my palms. I waited until Dwayne was looking at me before speaking in flat, emotionless tones.

"I give up. Stop. I can't take any more. I've had enough."

Dwayne looked at me with nothing less than contempt. As he sat himself up and he made a few statements questioning my lineage. He let several colorful phrases pass his lips. There was even a word in there that I don't ever remember hearing before, but I choose not to ask him about it.

Dwayne returned to his chair, and I returned to mine. Three or four minutes passed before either of us spoke.

Dwayne broke the silence first.

"OK, Chad, I'll ask again; what's the plan?"

I smiled. I smiled because we were back on a first name basis. That gave me some hope that he might cooperate with me just a little bit. And that's all I needed from him…just a little cooperation.

"I'm afraid it's not a very elaborate plan. It starts with you calling Lisa."

"Well, duh…" Dwayne look at me blankly. "Of course I'll call Lisa. I have to call her; she told me to."

"*Ohhh* Kay…"

I looked at Dwayne realizing just how crazy I must have sounded to my dorm mate, Kevin, when I said almost the exact same thing. I continued on.

"Dwayne, buddy, whatever voodoo, Lisa-do, is workin' in you."

Dwayne look at me puzzled, and I continued.

"After you call, I'll go meet her. I'll bring her back here. The three of us are going to have a conversation and start clearing this mess up."

Dwayne agreed. I retrieved my cell phone and the little slip of paper with Lisa's name and number from my backpack. I dialed the number and handed the phone to Dwayne. I jotted down the address as I heard it. He was supposed to pick up Lisa at five.

I made sure I had a couple of lengths of rope tied around my waist and under my shirt. I put Dwayne's folding knife in my pocket. I donned my backpack and looked over at Dwayne.

"I'm going to head out. When I bring Lisa back we may as well eat. What kind of pizza do you like?

"Anything guy, just lots of meat. But before you go, what do I do about the bathroom around here? I can't hold it much longer."

I tossed him the box of small trash can liners and a pack of hand wipes I bought on my last excursion.

Dwayne looked at me and said pathetically, "Dude,

you've got to be kidding!"

"Not at all, my friend. Nothing but the best for my guests here at the Fury Inn and Suites."

Before I had to listen to any objections, I disappeared out the rear window and began scaling down the wall. Dwayne stuck his head out the window to watch. He gasped, "Dude, you're not human!" I didn't know what he meant by that remark, but I let it pass and continued my descent.

I hit the ground and immediately started to run. I had a pretty good idea where the address was, and I wanted to get there in time to scope out the lay of the land.

The address was on Farmington Street was about sixteen miles away, and I made it in a little less than twenty-five minutes. It was now two-thirty PM.

The neighborhood was average, and the street number was associated with a rather plain looking two story house. There was one car in the driveway. I had to know if Lisa was alone.

I pulled the brim of my ball cap low over my eyes and looked up and down the street. A man was washing his car a couple of houses down, and he saw me. I had to keep moving.

I walked the length of the street down to the intersection intending to cross over to the adjacent street. When I arrived at the intersection I saw that there was a drainage ditch separating the houses on Farmington from their neighbors behind them. The best part was that all of the houses had privacy fences. I walked quietly along the drainage ditch until I was at the back yard of the house I wanted.

After all of the wall climbing I'd done, a six-foot privacy fence wasn't much of an obstacle. I was over the fence and across the back yard in seconds.

I leaned against the back of the house and listened. I couldn't hear anyone; I couldn't tell if anyone was in the house.

I pulled out my cellphone and dialed Lisa's number. I didn't bother putting the phone to my ear. I heard the ringing through the cell phone speaker, then a split second later I heard a phone start ringing inside the house. I hung up as soon as I heard Lisa say "Hello". I strained to listen inside the house again. I heard no conversation, no voices. I took that to mean Lisa was alone inside the house.

I evaluated different methods of gaining access, from breaking through the back door to shattering windows. I finally settled on the direct approach.

I walked around the side house, through the gate and strolled up to the front door. My heart was pounding as I rang the bell. I saw movement through the frosted glass along the edge of the door. A few seconds later the door opened.

I lifted my head and said, "Hello, Lisa. How have you been?"

Lisa gasped and tried to slam the door, but my right foot was planted firmly in the opening. I pushed the door open quickly, entered and slammed it behind me.

Lisa was standing about ten feet from me backing up toward what looked like the kitchen at the far end of the house. She stopped suddenly, gained her composure, and spoke.

"You will leave me and never return. You will go to the police and turn yourself in."

I winced in pain and instinctively put a finger in my ear.

"What the hell, Lisa? I will not! And what was that awful whistling?"

She stood there looking shocked.

"You heard that?"

"Of course, I heard that. "What was it?"

"No, you shouldn't be able to…" She paused and tried again. "Leave. Go to the policed. Turn yourself in."

"Will you please stop making that noise?! And no, I'm not leaving without you!"

"Look", Lisa said, "You shouldn't be able to hear that,

and I don't have time to explain. I've got people coming over, and they won't want you here. For your own sake, you'd better leave now!"

"I can pretty well guess who you've got coming over. One or more of your 'witch' friends are coming over to wait for Dwayne. You're going to drug him and take him away for some kind of ritual."

Lisa's look changed to anger.

"Now look here, Chad, neither I nor my sisters are witches! There's no such thing. As for what we're doing. Stay out of it!"

I lifted up my shirt and removed a length of rope tied around my waist.

"No way lady. You are coming with me. If I have to tie you and carry you out, you're coming. I'll give you a choice. You can give me the keys to that car and we can leave in a civilized manner, or…"

I gripped the rope, one end in each hand, and pulled sharply removing the slack with a 'snap'. I stood silently while she considered it.

"Let me get my purse."

Lisa pushed past me, and I followed her to a bedroom. She snatched her purse angrily, and said, "Let's go!"

"Not so fast. I want the keys and your cell phone."

She glared at me. After a few seconds she dug through her purse and handed the keys and cell phone to me. I threw the cell phone on the bed, and clenched the keys in my fist.

"I'm taking you to Dwayne. The three of us are going to have a nice long talk."

We walked out of the front door and over to her white sedan in total silence. I did the gentlemanly thing by opening her door for her.

Before getting in the driver's side, I threw my backpack in the back seat. As soon as I started the car, I remembered I had another task to perform. I dug my cell phone out of my pocket.

As a college student I had ordered enough pizza that I had the number for my favorite place committed to memory. I dialed and ordered three large pizzas. I informed Lisa that we were stopping along the way.

Lisa glared and scowled at me the entire trip. When we arrived at my place, I parked the car in the Imagine Ink parking lot. We got out, I took my backpack and the pizzas; I asked Lisa to carry the drinks. She grunted unhappily as she picked up the sacks containing the two large bottles of soda and the six pack of beer.

Lisa headed away from the car toward the rear of the studio. I cleared my throat, "Excuse, me. Just where are you going?"

She looked at me angrily, "Just where, should I be going?"

"This way," I said as I motioned with my head.

We hurried across the street and disappeared into the doorway of my abandoned building.

"Nice place you have here, Chad. But if it was up to me I'd add a little something, like, say, electricity? Just sayin'…"

"Yeah, well, you don't have to hide out because you're wanted for murder and the people who can corroborate your story are totally off the grid.

We're going up the stairs. It's probably too dark for you to see. Put your hand on my arm and follow me."

Lisa came to my side and took hold of my upper arm. I have to admit it felt good. It reminded me of the way Chrissy used to squeeze my arm and walk with me.

I started walking, and Lisa spoke up. "Slow down. Do you have this memorized or can you actually see in here?"

"Since recovering from whatever you did to me, I've been able to do a lot of things. Seeing in very low light is just one of them.

Careful, we're at the stairs."

We ascended slowly and exited on the second floor. There was more light due to the windows being nothing more than open holes.

"Where's Dwayne! I thought you were taking me to him!" I heard fear in her voice. "I've given you no reason to hurt me!"

"Relax. I seldom bring pizza to a murder. That's more of a hotdog and popcorn affair."

"So where is he?"

"He's on the third floor, but the stairs are rotted out. Give me a minute."

I leaned into the stairwell and yelled out, "Dwayne! Dwayne!"

Dwayne peered down through the gaping hole above our heads.

"Hey. What'cha doin' down there?"

"I brought food, and Lisa. I wanted to get the food as close as possible before throwing it to you. I hope you're a good catch."

I tossed the boxes up to him one at a time, and he caught them with ease. I took the drinks from Lisa, and pitched those to him one at a time.

Lisa stood there with one hand on her hip.

"Well, that's fine for Pizza, but what about you and me?"

I pulled off my backpack and took out the rope.

"Here, tie one end around your chest and under your arms." I reached out to help her.

"No way! You're not going to drag me up through some hole by a rope! How do I know you won't just leave me dangling there?"

I sighed.

"There is another way, if you're willing. But it might be a little scary."

"I'm listening."

"Put your arms out and interlock your fingers."

I demonstrated. When she complied I ducked between her arms, with my back toward her. I stood up, and her feet left the ground as she hung about my shoulders. I bent down, picked up the backpack and threw it through the opening. I proceeded to the rear window and started crawling out.

Lisa let out a yell as she realized what was happening.

I warned her, "Whatever you do, just keep holding on."

I had just started climbing, and Lisa yelled out again, "Chad! Your hands!!"

That was the first time I had looked at my hands while climbing. I had always been focusing on the wall, concentrating on my destination, but not looking at my hands.

I liberated my left hand and stared in amazement. Instead of four fingers and a thumb, there were only two fingers and a thumb. Fingers one and two were fused together forming a single new digit. Likewise for fingers three and four. The new fingers looked as though they were covered in shiny red scales. Each digit terminated with a single, golden yellow claw. I turned my hand, and saw that my thumb was a perfect mate for the other two fingers. I almost pulled my right hand away to examine it before I realized where I was and what I was doing.

"Look at it later!" Lisa shouted, "Just get me inside!"

I complied. I reached the third floor window; Lisa climbed off my back and through the square opening. I climbed over the edge, and stopped to examine my hands. They were already returning to normal and were back to their fleshy selves in less than a minute.

"That's…not…possible." I whispered.

Lisa reached out and stroked my right hand. "Well, obviously we were more successful than we thought."

"What the freak-in' hell was that?'

I looked into Lisa's eyes for answers, and found none.

Lisa cast a glance at Dwayne, and then back at me. "I guess you really do want answers."

"That would be nice." I looked at Dwayne; he was nodding his head in agreement.

Dwayne and I put the pizzas on the table. I lit a couple

of candles. Lisa and Dwayne sat in the chairs; and I sat on the window ledge. Once we all had food and drink in hand, I started requesting answers from Lisa.

"Lisa, tell me about Emily Smith…what did I…I mean, did I, well…

"What are you trying to say?"

"I need to know if I had anything to do with her death."

"Cha, You mean to tell me you don't know?"

"How could I know? The police think I did, and I don't know where I was when she died."

"Chad, you were passed out in the back seat of your car. Emily drove your car, and I followed in mine. I drove Emily back to her place and left her there, alone."

I exhaled in relief.

"Lisa, do you know who killed her?"

"*Know* them? No. Know of them? Yes.

They're hunters, part of the Abomination. It's a long story, Chad. I'm not sure where to start."

Dwayne cleared his throat and addressed Lisa.

"Lisa, why not start with what your little band of witches want with us and the animal tattoos?"

Lisa flashed Dwayne a dirty look.

"Don't call us that! There's no such things as witches."

"What should I call you? You tell me."

Lisa swallowed a bite of veggie pizza. "We're El-yanin. From El-yana."

Dwayne set his beer bottle down with a thud. "Really? Aliens! Don't go there."

I was in total agreement with Dwayne's sentiment. But, I decided upon a different tactic.

"Let's back up a bit. I want to try something. Lisa, pick a number between one and twenty."

"Fourteen." Lisa smirked.

"Stop it. I'm serious. Pick a number between twenty and forty."

I pulled pen and a notebook from my backpack and

gave it to her.

"Now write it down. I'm going to go ask 'is your number twenty?' You will answer 'no'. I will go through all the numbers, and you will answer no every time.

"I thought you wanted answers about what happened to you?"

"Please just do it. I'll explain after. Is your number twenty?"

Lisa replied, "No" and I repeated this for the rest of the series. When I hit thirty-seven I smelled onions, but I continued on to complete the series.

"Your number was thirty-seven."

Lisa raised a single eyebrow. "How did you know?"

I told Lisa and Dwayne how I learned that I could literally smell a lie. I had to demonstrate my ability four more times before I was believed. Afterwards, I demanded the truth from Lisa.

CHAPTER THIRTEEN

Lisa's story was a long one, and much to my surprise, I never once detected the onion-like odor of a lie. If it were not for the fact that I am able to smell lies, neither Dwayne nor I could have believed what we were being told.

Lisa made the claim that she and her sisters were descendants of visitors from another world, El-yana; they referred to themselves as El-yanin.

To help us understand her tale, Lisa gave Dwayne and me a short course in string theory. It was more difficult for Dwayne to keep up; he'd never had anything more than high school science and apparently had not done well in it. But Lisa did an amazing job of making the subject consumable for almost anyone.

According to Lisa, the El-yanin learned the nature of the universe thousands of years before humans began pondering string theory on Earth. Not only did the El-yanin perceive all matter as being comprised of vibrating strings, they made the great scientific leap of being able to manipulate string vibrations.

Lisa explained that if subatomic strings vibrate at one frequency they form protons, at another, neutrons, and so forth. By changing the vibrational frequency of strings, the fundamental nature of matter can be altered. It is even possible to change lead into gold, or salt into sugar. Lisa admitted that she made the explanation far too simple and there was a lot more behind the process.

For the El-yanin changing the nature of subatomic particles was, for nearly a millennia, as impossible as changing the nature of gravity.

The El-yanin eventually discovered the secret of altering matter, and through a resulting accident they discovered how to open portals between universes. The long supposed existence of parallel universes was finally proven when the El-yanin began opening dimensional portals. Lisa's group had come to Earth through a dimensional portal, and not on a space ship.

That answered how, but I was more concerned with why. Dwayne on the other hand was just lost and bored with the science, and had become restless. He had only two priorities now. First, he wanted me to let him go, and second wanted to make sure Lisa and her group were not going to bother him and his family. Lisa agreed to discuss that at the end of her story, which left Dwayne irritated and sulking.

Dwayne got up and took a trash bag into the shadows of the furthest corner behind a structural wall. I had to explain to Lisa what he was doing, and she tried to ignore it.

Lisa continued on with her story. She was born on Earth, but knew the history of her people. According to Lisa, the El-yanin had been able to cure all disease, and had put an end to most conflict. They did all of this by eliminating undesirable genes from the entire population. But the attempts to play God with their genetic makeup left them with a side effect. They had eliminated too much diversity in their gene pool, and we all know what happens when cousins marry.

The population of El-yana was too closely related. The number of live births was declining, and the entire species was headed for extinction. It would take generations, but eventually the El-yanin would become extinct.

The only course of action was to find new, compatible genetic material and introduce it into the population. For countless reasons, suitable donors were not found in their own universe. Portals were opened to parallel universes and Earth had proven to be the most promising treasure house of compatible DNA.

A contingent of two hundred scientists and volunteers made the journey through the portals to Earth about fourteen-hundred years ago. The volunteers, all female, were instructed to take mates who had been selected for specific desirable traits. It was a requirement that all of the offspring were to be female until after the return to El-yana.

The goal was to return to El-yana with enough female offspring to supply sufficient genetic diversity to begin cloning the new improved El-yanin. The cloning would be followed by a slow return to the natural reproductive order of things after the population was sufficiently salted with the new traits.

It was no surprise for me to hear about good plans going bad. The expedition party was not prepared for our uncivilized world. Regardless of how good of an act you put on, you can't fool all of the people all of the time. Things happen.

The El-yanin who came to this world were looked upon as practitioners of witchcraft and sorcery. They were hunted, and as a result they were driven into hiding.

The El-yanin broke into small groups they referred to as Sisterhoods, and spread out across Europe. They looked much less suspicious, but it created another problem. You can't control a large group of people from a great distance.

One of the volunteers fell in love with an unapproved male and had twin sons. The sons were born with the full genetic heritage of the El-yanin, and the human traits of deceit, callousness, greed, and other assorted ills of human nature. The sons were literally 'bad seed' and their descendants came to be known as the 'Abomination'.

The Abomination performed their own version of genetic enhancement. They mated freely, and destroyed their own offspring whenever their progeny appeared to be flawed or weak.

They began hunting the Sisterhoods, thirsty for their knowledge. They wanted to know how to manipulate matter. They wanted all of the secrets that would literally put them at the top of the food chain. The knowledge possessed by the Sisterhoods had the potential to make them god-like on this world.

The genetic project was a long-term project. In terms of overall length it was to take generations. It was finally nearing completion, but the Abomination still remained a problem. The Sisterhoods were not willing to leave the Abomination behind on Earth.

As long as the Sisterhoods remained on Earth, they would be the target of the Abomination's activities. If they left, the Abomination would have free reign to abuse humanity in any way they chose.

The ability of the Abomination to abuse was profound. Their El-yanin heritage gave them the same vocal abilities as the Sisterhood.

Humans have a normal set of vocal cords and a false set. The false set is used by singers to produce the falsetto tones we hear in music.

The El-yanin have a normal set of vocal cords, and a fully developed second set. With the second set of vocal cords they create tones that make the hearer subject to their commands, much like hypnosis, but vastly stronger than any post hypnotic suggestion.

As a group they can sing with their second voice and create the vibrations needed to affect matter.

The El-yanin also have the ability to share the memories and thoughts of another person through physical contact with that person's blood.

The Abomination had taken some of the secrets of the El-yanin, but not all. Opening portals and changing the nature of matter is complex; too complex to commit to memory. Those secrets were written in books, and the books were distributed among the Sisterhoods.

Each Sisterhood was responsible for guarding their book. When the time comes for them to depart they will assemble the volumes and use the combined knowledge of the books to open the portals for the return trip.

There are a total of sixteen books. Four had been stolen by the Abomination and their current location is unknown. Without all sixteen, the return trip is impossible.

But that only answered part of the questions. Dwayne was the first to ask what all of this had to do with the two of us. I agreed that it was an interesting story, but it was getting late and I wanted to get to why we were in the middle of this mess.

Lisa contended that Dwayne and I had stepped into the middle of a cat and mouse game that had been going on for hundreds of years. The Abomination would try to locate and trap the members of a Sisterhood, and the Sisterhood tried to protect its members. The Abomination would take the younger members for breeding stock, and bleed the older ones for information.

When the Sisterhood was threatened, they would select a human male to transform into its protector. The transformation was accomplished by encapsulating animal DNA in viruses, and infecting the selected male.

The Sisterhood would sing a transformation song over the man. If his mind was properly prepared by fixating on an animal matching the new DNA, the song would make the animal DNA merge with his own and bring about an immediate change in his physiology and behavior.

The new protector would be a kind of chimera, a blending of two species. His higher reasoning functions would be gone and the Sisterhood could control him easily with verbal commands. This new creation would hunt the members of the Abomination. The Sisterhood would have time to relocate and continue their work in peace.

It was at that point Dwayne stood up and gave us a demonstration of his excellent command of profanity, after which he started making full sentences.

"Damn it Lisa! What gives you the right to throw my life away?"

"They…we do it for the greater good. What is your life worth compared to the lives of billions…an entire race?"

Dwayne was glaring at Lisa, and I wasn't feeling much different about the situation.

Dwayne barked out, "Sure, billions of people I never knew existed, and who brought this entire mess down on their own heads!"

Lisa was silent. There was no arguing with Dwayne. There was a certain logic in not using others against their will, no matter how well intended the result might be. From our point of view, the ends did not justify the means.

I stood up and took the last beer before speaking.

"Lisa, what do we do? Dwayne does not want to be turned into some creature. I want my life back. I intend to get my life back, and you're going to tell me how!"

Lisa shifted uncomfortably in her chair. She looked at the floor, then looked away. She spoke without looking at either of us.

"Dwayne, you're problem's simple. Stay away from me and the Sisterhood. Eventually your body will flush the animal DNA out of your system. Chad, your situation's a lot different."

"I'm sure it is different. Just tell me what I'm up against. I want to know just how angry I need to get."

"First, I don't know if what we did can be undone. Only the Matron can tell you. To change you back may require having all sixteen copies of the book. You'll never get your hands on them. The books are being guarded by Sisterhoods around the world."

"Twelve", I corrected her. "Twelve copies are being guarded by the Sisterhoods. Four are in the hands of the Abomination."

"OK. Your right twelve. If you can be changed back, then the answer might be in any one of the books, or it might be spread out across all sixteen. You'd have to ask the Matron."

I inhaled deeply through my nose and slowly out through my mouth to keep from yelling. I waited until I knew I could speak calmly and rationally.

"Do it. Get me in touch with the Matron."

"That's not so simple since you abducted me."

"Enlighten me."

"My sisters don't know where I am. You abducted me, and I can't just pick up the phone and talk to them. We don't communicate that way; it's too risky.

Alice was abducted three days before we tried to turn you. Emily was killed after we took you back to your dorm at the university. Now that I've disappeared and did not deliver Dwayne to our meeting, the Sisterhood will assume that I've been abducted by the Abomination.

Three members lost is three too many. Add to that, we were not successful in creating a protector.

I'm certain Sisterhood will scatter now. They will flee and regroup at another location. I don't know where they will go, and I may not be able to contact them after they're gone. I'll be cutoff."

I clenched my teeth to keep from yelling profanities. My hand tightened around my beer bottle; it shattered in my grip. Beer and shards of brown glass sprayed across the table and golden liquid ran down my arm.

We all gasped. I was certain I was cut and bleeding. I opened my hand slowly only to reveal normal healthy skin and shards of brown glass clinging to my palm. The three of us stared in amazement.

Lisa looked at me. Her voice was almost a whisper, "Chad, if I can reach the Matron, you may have a bargaining chip."

"What do you mean?" I said sounding as confused as Dwayne.

Lisa smiled, "If you can convince the Matron that you can be our protector, she might agree to almost anything."

"Do it, Lisa. Do whatever you need to do. It's my only hope of getting my life back."

Lisa walked over to the wall where she had sat her purse down. She dug through the purse and pulled out a two-inch glass cube with gold and silver edges. She placed the cube in the palm of her right hand. She rested her left index finger on the surface of the cube and it glowed orange. It pulsed like a beating heart.

Lisa sang to the cube. The cube seemed to change color with the changing melody. When Lisa finished singing, she stood silent and motionless for several seconds. After a moment the cube glowed and pulsed in shades of green and blue. Lisa smiled, nodded, and put the cube back in her purse.

I've reached my contact and I let her know that I'm OK. I told her I need to speak to the Matron, it's being arranged.

I was in awe of what I had just seen and had to ask, "What just happened?"

Dwayne and I both gave Lisa our attention.

"The transresinator has several uses, but think of it as our smart phone, if you will."

Dwayne said it before I could.

"I didn't hear anything. Who were you talking to?"

"There's other ways to talk besides sounds coming out of your mouth. It would take too long to explain. There's a lot I have to do. Get me out of here Chad, I need to get started."

Dwayne looked Lisa.

"What about me? I need to go home."

Lisa nodded at Dwayne, but I spoke before she could make a sound. I explained to Lisa what I had done with

Dwayne's car and the corpse inside.

Lisa's spoke to Dwayne using her vocal talents.

"Dwayne, you won't tell anyone about Chad. You were taken by a gang. You barely escaped. You will forget about the Sisterhood and about your time with Chad."

Dwayne responded, "Yes, I was taken. Gang. Escaped. I will forget..."

Lisa promised to take Dwayne home. I carried them each down to the ground, one at a time. This time, I gave Lisa my phone number.

"Call me tomorrow. Let's talk about finding the Matron."

"I'll do better than that. I'll be back here before noon. Be prepared to leave, you're getting new accommodations."

CHAPTER FOURTEEN

It had rained during the night. A spring storm blew rain into my loft and I had a difficult time keeping both dry and warm. That morning I had a cereal bar and water for breakfast and I finally read the Saturday evening newspaper I had bought. I was curious what it had to say about my escape from the county jail four days ago.

Several pages inside the newspaper, I found a story telling that the access hatch in the shower room was now sealed and the cinderblock wall in the guard's locker room would be fixed in the next few days.

The article recapped the theft of the money and food from the convenience store, and stated that I had been seen buying camping supplies at a local store. The story went on to say it was likely that I was camping out in parks and wooded areas. It ended by saying that if I was seen, I should be considered armed and dangerous.

There was no mention in the paper of me trying to get to Amarillo and no reference of calls to my mother. But reading the paper did remind me that I still had an envelope to mail to Ronnie.

I didn't go out to the gas station to clean up. I stayed in my loft. I brushed my teeth with bottled water, and used the hand wipes to freshen up. I missed hot showers and running water. I was convinced that I needed a few more creature comforts and I was ready for this phase of my adventure to come to an end.

It wasn't long before I heard a voice yelling up from the second floor.

"Hey, Dragon Boy. Get your butt over here!"

I ran to the gaping hole over the stairwell to see Lisa looking up at me. She gestured with her arm for me to come down.

"Grab all your stuff; it's time to check out of here. I've made reservations at a nicer place to stay."

"Give me a minute", I yelled back. "What do you think I should do with the trash?"

"Leave it. It will be years before anyone finds it up here. Now move it. We've got a lot to do."

I put my things in my backpack, including the envelope for Ronnie.

I tossed my backpack down through the hole and onto the stairs below.

"Look out", I said, "I want to try something."

I jumped across the hole, caught the edge of the floor, and swung myself over to land firmly on the second floor landing.

"If you're done showing off, let's go."

Lisa was already heading down the staircase. I followed, carrying my backpack in hand. We went out the front door and I pulled my ball cap down over my eyes. Lisa made a clicking sound with her tongue against her teeth,

"We've got to do something about your clothes. As soon as we can, we need to burn everything you're wearing. You also need a haircut and a shave."

"Hey, priorities here."

"I am thinking about priorities. I'm going to arrange a meeting with the Matron, and you need to convince her that you're fit to be a substitute protector, and not a poster child for the homeless."

Soon we were at her car, and I was getting into the passenger side. Lisa got in, and started the engine.

"Where are we headed?"

Lisa smiled, "It's a surprise."

"Well, then, I don't even know your last name. What is it?"

"Smith", she replied. I caught the scent of onions.

"Hey, what happened to honesty?"

"We all go by Smith, or at least most of us do. It helps protect our identity. Smith's all you need to know."

I stopped talking and decided to enjoy the ride. Before long we were pulling in to a five star hotel near Oklahoma City's Brick Town area.

"Are you kidding me?"

I felt like I could cry at the thought of a real bed and a hot shower.

"We've got a room here?"

"Two rooms. You and I are in *separate* rooms."

Lisa stressed the word separate.

"I need a place to stay too. The Abomination is a real threat and I've been staying in a hotel since Emily's death."

She parked the car in a space nearest the entrance. She took something from the cup holder and handed it to me.

"Here's your key card, room three twenty-one. I've checked you in under the name Charles Fenton. I'm in the adjoining room, three twenty-three. The rooms face the parking lot. I thought you'd appreciate having a window on the third floor."

I laughed. "Thank you."

I go out of the car, grabbed my bag from the back seat and headed toward the door of the hotel.

"Hey, not so fast."

Lisa motioned me back close. She lowered her voice.

"There are security cameras in the hallways and just inside each door. Don't forget, you're still hiding out."

I gave her a sarcastic look, but I was actually glad she reminded me. I had been so overcome at the thought of staying in a room with running water and a decent bed that I had forgotten my predicament.

I waited for Lisa, and held the door for her. I followed her to the elevator. The ride up the elevator went quickly, and soon I was sliding my key card into the door lock on room three twenty-one.

I went inside my room and just stood there for a few seconds. The room was bright and clean. I sniffed the air; there were none of the noxious smells I had been enduring since my arrest. I tossed my bag on the bed; at the same time there was a knock on the door from the adjoining room.

"Hey, Charlie!"

I opened the door and Lisa came in carrying a notepad, pen, and a cloth tape measure.

"I've got some errands to run, and I thought you'd appreciate having some alone-time to settle in. Before I go, I need your measurements; you need a serious makeover."

Lisa took my measurements; waist, inseam, neck and arms. She even got my hat size.

"Now that I have your sizes, there's a few things we need to go over. First of all, you need to go by a different name. I'm going to be calling you Charlie for a while. You need to get used to hearing it and answering to it."

"That makes sense, I guess."

"Next, I know this isn't a prison, but try staying in your room. Please stay out of sight until your makeover's complete. Keep the 'Do Not Disturb' sign on the door. You don't need anyone walking in on you."

"I can do that."

"Feel free to order room service. Have the person who brings the food leave it outside at the door."

I was starting to get a little irritated, and it showed in my voice.

"I'm a big boy, I think I can watch my own back."

Lisa's eyes flashed and I knew I was in for a long, one-sided conversation.

"Look here, Chad. It's not just your back I'm worried about! You've still got to keep a low profile and you don't realize just how much your face has been plastered over every television screen in the city. The very minute you stop being careful is the minute we're both sunk! You'll be back in jail and headed for a prison sentence and possibly death row, and I'll be taken by the Abomination as breeding stock. There's not one part of that scenario I find appealing! And furthermore, you stink and need a bath. Now if…"

I interrupted her speech.

"I'm sorry, you're right. You're doing a lot for me. You're taking a huge risk and I need to be more thoughtful and appreciative."

Lisa's eyes softened. I stood there looking into her green eyes long enough that I embarrassed myself.

Lisa broke the awkward silence.

"Take your clothes off."

My mouth fell open!

"Uhmmm…I, Uhmmm…well…"

"Not that, stupid! Take you clothes off and give them to me. They need to be burned. Go in the bathroom, strip, and throw you clothes out the door. I'll take them with me and get rid of them; including that grimy ball cap.

But before you do that, empty that backpack. I want the clothes out of there too. I don't need to see what's in the bag to know there's not a single thing you've got that's fit to be worn to a worm wrestle."

I took the clothes from my backpack and put them in a trash bag. I went into the bathroom, stripped, and put my clothes in a second bag. I threw the bag out the door and closed it quickly.

"There you go. Don't say that I never gave you anything!"

"Gee, thanks. And before I go, one more thing…"

"Yeah, what?"

"Briefs or boxers?"

"I like the knit boxer briefs. Oh, and I forgot something too. On the bed is a large padded envelope that needs to be mailed, will you please drop it in a mailbox for me?'

"It depends", Lisa paused, "What's inside?"

"The envelope's addressed to an old Army buddy, Ronnie. Inside are a dozen postcards; I've addressed each one to my mother. They say things like, don't worry. I'm fine. I miss you. Ronnie's going to mail one every two weeks or so, each time from a different city."

"That's not bad. That's pretty clever. You got it, Dragon Boy!"

I heard the door between the rooms close, and I stepped into the shower.

After showering, I realized that I didn't have anything to wear. Lisa had taken everything. I wrapped a towel around my waist before placing the 'Do Not Disturb' sign on the handle outside of the room door. I went to the writing table and found the room service menu. I ordered a medium rare steak, baked potato, and two beers. If I couldn't leave the room, I might as well relax.

It wasn't until I put my backpack in the closet that I noticed two terrycloth robes hanging there. I put a robe on and sat down on the edge of the king-sized bed and just stared at the center of the room.

I don't entirely know what came over me in that moment. Maybe it was because after more than a week of constant stress I finally felt safe. I don't know what it was exactly, but whatever it was it came out in a flood of tears. I sat on the edge of the bed and wept.

I felt alone, and I felt a tremendous sense of loss. The life I knew was gone. I remember thinking that I was fooling myself to imagine I could get my life back. Even if I could clear my name, no medical school would ever accept me.

Chrissy and I were finished; there was no fixing that. And, my mother. I knew she would always love me, but I couldn't even talk to her right now. I didn't know how long it would be before I could see her again and tell her the truth.

I was still having my pity party when I heard a knock at the door.

"Room service."

"I can't get to the door right now. Please leave it."

"Yes, sir."

I wiped my face on my sleeve, went to the door and opened it. There was no one in the hall. There was, however, rolling cart with a try. The tray had a metal dome, a glass, two bottles of beer and a bottle opener.

I left the cart in the hallway, picked up the tray and carried it over to a little round table near the large reclining chair by the window. I took the television remote from the nightstand and found a news channel.

I sat in the recliner, ate my steak and potato and sipped my beer. A blonde anchorwoman on the television droned on about the deadlock between the Congress and the Senate and how the President wasn't taking sides. It seemed to me that the world had not changed much in a week.

After a while I heard some news about me. A picture of me flashed up on the screen behind the blonde woman and she started in.

"You all remember Chad Fury, the Oklahoma University student that was arrested for brandishing a gun on campus."

I got mad, waved my fork at the television and spoke loudly to the TV with my mouth still full of potato.

"I never pulled a gun!"

The anchorwoman ignored me and continued speaking.

"He was arrested on suspicion of terrorism, and was later connected with the murder of an Oklahoma City school teacher.

Fury was being held in the Cleveland County Jail pending formal charges. Before charges could be brought, he made a daring escape worthy of the film industry.

The Oklahoma State Bureau of Investigation, working in conjunction with the Federal Bureau of Investigation, is acting on credible evidence that Fury is making his way to Amarillo, Texas. He may be there now.

The citizens of Amarillo are asked to be on the lookout for this man. If you see him or have any information relating to him, call the FBI tip line. We're showing the number at the bottom of the screen."

That was enough for me. I sighed in relief. I figured the FBI and friends would be pretty busy. Now that the public had been told I was in Amarillo, sightings would start coming in, and some of the reports would sound reasonable enough that the FBI would convince themselves that I was hiding out there. It might be a few days before the FBI decided it was dead end. Shortly after that my mother should receive the first postcard from Shreveport.

I flipped through the channels and landed on an old black and white movie that I didn't care about. It was just nice to have some voices in the room for company as I finished my meal.

CHAPTER FIFTEEN

It wasn't until I heard a knock on the door from the next room that I realized I had fallen asleep in the chair. I shook off the sleep, adjusted my bathrobe, and went and opened the door between our rooms. Lisa was standing in the doorway with a suitcase in tow.

"Hello, Charlie. I brought you a few things."

Lisa crossed the threshold into my room dragging a rolling suitcase behind her. Suitcase wasn't really the correct term. It was a big, blue rolling duffle bag. It stood over thirty inches high.

"How many bodies have you got in there?"

"It's empty right now. But you needed something big; you're going to be living out of a suitcase for a while. It was the biggest thing I could get that could also go on an airplane."

"I don't know. It seems pretty big. I'm supposed to be hiding out. I don't need a bag of bricks slowing me down."

"You're right, Charlie. You are hiding out. And fortunately for you, I'm here to help."

I looked at her perplexed.

"Charlie, the Sisterhood's been hiding in plain sight for hundreds of years. We know how to do it, and I'm about to teach you. Pay attention, class is in session."

Lisa stood there, evidently waiting for me to do or say something, but I was speechless. She broke the silence.

"Put the bag on the bed and open it. You're going to try on your new clothes and pack the bag as you do."

I did as I was told, I put the bag on the bed and opened it. Lisa looked at me standing in my robe.

"Darn it! I should have told you to shave."

"I did shave." I rubbed my face with my hand.

"Not just your face, everywhere else."

"What the..." I cut myself off. I was trying to curb my use of profanity. "I don't shave anywhere else."

"We need to change your appearance. I have a tube of tanning cream in my room. It goes on best if there's no body hair in the way. You're going to be getting an all-over tan. I'll be dying your hair, including your eyebrows. And, you're getting a haircut."

Lisa went into her room and came back with a white plastic sack and dumped the contents on the bed. I stared at the assortment of boxes, gloves, creams and paraphernalia. She took a razor and a tube of shaving foam from the assortment and handed them to me.

"Charlie, that razor and foam is made for body hair. Put them in the bathroom and come right back."

I did as I was instructed. When I returned Lisa was setting out a pair of gloves. She pulled the desk chair into the center of the room and draped a towel over it.

"OK, what's next? I've got a feeling it's not much fun."

"I'm giving you a haircut, then I'm coloring your hair."

"Are you any good at cutting hair?"

"I have the memories of generations of women. And a few of those women have actually cut men's hair before. I think I can manage."

I seated myself and bent my head back to look at her.

"My fate is in your hands."

To my surprise she had all the accoutrements; electric clippers, a variety of combs, a spray bottle of water and even a pair of those pointy scissors barbers use. She snipped, and cut and ran the clippers. After a few minutes, she told me to take a look.

I stood up and went over to the full-length mirror on the bathroom door to look at myself.

"Not bad, high and tight on the sides, a little spiked on top. It looks pretty good."

"Thank you. Now, sit back down it's time to color it."

"What color?"

"Your natural color is a kind of a medium brown. We could go dark or light. Most people trying to hide their identity choose to go lighter. I personally think dark is better. Anything we can do to make it look like you're not trying to hide will be best."

"Dark it is. Do your worst."

Lisa poured a couple of chemicals in a squeeze bottle, and shook it to mix it up. She draped a towel over my shoulders, then she spread Vaseline on my skin at the edge of the hairline and all over my ears.

"Hey, what's that for?"

"The hair dye will stain your skin. And nothing makes hair color look more fake than stain on your face and neck. The Vaseline will keep the dye off your face. The dye is thin; it's going to run down your neck and face. If you need to wipe it off, just blot it with the towel. Don't rub off the Vaseline."

"OK. I got it."

"By the way, this stuff will burn your scalp. It's going to get uncomfortably hot. That's normal. Just be patient."

"Oh, great! I can't wait."

Lisa started working the color into my hair. She was right. It ran down my face and it burned my scalp.

"How long do I have to leave this stuff in?"

"About ten minutes. We're going black, so it won't matter if we leave it too long, it can't get too dark."

After she finished putting the color on my hair she brought out another box. It contained two small tubes of paste and a small brush. She mixed a little paste from both tubes and brushed it into my eyebrows. After another five minutes she gave me instructions.

"Ok Charlie, it's time to wash your hair. As soon as you're done, shave your body."

I stood there, dumbfounded at the thought of shaving my entire body.

"Go", she said. "Get started. We need to get this going. If you need help; if you can't reach something, let me know."

I did as I was told. Lisa was right, the Sisterhood's been around a long time, and as far as I knew they must be pretty good at hiding.

After washing my hair I stepped out of the shower and yelled to Lisa, "How much do I shave?"

"Shave whatever you think somebody is likely to see."

That was a relief. There are just some things I never want to touch with a razor. The shaving took longer than I imagined. When I was finished, rinsed and dried. I yelled for Lisa to bring me some underwear.

"Not so fast Dragon Boy. Underwear will just smear the tanning cream and you'll end up staining the underwear."

The bathroom door started opening and I pushed it closed.

"What in God's name do you think you're doing?"

"Let me ask you a question. Have you ever put on tanning cream before?"

"No."

"Trust me. Nobody does this right the first time. This needs to look real. Think of me as your doctor."

"At least hand me some underwear".

"Really Charlie? Are we that shy?"

"I don't know you. So, yes!"

Lisa was giggling like a school girl as she threw a package of underwear through the doorway. I put a pair on and let her in.

"OK, turn your back to me. Let's start there."

Lisa put on a pair of blue latex gloves, squeezed out a liberal amount of brown paste from a tube and began applying the cream just below my buttocks. She worked her way down my legs. It was cold and embarrassing. After my legs were done she stood up and did my back and shoulders.

Then it came time for me to turn around. I wanted to run away. Lisa smeared the goo on my face and ears, down my neck and arms, and torso. I closed my eyes tightly and bit my lip as she switched to my thighs.

When my feet were finished she said, "OK, you're done. I'm setting a timer for one hour. Don't sit down."

Time crawled as I waited for the hour to pass. I tried having a conversation with Lisa through the bathroom door.

"Lisa?"

"Yes, Charlie."

"So tell me some more about the Sisterhood. Why is it that the Sisterhood doesn't allow any of you to have boys? Why only girls?"

"I don't know all of the scientific reasons, but I do know some. And part of it is practicality.

From a scientific standpoint, men carry an X and a Y chromosome. Women have two X chromosomes. We take great pains to ensure that all of us carry one X chromosome that is pure El-yanin, and one that is purely human.

Also, remember what I said about memories being passed when we touch blood? When a baby is in the womb its blood and the mother's blood pass close to each other. The memories and knowledge of the mother pass to the infant.

We are born with knowledge from many generations. I have memories stretching back to my ancestors on El-yana. If an El-yanin male mated with a human female, then the children would be born without any knowledge of El-yana."

"You mean to tell me that you were born knowing how to speak, read, and write?"

"Essentially, yes. Infancy is difficult. I remember being helpless; unable to speak. It takes time for vocal chords to mature and limbs to strengthen. Infancy and old age are the most difficult periods in a person's life. I think infancy is the worst. And, by the way, your hour's up."

Lisa threw a pair a jeans through the door, which I put on. I looked myself over in the mirror. Not bad, it looked like a real tan. I stepped out of the bathroom to show Lisa her handiwork.

I smiled and turned three hundred sixty degrees for Lisa to see me. She smiled back.

"You should be able to do most of that yourself next time."

"Next time?" My smile receded a couple of degrees.

"Yes, in about three to four days, if you shower every day."

"Why are we doing this to me, if it's not going to last any longer than that?"

"Because, you need to look different now, not in three weeks from now. You'll keep this up and you'll go to a tanning bed. Before long you can stop the fake bake."

I took a seat on the edge of the bed.

"Lisa, what's next? I look a little different, but not enough."

"Have you ever worn contact lenses?"

"No, why?"

"Then you're not going to like this part. It's going to take some practice and some getting used to. I have to admit that I like your blue eyes. But we need to change them."

Lisa handed me a small plastic case with two lids.

"No, really?"

"Yes. Really. They're brown lenses, with no correction. I'll show you how to put them in."

The process took forty-five minutes just for me to get a lens in my right eye. After another fifteen minutes, I had them both in my eyes.

"Charlie, don't keep the contacts in for more than two hours at a time over the next couple of days. You have to get used to them. And whatever you do, don't sleep in them."

I had to admit, that the tan, the black hair, and the brown eyes made a huge change in my appearance. But the face was still mine.

"Lisa, should I grow beard and mustache?"

"Only if you really want to. If you do, then you'll need to color them to match your hair. It could end up looking fake."

"But I still look like 'me'. Just a different me; one with darker skin, dark hair, and dark eyes."

"You're right. You will always look like you. But you want that. It's OK if people say you look like Chad, that's different from saying you are Chad. That's how you hide in plain sight."

"You'll get the idea when you see your new clothes."

Lisa disappeared into the next room only to return with her arms bulging with shopping bags. She dropped her payload on the bed next to the open suitcase.

I was amazed by how much stuff there was.

"Is there anything left in the stores?"

"There's more in my room. Everything on the bed in there is yours. There's also some boxes by the window. Those are yours too. We might as well bring them in with the rest of the stuff. It's some tech that you'll need."

I followed Lisa into her room, and yes, there was more on the bed. I was able to take everything from the bed, and she took the boxes by the window.

I was looking at the mass of new clothes on the bed and shaking my head.

"I don't think we have the same idea of hiding out."

"I'm sure we don't, Charlie. I bought a couple of plain

white dress shirts for you. Find one and put it on while I explain."

I dug through the bags until I found one.

"Lisa, you spent a lot of money on all of this. This is a lot of expensive stuff. How much am I going to owe you?"

"You're not going to owe me…per se. Your debt is with the Sisterhood."

If I'd had any hair left on my body, it would have been standing straight up.

"I don't like this idea, Lisa. I don't trust those women. I'm not one hundred percent trusting you. I've gone along with this so far because I've got a clean room, hot food, and nobody's looking for me here. But me owing a debt to those witch…excuse me, I mean women. No. I don't want that happening; you can take all this stuff right back if that's the price. I'll manage just fine on my own."

I wouldn't be fine on my own and I knew it. The best I could do would be to stay off the grid for a little while, but somebody would eventually turn me in. And, I didn't have a prayer of getting my life back without the Matron.

"Sorry, Charlie. In for a penny, in for a pound, as they say. You need us, and I can see that you know it. You play the game our way, and you have a chance. You play by any other rules, and you're on your own. You can't do this on your own."

"You're right, but I don't have to like it. I reserve the right to remain skeptical."

"I understand, just don't let you skepticism get in the way."

"Agreed. Tell me about all the clothes. Why do I need all of these? Why not travel light?"

"The whole world's looking for Chad Fury. They believe Chad's on the run. If he's on the run, he has to travel light. One or two pairs of jeans, and one or two shirts. Everything he has to his name can fit into one backpack. Charles Fenton, on the other hand is a mildly successful independent investment broker. He travels on business. He wears nice clothes, keeps himself well groomed, and he is not running away."

"I get it."

"Good. Now try on the clothes. There's a new suit hanging in your closet. Put it on with the shirt and dress shoes, I'm going to mark up the suit and have it altered."

As I was putting on the suit, I got curious. "So, if all of this was paid for with the Sisterhood's money, just where do they get their money?"

"Most of it is from investments. Every once and a while they get a patent on a new product and sell it. The inventions are for simple things that won't put dangerous technology in the hands of people that aren't ready for it."

"Inventions? Like what?"

"Ever hear of Velcro? How about paper clips?"

I laughed.

"What's so funny?"

"Advanced alien life comes to Earth and bestows upon humanity the great gifts of Velcro and paperclips!"

Lisa laughed too. In that moment, she seemed a little softer and I thought I might be able to start making a friend.

Lisa marked the suit for alterations and took it to her room. While she was there she yelled back across to me.

"I'm getting hungry. I'm ordering up the salmon for myself. What do you want?"

"Salmon sounds good. I'll have whatever you're having."

I had finished packing all the new clothes in my suitcase, and was setting it in the closet when she came back carrying one more sack.

"We missed this earlier. It's a grooming case. I stocked it with razors, hair gel, toothpaste, and etc."

I thanked her and took it to the bathroom. When I came back she was setting more boxes and bags on the bed.

"Not more clothes, please. I think I have enough."

"You have enough clothes, you need to be equipped with technology. You're not going off the grid. You are going to hide within it."

"So, is this where you offer me the red pill or the blue pill?

Lisa looked at me blankly. "What?"

"You know that movie…The movie? The red pill, blue pill scene?"

"I never saw it."

"You never saw it! OMG! That's got to be fixed. I'll work on that."

"Whatever. Can we get back to this?"

"Sure. What is this stuff?"

"I have two hats for you."

Lisa opened the first box and pulled out a dark fedora. She opened the second, and pulled out a simple blue ball cap with no logos.

"What do you notice different about these, Charlie?"

I took the fedora and looked it over. On the front of the hat, underneath the brim were several led lights. There was bulge that felt like a button inside the hat.

"What's with the lights?"

"Those are infrared LEDs. Most digital cameras used for surveillance in low light are infrared cameras. If you see a camera with a ring of LED lights around the lens, that's an infrared light source. It's lighting up the area to get a good picture."

"So, this does what, exactly?"

"It blinds the camera. Turn it on, and there's too much light. Your face will be one big bright spot. Inside are two watch batteries and a small indicator light to tell you if the lights are on or off. The ball cap's the same."

"That's pretty cool."

I put on the fedora. "And I look cool too!"

"Moving along, Charlie."

Lisa handed me a black plastic case about eight inches long, three inches high and three inches wide.

I opened the case, and inside was an aluminum tube with a switch on the side and a lens on one end.

"You gave me a flash light?"

"No. It's a two watt blue laser. Don't point it at your eyes!"

"This has to be a joke, there's no such thing, unless you're giving me alien tech?"

"It's no joke, there is such a thing, and it's not alien. You can find this stuff on the internet. You've got to use human tech.

The laser's powerful enough to start a fire. But its main purpose will be to burn out video cameras. Point it at any camera lens for one or two seconds, and the camera's toast. The battery will last about forty-five minutes."

"This is really cool. I feel like a regular movie spy."

Lisa cleared her throat.

"Don't let all this stuff go to your head. Here's three burn phones…prepaid cell phones. Use one once, and throw it away. Buy your phones in three's. I find it better that way."

I put the three phones, still in their blister packs, in my backpack in the closet. When I turned back around Lisa had taken the last of the packages and laid them on the bed.

I walked over and stood next to her. She spoke without looking up.

"And now for the real education."

Lisa pulled a laptop carrying case from thin cardboard box.

"You'll want to carry this around more often than that backpack. It looks more like Charlie and less like Chad."

"Got it."

"This is a notebook computer." Lisa handed me a plain cardboard box.

"Get outta here. Really?"

"Really."

I opened the box and extracted the computer from out

of its plastic cushions.

Lisa began telling me all about it.

"It's a dual core processor, has eight Gig of ram and a three hundred twenty Gig hard drive. It's been preloaded with a word processor, a spreadsheet, and email client software. I need to show you how to use it."

"Begging your pardon, but I know how to use a computer. I've been using one since I was a kid."

"Yes, and you've been leaving a digital trail that any kid with a computer could follow. I did a little digging yesterday. You're Social Network accounts are still up. You have two web based email accounts, and I bet you even bank online."

"Yeah, but doesn't everybody?"

"Not the people who don't want to be found. I repeat, I need to show you how to use a computer. I didn't have time yet, but I'll be putting files on your computer that make it look like Charlie's computer. I'll need some help from the Sisterhood, but we can build a digital footprint for Charlie on the social networks.

One of your jobs is to use this computer like Charlie would use it. When it's booted up with the resident operating system, it's Charlie's PC. When you have this computer in your hands, Charlie's the one using it, not Chad. Understand?"

"Perfectly."

"Good. Now I'm going to show you how to use Chad's PC."

At that moment there was a knock on Lisa's door. Dinner had arrived. We brought the food into my room and ate as my education continued.

Lisa took the computer and the power cord, and sat at the writing desk. She plugged in the computer and made sure I was looking over her shoulder.

"When I turn on the computer I'm going to keep hitting the 'F12' key. That will bring up the BIOS, Basic Input Output System, settings. You want the boot order to be USB drive first, then hard drive. I'm setting this for you now, and you shouldn't have to do it again on this machine. You may have to do it on another PC, if this one's not available."

"OK…show me that again."

I watched a second time paying much closer attention.

Afterwards, Lisa started with new instructions.

"Now that you've set the boot order, exit and save the BIOS settings. The computer will try to start the operating system. Don't let it. Hold down the power key until it shuts off."

Lisa handed me a small black zippered case. I opened it. Inside were a half-dozen USB drives in individual pockets. They were all different sizes, shapes, and colors."

"Give me the little blue one. It's a four Gig drive, and Tails has been installed on it."

"Tails?"

"Tails. It's a flavor of Linux. The tails operating system is designed for anonymity. Nothing you do while using it will be saved. There will be no record of your computer use. If anyone ever gets their hands on this computer, they will never know what Chad has been doing with it."

"Wow. I mean, this is like spy stuff."

"No, this is old school spy stuff at best. This is advanced hacker and terrorist stuff. Spies have better toys."

Lisa inserted the drive into a free port and started the computer. A bunch of white text flew across a black screen; a few seconds later the words "Starting Tails" stood alone in the center of the screen. In another fifteen seconds or so, the screen changed to what looked like the familiar computer desktop.

I tapped Lisa on the shoulder.

"Wait a minute, could we back the truck up a few feet?"

"What?" Lisa turned toward me. "Do I need to do this again?"

"No, it's something else."

I scratched my head.

"I understand that this is Charlie's computer, and when I'm Charlie, I need to use it only like Charlie would use it. What I don't understand is why Chad needs to use a computer and," I pointed to the laser still sitting on the bed, "all this cloak and dagger stuff."

"Oh, I guess I did get a little ahead of myself.

Back in the abandoned building, I was able to use the transresinator just in time. What you saw me doing was speaking with one of my contacts. Each of us knows how to contact only two other members of the Sisterhood. I reached one of my contacts just in time. Another thirty minutes and the group would have started evacuating.

But, more to the point, since then I've been communicating with the council; it's composed of four members of the Sisterhood plus the Matron. The council feels some responsibility for the predicament you're in."

I interrupted, "Only some?"

"Take what you can get, and don't push it. If you push the issue you're apt to end up with nothing more than a strip of Velcro and a couple of paper clips." Lisa gave me a wink.

"Anyway, Charlie, the Sisterhood is willing to help you get a new identity, and it's my job to do it. After we have your new identity fully established, you will meet with the council. If there is any further obligation or association with them, it will be decided then.

Regardless, there may come a time when you need to contact me or the council. And this is how you will reach the council. Through the Deep Web, or the Dark Net."

"I've never heard of those things."

"They're two different names for the same thing. Most people only know about the Clear Net. That's where you get to the big search engines, the social networks, all the stuff people think about when they hear the word 'Internet'. But most of the information on the internet is sitting in computers not directly hooked up to the Clear Net. None of the places that the big search engines take you are part of the Dark Net, residing in the Deep Web."

"Alright, then how do I get there, and what do I do once I'm there?"

"You can't get there through a normal browser. That's what Tails and TOR, The Onion Router, are for. Tails is the operating system on the USB drive plugged into your computer right now. TOR is a private network that retains no information about the computers connecting to it. When you connect to a TOR server, the server passes your connection information on to another server, and then another, and so forth. A minimum of seven hops are made to different locations at any point around the globe until you are finally connected to your destination. If your initial connection is made correctly, and you don't do something stupid to disclose your identity, no one will ever know who you are or where you've been on the Dark Net."

"Whoa. My head's spinning."

"You don't need to know all of the details, not right now. Just focus on connecting the way I do, and you'll be fine."

Lisa started a browser called "ICE Web", and within seconds it said we were connected and my IP address had been anonymized.

"Next, you need to know how to leave a message for the council, and how to read a message from them. Grab the clutch of drives I gave you."

I handed Lisa the black case and she removed a red USB device.

"Ha! I knew it! Red pill, blue pill, red USB, blue USB. It is the movie!"

Lisa just shook her head from side to side and continued on.

"The red pill, as you call it, is an encrypted thumb drive. You cannot use the drive without entering a password."

Lisa, attached the drive, and a box came up asking for a password. Instead of entering a password, she clicked a button and brought up another box where the password could be changed. She put in her old password where it asked for it, and then got up and told me to sit down. She had me select a new password that was at least twenty characters long, and used uppercase, lowercase, numbers and symbols. She also made me write it down where I wouldn't lose it. Before I hit enter, she stopped me.

"You need to be a little more secure than that."

"You're kidding me…more secure than that nonsense I just typed in?"

"Yes. You see the button marked 'Use Key Files'? Click that."

I clicked and a window popped up with drive letters and file names.

"Chad, navigate to the drive labeled 'TAILS'. Find the file named 'grocerylist.txt', and double click."

I did as told, and asked, "What did I just do?"

"That TAILS drive is now your dongle."

I couldn't help it. I laughed out loud.

"Chad, stop it! You're not fourteen. Dongle is a perfectly acceptable word."

"I think here on Earth it might mean something else…"

"Men!"

She shook her head and sighed.

"Chad, you told the encrypted drive that no matter what, even if the password is correct, that file named 'grocerylist.txt' must be in that location on that 'TAILS' drive. If that doesn't happen, the login will fail. After ten failed logins, software on the drive will wipe the drive clean; there is no recovery."

I wasn't addressing Lisa, it just kind of came out.

"This is serious stuff."

"Yes it is. Your life, and the lives of the Sisterhood may depend on it. Let me show you what's on the drive…"

One file was a list of web addresses ending with ".onion". They were bulletin boards on the Dark Net where I could place a message intended for the council. Another was an encryption program. The program would take any text I typed and encrypt it. As far as I could see, encryption looked like a set of random keystrokes. I could copy and paste the encrypted text into a bulletin board message.

Any message I posted was to have the subject line, "For Your Consideration –SHC". Replies would be posted with the subject. "Considered Proposal – CFF". I was to copy the reply into the encryption program, and it would show me the message.

"Lisa, are we done with this? Please? My brain is full."

"I suppose so. I forget just how much information this is when it's all new. I can walk you through again tomorrow, if you're not sure about any of it. Right now there's one other thing we need to do."

Lisa left the room and came back with a digital camera.

"I need to take some pictures of you. We need them for ID cards, drivers' license, and social media. Without it, we can't give Charlie any history beyond today. Oh, and the camera is yours too. Tomorrow I'll show you how to hide messages inside pictures."

CHAPTER SIXTEEN

I awoke Tuesday morning, peaceful. I had gone to bed early and I had slept in a warm bed, in a safe clean room. The previous day I had eaten my fill of good, hot food. I now had new clothes and soon I would have a new identity. Chad Fury could become just a fading news story. Charlie was how people would know me from now on.

I looked at the clock; it read six-thirty-four AM. I started to get up, but realized how sore I was. I laid there. The soreness had to be from the constant stress, sleeping on unforgiving surfaces, and tension of trying to figure out my next move. I still had as many questions about my future as before, but at least, for the moment, I had peace.

At seven-thirty there was a knock on the door from the Lisa's room.

"Charlie! You up?"

"Yeah, just barely."

"Throw on some clothes and let's get downstairs and have some breakfast. We have a full day ahead."

I was disconcerted by her use of the words 'full day ahead'. After the previous day with the makeover, the computer lessons, and the spy toys I was certain full was an understatement.

I put on my robe and opened the door between our rooms. There was Lisa, in a white blouse and black jeans.

"Why not call in room service?" I yawned.

"Because this won't take as long, and Charlie needs to start introducing himself to the world."

"Give me ten minutes."

I tried to close the door, but her foot was in the way.

"Make it five."

"Do you want me with or without my teeth brushed?"

"OK. Ten... But not ten and a half!"

It took me nine minutes to do everything I needed to do. I exited into the hallway to find Lisa standing there waiting for me.

"Let me look at you."

Lisa shook her head in disapproval.

"What's wrong?"

"You forgot something."

"I've got shoes, socks, everything…What?"

Lisa pointed to her eyes.

"Contacts. Charlie isn't ready."

"It's just breakfast. I can get them after."

"No. You can't. That's the kind of thing that gets people hurt. You can't afford to be sloppy."

"Hey, we're in no danger here. I need a break."

I slid my key card in the lock, and reentered my room. Lisa followed.

"Look. I get it. Chad's been under a lot of pressure. He does need some time to adjust to everything that's happening. But we're on a tight schedule. If this falls apart too soon, you'll be back where you were this time last week."

"You win. I know you're right. It's just that this was the first peaceful night I've had since I met you."

I went into the bathroom and struggled with the contact lenses. It took fifteen minutes to put them in. Lisa assured me it would get easier.

We took the elevator to the first floor. The breakfast

buffet was set up in a large room that seemed more like an outcrop of the hotel lobby than another room.

It was a Tuesday morning and I was surprised that the place wasn't packed with businessmen pouring in coffee in preparation for the day ahead.

Lisa and I each took a plate, forks and knives and paraded ourselves along the buffet. There were the obligatory pastries and cereals on display, but I was very happy to see warm scrambled eggs and breakfast meats. I took a large helping of each. And, I took a liberal supply of coffee.

Lisa, on the other hand, took a few pieces of fresh fruit and a little cup of Greek yogurt. I could never figure out how anyone got enough nutrition eating like that.

Lisa led the way to a secluded table at the back of the dining area.

I took a sip of coffee before speaking.

"What's on the agenda for today? I remember the first time we met....it's really ironic. Your plans then were to change me, and that's exactly what you're doing now. Isn't that what every woman wants, to find a man and change him?"

"Not exactly. Women want to meet men who are mature enough to let a woman enlighten him, and he will therefore want to change. See the difference?"

"Sure, I do. And, if I had a great big sarcasm sign I'd be holding it up too. But, back to the real subject at hand, what's happening today?"

"Not so fast, you don't get to change the subject that quickly."

"Can I apologize? Will that help?"

"An apology would help, if I were willing to accept it."

"And you won't accept my apology because…"

"Apologies are for when people do something wrong. There is no way to apologize for stupid."

"There's no way for me to get out of this, is there."

"No, Chad. None. But, that's all I wanted, for you to

know just how much you don't have the upper hand."

"Now that you've successfully taken me down a few pegs, what do you have planned for me today?"

Lisa stood up.

"Give me a minute. Just wait here."

Lisa was making her way to the front desk, and I decided I should watch and listen.

There was a young man in his early twenties working behind the counter. It looked like Lisa was reading his name badge.

"Excuse me, Jimmy?"

"Yes, what can I do for you?"

"I believe somebody left a package here for me. My name's Lisa Smith. My room number's three twenty-three."

"Just a minute, I'll check."

Jimmy finished doing something on the desk computer before he disappeared through a doorway in the wall behind him. Less than a minute later, he returned with an oversized yellow envelope in hand. Lisa thanked him and headed back to our table. She handed the envelope to me and smiled.

"Here, this belongs to Charlie."

I took a moment to examine the bulging package before opening it. There was no address label. The only identifying feature was the name it bore on the front, "Lisa Smith", printed with some sort of black felt marker.

I took out my knife and cut open the top. I looked inside, then I looked questioningly at Lisa and waited. Lisa simply nodded her head, so I dumped the contents on the table.

Out of the package spilled three items, a man's black leather billfold, a small stack of business cards held together by a rubber band, and a key ring containing five keys and a silver fob. The key fob had the letters CLF inscribed on one side, and was blank on the other. Two keys looked like house keys, two looked like a car keys, and one was a small brass key with the number one hundred nineteen stamped into both sides.

Lisa was taking a sip of coffee when I asked, "What's with the keys?"

She swallowed her coffee.

"Those are Charlie's keys. Every man has a set of keys in his pocket. Some men carry such a wad of keys it looks like they're collecting scrap metal. Most men wouldn't go anywhere without their keys and Charlie's no different than most men."

"But the house keys, does Charlie really have a house?"

"No, not yet. That will be entirely up to Charlie. Charlie will be able to live anywhere or any way he chooses, eventually. But for now, anyone you should happen to meet should believe he has a home."

"The same goes for the car keys, right?"

Lisa nodded and took another sip of coffee. I started to put the keys in my pocket when she stopped me.

"Aren't your curious about the small key?"

"Isn't it just another stage prop?"

"No, it isn't. It opens a mailbox at 'The Mailbox Store' near the Penn Square shopping mall.

"Charlie has this because?"

"That key belongs to Chad. If the Sisterhood needs to send something to Chad, that's how they'll do it. I suggest you check the box a couple of times a week. Don't make it a regular routine. The place is open twenty-four hours a day, so go at any time, just not on a fixed schedule."

"What about the initials, CLF?"

"Charles L. Fenton", Lisa replied. "The 'L' can stand for whatever you want it to."

I put the keys in my pocket and picked up the business cards. I liberated a single card from its elastic bond and examined it. It was very plain. Shiny black ink on plain white paper with the words:

'Fenton Investment Services

Charles L. Fenton, CFP'

The card was blank on the back.

"That's not much of a business card…"

I threw a disappointed look at Lisa.

"We couldn't give you an address and phone number. You can hand write those if you want to or need to. Lots of people have understated business cards."

"Whatever. It's a prop anyhow." I dropped the cards in my shirt pocket. "I'll make sure I have a couple on me whenever I need them."

I turned my attention to the billfold. It was a rather ordinary black leather billfold. I opened it; a Texas Driver's License was proudly displayed in the plastic window on the left-hand side. The license had the picture of me that Lisa had taken the previous evening.

"That was really fast. And it looks real."

Lisa finished another sip of coffee.

"It is real, sort of. It's real card stock used for Texas Driver's licenses. The only fake part is the information on it. Just don't let anyone run the license number. The results won't be good."

I thumbed through the other contents of the billfold. There was a Social Security card, two credit cards, and a bank debit card. I looked at Lisa for an explanation.

The credit cards work, for now. Don't go crazy with them. They are for emergency use only. Use the debit card to get cash from ATM's; you need to operate on a cash basis because money is fungible."

"Fungible?"

"Yes, fungible. One bill is like another, they're interchangeable. You don't want to leave a paper trail to follow. Your bank account has three hundred thousand dollars in it."

My jaw dropped so hard that I nearly lost some teeth.

"Charlie close your mouth and pay attention."

I regained my composure.

"The cash is for you to use to start your new life. As long as the Sisterhood feels that you're not taking advantage of them, they will keep the account funded."

"I don't know what to say."

"Look, until Charlie is able to get a job and have his own life, he shouldn't have to worry about money. He's supposed to be here on business, and that means that he would be using his company's money to pay for everything. Just think of the Sisterhood as your employer right now, and that's your salary."

I returned my attention to the contents of the billfold. There were photographs in the little plastic pockets. A woman in a ball cap and team jacket was on top. The rest of the pictures were of other men and women I had never seen before.

"Who are these people?"

"Who do you want them to be, Charlie? Take some time and make up a few back stories. Make the stories simple. Elaboration is both a skill and a trap."

I put the billfold in my hip pocket and was about to take a sip of coffee when we both heard a voice through the television mounted on the opposite wall saying, "And now for an update on Chad Fury, who escaped from Cleveland County Jail in Oklahoma last week."

I nodded to Lisa and whispered, "I want to hear this."

The man speaking said pretty much the same thing as the woman I heard the previous day. However, there were mentions of tips that the FBI had been receiving from the good folks in Amarillo.

Lisa looked puzzled.

"Amarillo, why on earth do they think you…he's there?"

"Oh…I guess there's things I haven't told you either."

I lowered my voice and related the story of how I had let myself be seen stealing money, buying camping equipment, and that I had run to the Will Rogers Park and called my mother, and then to the Route 66 Park and called a motel in Amarillo.

Lisa asked, "What exactly did you mean when you said

that you 'ran' to the park? Did you drive or hitch a ride?"

"Neither. I ran."

"You ran? Explain that, please."

"I picked up and sat down one foot in front of the other, in rapid succession. I repeated the action until I arrived at the park."

Lisa whispered. "Just how fast do you think you were running?"

I matched her volume. "By my best guess, about forty miles per hour."

"Holy…." She cut her expletive short. "I want to verify that, later. Right now I need to change the subject. I was hoping this wasn't going to happen today."

"What?"

"Take a look at the man in the brown suit sitting near the buffet line and reading the paper. Do you see him?"

"Yes. So?"

"He was sitting in the lobby when we came down for breakfast. He moved there after we sat down, and he hasn't moved since. I've been seeing him at different places for the last few days. He's got to be one of the Abomination's hunters. They hunt in pairs, sometimes threes. They track and observe their victims. They don't let themselves be seen until they are getting ready to strike. Just before they strike they let you know they are hunting you because they enjoy making their victims afraid."

"What should we do?"

"Not a lot at the moment. I wanted to have breakfast down here because I needed to see how closely I'm being watched. I also wanted to make it clear to the hunters that I'm not alone; that's going to make them change tactics. We're going to try to flush them out.

I need to make a call. I'm going to the ladies room. Watch the man in the brown suit. Make eye contact. Let him know that you see him. If he tries to follow me, stop him. If you see him signal anyone. Take note. If a man comes toward the bathroom door, distract him."

Before I could reply, Lisa had her purse and was off to the ladies room, just down the hall.

The man in the brown suit put down the paper, and kept his eyes on Lisa as she disappeared into the restroom. I took my coffee cup and headed over to the pots behind the man. I kept my eye on him as I put my cup under the spigot and refreshed my coffee. As I passed near the man on my way back, I bumped into him and my hot coffee spilled down the back of his neck.

"Watch it! You son-of-a…"

Everybody within earshot looked at us and gawked. Everyone except for a man sitting in the lobby, wearing blue jeans and a black ball cap. The man never so much as glanced over but kept his gaze fixed on the ladies restroom door.

I made my apologies to the man in the brown suit, and went immediately down the hall to stand guard by the restroom door. I knocked.

"Lisa, you OK in there?"

There was a long pause, almost too long. "Yeah. I'm OK. What's up?"

"I think we need to move it along. I saw your friends."

Lisa came out the door.

"Let's go back to the room. You can fill me in"

I turned back to point out the men to Lisa, but they were both gone. She wasn't surprised.

I reported the details to Lisa during the elevator ride back.

We went to her room sat down to talk over the situation.

"What was that call about?"

"I was leaving a message for the Matron on…well, it's complicated. I had to let her know that I am definitely being hunted."

"What do we do?"

"Chad, I honestly don't know. The hunters have been trying to make me afraid, and they are succeeding.

I'm going to wait here and check my messages; hopefully I'll hear from the Sisterhood.

Go back to your room and wait, but let's keep the doors open between our rooms; if you don't mind."

I agreed and I exited Lisa's room and entered the hallway. As soon as I walked through the door, facing me was the man with the ball cap who I had seen in the lobby.

We looked each other squarely in the eyes, and I caught a distinct odor kind of like burnt cinnamon. I didn't know what to do. I wondered if I should hit him. Before I could make up my mind he spoke, and I heard a high pitched whistle.

"You will forget me. You cannot talk about me. You will check out of this hotel, and you will not come back. You will leave the girl. You will leave without speaking to her again."

I repeated back my instructions in broken sentences the way I'd heard Dwayne respond to Lisa. I turned away from the man and went into my room.

Once inside my room I opened the door between us and told Lisa what had just happened.

Lisa frowned. "They're planning on moving quick. They're separating us."

"Yes, but maybe we can use that. They're watching your room. They know you're inside. What if you're not here when they come?"

"It's broad daylight, you really shouldn't be scaling the walls with me."

"I don't plan to. Do you trust me?"

"To a point, yes."

"I have a plan to get you out of here. But first, I'm calling the front desk; I'm checking out."

CHAPTER SEVENTEEN

A short ninety minutes after I had told Lisa I was checking out, I was standing in the lobby with my bags on a luggage cart. I had asked the clerk on duty to print my final bill, and I paid my room service charges using a credit card courtesy of the Sisterhood. I also inquired about the shuttle to the airport.

The clerk was kind enough to let me know that the van outside would take me to the airport for no charge, and I could leave in five minutes. I exited the hotel lobby, pushing the cart ahead of me.

The van driver had all of the doors open, and was gracious enough to assist with my bags. I declined help with the large rolling duffle and laid it on the floor of the van myself. I took note that a man in a brown suit had observed everything I had done from the moment I entered the hotel lobby. He was now standing in the parking lot watching me get into the van.

The ride to the airport was uneventful, aside from a white sedan that followed all the way. The sedan was being driven by a man in a brown suit.

At the airport the driver helped me retrieve my bags, and I placed the rolling duffle on a luggage cart with my other bags. I tipped the man liberally.

Inside the airport, I found a seat and waited with my bags for about thirty minutes. I saw no one I recognized from the hotel; I assumed it was safe to proceed.

I looked for a quiet place where I could work unobserved. That's when I realized that I should have thought things through just a little more thoroughly. The airport was so busy there seemed to be no quiet spot to be found.

I headed to the baggage claim area, thinking I might find quiet nook or alcove along the way, but the building was bustling with travelers and airport employees. By the time I reached baggage claim I still had not found any place where I would be unobserved. I thought that if I couldn't work unobserved, then perhaps I should make a production out of it.

I reached into my laptop bag and found the digital camera Lisa had given me the day before. I pulled my baggage cart in front of a luggage carousel, and arranged some unclaimed bags in a semi-circle around my large bag. I called for volunteers.

There was soon a crowd around me, and I explained that this was an advertising stunt; I needed to take some still photos for a concept shoot. I selected an older couple to do the honors, while the remainder of the folks stood around with instructions to react to what they saw. I had the older man and woman undo the zippers on the large bag very slowly as I snapped pictures as fast as I could.

As soon as the opening was large enough, an arm appeared, then a head, and finally Lisa pulled herself out like a large, awkward bird hatching from a blue canvass egg.

Lisa tried to take a step and landed flat on the floor. The entire time the crowd laughed, cheered and applauded. I went over to Lisa, helped her up from the floor, and thanked everyone for their assistance.

Soon the crowd had dispersed, and Lisa and I with our

luggage on a cart, were headed out toward the taxis. Lisa was not happy and her eyes were letting me know about it.

I tried to change her mood.

"I think that went really well, don't you?"

Lisa scowled. "I didn't like it when you described it, and I like it even less now! You didn't have to leave me in there that long!"

"I couldn't let you out while we were in the van, we were being followed. When I got to the airport, I had to make sure 'brown suit guy' didn't follow me in. I looked for a secluded spot to free you, but there wasn't one. This was the best I could come up with."

"Oh great! The best you could come up with was me falling on my ass in public! And with me all sweaty and my makeup running! And did I mention I'm claustrophobic!"

"No, I had no idea. Why didn't you say something?"

"Because I wasn't, until you talked me into this stupid stunt!"

"Alright, Lisa. I apologize. But we have a big problem and not much time to solve it."

"What?" Lisa sighed in exasperation.

"We escaped from the hunters. And now, what do we do?"

"Charlie, you say 'escaped' like it's a bad thing. I don't think you get the concept of what escaped means."

"I know what escaped means, but any time now the hunters will know, and they'll choose a new target. We don't know who that will be. Somebody will be abducted or killed, and we won't be able to stop it."

Lisa's smirk disappeared.

"I see what you mean. Right now we're one step ahead of the hunters. We know where they are, and they don't know where we are. But how do we put that to our advantage?"

"Exactly. We need a plan, and we need it fast. Any suggestions, my dear Lisa?"

"Well Charlie, I suggest we get a room where we can

keep an eye on the hunters."

"Agreed. Let's get a cab."

It wasn't until we were seated in the back of a cab and on our way toward Brick Town that Lisa realized it.

"You took pictures!!! You have pictures of me coming out of that portable coffin!!! If any of those pictures ever see the light of day, so help me God, I'll…"

And that's when it happened. That's the moment in my life that I developed selective hearing.

CHAPTER EIGHTEEN

It was four-thirty PM when the cab dropped us off at our new hotel. Lisa was still making noises to express how unhappy she was with the suitcase stunt.

Our new hotel was directly behind where we had been staying. We took a room with two beds, under Charlie Fenton's name. My new room was very much like the last one, just not as big and not quite as comfortable. Lisa sat on a bed, and I sat in the desk chair, staring out the window.

"Lisa", I said without taking my eyes away from the window. "What do you think the hunters are doing right now?"

"Charlie…"

I cut her off. "Call me Chad. We're alone, and I'm tired of pretending to be someone else. I want to be Chad, again."

"OK, Chad…I think they're watching the room; trying to increase the fear factor. They may be knocking on the door a few times and making a few phone calls. They'll keep watching for a while. They'll probably make their move after dark. They won't risk trying to abduct me during broad daylight."

"That's good. It gives us some time. Time to get a bite to eat, and time to figure out how", I said pointing out the window, "I can get inside your room before the hunters do."

We ordered sandwiches and iced tea, and we continued to talk. We agreed that I could probably scale the wall, but I'd be seen. And even if I wasn't, I'd have to break out the window to get inside. I didn't need to attract any attention.

We examined several options and were in the middle of exploring another dead end plan when there was a knock at the door. Our sandwiches had arrived.

As I let a young man in carrying our tray, Lisa and I looked at each other. I could tell we both had the same idea.

"Excuse me", I said.

I took a moment to read the man's name badge.

"Tony, I can give you a five dollar tip, or, we could give you a lot more money if you're willing to do something for us."

"I don't know." Tony looked uncomfortable with my suggestion.

"How does three hundred dollars sound?"

"It sounds pretty good. Just what does old Tony here have to do for his new friends?"

Lisa chimed in.

"Well, Tony. We're trying to surprise a couple of friends of ours. Could you give us your clothes?"

"Uhhh….no."

I interrupted.

"They don't have to be yours. Would there be some like yours, say in the laundry somewhere? And a name badge?"

Tony grinned.

"For four hundred bucks, old Tony here can make it happen."

I frowned.

"I said three hundred."

"I know. I heard you. And I just said four hundred bucks."

Between the two of us, Lisa and I scraped together four hundred dollars in cash. I started to hand it to him, and then told him, I'd pay him after I got the clothes.

Tony left, and twenty minutes later he was back with the clothes and a name badge. He tried to get another hundred out of me, but I wouldn't budge.

I put on the pants, white shirt, and vest. It was a pretty good fit. Lisa pinned the name badge on me. My new name was Allan.

Lisa handed me the key card to her room across the road. I left as quickly as I could, carrying our serving tray with the silver dome sitting on top.

At the hotel where Lisa's room was, I dodged the line of sight of the cameras in the parking lot. I entered through a glass door on the end of the hotel and hugged the wall so I would not be seen by the security camera. I took the stairwell up to the third floor. There was no one in sight. As I approached room three hundred twenty-three a man in a brown suit came out of a door at the end of the hall. He looked my direction.

I calmed myself, held the tray up at face level, knocked on the door of Lisa's room and said, "Room Service."

Out of the corner of my eye I saw the brown suited man go back into his room. I slid the key card into the lock and walked inside.

The room appeared to be undisturbed. I was glad to know that no one had been in there while we had been away. After I had placed the tray on the writing desk I opened and closed the curtains one time to signal Lisa that I was inside.

Lisa had warned me that the room might be bugged, so I was cautious about the sounds I was making. I turned on the TV so that if anyone was listening, they would at least hear something.

I removed six lengths of rope I had tied around my

waist, and laid them out on the bed. I lifted the sliver dome from the tray and picked up the two watt laser I'd hidden underneath.

I kicked off my shoes and sat in the big overstuffed chair to wait. The phone rang, and I didn't bother to answer it. A few minutes later there was a knock at the door.

The sun finally set. According to the clock on the night stand, it was seven twenty-two when I heard the sound of glass breaking coming from the room that I had previously occupied.

There was a knock on both doors. I hadn't expected that. I thought they would come through the main door one at a time. But now I was faced the possibility that both of the hunters would force their way in the room at the same time. I picked up the laser and I turned out the lights.

I sat in the dark as the knocking on the doors and the phone calls continued through the evening. I finally unplugged the phone.

Around two AM, it happened. I heard the lock on the door click as a key card slid through it. The handle turned slowly, and the chain on the door went taut as the door cracked open.

All at once the chain gave way as one of the men burst through. I was standing by the window and had a perfect line of site; my laser passed across the man's eyes. The brown suit guy was blinded. He let out a yelp and stumbled into the room groping in the darkness.

The second man was in the room by this time; he had a knife drawn. I dropped the laser and ran past the foot of the bed. The man came toward me with his arm partially extended and the knife point leading the way.

I stopped in front of the man, spread my arms like a giant bird about to take flight and made my palms flat. When the knife came close to my belly I brought my arms down. My left palm struck the outside of his wrist at the same moment my right palm struck the inside of his forearm. I heard a snap and knew his arm was broken. It took a moment before he cried out in pain. I give the man an upper cut that lifted his feet off the floor, and left him unconscious.

The first man was still stumbling around; he was waving a gun with his right hand while rubbing his eyes with his left. I gave him a helping of what I had given his friend.

I didn't have much time. I had made a lot of noise, and I didn't want to be here when the police arrived. I called Lisa's cell phone.

Lisa had been waiting outside in her car with my large suitcase. By the time she entered the room, both men's hands and feet were tied. We only had room for one man in the suitcase, so I began stuffing brown suit guy into the bag. Lisa went over to the man on the floor and gouged is face with her nails leaving deep marks. There was blood; she touched it.

On my way out of the room I whispered, "Find his room key before you call for the police."

Lisa nodded and I left.

The plan had been for Lisa to stay behind and provide a back story for the police and anyone else that might show up. She had several things working to her advantage. It was after all, still her room, and with her vocal talents she could make anyone believe any story she told. Her tale would be about how the man lying on the floor had broken into her room, and an unknown man came to her rescue and left.

I, on the other hand, transported my new friend back to my place to see to his comfort. To successfully move him into my quarters required using my laser to blind a couple of security cameras along the way.

Inside my room I unpacked my sleeping friend. I laid him out on the floor between the bed and the window. I tied his wrists to the bed frame and left his ankles tied together. I found a sock and stuffed it in his mouth as a gag.

With my new friend resting comfortably, I changed clothes. I decided to check my sleeping friend's pockets. They were empty. No ID, no hotel key card, nothing. I sat down on the bed, leaned back and waited for Lisa to arrive.

CHAPTER NINETEEN

I hadn't rested well. My new roommate, the man in the brown suit lying on the floor, didn't seem to be appreciating the accommodations. He was squinting, blinking his eyes, and making noises. I figured the lights in the room were bothering him, so I turned them off.

My friend in the brown suit was struggling pretty hard against his ropes so I removed the sock from his mouth to try and reason with him. The moment he could speak he started giving me orders using that high pitched tone of the El-yanin.

"You will untie me."

I droned back, "I will untie you…when hell freezes over."

The man looked at me, stunned, and tried again.

"You will let me go; you will jump out the window."

"Look fella, your parlor tricks don't work on me. Don't ask me why, because I don't know."

I waited for a response.

"What the hell are you?" He barked.

"I don't know the answer to that either. I do know a little about who you are. I thought I might get your side of the story. I know some ladies that call you the

'Abomination'."

I waited, and he didn't answer.

"Let's try this again. You see, I ask a question or I make a statement and you're supposed to say something back; something related to what I just said. That's called conversation. How about we give it a try? Who are you?"

The brown suit guy obviously had decided not to participate in polite conversation. I gave him one last chance.

"Say something useful, or I put the sock back."

He opened his mouth and waited, so I obliged.

With nothing else to do I laid down on a bed and slept a little, on and off. After a while I decided that breakfast and coffee were in order. I looked at my guest in the brown suit, still tied to the bedframe, lying there awake, still squinting and blinking. I think his eyes must actually have been hurting.

"Listen, I'm going downstairs to get us some breakfast. Is there anything in particular you'd like?" I waited, he didn't acknowledge me. "OK. I'll just pick something out for you."

I returned with a plate of assorted pastries, two coffees, and two bottles of water. I had every intention of playing nice and letting my guest eat. I sat our food and drink down on the dresser, next to the flat screen television.

"Since I don't know your name, and you won't tell me, I need to call you something. I'll call you Mr. Brown Suit, until you give me a name.

Mr. Brown Suit, I have coffee and pastries…Mmmmm, pastry. I'm happy to share. I'm going to take the sock out of your mouth, and you can tell me your name. In return, you can have water, coffee, and pastry! Isn't that simple?"

I pulled the sock out of his mouth. He coughed.

"Go to hell!"

I shook my finger at him, "Bad puppy! No biscuit! Since you won't talk, I will."

I picked up a cup of coffee and sipped it.

"Until yesterday, I had never met you. I had met some people who don't like you, but I'm not one to judge people before I meet them. I was hoping to meet you, get to know you, and hear your side of the story.

You see, I'm in a pickle. I've been blamed for something that someone else did. These women who don't like you say you did it. I wasn't there, so I honestly don't know. I half expected that you would be saying they did it. So, it's your turn. Did you or your friends kill Emily Smith?"

He didn't answer but I saw his expression change. I assumed he finally put together who I was. I continued to eat and drink my coffee. After about ten minutes of silence I heard something.

"Eric. My name's Eric."

"Nice to meet you Eric. What would you like?"

"Water."

I pulled out a knife. Before I cut his hands free I reminded him of something.

"I'm about to cut your hands loose so you can sit up. I'm the one that blinded you and applied the sedative with my fist. Doing that hurt you more than it did me."

I could tell he understood my meaning; he nodded. I severed the rope, sat him up, and let him have a bottle of water.

"Would you like to tell me about your group?"

"Not really."

"Is there anything you would like?"

"I need to take a leak."

"I figured something like this would happen."

I took off his shoes and threw them in the corner. I took his brown jacket from him. I told him to take off his tie, and he did.

"I'm going to cut your feet free. You're going into the bathroom and I'm following behind."

"How about a little privacy?"

"I spent a few days in the Cleveland County Jail. I

learned something while I was in there; there is no privacy. Do you know what I did when I finally got a few minutes alone?"

Eric shook his head.

"I escaped."

Eric and I went in to the bathroom; he did what he needed to do, and we walked out.

I wheeled the desk chair by the window, and said, "Why don't you sit here?"

Eric moved politely to the chair, and then turned suddenly. I don't know how he had done it, but he had my knife in his hand. He slashed the knife across my chest, and I felt a hot sting. Instinctively my right arm extended and with a broad stroke I back handed him across the face. Eric toppled backward over the chair.

I put both hands on his chest and grabbed two handfuls of his white shirt. I pulled him up, off the ground and sat him forcibly into the chair. He was unconscious.

I took the last of my rope from my backpack I tied his hands together behind the chair, and I tied his ankles to the chair legs.

I had just finished securing Eric when I heard a knock at the door and familiar voice announced itself.

"It's Lisa!"

I opened the door and Lisa drug herself in carrying a half full cup of coffee.

"Good morning, Lisa. Might I say that you look pretty terrible this morning?"

"That plan of ours didn't account for not getting any sleep because of all the questions that had to be answered. Plus the hotel was kind enough to find me another room and help move my things. All of that takes time."

Lisa looked at me, "You don't look a lot better. What happened to your shirt?"

I had forgotten that Eric had slashed me with my own knife. I didn't know how badly I was cut. I went to the bathroom mirror to check it out before I answered. I looked at my chest, and there wasn't so much as a mark.

"Eric, that's our friend in the chair, took my knife from me and slashed my chest. But, I'm not cut. I had to give him a sedative."

I related the morning's events to Lisa who listened politely. I then returned the favor and listened to her. She informed me that after she had relocated to a new room on a new floor, she picked up her messages from the Sisterhood. We would be meeting the council at seven PM.

We stood there and looked at each other. Not a single word needed to be said. Lisa opened the door and hung out the "Do Not Disturb sign". I rolled our friend Eric into the bathroom, turned out the light, and shut the door. Lisa and I each laid down on separate beds and slept.

CHAPTER TWENTY

I woke up to someone shaking my shoulder.

"Wh…what?" I rolled over to see Lisa smiling at me.

"Chad, it's four PM. We have to meet the council at seven. I think we should both change into something decent."

"Right. Meet the council." I yawned.

"I'll go back to my room and change. I'll meet you back here. What are we going to do about taking our friend with us?"

"I've got it figured out…could I ask you to buy some rope? I'm fresh out."

Lisa nodded, said goodbye and let herself out. I opened the bathroom door and turned on the light.

I wasn't prepared for what I saw in the bathroom. I laughed out loud. The sedative I had given Eric had worn off, and he had decided that he didn't want to stay there in the dark. Eric was no longer seated in the chair. The chair was no longer standing upright, it was on its side, and Eric was lying on the floor in front of it.

"Hey buddy, you're not looking too well. You going to be OK?"

I grabbed his shirt collar and the arm of the chair, and

lifted them both upright. Eric gasped and saw my cut shirt. "You're not even scratched…I cut you. I know I cut you! What are you?"

"I told you before. I don't' know."

I rolled the chair out of the bathroom and over by the window.

"Eric, you stay put now. I've got to clean up and get a fresh shirt. And afterwards I get to introduce you to the ladies you've been hunting."

Eric didn't speak; he didn't have to. Even with the bruises on his face, it was easy to tell that the blood had drained out, and he was feeling sick.

It was five-thirty when Lisa returned. She looked like a new woman.

"Lisa, I'd like to introduce you to Eric. Eric, this is Lisa."

Eric ignored me and looked away.

"My goodness, Chad. He looks terrible. Whatever do you suppose is wrong with him?"

"He's had a few too many sedatives. I'd like to be able to take him for a ride. Eric, we're going for a ride now, do you need a sedative before we go?"

Eric refused to look at either of us.

"Lisa, I'll take that as no for now. But if he acts up, he can have another."

"That sounds perfect, Chad! What can I do to help?"

"Take the bedspread off of the bed. Leave the blanket; we'll use that."

I cut Eric's legs free from the chair and led him to the bed.

"Lay down."

"No."

"That wasn't a request."

I grabbed his shirt collar in one hand and his belt in the other. I lifted him up and laid him on the center of the bed. He started to squirm, and I said one word, "Sedative?"

Eric settled down, and I tied his ankles together one last time.

I threw one edge of the blanket over Eric, and rolled him in the blanket.

Lisa took the laser to blind the security cameras along the way, and I put our friend over my shoulder in a fireman's carry.

We made it to her car with only a couple of people glancing at us, but no one stopped us. We were soon on our way; Eric was safely in the trunk, Lisa was driving, and I was riding shotgun.

The way Lisa drove, it didn't take long for us to arrive at Oklahoma City's baseball field, the Bricktown Ball Park. We drove past the front and around to the side entrance where the statue of Johnny Bench stands.

Instead of parking on the street, Lisa pulled the car over the curb and up near the front door. We got out of the car and waited by the statue. I looked at my watch, it was exactly six fifty-five PM."

"Lisa, how long do you think we'll have to wait?"

"As long as it takes. We're being watched. As soon as they're satisfied that we're alone, they'll tell us what to do."

"You mean we're not meeting here?'

"I don't know. We'll find out when they're ready."

We continued to wait. I checked my watch frequently and impatiently.

At seven forty-eight PM, a police cruiser drove up. Two officers exited the car and approached us cautiously, one leading the way.

The officer in front spoke first.

"Good evening. Is everything OK here?"

I started to speak but Lisa signaled me to keep quiet. Lisa replied with the high pitched whistling voice.

"Everything's fine here. Nothing to see. There's no one here except the two of you."

The two officers looked at each other blankly and returned to the car. I heard the driver call over the radio,

"…Nothing to see here. The place is empty. Whoever was here is gone now."

It was another twenty minutes before I heard someone moving inside the building. Soon a door opened, and a woman in her mid-forties gestured for us to come in. I held up my index finger to indicate that she should wait.

Lisa and I went to her car, she opened the trunk, and I extracted our package. Eric was still wrapped as snug as a bug in a rug.

The woman holding the door blocked the entrance as we approached. She grimaced and whispered, "What's that?" It was more of a statement than a question.

Lisa responded to her while I balanced Eric on my shoulder.

"Consider it a gift, from Chad. By the way, it's good to see you Fran."

"It's good to see you too. I'm glad to know that you're alright. You are alright, aren't you?"

"I am, and I think things are going to be good for all of us."

Fran escorted us up an elevator to the second floor, down a hallway, and into a very comfortable room with overstuffed chairs along the walls. Eight round tables with chairs were equally spaced throughout the room.

I placed my package on the floor and it made a slight groan. Fran raised an eyebrow and asked us to make ourselves comfortable.

It was scarcely a minute before four other women entered the room, one of which I recognized as the Matron. I was struck by how feeble she looked dressed in ordinary clothes. But her steel blue eyes blazed and I was absolutely certain that there was an iron will behind them.

I stood to be polite and the ladies took seats on the sofa and chairs along the far wall. Lisa and I pulled chairs away from the table nearest them, and seated ourselves. No one bothered with introductions.

The Matron spoke first.

"Mr. Fury. Let us begin by acknowledging that the council and I feel some level of responsibility for the predicament you find yourself in right now."

I interrupted.

"Some responsibility? None of this would have happened if it hadn't been for you and your w…"

Lisa cut me off and warned be about my choice of words. I acquiesced, knowing that if I made them too mad, I wouldn't get anywhere.

I continued, "Your women's club."

The Matron looked at me and her mouth drew up slightly.

"Mr. Fury. We did not influence you to bring a gun on your campus. We are not responsible for your choices."

"No, Matron, but I was driven back to the campus in my car by someone from your group. That someone was murdered later that night, and the police want me to explain where I was when she was killed. You could clear my name, but I doubt you're willing since you'd have to confess to abducting me and doing God-knows-what to me against my will."

"You're right, Mr. Fury. We're not willing. We are willing to assist you in setting up a new identity for yourself and giving you the funds to make a new start."

"With all due respect, a fictitious life is a poor substitute for the real life I had before I met you and your Sisterhood."

"That's all we're offering. We can't help you with anything else. I've given you an opportunity to accept it willingly. Now I will force you to accept our offer."

Her next words came with high pitched, shrill whistles.

"You will forget being Chad Fury. You will accept that you are Charles Fenton."

"I will not! And your whiny voice can't make me!"

The Matron and the council gasped in unison. The Matron tried a second time, then the council tried in unison. After a few more tries they finally conceded the battle.

"Matron, and ladies", I stood up to make my case, "you changed me. You can no longer use your voice to compel me to do your will, but I may be able to use mine to compel you. No, I don't have your vocal talents. What I have is a very valuable bargaining chip."

I went on to describe the events from the time I was driven back to the campus up to and including the events of that day. When I came to the part about bringing Eric to our little meeting I grabbed the edge of the blanket and unrolled our guest onto the floor.

Eric greeted the room with coughs as he inhaled the cool fresh air a little too deeply.

The council glared at one another, then at me. Fran broke her silence with a loud, "This is preposterous!" The rest of the council voiced agreement with her opinion.

"Mr. Fury."

I could tell the Matron was choosing her words carefully.

"Just what, pray tell, are we supposed to do with that!"

She pointed at Eric lying in the floor.

"You're the advanced race from another planet. You shouldn't have to ask me. Put him in stasis…beam him into space…Open the pod bay doors and shove him out! I honestly don't care what you do with him. But if I were in your shoes, I'd bleed him a little and gather up all the memories and knowledge I could."

The ladies didn't respond, so I kept talking.

"I really thought you would be more appreciative of my gift. After all, in the last two hundred years, how many hunters have you captured?"

My question was met with thunderous silence.

"I'll take your lack of response to mean that this is a pretty rare gift. I'm giving you a possible clue to the location of your missing member. I believe her name is Alice? I'm also giving you the possibility of locating your missing books."

The ladies broke into an uproar. It was a cacophony of dissention and differing ideas until the Matron called for silence.

"Chad Fury!"

"Yes, Matron."

"You have not brought us a gift, you brought more trouble down upon our heads! The hunters travel in pairs, sometimes threes. Where is the second hunter?"

"He had a badly broken arm. The police carted him off. And yes, I'm sure he will use his vocal talents to escape."

"You are correct he will escape. He will report the events to the Abomination and they will come in force. If we had been able to transform you into our protector, both hunters would be dead, and our presence here would remain unknown."

"Then, Matron, it appears you need my help."

"You insolent, arrogant man! The Sisterhood does not work with outsiders."

"No, Matron. The Sisterhood uses them."

"What, sir, exactly are you proposing?"

"I can help you. I can help retrieve the books. I may even be able to help Alice."

The Matron lowered her voice.

"And, I assume, there is a price?"

"Ah yes, the price. You will give me my life back. Clear my name and change me back."

"Mr. Fury. Changing you back may not be possible."

"True, but you could try. If you had all of the books, you might know for sure."

"We could refuse to help you."

"Until just now, it had not occurred to me that I have options. Letting Eric fall into your hands and hoping for your gratitude is only one of three possibilities. I could let Eric go; I could escort him out and offer my services to his band of merry men. They might accept the same offer that I have presented you."

I looked at Eric. "Eric, would your friends consider my

terms?"

Eric lifted his head.

"They will."

I addressed the ladies.

"And if they will not, I still have another option. I could go after the books myself. It is true that I can't use their knowledge. But I could burn the books. I may not need to destroy more than one. If I do destroy just a single book it might mean you can't return, and you would be stuck here forever."

I had more to say, but the Matron interrupted.

"The council needs to consider the situation."

"Please, by all means. Take all the time you need, say two or even three minutes."

The council left the room. While they were out, Lisa and I discussed the possible outcome. Lisa informed me that the Sisterhood does not like being backed into a corner, and people backed into a corner do not always react rationally.

It was nearly an hour before the ladies returned. Their response was encouraging and unexpected.

"Mr. Fury we have considered your offer. You have left us with no choice but to accept. However, we will add one stipulation. You will not deal with the council directly. We want some distance. Lisa will be your handler. Communication between the council and you will pass through Lisa."

"Fine, how do we proceed?"

"We will digest the information we get from this thing you brought here. When there is something that can be acted upon, we will contact Lisa."

That was a major victory. Lisa and I returned to our respective hotel rooms. We agreed that we needed our own space for a while and decided to spend the next day apart

CHAPTER TWENTY-ONE

After having my audience with the council on Wednesday, I spent the next three days doing almost nothing. Let me correct that. I did things, but nothing at the same pace I had been doing them. To the rest of the world, I was still presenting myself as brown-eyed Charlie Fenton, and Charlie had things he wanted to do.

On Thursday was a small matter of relocating. Lisa and I were in separate hotels, and since she was my contact to the Sisterhood, it only made sense for us to be in the same hotel. I checked out of my room and migrated across the street. Lisa's new room was on the second floor, and I was able to get a room across the hall from her.

Then there was the matter of clothes. Yes, Lisa had bought me some new clothes, but there were some things missing; pajamas, a bathing suit, and some workout clothes. That afternoon I took a taxi to the Penn Square Mall, and picked up the few things I wanted. But mostly I had wanted to get out and feel normal.

On Friday, I informed Lisa that I had relocated to her hotel and had taken the room across from hers. I also asked her for another computer lesson, to which she readily agreed. It was a tedious, five hours, but I figured it was worth it because I didn't know how long it would take for me to get my life back. Knowing how to work covertly on the internet seemed like good skill to have.

That evening I went alone to a club. There was loud music, drinks, and a lots of people milling around in the dim light. I chatted up a couple of girls, which all led to nothing. Not that it couldn't have been more, but I realized I didn't want to have a one night stand or a long term relationship as Charlie. Chad needed relationships, and Chad was still grieving over the loss of his old life.

Saturday was when things got a little more interesting. I woke up anxious for whatever might be coming, and I needed to work off a little nervous energy. Parkour and free running had been gaining popularity in the city. I had seen the videos on the internet, and I had always wanted to try, but never did.

I changed into my new workout clothes, and headed off north, toward the Oklahoma City memorial, on foot.

I never made it to the memorial. I had forgotten that the Botanical Gardens and park was along the way. When I saw the gardens I decided it was the best place to see just what I could do.

I played. I jumped the split rail fence several times, and then ran along the top edge. I approached the giant modern art, metal sculptures and ran up them and leapt off, doing flips in the air. I felt as though I was flying. It seemed like there was nothing I couldn't do. I had balance and agility.

After a while of doing stunts, I noticed a crowd had gathered. I did a few flips for their entertainment. It was late afternoon before I decided I'd had enough, and ran back.

Back in my room, I showered, ordered room service and settled in for the evening. I was at peace.

CHAPTER TWENTY-TWO

Sunday morning I awoke to furious pounding on my door. I could hear Lisa's voice.

"Charlie! Open this door! Now!!"

I bolted out of bed and opened door. Lisa rushed past me, grabbed the television remote from the dresser and turned on the TV. As she was searching the channels, she kept repeating, "Idiot! Chad is an idiot!"

Lisa stopped on one of the twenty-four hour news channels.

"Chad! Sit yourself down. Watch. Then explain to me just how you could be such an idiot!"

A couple of minutes passed before a familiar looking blonde anchor woman came on the screen talking about me.

"Remember the name Chad Fury? That was the man who broke out of an Oklahoma jail almost two weeks ago and is suspected of murdering a school teacher. Authorities had believed that Chad Fury had fled to Amarillo, Texas. However, this video taken yesterday, was posted on the internet yesterday evening. Authorities quickly identified the man in the video as Chad Fury.

Although the man in the video has black hair, he has

the same dragon tattoo on his left arm as Chad Fury. Chad Fury is believed to be in Oklahoma City. Anyone having any information about this man is urged to call the number on the screen below. A reward is being offered for any information leading to his capture."

My stomach caved in, and my heart sank to fill the void. Lisa just stood there. "Well?"

That one word was a thunderous condemnation.

"Lisa. I'm sorry. I was anxious. I needed to blow off some steam."

"The point of hiding in plain sight is to blend in. That…was not…blending in!"

"I know. It seemed harmless. It was just a run."

"Chad! That was no ordinary run. You were doing things I didn't even know were humanly possible!"

"Yeah." I grinned. "It was pretty cool."

"It was also pretty stupid! The only thing that could be worse is if you told someone your name...You didn't tell anyone your name, did you?"

I sat there in silence. I just couldn't bring myself to say anything.

"Oh my God, Chad. NO! How could you? You moron!!!"

"Lisa, it was Friday night. I wanted something to do. I went to the club down the street. I had a couple of drinks, and talked to a couple girls. I told them my name's Charlie."

"Moron! I'm keeping watch over a moron…who can't keep his hormones in check!"

"Ok. I screwed up. I get it. I can't undo it. What do we do now?"

"First, let's both get packed."

"Where are we going?"

"We're trading rooms. If we check out and run, it'll look suspicious. If the police come here, they'll come to your room, not mine. They need to find someone in this room who can convince them that Charlie Fenton and

Chad Fury are two different people. I think I have a better shot at that than you do.

You stay in my room and don't come out! Don't show your face until I tell you to. In the meantime, be thinking of a plan to put the police on a new trail. I'll be doing the same."

We worked in silence; Lisa refused to speak to me the entire time we were changing rooms. I took advantage of the icy silence by trying to come up with a way to make the world think I was somewhere else. As I was putting the last of my things in the closet I realized I had another problem and Lisa needed to know about it.

I hurried across the hall and knocked on Lisa's door.

"Lisa, it's Charlie. Open up!"

The door remained closed.

"Charlie. Go back to your room. Stay inside until I say otherwise!"

"This is important! I wouldn't be out here harassing you if it wasn't, now open up!"

The door opened and Lisa reluctantly stepped aside for me to pass by. I took a seat in the rolling chair at the writing table.

"You might as well sit down too. This could take a while."

Lisa went to the large stuffed chair by the window, and I turned in the desk chair to face her.

"Lisa, the envelope I gave you on Monday…did you mail it?"

"Yeah, why?"

"Do you remember what I said was in it?"

"Postcards for a friend in Louisiana to mail…back…oh, my, God!"

"I think we're on the same page now, Lisa, but let me spell it out just to be sure. When did you mail the package?"

"Monday afternoon; I dropped it in a slot at the main post office."

"There's our problem then. Mail delivery to Shreveport shouldn't take more than three days. If Ronnie has sent one of the postcards, and its postmark is too close to my Sunday run, then which one will be believed? I think they'll believe their eyes. I also think they'll know somebody's sending the postcards for me, and Ronnie could be at risk."

"That's only part of it, Chad. We can't go changing your identity too many times. You'll start leaving a very visible trail if you do. We have to break the connection between Charlie and Chad. We have to prove they were in two different places at the same time.

And, Chad, there's one more thing. You're so obsessed with the police hunting you you've completely forgotten about the Abomination."

"I don't follow. What's the problem?"

"Chad, do you realize why you worry about the police? That's a rhetorical question. I'm going to tell you. You worry because you have some understanding of how they operate. You've gotten information all your life from news, fiction, second-hand accounts, and now some first-hand knowledge; your own experience. But, you don't know anything about the Abomination."

"I think you'd better fill me in."

I had a sinking feeling that I wasn't going to like anything I was about to hear.

Lisa shifted in the chair, and leaned back.

"Chad, the hunter, whose arm you broke. He's probably already escaped, and he will report back to his brothers. He'll share his memories of you with them. Soon a lot of hunters will know your face, and add to that your face has been on the television and the internet. It won't be long until they have the name 'Chad Fury' to put with the face.

They will make the assumption that you're in contact with the Sisterhood. They will be coming after you. They won't care if the police find you first; eventually they will get to you. And because they can't bleed you, God only knows what they'll do to you."

I was right. I didn't like what I heard.

"What do we do?"

It was less of a question I was asking and more of an expression of despair."

Lisa closed her eyes and pressed her head back into the chair.

"We need information. You call your friend on a burn phone. Find out if and when he mailed a post card. If he asks if he's to stop, tell him no. Just wait two weeks before sending another."

Lisa's eyes remained closed. She tapped the arm of the chair slowly with her right index finger. I took one of her burn phones and dialed.

I heard Ronnie's voice after the second ring.

"Hello. You got Ronnie."

"Ronnie, it's Chad."

"Should we be talking?"

Ronnie's voice was flat and his words were terse.

"I won't keep you. I just wanted to know if you got the package I sent."

"I did."

"What did you do with it?"

"I sent a card on Saturday, just like you said."

"Thanks, guy. Just wait a couple of weeks before you mail anything else."

"I will, but one question. Was that you I saw doing all those flips and jumps on the TV?"

I made a choice to lie to my best friend.

"No, man. It wasn't."

"OK then. Stay safe."

"I will. You too."

The call ended with that; neither of us actually said goodbye.

When I turned back to Lisa, her eyes were still closed, and the finger tap had switched to the other hand.

"Lisa, Ronnie said that…"

Lisa put up her right hand and waved me off. I laid down on the bed and waited. It was more than twenty minutes later before Lisa spoke.

"Chad, I have something."

"Just what were you doing? What was all the finger tapping about?"

"I was talking with my memories. The tapping helps me focus. As an El-yanin, I have the memories of more people in my head than I can count. I was searching for similar situations and studying what the others did."

"Did it help?'

"Yes. Based on what I've seen, our best course of action is to let some people see Chad Fury. The same Chad Fury that escaped from Cleveland County jail. Here's the problem. He needs to be seen in Louisiana, not Oklahoma."

"That's about a 6 hour drive, let's go."

"I can't go with you. I'm betting that the police will show up here; it could be any time, tonight or tomorrow. I need to be right here when it happens. That's why we changed rooms; when they find me here I'll convince them they saw Charlie, and Charlie is not Chad."

"Yeah, I get it. Give me the keys to your car, I'll go alone."

"That's not happening. I may need the car to get away quickly. Also, if you get stopped, it's game over. Since the video's been aired on the news, the police are expecting you to run. They'll be watching bus stops and checking highways. You need to go on foot. How fast did you say you could run?"

"I'm guessing it's about forty miles an hour or so."

"We're going to find out just how fast and how far you can run. But, that's later. For now, go back to your room and stay inside. I have some shopping to do for you. Be ready to leave as soon as I get back. If you want to do something useful while I'm out, get on the internet and map out how you want to get to Shreveport.

CHAPTER TWENTY-THREE

It was almost five PM when Lisa knocked on my door, and I let her in. She was loaded down with packages. I looked at her more than a little amazed.

"Does every solution to every problem involve 'shopping'?"

"No, only the solutions that are any good."

Lisa unloaded the packages and explained what they were and how they were to be used.

First there were three pairs of running shoes. It was a long trip, and I was likely to need a couple of shoe changes.

Then there were two jogging suits. I might be in the sun a long time, and I didn't want to be sunburned when I arrived. She also gave me a tube of sunscreen and told me to use it on my face, neck and hands.

Lisa reminded me to take my ball cap. It was imperative that no camera in Louisiana saw anyone other than Chad Fury.

She had bought a collapsible water bottle; that was self-explanatory.

She had been to a homeless shelter and picked up some clothes for Chad. There was a pair of faded jeans with holes in them and some very old looking t-shirts. I was to change into those in Shreveport.

Out of another box came a wig in my original hair color and Lisa told me she would cut and shape it before I left.

I informed her that she forgot about my eyebrows, and she smirked as she tossed me a box of beard dye.

After that was some small stuff. A GPS unit, a tactical flashlight, extra batteries, and some protein bars. Lisa reminded me to take my laser and a couple of burn phones.

I made a mental note to take some cash.

There was one last thing. There was something that looked like a pantyhose leg. She told me it was for my left arm; from now on, whenever I was being Charlie, I needed to wear it. It was the kind of thing used in movies when an actor needed to cover tattoos.

I had been packing my backpack at the same time Lisa was showing me what she had bought. In another thirty minutes I was ready and heading out the door.

I looked at my watch; it was seven PM. According to the internet, the most direct route was a distance three hundred fifty miles. If I could maintain a constant speed of forty miles an hour, I would be there in less than nine hours. With stops, I might make it in ten. I wondered if I could do it.

As soon as I was out of the hotel, I was jogging. In another two minutes I was running southeast, in the fairly straight line the GPS had mapped out. It would have been easier to stick to the roads because it was dark and getting darker. It was especially dark because of heavy clouds between me and the stars.

After seeing a flash of lightning in the distance, I knew I was in for an Oklahoma Spring storm. In a deliberate effort not to jinx myself I refrained from yelling out 'Storms Suck!'

I had started out with the GPS hanging from a lanyard

around my neck. I soon realized I couldn't do that. The GPS was bouncing as I ran; I stopped, plugged the earphones into the GPS, and put it in my back pack. I was able to hear the synthetic voice giving me course corrections and turns as I ran.

I had to slow down at the Canadian River, about 25 miles outside of Ada, Oklahoma. The Canadian River is a little unpredictable. The riverbed is mostly silt and sand, and it can be very soft in spots. In a few places it's like quicksand. In some places it's shallow and wide. In other places it's deep enough to swim across. It's muddy most of the time.

Where I was crossing was at one of the shallow areas. I removed my shoes, socks, and pants, and put them in my backpack. I threw the backpack across the river, and it landed on the other bank.

My feet hit the water, it was warm. As my feet sank into the mud and silt small air bubbles rose up around them. The mud sucked my feet down, and my body weight forced them to sink down to my ankles. I moved carefully, testing how far my feet sank. Ribbons of dark brown mud flowed from my feet when I lifted them and the water took the muck away.

I made it across. When I lifted my right foot a thick layer of the slimy silt clung to the sole of my foot. I sat my foot on the sloping dry bank, and my foot slid back into the river. I fell face first onto the bank and slid back into the river, up to my waist. I could get no firm footing. I crawled on my hands and knees out of the river and up the bank.

My legs and feet were covered with mud. I scraped off what I could with my hands before going to the backpack and getting my shoes and pants. I made a mental note to always have towel if I planned anything like this again. I was also going to stick closer to the roads for the rest of this trip.

When I reached Ada, Oklahoma it was a little before

nine PM and I crossed over Sandy Creek on highway nineteen. The storm I had seen earlier was about to greet me; the winds were picking up. I looked around and there was an old barn in a field on the south side of the highway. I left the road and ran to the barn for shelter. I made it into the barn just as it started to hail.

The barn was everything you might come to expect in an old abandoned barn. But at least it was dry. I took off my backpack, sat down on the ground and leaned against an old feeding trough. It was the perfect time to rehydrate and have something to eat.

While the storm intensified I decided to take a look at the GPS. It said I had traveled eighty-one miles, and my average speed was forty-two miles per hour. How was that even possible, I wondered? What really had happened to me? I still couldn't wrap my head around it.

It was over an hour before the storm let up and I was back on my way. The GPS had me routed through the center of town and on toward Hugo, Oklahoma. About every two hours I found myself stopping for water and food. I found I didn't need long to rest. Only ten minutes or so and I was ready to go again.

I ran on through the night. Sunrise found me on Pin Hill Road, headed toward Highway One on the outskirts of Shreveport. All through the night, as I ran, I had been thinking about how to let the authorities know I was here without getting arrested. I supposed I could have done what I did the first time and rob a convenience store, but I don't like being a thief. I was too tired to know what to do.

Although I was still able to maintain my speed, I recognized the signs of my blood sugar dropping. I was no longer able to think clearly; I needed food and rest.

I stopped at the first convenience store I came across and bought a two liter bottle of soda, three candy bars, a box of mini doughnuts, and two prepackaged sandwiches of whatever they had. The clerk accused me of having the munchies, I was too light headed to respond. I walked outside, sat down on the curb and consumed half of the soda, the sandwiches, and all three candy bars.

After about thirty minutes I was feeling a little better. I started walking. I continued down Highway One; its name eventually changed into Market Street. That's where I saw the Southern Comfort Inn. It was one of those old motels that had seen better days. It was a single building divided into maybe twenty rooms. I didn't much care what it looked like. I just needed a place to rest.

Inside the motel office, a greasy little man asked me how long I wanted the room; he informed me that I could get it by the hour. I looked at my watch; it was nine AM. I told him I wanted it for a day; he charged me thirty dollars and I paid him in cash, up front.

On the outside, room number fifteen wasn't much different than number fourteen or number sixteen, except the five was missing from the door. The door lock was in such bad shape that I scarcely needed a key to open it. Inside I was greeted by a dirty brown carpet, stained curtains and stale smoke odors. It looked like the kind of place I imagined I would be hiding out in if I were on the run with very little money and no friends.

I didn't know what kind of creatures might be living in the bed, so I left my clothes on, and left the bedspread in place. I pulled a burn phone out of my backpack, turned it on, and set an alarm for three PM.

There were enough outlets to plug in my electronics, so I charged my three phones, my laser, and made sure everything thing else had fresh batteries.

When my head finally hit the pillow, I was asleep.

CHAPTER TWENTY-FOUR

I had slept so hard that when the alarm went off I didn't feel like I had even been asleep. My body ached. I was still tired, but I decided I could function; I had to. I emptied my backpack, and picked out what Chad would be wearing when he made his Shreveport appearance.

I took off my clothes for a shower, and then remembered I needed to change the color of my eyebrows. I put the color on, and ate the doughnuts I had bought that morning. As I ate I was missing my coffee. Whatever I did as Chad, it was going to include coffee.

I left the room as Chad Fury. I was wearing a plain blue ball cap, the wig, an old t-shirt that boldly displayed the dragon tattoo on my left arm, worn looking jeans, and a new pair of tennis shoes. I headed toward downtown with my backpack and still no plan. What I did have was hunger and an overwhelming need for coffee.

I didn't have to walk far before I saw an old Pancake House restaurant. I always loved those kind of places; I could get a plate of eggs, meat, and hash browns cheap, any time of day. That was perfect. I went in, sat at a booth and ordered the steak and eggs, and lots of coffee.

The waitress was chatty, so I chatted her up. It wasn't

part of the plan; I was making everything up as I went. In passing conversation I used my first name, and I flirted. I just hoped I would be remembered. After paying and leaving a generous tip, I continued toward downtown. I walked a couple of blocks and decided to make a phone call; I dialed my mother and kept walking.

On the fourth ring, my mother answered.

"Hello."

"Hi mom, it's Chad."

Mom began to cry. She tried to talk, but real words weren't coming out.

I cried too.

"Mom. Stop it. It's OK. I'm OK. I just can't come home yet."

"Chad, my baby. Please come home. Give yourself up. You're only making it worse."

"Mom, I can't explain, but it's going to be OK. I'm going to fix this."

"Where are you sweetie? Was that you I saw on the news, running in the park?"

"No mom. That wasn't me. I'm in Shreveport."

"Why Shreveport? How does being in Shreveport help?"

"I can't explain it now. But someday I will. Listen, I just wanted to say I love you."

"I love you too Chad. Just please be careful, and please come home."

I ended the call and put the phone in my pocket; I thought I might make a few more calls just to leave a solid trail.

Now for the hard part. I was still working on how to be noticed by the law, make it look accidental, and yet not get arrested.

I continued on down the road and the neighborhood changed. There were fewer abandoned buildings and more people actually living and working here.

I saw a grocery store and I got excited when I saw that

there was a bank inside the store. I trotted into the store, made a left-turn and found myself standing at a counter with a bank teller on the other side.

I took off my cap so the cameras could get a good look at me. I reached into my pocked and took out a hundred dollar bill. I asked for change. I made a pretty big deal out of it so it would take a long time. I also made a point of frequently looking over my shoulder and commenting on the security guard about thirty feet away.

With my change in hand I hurried out of the store and into the street. A couple of blocks further along I saw a dark building with a neon sign reading, "Fat Daddy's Bar and Grill".

That looked just like the kind of place Chad might get in trouble, so went a little closer. I walked around back and looked for a place to hide my backpack. There wasn't anything at ground level; I tossed my bag up on the roof. I walked back to the front door and went inside.

The place was dimly lit, and there were all the familiar smells of alcohol, greasy food, and perspiration. It was still early, I decided to wait to see what kind of clientele might show up.

I sat at a booth, ordered a beer in a bottle, and just watched for a little while. The beer turned out to be what my Army buddies called 'beach beer' because it was close to water. After a while I ordered a burger and more beer.

I continued to watch. Sometime after sunset I saw it; trouble. A man, about thirty years old walked in and went straight to the pool table. His face looked like ten miles of bad road. He stood six foot three, and there wasn't an ounce of fat on him. He had a red paisley bandanna tied over his head in the do rag style and wore a black leather jacket. He reminded me of some of the people I'd seen in the Cleveland County jail.

I felt sorry for what I was about to do to the guy, but I needed to be noticed and remembered. I left plenty of cash on the table to cover my meal and tip. Then I walked straight up to the man with every intention of making him as mad as I possibly could.

"Hey." I belched, and I slurred my words. "You...yur thu guy…you owe me…two hun-red bucks!"

"Look man, you're drunk. I don't know you."

"No…no. I know you!" I pointed in his general direction. "I want…my money." I stumbled toward him.

"Back off dude. Let it go. You don't want this."

"Tha name-sss not 'Dude'. It'th…Chad. Chad Fury."

I pulled a pool cue off the wall and snapped it over my knee. I threw the small end away. I took two steps forward. The man was already coming toward me, ready to swing his cue like a bat.

I watch him start his swing. I raised my left forearm and his cue snapped around it. In that same moment, I dropped my stick, took a step closer and my right fist landed a solid punch in his stomach. The blow knocked him back but didn't injure him. I was intentionally trying not to hurt him. This wasn't his fault. I was just using him.

Another man came up behind me. He was a little shorter than me, and carried about seventy-five pounds more than he needed. I spun around and faced him. With both hands I grabbed his shirt on each side of his collar. I spun back around dropping to a squat at the same time. The result of my sudden drop pulled him over and as he started to fall, I threw him forward. He made one flip in the air and his feet hit the first man in the stomach.

I didn't stay around for more. I ran out the door and around the back. It was an easy jump to catch the edge of the roof, and I pulled myself up to retrieve my backpack. I almost ran away, but then I thought I should lay low on the roof and wait.

Waiting paid off. After about ten minutes a police car pulled up and two uniformed officers got out. I listened as best I could. I couldn't hear everything, but I did catch enough to know that they were given my description and my name.

I waited until I saw one of the officers come outside. I took that opportunity to jump off the roof and onto the squad car below. The roof of the car dented with my impact.

I waited for the officer's shock to wear off. I jumped off of the trunk of the car and ran across the street behind a building. I heard the officer yelling for his partner, which was followed by rapid footsteps headed my direction.

I needed to run, but not too fast. I wanted to be chased; I wanted to be seen by more than one officer. I started jogging down the alley, with the two officers running behind.

I heard a voice behind me yell, "Stop! Police!"

That warning made me realize what I hadn't taken into account was gunfire. I froze and turned slowly to face the two men. The first man was standing motionless, pointing his gun at me. His feet were slightly apart, and he was gripping his weapon with both hands. It was a classic stance. His partner was approaching slowly with his hand at his holster, ready to draw his sidearm.

I ran two options through my head. One, I could let myself be cuffed and put in the cruiser, and try to escape. Two, I could make a run for it. I figured that if they took me, I might not be able to escape; it might be game over. If I ran, I might be shot. I chose to see what was behind door number two.

My eyes scanned the dark alley. On my left was a large metal dumpster. The building next to it was four stories of brick. To my right was a row of small, run-down houses, most with low chain link fences.

To this day I don't know why I did it; it was like instinct. I put my left foot against my right heel and slipped my right foot out of its shoe. The officer approaching yelled out "Stop whatever you're doing!" I ignored him and liberated my left foot.

I bent my knees slightly and prepared myself. The second officer drew his gun. I ran for the dumpster and leapt for the top. Shots rang out as my feet left the ground. Something hot stung my right shoulder, as the soles of my feet found the dumpster lid.

I sprang up and toward the wall. My fingers and toes found anchor points and I climbed as fast as I could into the darkness above. Two more shots rang out, and brick shards flew around me. I climbed on until I was on the roof.

While on the rooftop I took the opportunity to look at my shoulder. There was a round hole in my t-shirt, but no blood. I remove my backpack and pulled off my shirt to find only a red whelp. "Huh..." I said, "Not bullet proof; more like bullet resistant."

I needed options. Being trapped on a rooftop didn't seem like it was much better than being trapped on the ground. I did have one advantage, time. I guessed it would be a few minutes before the officers found their way up to the roof.

I had to leave, and I had to do it quickly; but if I could do it unseen, all the better. I kept low to the rooftop, watched over the sides, and I listened. I gathered from the conversation filtering up from the street level that one of the officers was headed back to the car to call for backup. The second officer was circling the building to watch the doors and windows.

Luck was with me. The moment the first officer was back at the squad car, the other officer happened to be on the far side of the building, away from the downtown skyline.

The building on the unobserved side was a little shorter, only two stories. I threw my backpack over to the other building. I backed up, took a run toward the edge, and quite literally took a leap of faith.

I sailed through the air with the downtown lights in my eyes. I landed on the roof on all fours, and rolled once. I was back on my feet, wearing the backpack, and headed down the far side of the building before the officers realized what had happened.

Back on the street level I stayed to the shadows until I came to Thatcher Street. I ran down Thatcher. It looked like an industrial park. Some of the metal buildings looked like bus barns. Most of the buildings had security cameras.

I let myself be seen by a camera as I was climbing over a chain link fence. I then ran into the shadows of a building that did not have any cameras pointed at directly it. That's where I changed clothes.

I put the wig in my backpack, removed Chad's clothes, and put on a running suit. I pulled out the ball cap with the infrared led lights in the brim, and made sure it was powered on. I grabbed my laser, and I was off again.

I blinded the cameras on the way out, and I didn't worry if some camera from a across the street saw me. I continued down Thatcher until it dead ended as a one lane strip of black asphalt. I continued straight on and through a small stand of trees. On the other side of the trees was a large highway. I could smell the water all around me. I figured the Red River had to be close.

As soon as I crossed the highway I could see the river. After I descended the bank, I pulled out the phone I had used to call my mother, and I left it there. I wanted to make another call, but told myself it was too late. The truth was I couldn't bring myself to upset her again.

I decided to follow the riverbank away from Shreveport. After a few minutes of running along the bank, I saw the airport. I stopped there to make a call back to Lisa. I pulled out my second burn phone and dialed.

The phone rang five times, and no one answered. I hung up. I got little worried.

I sat down by the river, drank a bottle of water and ate a protein bar, all the while telling myself that everything was OK. I tried calling again, but there was still no answer. I kept trying to reassure myself that things were OK, but the more I tried, the more concerned I actually became.

I eventually realized that I could sit by the river and call

all night, or I could start heading back and call along the way. I'd have to stop every two hours anyway, I might as well call then.

I pulled out the GPS and programmed my destination. It was a little after ten PM according to my watch. With any luck I'd be back at the Hotel before eight AM.

I said a quick prayer before I started running. Lisa was my connection to the Sisterhood, and without her I could lose every chance of getting my life back. But as I was praying I realized that I wasn't just concerned about me. I was genuinely worried for her. I just hoped that she had been wrong and the hunter hadn't come back for her.

I ran down Jack Wells Boulevard, past the airport and to Grimmer Road. I stayed on the Grimmer until I passed under Highway 220 and then made my way back to Market Street and toward Oklahoma City.

I pushed myself as hard as I could retracing my route. At each stop I called Lisa's cell phone. Each time, there was no answer. I had to start ignoring the sick feeling growing in my stomach and just keep going.

CHAPTER TWENTY-FIVE

It was just after six-thirty AM when I entered the side door at the hotel. My blood sugar was low, and I was light headed. I still felt like I was running. I could still feel the pounding of the road under my feet. I took the elevator to my floor. I went immediately to Lisa's room and knocked. There was no answer.

I stood at the door and knocked three more times. I called Lisa's name and listened closely; no sound came through the door. My emotions passed from concern into full-fledged worry. I considered breaking down the door, and then realized that this was my room, or at least it was the room the front desk had given me.

I quickly returned to the room I was occupying and threw my backpack on the bed. I pulled my wallet from the top drawer of the dresser and headed for the front desk.

At the front desk I tried to act calm and got the attention of the young girl behind the counter.

"Excuse, me. I'm Charlie Fenton. I've lost my room key."

After she had looked at my driver's license, she made two key cards and gave them to me with a smile. I thanked her. On the way out of the lobby I grabbed a pastry from the buffet and shoved it down my throat during the elevator ride back.

When I arrived at Lisa's door, I slid the card in and out of the door lock, turned the handle and stumbled into the room; there was no Lisa. I started to panic, but soon got ahold of myself.

"Chad", I whispered. "Only you can help, you, right now. Calm down. Make a plan."

I stood there with my eyes closed letting my other senses report back to me what they observed. My ears heard a drip in the bathroom. My skin felt the warmth of the sunlight coming through the window. My nose caught the scent of burnt cinnamon. The hunter whose arm I broke had been here.

I scanned the room. The signs of a struggle were obvious. The desk chair was on its side, on the floor. Lisa's purse was on the floor, and its contents had been flung out. Both her cell phone and the transresinator were in the trash can. I picked up the phone and looked it over. It showed nine missed calls from my number.

My emotions were in my throat, but I wrestled them back down. I looked more closely at the room. It didn't look like the crime scene photos I was shown in the jail. If the hunters had killed Lisa, there would have been blood, lots of blood.

I righted the desk chair. On the back of the chair was a bloody palm print. My heart froze. When I breathed again, I thought, "Sure there's blood. They wanted her memories. But they want her alive too."

This wasn't going well; I was too tired and hungry to think this through properly. I heard myself say aloud, "Forgive me, Lisa…"

I returned to my room, called room service, showered and changed clothes. I felt guilty for taking care of myself, but I needed a clear head or I wasn't going to be any good to anyone.

When room service arrived, I had my laptop open and was posting an encrypted message for the Sisterhood, just the way Lisa taught me to do. I created my message in plain text.

"Lisa was taken by the hunters sometime on Monday evening. I don't know where to start looking. Post back if you can get anything from Eric.

--Chad"

After running the encryption program, my message looked like someone had run a dictionary through a blender and poured the contents out on the computer screen.

I posted the message to each bulletin board just like Lisa had shown me. I was going to have to wait to hear back from the Sisterhood; and I really didn't feel like waiting.

I pulled out a piece of paper and pen. I decided that I should write down everything I could as it crossed my mind. I was hoping that seeing it on paper would help me sort it all out.

What did I know?

1. Lisa is missing, and did not leave of her own free will.

2. I smelled burnt cinnamon, the same odor as the hunter who came at me with the knife.

3. The bloody handprint. Someone touched Lisa's blood…to get her memories. That means someone knows what she knows; that person knows about me.

The thought that a hunter knew about me, and what I can do, frightened me. I had to assume he knew what I had done with Eric; he knew about the bargain with the Sisterhood.

I sat paralyzed for a while. How was I going to fight an enemy that could be anyone on the street? What do I do if that enemy knows everything there is to know about me? How do I find an enemy when I don't know where to start looking?

It finally hit me. I had something he didn't know about. I never told Lisa I knew the scent of the hunter. I recognized that same scent in her room. At least I might be able to pick up some kind of trail.

But something else was bothering me. How did the hunter know that Lisa was here, and that she was alone? After breaking the one hunter's arm, and capturing Eric, anyone would have assumed that we would have left the hotel. I assumed that Lisa stayed because she thought it was safe now, that no one would expect us to be here. I had to be missing something.

"No!" I said it again. "No! The Matron said hunters always hunt in twos and sometimes threes. Before I left for Shreveport, Lisa said she needed the car in case she had to leave quickly. Was Lisa trying to draw out the third hunter?"

I got up and returned to Lisa's room. I sat on the edge of the bed and closed my eyes. I paid close attention to every smell coming across my nose. I let my memories and imagination run with every scent. There was a sweet cinnamon smell, which my mind connected with Lisa. I sniffed the pillow. Yes, the same smell. It had to be Lisa.

I focused again. There was the burnt cinnamon again, the hunter I faced in the hallway. I focused a little harder on the scent. The more I focused, the more it seemed like two voices singing in harmony. The odor had to be from two people…there must have been two hunters. One of them I could recognize by site, but I would definitely recognize both of them from their scents.

I had the faintest glimmer of a plan. It was a longshot, but I had little to lose. I spent the next two hours walking up down every hallway in the hotel. I remembered that I had seen Eric coming out of a room at the same time I was sneaking in to set my trap for him. I was hoping that the hunters were creatures of habit, and had once again taken a room in this hotel.

There was no scent in the hallway where Lisa's room

was, so I choose to start on the first floor and work my way up. I walked up and down a couple times. I stood in front of every door and sniffed the air. I had worked my way up to the eight floor when I caught the faint smell of burnt cinnamon at the far end of the hall. I sniffed the first door; nothing. Nothing on the second. And then, pay dirt! I had to see what was behind door number three. But how?

I listened for sounds on the other side. There was nothing. I thought it was best not to knock.

I felt my back pocket and verified that my wallet was there. "Good", I whispered. "Kevin, I'm beginning to think you were right. I sincerely apologize. It looks like I need to use a little gold to get a girl."

I ran down the stairs to the hotel lobby and located the ATM machine near the front door. I slid in my bank card, entered my pin, and checked the balance. I could scarcely believe my eyes, the machine was showing me there was three hundred thousand dollars in the account; I took out five hundred dollars. I walked up to the man at the front desk and read his name badge so I could call him by name.

"Hello, Tim."

"Hello, sir. Is there something I can help you with?"

"Yes, Tim. I need to get into room eight forty-three."

"Just let me see your ID, and I'll be happy to make you a new key to your room."

I counted out five, twenty dollar bills and said, "Will this work as an ID?"

"I'm sorry sir, I can't let you into a room that's not registered to you."

I counted out another one hundred dollars.

"You really don't understand. I need to get into that room."

"No sir, you don't understand. I can't."

I counted out another one hundred dollars.

"Uhm, maybe I'm going about this the wrong way. Could you tell me who the room is registered to?"

Tim took the three hundred dollars from the counter and typed on his keyboard.

"The room was registered to Samuel Smith. He checked out this morning."

"Then there's nobody in the room?"

"That's correct, sir."

"Then I'd like to rent the room, for one day."

"Very good. The room will be ready for check in after two PM.; in just about two hours."

"I'd like to check in now, before it's cleaned."

"I can't do that, sir."

I put my last two hundred dollars on the counter.

Tim took the cash and said, "Very good, sir. How would you like to pay for the room?"

"I have a room. Add it to Charlie Fenton's bill."

I returned to room eight forty-three, with a key card in hand. I opened the door, and immediately hung the 'Do Not Disturb' sign on the handle. I closed the door behind me.

I went across the room and stood by the window. I closed my eyes and listened to what my senses were telling me. The burnt cinnamon odors were stronger in here than in Lisa's room. It was simple now to tell that the scents belonged to two different men. My sensitive nose told me nothing else that seemed relevant. There were no unique sounds; I opened my eyes.

I scanned the room. The bed was unmade and turned down on the side nearest the window. Whoever had slept here preferred the more open side of the room. There seemed to be nothing left in the room that could help me to help Lisa.

I started to leave, and thought better of it. I remembered a friend who took a criminology class a couple of years earlier. He told me about the Locard Principal; it's impossible to commit a crime without leaving some evidence behind or taking some evidence of the crime scene with you. There had to be something left behind; something useful.

I opened the dresser drawers, they were empty. I opened the drawers of the night stands; all I found was a phone book and a Gideon's Bible. I continued searching. I looked behind the furniture, and under the bed.

Finally I thought to look through the trash can. It was full of fast food wrappers, and I dumped the contents of the trash on the bed. A half-drunk cup of old coffee poured out on the bed, and stained part of the trash. I sorted it out. I immediately learned that somebody liked cheeseburgers.

I was about to give up when I noticed something in the bottom of the can that had not come out with the rest of the trash. It was the size of a business card and had a single word hand written on one side, "okhotnik". I removed the card and turned it over. On the opposite side was what I recognized as a TOR internet address, "kzr2p74hgarn453x.onion/rev228", because it included the ".onion" in the address.

This seemed like the only thing that might possibly be a clue. I put the card in my pocket and the trash back in the can. I went back to my room for some sleep. I was exhausted. I wanted to push on and not stop, but my head felt like it was full of cotton, and I wasn't going be able to go on much longer.

CHAPTER TWENTY-SIX

I awoke at five PM to the alarm I had set. I was better, but I could have used a lot more rest. I called for room service, again.

While I waited on room service to bring my meal, I set about deciphering the card I had found in the trash. I figured that the best place to start was with the web address. I fired up the computer and connected to the TOR network.

I typed in the web address, but the browser told me that the address didn't exist. I tried again, only leaving off everything after the slash. That worked; I was looking at a logon screen for some site named "Dark Realms", but I needed a user ID and a password. I was really starting to miss having Lisa around.

I took a few wild guesses in hopes that I might get lucky. I entered okhotnik as a user ID and took a stab at passwords, everything from "password123" to "Abomination". It didn't take long for discouragement to set in, so I chose to leave that for a moment and see if I had a reply from the Sisterhood.

I was excited to see there was a message posted on the message board with the title "Considered Proposal –

CFF", dated today. I copied the text into the decryption program, and the message appeared.

"We are sorry to hear about Lisa. We have started working on your problem. Eric does not seem to know an exact location where Lisa might have been taken. He does know that she was to be brought to a place called 'the Hub'. The Hub appears to be a place where human traffickers and people dealing in contraband take their merchandise to be shipped off to other locations.

We are making plans to relocate. Please continue to use the message boards."

The message gave me chills. I couldn't imagine the depth of what I had stepped into.

I was still thinking about the connection of the hunters with human trafficking when there was a knock at my door followed by the familiar words, "Room Service."

I don't remember enjoying my meal. I only remember that I was very hungry and eating changed that. I had turned on the television to catch the news while I ate. I was pleased to hear that the FBI was acting on credible evidence that Chad Fury was in Shreveport, Louisiana, and it was also now believed that the person in the recently posted video was not Chad Fury.

"At least something went right", I said aloud.

I leaned back in my chair and closed my eyes to try and consider a login ID and password for the TOR site, Dark Realms. It seemed fairly obvious that "okhotnik" might be a login ID. If that's so, what do I do for a password? I couldn't come up with anything. I picked up the card and turned it over and over in my fingers. I needed help, and I knew it.

Instead of me trying to figure this out, I wondered who I knew that was good at solving puzzles. Two names came to mind. Corey Cooper, a geek on campus that had a mind for this kind of thing, but he might turn me in. And also, dad's brother, Uncle Allan.

Dad had always looked up to Uncle Allan, his younger

brother. He had always considered Allan to be the smartest man he ever knew. Allan Fury never married; he went into seminary to become a priest. He eventually got his doctorate and became a professor at Oklahoma Catholic University.

I debated making the call for quite some time. If taking a run in the park nearly destroyed my alias, then this could be disastrous. I finally made up my mind; I needed help from somebody I could talk to face to face.

I picked up the burn phone and called information; then I dialed Uncle Allan's number. The phone was answered on the fourth ring.

"Hello?"

I tried to speak, but the words caught in my throat. After a long pause, the voice on the phone repeated itself.

"Hello?"

This time I forced the words come out.

"Uncle Allan…it's Chad."

"Oh my God. Is that really you, son?"

"Yes, Uncle. It is."

Uncle Allan's questions came quickly; "Where are you? Are you OK? What's happened to you?"

"I need to talk to you. I need some help."

"You know your mother's worried sick. Where are you? I'll come get you and we'll go to the police together."

"No. I can't do that…"

I paused. There was no response through the phone, so I continued.

"Listen, I'm in Oklahoma City. A lot has happened. I need to tell you in person, or you won't believe it."

"Chad. There's no good way out of this, but the right thing to do is to turn yourself in."

I could tell this was going nowhere, so I changed tactics.

"Uncle Allan, if you promise to first let me tell you everything face to face, then I'll let you call the police. You need to hear the whole story first."

"I'm listening."

"Do you promise? Will you let me tell you the whole story first? Before you call the police?"

There was a long silence. I almost expected to hear a dial tone before he spoke again.

"Alright. Do you want to come to my place?"

"No, can we do this in your office, at the university?"

"Why there?"

"I just think it's better. Can you meet me at eleven PM?"

"OK. In my office, at eleven. You remember where it is?"

"I do. I'll see you there."

I ended the call and swallowed hard to push my emotions down out of my throat.

I took the laptop case out of the closet, and put the laptop, thumb drives, and the little white card inside. I headed out of my room, and into Lisa's room to get her car keys. I thought it might be nice to drive somewhere for a change.

I arrived at the university at exactly nine forty-five PM. I parked the car in the shadows at the rear of the mathematics and computer science building. The building reminded me of an old, English castle and just being there made me feel as though I had traveled back in time.

I got out of the car and looked around. I walked around quietly, looking for surveillance cameras and people.

The grounds appeared empty. There were a few cars around other buildings but they looked lonely and abandoned. There seemed to be no activity.

I was beginning to let my guard down when I heard a car approaching. I moved quickly into the deepest part of the shadows against the building and waited. A campus security vehicle passed slowly. Once the car was out of site, and I heard no more signs of life. I threw my laptop bag over my shoulder and ascended the wall to the rooftop.

The roof afforded me a perfect view of the university grounds; I would be able to see my Uncle approaching. I would also be able to tell if he was alone. I waited patiently for eleven PM to arrive.

At ten forty-five, a car drove up and parked by the east side entrance. A lone figure stepped out and approached the building. As the door opened, enough light came out that I could see it was my uncle. I waited another twenty-five minutes, and no one else came. I descended the eastern wall and entered through the side door.

The hallway was dimly lit, and the normally white linoleum tiles took on a pale yellow tint. I walked quietly down the hall to the fifth office door. Bright light was pouring out under the bottom of the door.

I hesitated as I considered turning back, but decided that this was the best course. I had no other options. I knocked on the door with two soft taps and said quietly, "Uncle Allan?"

A soft baritone answered me back, "Come in Chad. Sit down, and tell me what this is all about."

I opened the door cautiously and slowly crossed the threshold.

"I will, but first, please tell me something. Did you call the police?"

I started taking note of the smells in the room before Uncle Allan had time to respond to my question.

Uncle Allan looked me straight in the eyes. His brown eyes softened, and his forehead relaxed beneath his salt and pepper hair.

"No, son. I've not called anyone. I'm not going to call anyone until you've had a chance to tell me everything you need to."

The smells in the room remained unchanged. There was no unpleasant odor of any kind. I removed my laptop bag from my shoulder and took the seat in front of the large walnut desk.

"Uncle, there's something I need to show you. You're not going to believe anything I have to say unless I show you this first. Please clear some space on your desk."

Uncle Allan appeared a little reluctant, but he did as I asked. He moved a few papers into a stack and placed them at the right-hand corner of his desk. "Is that OK?"

"Sure. That's fine."

I pulled my right sleeve up to my elbow, raised my hand above my head, curled my fingers, and brought my fingertips down swiftly and firmly onto the desktop. Immediately, my hand transformed. Uncle Allan and I were both looking at two large fingers covered with shiny red scales. The digits terminated in golden claws. The thumb at the side matched perfectly.

I kept the pressure against the desk so that Uncle Allan had time to take in what he was seeing. His chin dangled loosely. After a moment his mouth slowly closed. When he opened it again Latin sounding words poured out. His speech ended with him making the sign of the cross over his chest.

"Was that a prayer?" I asked.

"Uh, no. I was swearing…"

I chuckled, he didn't. He put a hand out and gently touched the back of the red fingers. I released the pressure, and in about thirty seconds, they began returning to normal. In less than a minute, my hand was mine again.

"What did I just see, son? What was that?"

"That was what I needed to show you. I'm not sure exactly what it was. I don't understand everything that has happened to me."

"Is this why you're wanted by the police?"

"No. The police don't know about this. But it is related. It's a long story. I'll be glad to tell it over a cup of coffee."

"Sure, I guess. Walk with me to the faculty lounge. There's a pot down there. But I've got to warn you, the coffee's not very good."

"That's OK. As long as it's strong and hot…that's all I need."

Uncle Allan led the way, but kept turning to look at my hands the whole time. When we got to the lounge, he stopped.

"I'm sorry, but I have to ask. Does it hurt, I mean the change? Does it hurt when it changes?"

"No. I don't feel a thing. But changing the subject, you might as well know everything. Let me tell you how this all started."

Uncle Allan did his best to focus on making a fresh pot of coffee while listening to my tale. There were lots of questions, which caused entire process of making coffee take a lot longer than it needed to.

We were each sipping our third cup of coffee comfortably in his office when I finally came to the part about the little white card. I reached into my laptop bag and produced the card. I handed the card to Uncle Allan, who took it carefully by the edges and placed it gently on his desk. He pulled a pair of reading glasses from his shirt pocket and examined both sides of the card.

"Well, Uncle. What do you think?"

"Hmm. I don't know. I honestly don't know. Do you mind if I keep this?"

"No. Go ahead."

Uncle Allan looked across the desk at me. "Russian."

"What?"

"Okhotnik. I think it's Russian."

I was genuinely surprised. One look and Uncle Allan had more information from the card than I would have had in a month of staring at it. "Russian for what?"

"Well, my Russian is a little rusty. I need to look it up to be sure."

Uncle Allan turned his chair around to face the bookshelf behind him. There at eye level was a Russian – English dictionary, which he took from the shelf and turned his chair back around. Uncle Allan held the card in his left hand while he turned the pages of the dictionary with his right.

"There you are!" Uncle Allan chuckled, "Hunter. It's Russian for hunter."

"So the user ID is hunter."

"Not so fast. Maybe it's hunter, maybe that's the password. Maybe it's a clue."

"How do we know?"

Uncle Allan flicked and tapped the desktop with the edge of the card.

"We look at the rest of the card. Tell me about the web address again. You said the entire web address doesn't work."

"Yeah. The only thing that works is the first part, the stuff before the slash."

Uncle Allan handed me the card.

"Look at the web address. What do you make of 'Rev228'?"

"I don't know. What should I make of it?"

"You're religious studies are lacking. It could be a reference. Hand me a Bible. There's one on the small table behind you."

I handed him the black leather bound book. He turned to the end of the book.

"Let's just see what we have here. Revelation two, verse twenty-eight: 'And I will give him the morning star'."

"I don't get it. Is the user ID 'hunter' and the password Revelation 2:28?"

"Maybe, maybe not."

"You're just full of information, aren't you, Uncle?"

"We won't know until we try. Fire up your computer, son. We've got wireless here."

I pulled out the laptop and fired up TOR. In less than two minutes I was trying our new information, and finding out that it didn't work.

"Well, that's a bust, Uncle. What next?"

"Next we read."

"Read what?"

"You're connected to the internet. Find out everything you can about hunters and about the morning star. I'm going to check some of my books."

We worked in silence, I came up with 'Sirius', 'Venus', and 'Canis Major' for morning star. I also found several names of mythical goddesses for hunters. None of it struck me as the correct answer to our puzzle. I gave up and looked up at Uncle Allan.

Uncle Allan was leaning back in his chair with his eyes closed.

"Excuse me, Uncle?"

"Yes Chad?"

"I guess this means you didn't find anything."

"On the contrary, son. I had it figured out fifteen minutes ago."

"Then why didn't you say something?"

"You were so busy with your computer I didn't want to interrupt."

"If I wasn't so tired, I'd be angry. So, what is it?"

"In the Bible, the morning star is a reference to two things. In Revelation, it is a symbol of eternal life. In the Old Testament, it's a name for Lucifer.

The address takes the user to a site named 'Dark Realms'. That tells me that the morning star reference is probably the darker reference; Lucifer.

The last piece of the puzzle is who is the hunter? Is there a hunter in the Bible who is equated with Lucifer?"

Uncle Allan sat silently.

"Uncle? Is there?"

"Well, of course, don't you know?"

"No. I don't."

I was starting to get irritated. I wanted answers, I didn't want a classroom lecture.

"Nimrod. Nimrod is a type of Lucifer in the Old Testament. So give it a try. User ID is Nimrod, password is Lucifer."

I gave it a try…A few seconds later I was in and looking at the full Dark Realms website. My only experience with the TOR network up to this point had been accessing the few message boards Lisa had shown me. I honestly expected this site to be the same. I was staring at the home page when I heard my Uncle trying to get my attention.

"Chad…Chad…What's wrong? You're white as a sheet!"

I couldn't speak. I just turned the laptop toward him and pushed it across the desk.

"Oh, my…Oh!"

Uncle Allan was motionless. I can't describe his look exactly, but it did look like he was about to be ill.

"That's what's wrong, Uncle. I never dreamed such things existed."

"Chad, do you think this is real?"

"I really hope it's not, but I'm afraid it might be."

"I have to call the police."

"I know, but please, not just yet. This is my only clue to finding Lisa and to clearing my name. Can we wait just a little bit? "

"Chad, this whole site's about buying and selling children, drugs, and military arms. I've got to tell somebody. This thing's got to be shut down."

"I agree, but you're not thinking. What are you going to tell the police? What are they going to think when you report this? If you don't tell them about me, they're going to think you've been involved in this stuff. If you do tell them about me, they won't believe the story I told you, and they'll be coming after me for crimes against children."

Uncle Allan frowned. He put his right elbow on the arm of the chair, and supported his forehead with his hand. He sat there, motionless for four or five minutes before he raised his head and spoke.

"It will have to be turned in anonymously."

"I agree."

"Chad, son, you've stepped into some scary stuff here. Are you safe staying at that hotel? You might want find a new place. You're welcome to come stay with me for a while; we could work on this thing together."

"I'd like that, very much."

CHAPTER TWENTY-SEVEN

I hadn't gone to bed until after sunrise, so it was only natural that I woke up shortly after noon in Uncle Allan's guest bed.

The room was small; only large enough to accommodate a double bed, a dresser and one night stand. Since I was no longer staying at the hotel, I made my own bed before heading to the bathroom to perform my daily ablutions.

In the bathroom there was a note taped to the mirror above the sink.

> "Chad,
>
> Help yourself to anything in the kitchen, and the rest of the house. There are clean towels in the hall closet. Make yourself at home. I will be home before four. I'm taking the rest of the week off.
>
> -- Allan"

After performing the necessary cleansings, I dressed and headed to the kitchen for something to eat.

Helping myself and making myself at home was a little more difficult than Uncle Allan would have wanted it to be. Uncle Allan was meticulous in some things and a totally disorganized in others. Although his home appeared uncluttered and clean, his refrigerator, kitchen drawers and cabinets were a mess. There was no organization of any kind.

I found a carton of eggs and a loaf of bread in the refrigerator. I couldn't locate any breakfast meat. I had to go on a search for a pan to cook the eggs. I finally found a skillet in the dishwasher, which was full of dirty dishes. I washed the skillet by hand, and started the dishwasher.

It took a while, but I finally succeeded in consuming a plate of eggs and toast. I made a mental note to do some grocery shopping for Uncle Allan, and see if I could organize his kitchen for him later. But for now, the matter of the Dark Realms website was my priority.

I set my computer up in Uncle Allan's office. I sipped on a cup of coffee while I looked at the site. The initial shock of what I was seeing had worn off, and I was able to start processing the content.

The site was set up so that a person could fund an account with an electronic currency known as Bit Coin, and then bid on anything posted on the site. The sellers had accounts complete with profiles and customer testimonials.

I was at a loss as to how any of this would help me find Lisa. I was on the verge of giving up when Uncle Allan came through the front door calling for me. I ran into the front room to find him struggling with three grocery bags. I grabbed two of them, he closed the front door and we proceeded to the kitchen.

"What's all this, Uncle?"

"I figured we could use some more food in the house. Now get the trash can from under the kitchen sink and put it by the refrigerator; I've got to throw some of the old stuff out to make room for the new."

I pulled out the trash can, and Uncle Allan started dumping left overs as fast as I could unload the grocery bags. While we put the groceries away, we talked about our problem.

"So, Chad, what have you figured out? I'm sure you've been looking over the website."

"It looks hopeless to me. I don't know anything more than we did earlier; It's a site for buying and selling children and contraband. I don't know how that gets us any closer to finding Lisa."

"What was it the Sisterhood told you in their message to you? Didn't they say that they were going to take Lisa to the 'Hub'?"

"Yes they did. I don't understand what that means."

"Chad. You told me that the Sisterhood said that this Hub is a kind of staging area for human traffickers. Maybe the hunters didn't know where it was either, and they needed the traffickers to get them into the Hub."

"Spell it out for me, please. I'm not connecting the dots here."

"Chad. Somebody, or maybe several people on that website know where this Hub is. Instead of focusing on finding Lisa, we need to focus on finding the Hub. And when we find the Hub, we might find Lisa."

"That's something at least. But how do we find out where this Hub is? I don't think anyone's going to just up and volunteer that information. Only traffickers know that, and I'm sure they want to keep it a secret."

"You've just solved your own problem, Chad, and you didn't even see it."

"What are you talking about?"

"If traffickers only share that information with other traffickers then…"

Uncle Allan made little circles with his hands like he was trying to pull information out me.

"Oh no. We're not going there. I can't… I won't do that."

"Won't do what?"

"I won't make people think I'm trafficking children so

I can get information."

"What are your choices, Chad?"

"Well, I could…"

I was at a loss for words. I didn't have a plan, and I didn't like where this was heading. I relented.

"You win. You're right. It may be the only way I can find out where Lisa has been taken. What do we do?"

"We have to learn everything we can about human trafficking. We have to learn the slang and the inner workings of the trade. To find out what we need to know, we've got to talk to the people in the business; we can't afford to look like outsiders."

"I can do that. What else?"

"You'd better contact the Sisterhood; post another message and bring them up to speed. Let them know everything you've found out. They may have some input"

"So far, I'm with you. But I've got a feeling I'm not going to like what comes next."

"You probably won't like it. I don't like it either. I need you to show me how to use TOR and how to set up that anonymous email you told me about. To begin with, I'm going to post some ads on your behalf on the Dark Realms site. You need these people to contact you. It might help if they think you're looking for a job, maybe as a driver or something. I need to give it some thought."

"Yeah, just keep thinking. I don't like where this going. But even if you post ads, that's hit and miss. It might be months before someone responds to the ad, if ever."

"I know. I also think you need to do some old fashioned street pounding. We're looking for a distribution network. If we were talking about a legitimate business, and we wanted to find a distributor for a product, we'd ask a retailer about their supplier. Same thing here."

"What you're really telling me is that I need to find some pimps and shake them down for information."

"That's part of it. You may not need to shake them down. You might be able to gain their trust and get more information that way."

"I was right. I don't like this; I feel like you're telling me I have to take a swim down a sewer pipe."

"In a way, you do. Some very dirty people are involved in this, and unfortunately, we've got to get pretty close to them. We also don't have a lot of time to debate and make elaborate plans. The clock's ticking for Lisa. Either we find her soon, or we don't find her at all."

"I know you're right. How do I start?"

"Let's go lay out your clothes for tonight and plan our evening. I've heard rumors of where the prostitutes hang out. Unfortunately, it shouldn't be too hard to find one; after that, we track down the pimp and ask some questions."

"You keep using the word 'we'. I'm going out; you need to stay here."

"We'll see, Chad. We'll see."

"Look. If things get rough, it's less dangerous for me. Besides, if someone sees you in the wrong part of town, it could ruin your career."

Uncle Allan sighed, "I suppose you're right. But I don't like it."

We argued the point for a few more minutes, but ten PM found me driving Lisa's white sedan into the seediest parts of the city, alone.

I was stunned by the number of girls I saw standing on street corners and waiting for a car to stop and a window to roll down. After a second look I started to notice the ages. Some of these girls were just girls, not even sixteen years old.

I parked the car a couple of blocks away and walked back to try and talk to the girls. I tried to get information out of them, but not a single one would talk to me. They were there for business, and even the offer of money for information was fruitless. They seemed, for the most part, loyal to their pimps and would not come forth with any information. I gave up in less than an hour's time.

Back in the car I sat and thought about my alternatives. I began to believe that the streets were the wrong venue; perhaps I seemed a little too threatening out here.

I started the car and drove on a little further down the street. I saw what some people call a gentlemen's club. I pulled into the parking lot of the Nirvana strip club. I had never been in a strip club before so I wasn't quite sure what to expect. I sat in the car for a full minute debating if I really wanted to do this.

When I opened the car door and my feet hit the ground I felt the vibrations coming from the music inside the building. I dreaded how loud it was going to be inside, but I made myself go in.

The place smelled of alcohol and cigarette smoke and the flashing lights on the stage were a little disorienting. There were about twenty or so men at tables around a stage which seemed to occupy too much space in the center of the room. The people at the tables were mostly men. I was surprised to see a few women, but then realized from the way they were almost dressed that they must work here and paying attention to the guests was part of their job.

I sat down at the bar with my back to the stage where a mostly undressed blonde was making rude gyrations around a brass pole and accepting tips.

The black haired bartender facing me stood about five feet seven inches tall and looked to be no less than forty years old. He came up to me and robotically asked "What'll ya have?"

I pulled out a fifty dollar bill and slid it toward him.

"Information."

He pushed the bill back toward me.

"We only sell alcohol."

I pushed the bill back to him again.

"Anything you recommend."

The bartender turned his back to me and took a thin clear bottle from a shelf. He placed a shot glass in front of me and poured it full without saying a word.

I pushed the bill closer to him. He took the fifty as I took a sip of the clear liquid. I nearly choked as what felt like lava filled my mouth slid down my throat. I coughed and sputtered.

"What the hell…is that!?"

"Jalapeno tequila."

"The least you could do is warn a fella!"

The bartender laughed and brought my change. I told him to keep it. He raised an eyebrow. I cleared my throat and tried again.

"I need information."

"I don't know much", the main said. "You're going to be pretty disappointed. What kind of information are you looking for?"

"I have a client. He's looking for some companionship."

"Have him stop in sometime. There's plenty of girls here; he might get lucky."

"His tastes run a little more on the exotic side, and he likes them a little younger."

The bartender frowned.

"You might want to consider moving along. This ain't no Sunday School, but we don't go in for that kind'a thing around here."

"I didn't say you did. But a man in your position hears things. I bet you know a guy somewhere that knows a guy."

I laid another fifty on the counter.

"Yeah, I think I do. You're looking for big Al."

I smelled onions, and snatched up the fifty.

"Don't bother. If you're not going to tell me the truth, then I'll just go somewhere else."

"Now hold up a minute. OK. I admit I was yankin' your chain. But how do I know you're not a cop?"

"You don't. But, I'm not. If you're not interested in my money then I'll just leave."

I stood up from the bar.

"OK. Tell me little more, I might be able to help."

I laid a hundred bucks down on the counter and sat down.

"I'm in the business of finding things for people. If somebody wants something, and they can't get it, I can. My client wants a girl. A young girl. Now I could find one on the street, but he wants one that's trained to do what she's told."

"Look, around. All the ladies here are adults. Some of them make deals on their own, but nobody here is in the game."

"Sure. I understand. But my client has a lot of money. I'm willing to pay for information that gets my client what he wants."

I put another hundred on the bar.

The bartender looked at the money and then at me.

"What did you say your name was?"

"I didn't, but you can call me Charlie."

The bartender picked up the money.

"Charlie, My name's Tom."

"Pleased to meet you, Tom."

"One of the girls here used to be in the game. She got out. That doesn't happen very often, and she doesn't talk about it much. I'd be happy to introduce you, but that's all I can promise."

"Sounds good."

I sat there waiting, and Tom just stood there until I figured out what he wanted. I laid down another hundred dollars.

"Follow me."

Tom came out from behind the bar and led me to a table in a dark corner away from the noise of the stage. He walked away and in a few minutes he came back with a blonde woman trailing him.

"This is Cherry. Cherry, this is Charlie."

Tom left and Cherry took a seat. I wasted no time

displaying another hundred dollars on the table.

A squeaky voice cut across the table,

"What's that sugah?" Cherry smacked the gum in her mouth. "I thought we was just talkin."

"We are. But I'm very appreciative of good conversation."

Cherry grabbed the money.

"Tom says you're lookin for somebody that can fix you up with the young ones. But you don't look the type."

"I'm not. I'm going to level with you. A friend of mine was taken. I don't know where they took her, but I know they took her to someplace called 'the Hub."

Cherry looked down at the floor for about twenty seconds without speaking.

"I'm sorry, but if she's at the Hub, then she's gone."

Her voice had lowered to normal tones and she had lost the air-headed bad grammar.

Cherry shifted in her chair and laid a palm flat on the table.

"Look, I don't know where the Hub is. Not many people do. But those kids that go through there are never seen again. I can't help you. No one can."

"Maybe that's true, but I need to find that out for myself. I can't just walk away."

I put another fifty on the table.

"I don't know what Tom told you, but I used to be in the game. Do you know how old I was when I started?"

I shook my head and replied, "No."

"I was fourteen. That was almost twenty years ago. I was lucky to get out alive, and I don't know those people anymore. Those men that made me turn tricks are gone, and this Hub wasn't around back then."

"The fact that you know anything about the Hub means you know more than I do, and I'd really appreciate knowing what you know."

Cherry thought for a minute and told me to wait. She got up from the table and came back with a dark skinned young lady.

"Charlie, this is Trixie"

Trixie was thin in all the right places and not so thin in the others. She was dressed in a pink bikini with some kind of see-through negligee on top.

Trixie spoke up proudly to announce to me, "That's Trixie with three X's. I'm Triple X Trixie!"

I looked as pleasantly as possible at Trixie.

"Pleased to meet you, Triple X, or should I just call you Triple?"

Trixie giggled as both ladies sat down and I laid another hundred out on the table.

Trixie turned to Cherry.

"You were right, this guy has more money than sense."

She turned to me. Her face was serious and cold.

"Look, you're asking questions that could get you seriously hurt."

Cherry took her money and excused herself; I looked into Trixie's brown eyes.

"I understand it's dangerous. It's even more dangerous for my friend. Is this really the way it works? These people take whoever they want and nobody does anything about it?"

"I know you can't understand it, but yes. The men who run the Hub don't have any rules except their own. And the people who run the Hub, and the ones who use the Hub only care about money. If you stand between any one of them and a single dollar bill, you and everybody you know will suffer."

"I hear what you're saying, but what I'm getting is that you're scared. You're too scared to even give me a name."

I put another hundred on the table.

"How much is it going to take to overcome your fear?"

"Save your money, Charlie. It's not worth my life."

"If you give me a name, or just tell me where to start looking, I don't have to remember your name or what you look like. Hell, I probably found it in fortune cookie."

Trixie over exaggerated a smirk. She took a deep breath and said, "You're looking for Vitaly. They call him 'The Wolf', but of course, nobody calls him that to his face. He hangs out at a joint called The Port."

"I've heard of it. It's a nice place."

"It's only nice on the outside. Inside it's dangerous. The kind of business that goes on in there is the kind nobody talks about."

"Is there anything else I need to know?"

"You didn't need to know any of this. But here's new word for you. 'Bratva', look it up. If you decide to do anything, plan your funeral first."

Trixie took the money off of the table and left.

CHAPTER TWENTY-EIGHT

Wednesday had been long and exhausting. I don't know what time I had gotten in, but Uncle Allan was waiting up for me and had demanded a debriefing before I went to bed.

When I woke up around noon I could smell eggs, bacon, and coffee. The smell was enough to motivate me to leave the comfortable bed and place my bare feet on the cold hard floor.

Uncle Allan was in the kitchen. He was dressed, but he wasn't smiling.

"Good morning, Chad."

"Morning."

I squeezed my eyes tight and opened them again.

"Grab a plate, Chad, and fill it up. Let's talk in the dining room while we eat."

I took a healthy portion of scrambled eggs and bacon, poured my coffee in an oversized mug and took my plate to the dining table. There were already two sets of silverware and two glasses of orange juice waiting for us.

I was already eating when Uncle Allan sat down and stopped me to say grace over his meal. When he finished praying he tore a piece of toast in half and laid both pieces back on his plate. He looked at me from across the table.

"Chad. You need to back off. The Sisterhood gave you the opportunity to go away and start a new life as somebody else. I really think you should take it."

I sat there stunned. I held my fork in midair with my mouth just hanging open.

"I can't believe you're saying that."

"I am saying it. I didn't want to get into it last night; we were tired and you had a lot to tell me. But, I know what the Bratva is, and you can't go up against that."

"We're talking about Lisa's life, and the lives of children here, and the possibility for me to get my life back. I don't care what this Bratva is, I have too much at stake to just walk away."

"Chad, son. The Bratva is the Russian Mafia. It's Russian organized crime. They fear nothing and no one. They give their lives to the organization, literally. They've been around in some form since the time of the Czars. No government has ever been able to bring them down, and I don't think a government ever will. You don't have a snowball's chance of getting information out of any of them."

"I'm going to try. I promise I'll keep you out of danger. I'll move out if it will make you feel safer."

"Stay. I'm not worried for me. I don't want to see you hurt. And I don't think you can win this one. It's better to accept defeat up front than to spend all your energy on a battle you can't win."

"Look. I don't even begin understand why you're saying all of this. This just isn't you. It's not the Allan Fury that I remember."

"I don't know what you remember, but this is me. It's me telling you to walk away. You could even go to another country."

I looked Uncle Allan in the eyes as coldly and with as much steel as I could muster.

"No. I'm not dropping this. I'm moving forward. I've

already lost my life. I refuse to live the rest of my life as someone else, always looking over my shoulder wondering if I'm going to get caught. And I'm especially not running off to another country!"

Uncle Allan leaned over his plate and matched my gaze.

"Ok then. You just promise me one thing."

"What's that?"

"Don't drop your resolve, not even for one second. People's lives are at stake here. Innocent lives of children will be hanging on the decisions you make. If you walk away. If you say the wrong thing to the wrong person, then people around you will die."

"I promise."

After that, Uncle Allan started eating, and I continued working on my plate. When I had finished, it was my turn to initiate a new conversation.

"Uncle. What did you do while I was gone last night?"

"I used your computer to search TOR, and the Dark Realms site. I posted an ad for you.'

"Really! What kind of an ad?"

"It said that you are an independent contractor for hire. You specialize in recruiting and transportation, and you're currently looking for work in Oklahoma."

"You obviously chose the words carefully, because I don't understand what you're saying that I'm offering."

"I was letting people know that you are willing to abduct children and take them across state lines."

"Oh, that's just lovely. What do I do if someone responds to your add?"

"You meet them, you talk, and maybe you find out about the Hub. Nothing says you have to actually take any job you're offered."

I conceded the point and changed the subject.

"Ok. You're right. Is that it? Did you find out anything else?"

"I looked over the message boards. The Sisterhood left you a new message."

"What did it say?"

"They gave you some new information; some new names. Eric you know and Samuel you know. The third hunter is Kane. He was giving orders to the first two; directing the hunt. It seems Eric didn't know much else. Everything Eric knew came through Samuel and Kane."

"That's not much help."

"Maybe not, but you never know. Oh, and there's one more thing, I almost forgot. According to Eric's memories, the Abomination refers to itself as 'The Company' when dealing with outside parties. So, if you're talking to someone, you might name drop 'The Company' just to see how close you are to the being on the right track."

I agreed and finished my coffee in silent thought, pondering what Lisa would be telling me to do right now. I imagined Lisa telling me that I needed to go to the night club I learned about, The Port, and find this Vitaly person. Then she would go shopping for new clothes so I would look the part.

That didn't sound like such a bad plan and I almost asked Uncle Allan if he wanted to go shopping with me, but then I looked at the way he was dressed. There was no way he could advise me on clothes for a night of clubbing.

"Uncle Allan, I have some shopping to do to get ready for tonight. Thanks for breakfast. Call my cell if you need me. I'll be back, when I get back."

"You be careful, Chad."

I assured him that I would be careful, and I carried my plate to the kitchen and then headed out to the car.

I spent the afternoon shopping for clothes in the trendiest stores. I never knew shopping could be so difficult. The biggest problem was that the clothes were for Charlie Fenton, and had to represent how I wanted Vitaly to perceive him.

I ended up at a shop called Dressed to the Tens, and the shop owner, Charlene, a lady in her forties, was most helpful. Under her tutelage I learned how to dress for a night at The Port. I was amazed at what her keen eye picked up.

"Charlie? Is that right? Let me get a good look at you. Tell me what you're after."

"What do you mean?"

"Are you after girls or guys? Not that it matters to me, but you need a major overhaul either way."

I didn't know whether or not to be insulted, and on how many levels.

"Girls, thank you."

"OK, then. What kind of girl?"

"Please forgive my ignorance, but there are 'kinds' of girls at a club? Girls are, well, girls."

"Charlie, my goodness. We are naïve. And your name, Charlie, we need to do something about that. Do you have a nickname?"

"Charlie is my nickname."

"Well, it's not very good for the clubs. It's fine for hanging out with the guys at the sports bar, but not for the clubs. I'll work on that while we get you fixed up.

Back to the kinds of girls. Do you know why men go to clubs? Don't answer that. You don't really know, you were about to say something stupid like 'to meet girls'. Men don't really know why they go. That's not true with women.

Women go to clubs for different reasons, and they dress according to why they're there. While they're at the club, they look around. They look at other women, trying to spot their competition. They look at the men to see who matches what they're after. They identify men based on how they're dressed, secondly by how they act.

The reasons girls go to clubs are:

One. They're with a boyfriend, and he brought them. That's usually a bad sign for a relationship; a stupid thing for a guy to do unless they're with a group or other couples.

Two. They just want to have some fun. They've

dressed in their play clothes, and they want the music, the drinks, and the dancing.

Three. Then you've got the ones that are there looking for something long term. They'll say they're there to just see what happens. What that means is that they are looking for a stable guy, and they're hoping he happens to wander in.

Four. Finally you have the rest, who are looking for what most men are looking for. They fall into two categories, good girls and bad girls.

So, Charlie. What are you looking for?"

I think I was actually blushing trying to decide how to answer. I wasn't going to find someone for a hookup, but there was no reason to say 'to meet the Russian Mafia, how should I dress?' I froze and finally said, "Let's go for the last group, the bad girls."

"Well, I shouldn't be too surprised. Everybody has to sew a few wild oats. Lucky for you both good girls and bad girls are drawn to bad boys. For different reasons, of course, but I think I can make you into a bad boy.

I see that you've dyed your hair. You need to touch it up. You'd look better with a darker tan. Get a bottle of tanning lotion and use that too. You need to not shave quite so close, a day or two's beard growth would help you out. When you do that, go ahead and shave your neck. Make it look groomed. The hair cut's good. Put some product in it and let it spike a little. Just comb it with your fingers.

Now for your clothes. You need a pair of black loafers. We'll check the size, but I'm guessing size eleven."

Charlene yelled over to a clerk and had her go find a specific pair of shoes for me. After dressing and undressing me repeatedly, Charlene finally decided on black loafers, a pair of dark washed blue jeans, a black button down shirt, a light grey blazer and a black fedora.

She brought me over to jewelry case and warned me not to wear a watch. Wrist watches were fine other places, but according to her I shouldn't have one in the club. Instead she thought I should have a chain bracelet or some type of fetish jewelry. She sold me a silver and black bracelet that looked like a handcuff.

As Charlene was ringing me up, she said, "Chad."

I was stunned and prepared myself to make a hasty exit.

"You're nickname should be Chad. It suits you better."

I thanked her for the advice and the help with the clothes. Before I left she gave me one more piece of advice.

"Charlie, if you want to get into the club, you'll need to tip the man at the door very generously. If you're not on his list, you'll be standing in line for hours. I suggest no less than twenty dollars."

I thanked her again. On the way to the car I decided that I needed to take her advice and touch up the hair color and tan. I didn't need anyone else thinking my name should be Chad.

CHAPTER TWENTY-NINE

A bull. That's the only way I can describe the bald headed man guarding the entrance at the 'The Port'. He was dressed in dark suit with no tie, and had one of those earpieces in his right ear that connects to a radio somewhere under a jacket. His jacket was too small for his muscular chest and made him look all the more imposing. This man-bull was all that stood between the smoked glass double doors at the front of the club and a line of about fifty people, mostly men, winding its way down the sidewalk.

I walked up to the man-bull and very indiscreetly handed him a fifty dollar bill. He put the bill in the outside pocket of his jacket and granted me immediate access.

Inside the club it was loud. Dance music drummed its way through my body and tried to force my heart to beat in rhythm. The club was large. The open dance floor was full of more people than I could count. In some spots it was difficult to tell who was dancing with who. Circles of colored light moved across the dance floor in time with the music.

Groups of men and women stood around the edge of the dance floor just drinking and watching. Others sat at tables having conversations of their own.

The bar was against the far wall opposite me and I headed around the perimeter of the floor toward the bar. Along the way I noticed a set of stairs leading to a balcony encircling the club and what looked like office windows scattered along the second floor walls.

I seated myself at the bar, and waited for someone to take my order. A young blonde haired man came to take my order; he spoke just a little louder than the music.

"What'll you have?"

"Two things. A shot of whiskey, the good stuff, and I'm here to see Vitaly."

The bartender left and returned with a shot glass and a bottle. He poured a shot in front of me, and I put a twenty on the counter.

"Is Vitaly expecting you?"

"No."

"I'm sorry, but Mr. Dimitrievich doesn't see anyone without an appointment."

"He'll see me."

I pushed another twenty his direction.

The bartender lost his Oklahoma accent and sounded distinctly more Russian.

"Tovarish. People that see Mr. Dimitrievich without an appointment don't fare too well. You need to go back home to your mother's basement and hide in the shadows. You'll live longer."

The young man pulled up his left shirt sleeve to reveal a black ink tattoo on the inside of his left forearm. The gesture was obviously intended to send me a message of some kind.

I reached into my shirt pocket and pulled out the card I got from Samuel's hotel room. I handed it to the bartender.

"Listen, *com-rude*. Show that to Vitaly, he'll see me."

"Perhaps I'll tear it up?"

He pinched the long edge of the card between the

thumb and forefinger of both hands like he was about to tear it in half.

I took a sip of my drink.

"I'd read that first."

He looked carefully at both sides,

"Zadnitsa. Next time you should start with this. Who should I say is here?"

"The name's Charlie Fenton."

The bartender left and went up the stairs with my card in hand. I waited and sipped my drink. I didn't have my watch to look at, so I don't know how much time passed but I'm guessing it was maybe fifteen minutes or more before my new friend returned to his place behind the counter. He nodded at me and used his head to gesture in the direction of the stairs.

I stood up from the bar and a large man in a black suit came my direction. The man escorted me up the stairs to a door at the far corner of the building. I reached for the door knob, but the man stopped me and turned the handle for me. I entered; my escort followed, closing the door behind us.

The room was large as offices go. There was a leather sofa, coffee table and a couple of leather chairs at the end to my right. There were a couple of lawyer's book cases on the wall opposite the door, and oil paintings hung on every wall. The carpet was a green Berber.

To my left was a large mahogany desk and matching chair. Seated behind the desk was a man with short grey hair and steel blue eyes. He was dressed in a blue button down shirt, with no tie or jacket. On either side were two men with body builder physics in dark slacks and blue shirts. They each had a pistol in a shoulder holster; they stood motionless and expressionless with their arms behind their backs.

The man behind the desk looked my direction and said with a heavy Russian accent, "Tom, wait outside the door."

My escort left the room.

The man behind the desk picked up his right hand and gestured toward the chair in front of the desk. I took the seat without saying a word. I was afraid that if I did try to speak, my voice would crack. After I sat down, the man behind the desk spoke to me.

"We have an agreement with the Company. There are to be no surprise visits. Tell me what is so important that you violate our agreement."

That was so much more than I expected. I had run through several scenarios, but in none of them did I expect to hear Vitaly talking about the Company. I couldn't decide if I should pretend that I was with the Company or not. If I said I was, and I was discovered lying, it could be disastrous.

"I'm not with the Company."

There, I had said it. I waited. Vitally leaned forward, and sailed the card my direction.

"Explain yourself. How did you get that card, and what is it you want from me?"

"I got the card from Samuel and Kane."

When I mentioned Kane, I watched disgust flash across Vitaly's face and he spoke only one Russian word, "Govno."

"I want a job." It was the only thing I could think to say.

"You have a pair, I grant you that. If Kane sent you, then he murdered you."

My heart pounded in my chest when I heard him say that. He continued.

"But if Kane wants it, and I have no direction from the Company, I'm not particularly inclined to give him what he wants.

I'm in no mood to hire anyone, especially someone who is not Russian. I tell you what. I'm going to give you a chance to live. Serge here," Vitaly gestured to his right, "Is going to try to kill you. Survive, and we may talk about a job. Otherwise, well…"

Vitally said a couple of sentences in Russian to the man on his right, and the man came around the side of the desk. I stood up from my chair and backed to the center of the room. Serge had three inches and several pounds on me, and was coming toward me like a bear. Vitaly give him one instruction.

"Don't use your gun. Keep it neat, the carpets have just been cleaned."

Vitaly laughed at his own joke.

Serge took me by surprise. He telegraphed a punch with his left, and instead landed his right in to my stomach. I doubled over. He brought either a fist or an elbow down on the back of my neck, and I landed face first on the floor.

I rolled over quickly, just in time to see a foot headed for my throat. My hands caught his foot, and I pushed it away with enough force that Serge lost his balance and toppled backwards. I was on my feet in less than a second and standing over Serge's head. I made a fist with my right hand, and pulled my hand near my left shoulder. I brought the back of my knuckles sweeping down across his temple. He was out.

I grabbed his pants by the belt buckle, and a handful of shirt at his collar. I lifted him like a sack of potatoes, carried him to Vitaly's desk and deposited him on the desktop.

Vitaly's lips were pursed together, and he did not speak for several seconds. He looked at me.

"Wait outside with Tom."

I exited and stood near the door on the opposite side of Tom who had been my escort into Vitaly's office. I closed my eyes and listened for what was happening in the room. It was difficult to hear over all of the dance music, but I found with enough concentration I could make out what was being said.

Vitaly was speaking.

"Robert. Bring Pavel in here."

A moment later the man who had been standing at Vitaly's left side exited the office.

I heard Vitaly speaking again. Since he was alone, I assumed he was on the phone.

"I need to tell you about an issue. It involves the Company…Yes, I know…Yes, I will do whatever the Company says…Yes, I know the Company can destroy us…It's about this. A man was just in my office. He claims to know Kane, and said that Kane told him to come to me and ask for a job…No. I don't intend to give him a job. I put one of my men on him, to rough him up so his tongue would be loose. He took care of my man with no more difficulty than beating a dog...No, it was Serge…No. I don't know if he is FBI or CIA. No…but I will find out.

The name he used is Charlie Fenton. I would like you to check and see if anyone knows that name. I want to know who it is I'm killing."

That was all I heard until Vitaly's man Robert returned with another man following closely behind. They entered the room and shut the door. When the door was closed Vitaly started speaking.

"Robert, Pavel. I'm going to bring that man back in here and ask him some questions. When I am finished, I will send him away. I want the two of you to follow him. Wherever he stops, kill him and everyone he's with. I don't care how messy it is. I don't care what it looks like. I'm sending a message and I want it clearly understood."

A moment later the door opened, and Robert gestured for me to come inside. Serge was no longer on the desk, but was lying on the leather sofa. Vitaly was seated at the desk, and he gestured for me to be seated in front of him.

I took my seat, and Vitaly started talking.

"Charlie, tell me what kind of a job you are looking for. What do you do?"

I didn't expect this; the only thing I could think of was the job ad that Uncle Alan had posted on the Dark Realms site.

"I've been doing independent work, as a recruiter and a transporter. Kane told me that I might fit in well at the Hub."

Vitaly's face flared momentarily with anger when I mentioned the Hub. His response was controlled.

"The Hub is not for outsiders. Kane was out of line by mentioning it. But I'm not convinced. Describe Kane for me. Tell me what he looks like."

I could do a lot of new things, but so far mind reading was not in my bag of tricks. I tried calling his bluff.

"Kane, not much to tell. I've shown you the card. That's enough. I'm not inclined to say much to someone who might have me followed and killed just to send a message."

Vitaly was cool. He never took his eyes off of me and his expression didn't change.

"I don't know that you're not FBI, or CIA, or something else. No ordinary person could have taken down Serge so quickly."

Serge groaned on the couch when Vitaly said his name.

"Neither of us trusts the other, and it's obvious that we're not going to share any information tonight. Go home. Come back in a day or two, and show your card to the bartender. We will talk then if I feel so inclined."

Vitaly gestured toward the door; I got up and walked out. All the way to the car I wondered where I should go and what I should do next. I could always abandon the car and run away, but that would not earn Vitaly's respect. I needed some way to get information out of Vitaly.

When I got to Lisa's car I took off my blazer and got inside. I had decided where I was going, but I didn't know exactly what I was going to do.

I drove to Imagine Ink and parked the car in the street. I had driven slow enough that there was no way my tail could have lost me. I turned off the engine and watched a black sedan pull to a stop a block behind me. I got out of the car and headed into my familiar abandoned building across the street.

Inside the building, I waited crouching in the shadows. My legs were bent, ready to spring and my right hand was a fist with my knuckles pressing against the concrete floor. My eyes were seeing just fine, and I knew I would have the advantage.

I didn't have long to wait before the plywood door opened. The first man inside was Robert. His pistol was drawn, and a tactical light was shining from the end. Pavel followed.

The men scanned the room with the lights at eye level. I was crouching just below the bright circles put out by the tactical lights. As soon as a light hit me, I sprang toward the source. An inhuman roar passed out of my lips. The guns fired, and hot bullets struck my skin. The searing heat only served to make me angry. My body made contact with Robert and sent him backward into Pavel.

Both men lost their guns, fell to the ground and scrambled to their feet. I was on them before they could get their balance. I landed a solid punch into Robert's chin and he went backward into Pavel one more time, sending them both to the concrete floor again. Robert was out. Pavel stood to his feet, pulled a knife and started toward me in the dark. He was moving slowly letting his knife blade lead the way. As soon as he was in reach, I grabbed his wrist with my right hand, and pressed my thumb into the back of his hand. His wrist bent, and the pain sent him to his knees.

Pavel's fingers let go of the knife handle, the blade clinked as it hit the concrete. I let go of his hand and delivered a blow to his temple that sent him off for some much needed rest.

With Robert and Pavel asleep I took a moment to decide how to send a message to Vitaly. I took off the men's belts and used them to tie their hands. I carried them one at a time back to their black sedan.

I drove the long black sedan back to the club. I pulled the car up on the sidewalk, and parked it at the front door. The man-bull at the front door just stood and stared blankly as I got out of the car. I started to walk away and he yelled, "Hey, you can't leave that here!"

I threw him the keys.

"It's not mine. It's Vitaly's!"

CHAPTER THIRTY

I woke up that Friday morning to the smell of pancakes and syrup. I threw on some clothes and headed off to the kitchen. Uncle Allan was filling a tray with warm pancakes to set on the dining table when I gave him a hearty "Good Morning."

"Good morning, Chad. Now that we both have had some rest, I can't wait to hear about your evening. You looked pretty excited when you came in, but I was too tired to listen; I apologize."

"No worries. The story didn't change much in the last few hours."

We seated ourselves at the table and I recounted the evening's events while sipping my coffee. I couldn't help but notice that as my story progressed, Uncle Allan's mood became increasingly darker. When I got to the part about putting Pavel on Vitaly's desk. I stopped to ask him what was wrong, and he simply said that he would weigh in when I was finished.

I finished my story, and Uncle Allan's face looked grim. He got up from the table silently, and left the room. I sat there wondering what was so disturbing about my story. Sure, I knew I was in a spot, but at least I now knew who was in charge of The Hub. I was a little closer to finding Lisa, maybe.

Uncle Alan returned and sat in front of his mostly uneaten breakfast. His face was serious. I started to speak, but he put up the palm of his hand.

"It's my turn. You need to listen to me, now."

"OK. I'm listening."

I pushed my breakfast plate away from me, sat up straight in the chair, and gave him my full attention.

"Chad, I just can't believe you. Instead of making things better, you seem to insist on making things worse at every turn. You've got to stop this pattern, and you've got to stop now."

"I don't understand? I…"

Uncle Allan cut me off.

"I agree, you don't understand. Just be quiet and listen. What I'm about to say, I'm saying because I love you.

Your father, my brother, Robert, did an excellent job raising you. He prepared you well to be a decent and respectable man, living a normal, average life.

Nothing that's been happening to you since you've stepped into this mess is normal. You're not prepared for it; nobody would be, so don't take this as though I'm saying you're a bad person. You're just a person, and you've not had time to come to terms with what's happened to you.

So let's talk about you. You are where you are right now, primarily because of you. You were arrested for bringing a gun onto a State University…"

"But, Uncle Allan, that's because…"

"Chad, don't interrupt."

"Yes, sir."

"You brought a gun onto campus because you were scared, and paranoid. I would probably have bought a gun too.

Next, you broke out of jail and eluded law enforcement. You broke out in such a way as to make fools of the Sherriff and the guards. You're fooling the FBI and OSBI with your little post card stunt, and they won't like it when they discover how easily they were led astray.

You went off for your little run in the park, and almost brought everything crashing down that Lisa was trying to do for you. While you were showing off for the local law in Shreveport, you left Lisa exposed, and now she's missing…who knows what's happening to her.

And now this. You go to a nightclub used as a front by a member of the Russian Mafia, and brazenly affront him. You should have been observing, listening and learning, not walking in like you own the place. On top of that, you beat up three of his men. You dropped the first one on his desk in an arrogant display of testosterone. You beat up the other two, and left them at the front door of Vitaly's club. You sent him a message alright, but not one that's going to influence him in any way that's helpful to you.

Chad, you've changed. When you got out of the Army, you were saying 'yes sir' and 'no sir', just the way you were taught. The service engrains that kind of behavior into a person. But you're different now. You're getting arrogant. You're thinking about Chad, and not about the people you're dealing with. If you don't stop right now, you're going to end up running for the rest of your life.

You're running right now. You're running from law enforcement. Eventually, they will catch you. It might take years, but eventually it will happen.

You've made enemies out of the Russian Mafia! They don't give up! You're going to be running from them for the rest of your life unless you can find a way to fix what you've done.

I don't even begin to understand what this other group, this 'Abomination' is. Whatever else they may be, they are ruthless, and you're responsible for one of their hunters being in the hands of their enemy. Eventually they'll come for you. I'm surprised they haven't already."

I was sinking low in my chair. Uncle Allan was right. I wasn't handling anything very well. I had felt totally justified in doing everything I had done. I had rationalized my way through every action, from the jail break to now, and I was only making things worse.

"I'm sorry. You are totally right. I've acted like a fool. What should I do now?"

"OK. First, clean up your breakfast plate and help me clean up the kitchen. Then, go to your computer. Send a message to the Sisterhood. Tell them what you've learned, but leave out the details about making a fool out of Vitaly. Just stick to what you've learned about him and his operation. The Sisterhood might have some insights.

Secondly, get on the internet and read up about the Bratva. Find out everything you can about how they operate. Look for Vitaly's name…see if there's any information about him, anywhere.

I need to think by myself for a while. I'll come get you when I'm ready for us to think through this together."

After the dishes were done, I spent the next four hours researching the Bratva and Vitaly. I learned about the Bratva's roots during the time of the Czars, about the efforts of the Communist government to dismantle it. I learned how the Bratva created a black market that helped provide food, goods, and services to a needy population suffering under government imposed austerity.

I was still lying back on the bed, reading, when Uncle Alan came into my room.

"We're going to need to eat, and I don't want to take the time to cook. I've ordered pizzas for lunch and dinner."

I looked at Uncle Alan with surprise, "Lunch and dinner? Just how long is this going to take?"

"It will take, as long as it takes. Let's move to the den. I've set up a white board for us."

I followed Uncle Allan into the den. The furniture had been rearranged, and a large white board was now occupying the wall space where three Van Gogh prints used to hang. Two comfortable chairs were facing the whiteboard, and the coffee table was between the chairs and the board.

Uncle Allan gestured toward a chair, and I got comfortable while he uncapped a marker and stood next to the board.

"Chad, it occurred to me that we might find our greatest help in game theory."

"I'm sorry, you've already lost me. Game theory?"

"Yes, game theory. Game theory analyzes the interactions between competing people and groups. It comes in especially useful when the actions of one or more groups depends upon the actions or possible actions of the others. That's exactly the situation we're facing. There are several players in this game, and each one has different objectives."

"I follow so far. How do we use this game theory?"

"Let's start by listing the players, then we'll look at their goals, what's motivating them. So help me list the actors; the players of this game. The first one is easy."

Uncle Alan wrote "Chad" at the top of the board, and drew a line underneath my name.

"Alright Chad. Tell me what your goals are in this game. What constitutes a 'win' for you?"

"I thought you knew that? I want my life back."

"You keep saying you want your life back, but for the sake of this exercise please be very specific. Tell me what 'I want my life back' means. For instance, do you want Chrissy back? Do you want your relationship with her back the way it was before all of this started?"

I thought for a minute, and then realized what Uncle Allan was doing. I hadn't considered it but what I wanted at that moment was different than what I wanted when all this started.

"No. I don't think I want that anymore."

"I don't blame you. You need someone on your side,

and when the chips were down she wasn't standing by your side. It's totally your decision, but I understand how you feel. So moving on, what does getting your life back look like for you now?"

"I want to not be on the run, not wanted by the police, not chased by the Bratva, and to not be hunted by the hunters."

"Good. Do you have to have all three to have a win?"

"It would be nice, but I know why you're asking. It may not be possible to have all of them right way. I'll take whatever I can get. But there is something else. I want Lisa. I need to get her back from the hunters."

Uncle Allan smiled. "It all takes time. Who else is playing?"

"There's the Sisterhood."

"What do they want?"

"Well, Uncle, that's complicated. I'm not sure I know all of their goals. They want to complete their genetic project and return home. They want to protect their books and their members. That's all tied to the genetic project, somehow."

"We can come back to that. Who else?"

"The hunters. They want the knowledge of the Sisterhood; they want their books so they can manipulate matter and open portals."

"Next."

"The Bratva, and Vitaly. They want me dead, and they don't seem to like the hunters. I think they would be happy to have them out of the picture."

"Next."

"That's it."

"No, you're forgetting at least two more."

Uncle Allan wrote Lisa's name on the board, and then 'Law Enforcement" in the remaining space.

We spent the remainder of the day going over goals and motivations of each of the groups. It was long and exhausting. Around ten-thirty that night I was ready to give up, when it finally struck us both that there was something I could do. I had something to offer Vitaly and it might just be enough.

We discussed it well past midnight, and finally agreed it was the only plausible option. I left the den and returned with my laptop. I sat the computer on the coffee table, inserted the flash drive with the Tails operating system, and started the machine.

In a few minutes we had composed a message to the Sisterhood telling them about our plan. Less than a minute later, the encrypted message was sitting on the message boards waiting for them.

Step one was underway. If they agreed and would send us what we were requesting, then I had a chance.

CHAPTER THIRTY-ONE

Uncle Allan and I both slept in on Saturday morning; there was nothing that could be done until the afternoon. I brought my computer with me to the breakfast table and checked the message boards before we ate. There was no reply.

Uncle Alan was very interested in the Sisterhood and the claim that they had the ability to alter matter from the sub atomic level. I did my best to answer his questions based on what Lisa had told me, but I failed miserably. His knowledge of physics and quantum mechanics was well beyond my grasp.

Before we cleared the table, I checked the message boards again. I grinned and turned the computer where Uncle Allan could see the screen.

"It's here. They've replied."

"Well, don't keep me in suspense; decrypt the thing."

I started the decryption software, and in a few more seconds was reading the message aloud.

"Agreed. Go to your mailbox. A package will be waiting for Charlie Fenton behind the counter. Instructions enclosed."

I was puzzled, and so was Uncle Allan.

"Uncle, I don't understand. They could have given us what we asked for in a download."

"I know. Perhaps they have something better to offer. We'll only know when we get the package."

We left the dishes on the table and headed off to the Penn Square Mall and the Mailbox Store. I drove; we took Lisa's car.

On the ride over, I decided to ask about something that I had always been a little curious about.

"If you don't mind, I was wondering why you never entered the priesthood after seminary."

"I don't mind at all. Truthfully, it's Noah."

"You'll have to explain that one a little more."

"I had the same problem that a lot of people have about God and religion. Just how can an all-powerful, loving God let bad things happen to good people? Specifically, the story of Noah and the flood. Why didn't God save more than just Noah?"

"And…"

"Well, Chad, I still don't have all the answers, but the questions don't bother me as much as they used to. Sometime after I started my PhD, I discovered that I was missing one of the more important points of the story. You see, It's not that God wouldn't save the world, He couldn't. But probably just as important, God didn't need to; He only needed to save one individual, Noah. It's a lesson for all of us. We can't save world, but sometimes saving just one is enough to give the world a second chance."

I had to admit I'd have to think about that for a while. Yet it somehow seemed very important in my situation. I was consumed with how to save Lisa and those children. As cold as it may sound, I was facing the possibility that I might to have to make a choice who I would rescue.

We arrived at the Mailbox Store, and inside I asked the clerk for a package being held for me. The little redheaded girl behind counter looked under her station and pulled out a box with my name on it. The box was about a foot square, and five inches high. I thanked her and headed back to the car where Uncle Alan was waiting.

I couldn't wait to see what was inside, so I handed the box to Uncle Allan before I got into the car, and asked him to open it while I drove us back. Uncle Allan took out his pocket knife and split the tape holding the box flaps down. I started the car and began driving us back.

"What's inside?"

"Polaroid pictures. Six of them, of a book, all taken from different angles. I must admit that's darned cleaver of those ladies."

"I don't understand."

"With all the computer technology available pictures can be faked pretty easily. But it's a lot harder to fake a Polaroid. This will be a lot more believable than what we asked for."

"OK, then. Anything else?"

"Some photocopies of what look like four pages from a book of some kind. I can't read the language. If you don't mind, I'll make a copy of these for my own study."

"Go ahead. That's a lot of box for some pictures and photocopies. What else?"

"A lock pick set, and an instruction book."

"Well that's unexpected. Anything else?"

"It looks like an external hard drive, five Terabyte to be precise."

"I wonder what we're supposed to do with that?"

"There's an envelope here too. It will probably tell us."

Uncle Allan opened the envelope and started reading.

"Enclosed are the pictures you requested. It should be very convincing. We thought it might help to have some copies of a couple of pages from our book. It should be enough to convince anyone that you know about our book.

We have also enclosed an external hard drive. There is every possibility that you will be around one or more computers that have data you will want. The drive contains forensic software. Plug the drive into the computer and boot the computer up to the hard drive, just like you do for the Tails operating system. The software will make a copy of the hard drive. Use everything at your discretion."

We continued to talk about the contents on the way home, and Uncle Allan was most interested in trying out the hard drive copier. He said it would be a good idea to test it; that we needed to know how long something like this might take to run. I left that up to him. I was more interested in learning to use the lock picks.

Back at the house I went to my room, sat the things down that the Sisterhood had sent me, and I made a phone call. I dialed The Port nightclub. The phone rang three times; it was answered on the fourth ring. A female voice on the other end of the line greeted me.

"Thank you for calling The Port, how can I help you?"

"I would like to speak with Mr. Dimitrievich, please."

"May I tell Mr. Dimitrievich who's calling?"

"Tell him it's Charlie Fenton. I'd like to make an appointment to see him."

"Please hold."

I was on hold for a very long time before I heard Vitaly's voice.

"Mister Fenton." The words were cold and sharp. "I did not expect to hear from you again."

"No sir, I'm sure you didn't, but I owe you an apology and an explanation. I would like to see you in person to attempt to make amends. I have a gift for you. I hope that it will make up for my inexcusable behavior."

There was silence on the phone. I started to doubt whether he would consent to see me. Even if he said yes, it still meant he might want to kill me on sight.

"I will see you. The club is closed on Sundays; you will come Sunday. Enter through the door in the alley at two PM. Someone will be there to let you in."

"Thank you Mr. Dimitrievich. I…" The call ended

before I could say anything else.

I had no sooner laid the phone down when Uncle Allan stuck his head through the doorway.

"Chad, I've been thinking about the things in the package; the lock picks and the hard drive."

"And…"

"And we know that Vitaly will probably want to kill you on sight. We need to find a way to make him want to talk to you, to get information out of you."

"What are you suggesting?"

"I think we need to change our plan. The plan needs to be for him to want you to stay alive long enough to let you talk to him. For that he needs to believe you know something he needs to know. You need to create a reason for him to interrogate you. That's the only way he's going to really listen to you."

"I don't like the word 'interrogate'. It sounds unpleasant, kind of like taser and root canal."

"Vitaly already wants you dead. Unless you can get him to listen, and I mean really listen, he might only be half-listening. If you want his full attention, he has to be motivated."

Uncle Allan went on to explain the why and the how of his plan. I listened and debated with him for almost two hours. The longer I debated with him, the less I liked his plan. The main reason I didn't like it was because it made sense. I had to make Vitaly want to hear what I had to say.

I decided to go along with Uncle Allan's plan, after all, I was in a tight spot and there wasn't going to be an easy way out of this.

I picked out clothes appropriate for the evening, and I practiced using the lock picks. Picking the door locks was difficult at first, and I was glad I had the instruction book. After a couple of hours I was able to feel the pins in the lock and open the locks all around the house.

As soon as I felt I was ready, I packed my backpack and included the hard drive the Sisterhood sent me, a couple of the Polaroid pictures and one of the photocopied pages from the book. I informed Uncle Allan that I was on my way.

I dove Lisa's car to Vitaly's club and parked a block away. I put on my ball cap with the infrared lights, put my back pack on my shoulder and walked to the alley behind the club. It was around eleven PM on Saturday night, and that meant the club was in full swing. The music poured through the cinderblock walls into the back alley. I noted the camera pointed at the rear door; I waited in the shadows for the door to open, out of view of the camera.

The alley was busier than one might imagine. Club patrons would occasionally wander past one end of the alley or the other. A police cruiser drove by once, but the shadows of the dumpster provided adequate cover. I had waited almost an hour before the door opened, and I heard my name.

"Chad, hurry up!"

I ran out of the shadows and slid through the door opening. The room I was in was dimly lit. There were a couple of old tables stacked on top of each other to my immediate right. Bags of trash were piled to my left. Uncle Allan stood in front of me.

"What took you so long, Uncle?"

Uncle Allan pointed to a bit of duct tape at top corner of the door. "There's a magnetic alarm on the door. I unscrewed the door contact and taped it together. You'll want to fix that when you get a chance." He handed me two small screws and a screw driver, which I dropped into a small pocket on the outside of my backpack.

"Listen Uncle, if I don't come home after this, then come back here the next time the club's open. I'll have hidden the drive in this room…behind something. It's time for you to go."

I said goodbye and put my ball cap on Uncle Allan's head. Uncle Allan hugged me and wished me luck before disappearing through the door and into the alley.

The small room I was in had a doorway with no door leading into a narrow hallway. I peered down the hallway. The music was coming from the far end of the hall, to my right. To my left was a metal door. I decided to try the door.

The door was locked; I pulled out my lock picks and started to work. I placed the tension bar in the keyhole and inserted the rake. I was a beginner and this wasn't happening fast. I was nervous and applied too much pressure to the tension bar; the lock pins sheared. At least the knob now turned.

Behind the door was a metal staircase leading down into darkness that was even too dark for my eyes. I pulled the tactical flashlight out of my backpack and let the door close behind me. I made my way quietly down the steps, listening carefully all the way.

At the bottom I shined the light across the room from my right to my left. On my right was a concrete wall, with two metal doors. The wall ahead of me was concrete, and had some kind of cabinet or case on it. To my left was a wall with filing cabinets. The center of the room had a large rectangular table with ten chairs, four on each long side, and one on each end. There was a simple light fixture with long fluorescent bulbs hanging over the table.

The place seemed quiet enough, and safe enough, but I decided to wait under the stairwell, in the blackness until I was certain I was alone in the building. I sat on the hard concrete with my knees pulled up against my chest, listening to the music filtering down from above. In the dark, my sense of smell seemed more acute. I detected burnt cinnamon. It was the same as one of the smells back at the hotel where I found the card in the trash. I decided that the smell must belong to Kane.

The music finally ended, and then I waited another two hours before moving. I searched the room with my flashlight, looking for a light switch, which I located at the foot of the stairs. The fluorescent lights blinked twice before coming fully on. I decided to see what was in the cabinet first.

The cabinet was mounted on the wall about two feet off of the floor and was only about a foot deep. What it lacked in depth it made up for in width and height. It was about ten feet wide and five feet tall. There were five doors across the cabinet. I put on a pair of thin surgical gloves and used my lock pick to open one of the doors.

I should not have been surprised by what I saw, but I was. The door opened to reveal an arsenal of weapons resting on wood pegs mounted into the back of the cabinet. I hadn't seen weapons like these since being in the military. These were not the ordinary guns that were found at sporting goods stores.

That was when I changed my mind on how this was going to play out. I knew these men were dangerous, but the number of guns and weapons made me realize that there was no respect for anyone outside of their organization. I decided not to hide the fact that I had been here. I was even toying with the idea of tripping alarms on purpose to let them find me inside.

After photographing the arsenal I turned my attention to exploring the file cabinets. The file cabinets were secured with a small lock mounted in the upper right corner of each unit. There were six units and each had five very wide drawers.

The lock on the first cabinet opened easily. I pulled the top drawer open. The first hanging file had a thin black book inside. I opened the book, it was journal of some sort, with various entries that were either coded or abbreviated. The page I was looking at had several entries.

"1 f – 13 loc 3
2 f – 11 loc 1
1 m - 7 loc 3"

I didn't have time to try and decipher the entries; instead I took some pictures with my phone and sent them to Uncle Allan. I took pictures of a total of ten pages from the book, and also pictures some of the papers I found in the other drawers. The rest of the contents I photographed with my camera. Everything I photographed, I laid out on the table and left there to be found later.

After photographing the contents of the file cabinets, I decided to check out the two other doors in this little dungeon. The rooms were empty. One had a couple of old mattresses on the floor, and nothing else. The other had a couple of chairs.

I ascended the stairs to look over the remainder of the club. I walked out of the hallway and into the main room. It was a creepy feeling to be all alone in such a large room. I hurried to Vitaly's office. The door was locked, but was no match for my lock pick. After about ninety seconds I was in the room.

On Vitaly's desk was a laptop computer. I pulled the hard drive from my back pack and connected it to the laptop. I booted up to the external drive, and the software on the drive took over. While the drive was copying, I went through his desk drawers. There wasn't much very noteworthy in comparison with the file cabinets in the basement, but I wanted the pictures.

With my evidence gathering complete, I headed back to the door I had come through. I stood on a mop bucket and put the screws back in the contact of the door, and removed the duct tape. After the repairs were complete, I put my backpack over my shoulder and opened the door. An alarm immediately sounded. I stepped outside, turned to face the camera and gave it wave.

CHAPTER THIRTY-TWO

I had given Uncle Allan my backpack as soon as I got back, and he had been sorting through the pictures I had taken and the contents of Vitaly's computer while I slept. Around ten AM he came into my room to wake me up and give me a cup of coffee. I greeted him, took a sip of coffee, and followed him into the den where he had been working.

"So, what did you find, Uncle?"

"I found out that you're poking hornet's nest with a stick."

"I kind of figured that, but tell me more."

"Chad, this Hub we've heard about is a lot more than human trafficking here in the United States. It's kind of like a global distribution node for all kinds of contraband. There're records here of receiving and passing along military arms, drugs, and stolen merchandise of all kinds, all around the world. There's even a reference here to taking grain alcohol, adding coloring, and shipping it overseas labeled as glass cleaner. The receiver removes the color, flavors it and sells it as liquor."

"That's an awful lot of work, and a lot of expense. What do they gain?"

"They avoid the alcohol taxes. It looks like that operation netted them over one hundred seventy-five million dollars last year."

"Holy crap!"

"They're using this Hub to ship everything imaginable, to every corner of the globe. Vitaly's going to be very motivated to protect this operation. You're not going to be able to get any information about the Hub directly out of him."

"Surely there's something in there about the location of this Hub."

"There is, but it doesn't help us. The Hub isn't just one place. It moves. There are legitimate businesses being used as fronts, multiple warehouses, and even residences being used. They use different locations for different items, and the locations seem to change randomly. It's like trying to hit the proverbial moving target. And, every reference to any location is coded."

"Uncle, what do we do? Do we turn all of this over to the FBI?"

"It wouldn't do any good, for several reasons. First, this evidence was obtained illegally. The FBI would have to start investigating from the beginning. Secondly, they may already be investigating, and acting on this could ruin what they're already doing. Thirdly, you're still a wanted man; this would only make you an easy target. And, to top it off, this isn't the movies; in real life they're not going to assemble a swat team and swarm the place on your or my word."

"So what's the plan now?"

"Remember Noah? Saving everyone's not possible. The only choice you have is to save just the one. Keep your focus on Lisa. If Vitaly won't give you access to her, then you'll have to go through Kane."

I knew he was right, but I didn't like it. The entire situation was about to get very unpleasant.

Uncle Allan handed me two large manila envelopes.

One had 'Kane' written on it, the other was blank.

"Chad, the blank envelope has some printouts of the pictures you took, and copies of some files from Vitaly's computer. The other has a couple of Polaroids and the photocopy. Good luck, son. You'd probably better get ready to leave."

I cleaned up and left for the club. I parked the car in front, and walked to the alley with my envelopes in hand. As soon as I turned the corner, I saw Serge and Robert with guns drawn.

"Easy fellas. I know you want me dead, but Mr. Dimitrievich will want to talk to me first."

I walked slowly toward them. Serge held the door open for me with one hand. Vitaly was waiting inside.

"Mr. Fenton. Please follow me."

Vitaly led me into the main room of the club, with Robert and Serge following close behind. We stopped at the edge of the dance floor and Vitaly nodded to Robert. Robert holstered his pistol and patted me down.

"He's clean Mr. Dimitrievich."

Vitaly looked at me.

"Take off your shirt. I want to make sure you're not wired."

I pulled my shirt off over my head, turned around once and put it back on.

Vitaly nodded to both men, and they took me by the arms and forcibly seated me in a nearby chair.

Vitaly stood with his hands behind his back.

"Mr. Fenton, you will answer my questions. Who are you working for?"

"I'm not working for anybody; I'm acting in my own interests and in the interest of some ladies that don't like Kane and his people.

"Tell me why I shouldn't kill you right now."

I held out the two envelopes in my right hand.

"Here. This is why. One has Kane's name on it. Open it last."

Vitaly opened the unmarked envelope and pulled out a few papers half-way. He dropped both envelopes on the table in front of me.

"Let me guess. You have copies in the hands of a friend, and if anything happens to you then..." His voice trailed off and he waited for me to finish for him.

"Yeah. That's the general idea."

"I do not like being backed into a corner. I strongly advise you against it. Let's get to the point. What do you want?"

"Kane and Samuel took a friend of mine and put her in the Hub. She's part of a group of women that Kane and his people are hunting. I want my friend back, and I want Kane."

"I can't give you either of those things. Your friend is the Company's property now. I can't deliver her or Kane to you."

"Just tell me where they are, and I'll do the rest."

"I can't do that."

"Mr. Dimitrievich, I have something the Company wants. It's one of the reasons they're hunting these women."

I handed the second envelope to Vitaly. Vitaly opened the envelope and examined the contents.

"What is this? What am I looking at?"

"The pictures are of a book. A very old book. It's part of a collection. The Company has four of them. They want the rest. I can lead them to one of them, possibly more. The photocopies are pages from inside the book."

"And this book is valuable?"

"It is to Kane, and the Company. They've been killing for it, and they'll keep on killing to get it."

"That's an interesting proposition, but I choose to decline."

"I haven't proposed anything, yet."

"Let me guess. You want me to help you trade the book for your friend."

"No. I want to trade myself. Well, that' not exactly right. I want you to turn me over to Kane."

Vitaly raised both eyebrows. He walked over to a nearby chair, pulled it across from me and took a seat.

"Durak. Mr. Fenton. You are casting serious doubt upon your sanity. You affront me, assault my men, and break into my place of business for the purpose of blackmailing me so I will not kill you. Then you tell me you want me to turn you over to Kane. Kane will torture you and kill you."

"Mr. Dimitrievich, I see the events very differently. I came to see you without an invitation only because I did not know how to get an invitation. You put me in a fight against one of your men in your own office, and I did not kill him. You had me followed by two men, and you gave them orders to kill me and everyone around me. I on the other hand, did not kill anyone, and didn't even try."

"Why did you not kill Robert and Pavel?"

"Because I wasn't trying to make an enemy. I have enough of those."

Vitaly looked contemplative. He pushed his lips out and then relaxed them before speaking.

"If I hand you over to Kane, what do I gain?"

"It might be seen as a favor, and you might call it in sometime down the road. Plus, if I succeed, I'll take Kane out of the picture, and you won't have to deal with him ever again. That might even be a feather in your cap."

"Robert, Serge, escort our friend to one of the guest rooms below. I want some time to think."

The two men directed me to the back of the club, and down the metal staircase I had discovered earlier. At the bottom of the stairs they deposited me in the room with the two chairs and locked the door behind me. I settled in one of the chairs and waited.

What seemed like a couple of hours passed before the door opened. Vitaly came into the room, alone. He pulled up a chair facing me and sat with his hands folded in his lap.

"Tell me. If I turn you over to Kane and the Company, and you can take down Kane, what assurance do I have that you won't destroy the Hub at the same time?"

I thought for a moment before answering,

"None. I can't guarantee that. I'm going to get my friend, Lisa.

I've been thinking a lot about the Noah story. God destroyed the whole world just to save Noah. There's nothing to say that I won't destroy the Hub and everyone with it just to save Lisa."

"That's not the answer I was expecting."

"At least it's an honest answer. You might even take it as a warning and put some distance between you and the people who run the place where she is. You might even be able to make it look like somebody else, or even the Company is responsible for the operation…I'm just saying.

Vitaly stood up went to the door and called for Robert. Robert opened the door.

"Robert, I want you to have some food brought in. We're going to make our guest comfortable until morning."

Robert made some kind of noise that meant he would do as asked, and Vitaly returned to his chair.

"I'll get in touch with Kane. But it's going to be very unpleasant for you, even before you meet Kane."

"How so?" I asked with more than just a little concern in my voice.

"Kane has to believe that you did not go willingly. In the morning Pavel will be in to make it look as though I have been questioning you. It won't be pleasant. I want it to look like you've been questioned thoroughly before I deliver you to Kane."

"I'm finding this unpleasant already."

Vitaly smiled.

"You won't die. Not at Pavel's hands. I promise you

that."

CHAPTER THIRTY-THREE

I had slept very uncomfortably on the cold concrete floor. I had tested the door a couple of times during the night. I also heard someone snoring just outside the door. I don't know what time it was when Vitaly came into the room, but he greeted me with a smile.

"Well, my young friend, I slept well. I at least hope you slept. Forgive the accommodations, but we must make it look like you have suffered at our hands. A bad night's sleep goes a long way in that direction."

"I understand. I don't appreciate it, but I do understand."

"Is there anything I can do for you before Pavel comes in?"

"Yes. I need the restroom, and a cup of coffee, please."

"Very well."

Serge was outside the door, and he escorted me to the men's room. When I had finished, he was holding a fresh cup of coffee in a Styrofoam cup for me.

The coffee was exceptional. Not because it was all that good, I just needed it that badly. I drank my coffee sitting at a table by the dance floor. Serge escorted me back after I finished.

Vitaly and Serge handcuffed my arms to the arms of the chair. Serge produced ankle cuffs and fastened my legs to the chair legs. A sick feeling went through my gut as I remembered the last time I was restrained like this to a chair.

Vitaly looked me in the eyes.

"You must love her very much to go through all of this."

"It's complicated."

"Love always is. I've come to respect you for what you're trying to do. I think it is foolish and you will die trying, but I respect you. Just know this, there are things in this life worth dying for."

The Vitaly left the room. I started breaking out in a cold sweat. My mind was racing through the memory of being chained in that warehouse with those women singing. I could almost feel my body contorting and twisting. My heart was pounding in my ears. I didn't calm down until the door opened and I saw Pavel enter.

Pavel approached me and took a position directly in front of me. He drew his right hand into a fist and landed a blow firmly on my jaw. My head snapped to the side and I let out a noise. Pavel abused my face with his fists several times and stopped suddenly.

Pavel went to the door, opened it and said something in Russian. A minute later Vitaly entered the room.

Vitaly looked at me then at Pavel.

"When are you going to start?"

Pavel answered in an accent that was even thicker than Vitaly's.

"I deehd. He dose naht seehm to bleehd."

"Show me."

Pavel took his position facing me and began assaulting my face again. This time he struck much harder than the first. I cried out with each blow to my lips, nose, and cheek bones. He finally backed away and let Vitaly approach for an inspection.

Vitaly took my chin in his right hand and turned my head from side to side.

"Pavel, there's not so much as a mark on him. If I had not seen it myself…"

Vitaly's voice trailed off and he looked at me.

"Mr. Fenton. Why don't you bleed?"

I took a deep breath and let it out slowly.

"I honestly don't know. I assure you I do feel the pain. I can't explain why I don't bleed."

Vitally scratched his head and turned to Pavel. The two of them exchanged some sentences in Russian and then Pavel left the room. Vitally made a fist and struck me a few times, I suppose just to satisfy himself.

"Mr. Fenton. This would be much simpler if you would cooperate and bleed for us."

"I promise you, I'm trying to doing my part."

Vitaly bent down and pulled up my left pant leg to expose my shin. Pavel returned holding a twelve inch metal rod in his hand. He flicked his wrist and the rod expanded more than twice its size. The baton had a metal ball on the end. I swallowed hard in anticipation of what was coming.

Pavel approached and looked at Vitaly. Vitaly backed away and nodded to Pavel. Pavel drew back and sent the end of the baton crashing into my shin. I cried out as white hot pain shot up my leg and into my hip. It felt as though my leg was broken.

Vitally approached and examined my leg.

"Mr. Fenton. You are making this very difficult for us."

"It's not too easy for me either."

Vitally turned to Pavel.

"Don't hold back. Get some blood."

"Yes, Mr. Dimitrievich."

Pavel approached with his arm raised. I gripped the arms of the chair bracing myself for the impact. Pavel swung, and the shaft of the baton landed along the left side of my head and across my ear. My head bent over and

I cried out louder than before. My hands pushed against the arms of the chair; there was a loud snap and I felt my arms move freely.

Both Pavel and Vitaly gasped.

Vitaly spoke loudly, "Stop!" He walked over to me.

"Mr. Fenton. I think we had better try something else while I still have some furniture left."

I lowered my arms and let go of the arms of the chair. The broken chair arms dropped to the floor still hanging from the handcuffs.

"I'm in favor of that."

There was another exchange in Russian and both men left the room. I rubbed my face with my hands. The broken pieces of the chair dangled from the handcuffs. My face was sore and tender to the touch, even if there were no visible marks.

Vitaly returned with a glass and handed it to me.

"Here, drink this."

I looked at him and questioned him with my eyes.

"It's whisky and a little something to make you sleep."

"I'd rather not. I'd like to be awake when you give me to Kane."

"If Pavel cannot put you to sleep, then we need to do something else. Please, I insist."

I put the glass to my lips and let some of the liquid fill my mouth. I pulled the glass away and swallowed. It burned like whisky, and there was something bitter in drink too. I coughed.

I looked at Vitaly, and he merely nodded. I finished the drink in two more swallows.

CHAPTER THIRTY-FOUR

When I awoke, I was lying on my side in total darkness. There was a roar in my ears. I felt my weight shift toward my feet; that combined with the vibrations and noise made me realize I was in the trunk of a car.

My head was foggy from the drugs in my system. I pulled my right hand up to rub my face, and my left hand was unwillingly pulled along with it. I was hand cuffed. I moved my right leg. At least my feet were free.

I was drugged, it was dark and hot. I had no idea how long I'd been in the trunk, and no idea when we'd get wherever it was we were going. I closed my eyes and stopped fighting the drugs. After a while I was aware that we had stopped and the motor was no longer running.

I laid there, in the dark and waited. After some time I considered trying to kick the trunk lid open, but decided to stay quiet. If I was going meet Kane, it would have to be on his terms, whatever those terms were. It was growing uncomfortably hot, I could only assume that the Oklahoma sun was bearing down on the trunk lid. I would need to exit the trunk eventually due to the heat, but I figured I could last like this a little while longer.

I was just about to start trying to free myself when I

heard something outside. It sounded like footsteps on gravel. I waited and listened. A voice said, "Go ahead and open it." A moment later I heard the sound of a key working the trunk lock.

When the trunk opened I found the light to be blinding. My hands instinctively moved to protect my eyes. I caught the smell of burnt cinnamon as a voice full of gravel greeted me.

"Hello, Charlie, or do you prefer Chad?"

"Chad will do."

"Fine. Ed, Tim, get him out."

One pair of hands grabbed my ankles, another pair of hands took my shoulders. In moments I was standing outside the trunk facing the three men. The man in the center was holding an assault rifle I recognized from my stay in Afghanistan; an old Korobov with the distinct wood stock and curved clip. He pointed the weapon in my general direction.

"Mr. Fury. My name is Kane. Ed and Tim here are going to wait outside with Belgian F2000 rifles. You remember those from your military days, don't you?

"Yes. They were banned in most countries for being too lethal."

"Correct. You and I are going into my office where we can have a civilized conversation. If you come out of the office without me, they will cut you in half and the pieces will never be found."

"I understand."

I looked at my surroundings. The car I had been in was parked at some kind of a construction site. The building behind me was a concrete and metal skeleton, at least twelve stories high, with metal sticking upward which would serve as supports for more floors.

The two men to either side of Kane were both over six-feet tall. One with brown hair, the other blonde. Both wore overalls and hard hats. Behind them was a mobile trailer that served as the contractor's office.

Kane stood about five feet eight inches. He was dressed in blue jeans, a blue denim shirt, and work shoes appropriate for the construction site. His brown hair was neatly parted on one side, and his green eyes looked hollow and evil. There's no other way to describe the look than just evil. He was carrying a few extra pounds, but that didn't make him look soft in any way. There was nothing in his demeanor that would lead anyone to believe compassion or kindness had ever lived inside of him. He made a sweeping gesture with his old Korobov indicating that I was to pass by him and head toward the office.

Our feet made crunching noises on the loose gravel as we walked to the office steps. I ascended, and had to use both hands to pull the door open due to the handcuffs still on my wrists. A wave of cool air washed over my body as I entered.

Kane came in behind me.

"Take a seat."

I sat down in a wooden chair opposite the main desk. Kane stopped at a small refrigerator and pulled two bottles of water out. He brought one to me.

"Thank you for the water. Now what about the cuffs?" I said as I twisted the small plastic cap from the clear plastic bottle.

"We'll see. Maybe later. But first, we need to talk."

"I suppose we do. What would you like to talk about?"

I drained the entire bottle of water while I listened to Kane speak.

"You went to a great deal of trouble to see me. I would like to know exactly why. I can only come up with a few possibilities; tell me if I've missed anything."

I nodded and Kane continued.

"According to Vitaly Dimitrievich, You have information related to the Sisterhood and their book, and you are wanting to trade it for Lisa. I doubt that's the entire truth. So I'm going to discount that for now.

It may be that you want to switch sides, so to speak, to

see if the Company is willing to help you get your life back in exchange for working for us. I have Lisa's memory of the speech you gave to the Matron. It was amusing. But somehow I don't think that's quite all of it either.

You could be viewing yourself as some kind of hero, and you're trying to bring down Vitaly and the Company in one felled swoop. But, your current state doesn't look like you're in a position to take anyone down.

You could be one hundred percent loyal to the Sisterhood, and all you want is to kill Samuel and me, and rescue Lisa and Alice if they can be found."

I had to admit it. Kane had pretty much nailed down the possible objectives here. And the truth was that I hadn't thought far enough ahead to come up with a plausible motive I should tell my captor. I never considered that I would have to tell anyone, point blank, why I was here.

"Mr…."

"Just call me Kane. You don't need any other names."

"Kane, sir." I hesitated. "The truth is, that I've got too many enemies, and not a whole lot of options. The Sisterhood would be happy to pay me off to disappear, but that leaves me hiding out for the rest of my life and living under assumed names.

I've turned over Eric to the Sisterhood, and that can't make the Company too happy. I'm actually surprised that you've not been hunting me.

I've insulted Vitaly, and it wouldn't take much for the Bratva to come after me.

What I want is to find a way to live a normal quiet life. To do that, I need my name cleared. And to clear my name, I need the help of either the Sisterhood or the Company."

"Tell me Chad, what about Lisa? How important is she to you?"

"How I feel about Lisa isn't important."

"I don't believe you. You just admitted by inference

that you have feelings for Lisa. I'm going to tell you up front that she belongs to the Company. Whatever deal you want to make cannot include her."

I wasn't happy with that, and I tried to think of what to say, but I was speechless. Kane pulled open a desk drawer and pulled out a long, thin black box. He opened the lid.

"I want to show you something Chad. This dagger is very special."

He got up from his chair and moved around the desk toward me.

"Hold out your arm."

Since I was cuffed, I extended both arms. Kane pressed the tip of the knife against my forearm, and drug it about four inches across. It stung and burned and bled.

I gasped, "That's not possible!"

Kane grabbed my arm over the fresh, bleeding wound.

"Tell me about being beaten."

The memory of Pavel beating me raced through my mind. I watched Kane grin from ear to ear. He pulled back and laughed. When he finished laughing, he licked his lips. And wiped his bloody hand on my shirt.

"Deliciously amusing. Absolutely delicious. I so would have liked to have been there to see that. I'm sure they're still discussing why they couldn't make you bleed. I find it very interesting too, just how much pain you feel, and yet you don't seem to be injured. I think the Company is going to be very interested in you."

"How? How did you cut me?"

"Oh come now. Surely you've put it all together by now? No?"

I looked at Kane blankly.

"Very well. Let me fill in the details. You already know that we hunt the Sisterhood. You know that we want the memories of the Sisterhood and we want all sixteen books. You also know that we have four in our possession.

What you don't know is that we know where ten of the remaining twelve are. We are watching them. When they are moved, we know it. When we are ready, they will be taken. We just haven't bothered. We need only two more books; one them is guarded by this Sisterhood."

"Why haven't you taken the books if you know where they are?"

"Because they won't do us any good without the last one. The books are not just a collection of pages from a larger volume. Each book is a random collection of pages from the original book. None of the books make sense by themselves. The last book is an index of sorts. It tells how to order the pages in the collection so that they make sense. Once we have that, we will take the others.

By keeping our secret the Sisterhood is unaware of just how close we are to our goal. We keep them in the dark, pretending to search for the other volumes. We hunt a few of them for the sake of getting the memories and some new breeding stock, and to keep up appearances.

The Sisterhood abducts unsuspecting young men like yourself and transforms them into creatures to hunt and kill us. Long ago, those creatures were called bisclavret, garwulf, the werewolf.

The Sisterhood is the source of your legends of half-man, half-animal monsters. Even your vampire myths are founded in them and us. And what defeats the werewolf?"

"Silver. Silver bullets."

"Actually it's not silver. It's titanium. A few hundred years ago titanium was unknown and people mistook the silver-gray of titanium for tarnished silver. We are responsible for humans even having titanium. You probably don't know this, but the process that was used for many years to extract and refine titanium is known as the Hunter Process. That's no coincidence.

So take caution Chad. We have titanium clad bullets in our guns, and carry titanium blades. You are not invulnerable."

I swallowed hard. I hadn't counted on any of this.

"What are your plans for me? To take all of my

memories?"

"We don't do anything without orders. One of the memories we're all given as small children is of the punishments carried out upon those who disobeyed the Company.

One of my favorite memories is of a man named Randall. Randall was skinned alive. It is a particularly delicious memory. It took Randall hours to die. His skin was peeled off starting with the soles of his feet and the palms of his hands, and then slowly off of the rest of his body. There was so much blood and pain; it was exquisite!"

"I can't imagine."

"No, and it's obvious you don't approve. Suffice it to say that none of us want to live through the punishments."

"So what about me?"

"Oh yes, I was distracted. I don't have orders to take your memories. I was only given orders to verify that your memories can be taken. I've done that. You will be detained until I hear what is to be done to you, or with you."

Kane opened the center drawer of his desk and pulled out a small pistol. He stood and used the pistol to motion me toward the trailer door. I passed by the desk and made my way slowly to the door. I touched the doorknob and looked over my shoulder at Kane. Kane nodded his head and I exited into the Oklahoma heat.

Ed and Tim were waiting at the foot of the stairs. I sniffed the air again as I passed by them, just for sanity's sake; no smell of burnt cinnamon, these were ordinary men.

Kane spoke up from behind me.

"Ed, take Mr. Fury to the guest house and lock him in. I want both of you to guard it. Shoot him if he comes out."

The man to my right took the lead; I followed him to a metal storage building behind the contractor's office. Ed slid the door open, I walked into the shadows, and the door slid closed behind me. I heard the sound of what I assumed to be a padlock closing against the latch.

It was hot and dark inside. It took a few moments for my eyes to adjust to the light filtering in through the vents at the top of the building.

I was tired of the handcuffs and decided to test myself against them. I pulled halfheartedly, and they held fast. I decided that if it was possible for me be break these bonds I needed to put all of myself in the task. I closed my eyes, and began pulling my arms apart with as much force as I could summon. Suddenly, there was a snap and my arms flew apart, free.

I looked at my hands. The handcuffs were around my wrists like bracelets, but the chain that held them together was broken. Now that my arms were free, I felt that I could start doing something about my situation. I had no desire to sit and wait for Kane to hear what my fate was to be. I needed to get Kane and force him tell me where Lisa was being held. But step one was getting out of here alive.

I took a quick inventory of my surroundings. There were two pallets with bags filled with concrete. Seven plastic bottles of muriatic acid, some cans of paint, some shovels, and a tool chest. The tool chest contained an assortment of screw drivers and wrenches.

My big problem was the titanium bullets that might come through the thin sheet metal walls if I made any sign that I was escaping. I started moving the bags of cement. I lined several up against a wall as a barricaded against any flying bullets. After I had created a wall sufficient for me to duck and cover behind, I turned my attention to the door.

Fortunately, the door had been designed to keep people out, not to keep people in. The door latch was fastened to the door with sheet metal screws that had nuts on the inside. A wrench could remove the nuts, and the latch would fall free from the door. I could expect to draw attention to myself as soon as the latch fell to the ground. I would need to open the door and duck behind the bags of cement as quickly as I could.

I set about removing the nuts and the screws holding the latch. It was a little tedious; I had to wedge a screwdriver behind the nut to keep the screws from turning as I tried to take off the nuts. I was about to remove the last screw when I realized it was still daylight outside, and I might be better off waiting until dark to make my move. I placed a few bags of cement on the floor to make a chair, and settled down until dark.

CHAPTER THIRTY-FIVE

I woke up to gunfire and yelling. "It's over there! To your right! One o'clock!"

I heard myself say, "What the hell?"

I quickly removed the last screw on the door latch and hesitated before pulling the door open just wide enough to look out.

It was dark outside, the only lights were from work lights on the construction site. I listened and counted four different locations as sources of gunfire. From those locations men were yelling out where each other should be shooting. The first man I located was near me, half way between the storage shed where I was and the contractor's trailer.

I crept out of the storage shed and headed toward the nearest source of gunfire. I saw a man positioned behind a pickup truck. The man's right arm was in a cast, and he was firing a pistol with his left hand. The man had his back to me; there was no mistaking that it was Samuel. I was standing downwind from him, and I caught the smell of burnt cinnamon.

I had no idea what Samuel was shooting at, but for the moment at least, the enemy of my enemy was my friend. I whispered, "Friend, whoever you are, I'm going to help you."

I moved slowly and quietly up to Samuel. When I got close, loose gravel crunched beneath my left foot. Samuel heard the noise and turned toward me. I had no choice, I curled the fingers of my right hand and brought my hand down across his left arm which was holding his gun. Two claws tore through the flesh of his forearm and he dropped the gun. My left hand swung across his throat and his screams turned to gurgles as claws severed his trachea.

I picked up Samuel's gun and tucked it between my waistband and spine. I kept low as I crept away and crouched near the corner of the trailer. There were now three voices. The most distant voice screamed and went silent. The two remaining positions fired off rapid shots in the direction of the scream.

To my right was a sand pile at the opposite end of the trailer and near the building under construction. Kane's voice was yelling from behind sand pile, "Ed! Get that thing! It's headed for you!

About fifty or sixty feet in front of me were several fifty-five gallon metal barrels. A man was using the barrels for cover, taking aim at something moving in the shadows. Further in the distance my eyes caught the outline of something big, moving in cat-like fashion, circling around toward the barrels. I left my position and quickly moved behind the trailer so I could come up behind Kane who was cowering behind the sand pile.

As I rounded the corner at the far end of the trailer, I heard a scream in the direction of the metal barrels. Ed was gone. That left only Kane.

When I looked behind the sand pile, Kane wasn't there. My eyes scanned the area to no avail. My ears picked up the sound of an electric motor coming from around the corner of the building; I ran to investigate.

As I turned the corner of the building I saw a construction elevator ascending against the outside wall of the building. Through the wire cage of the elevator I saw Kane's outline.

I kicked off my shoes and leapt upward; Claws on my hands and feet caught the wall and I started climbing. I was soon parallel to the elevator. Kane pulled his gun and fired two shots in my direction. The cement wall exploded in small shards near my head. He fired again, and I heard nothing but clicks from his gun.

Kane quickly gave up trying to fire an empty gun and seemed to be focused on getting wherever the elevator was taking him.

I heard a growl from below. I looked down and saw what appeared to be a giant cat standing upright like a man, looking up at me and the elevator. The thing below walked around, looking for a way up.

The elevator finally stopped on what had to have been either the ninth or tenth floor. Kane ran out as soon as the gate opened. I crawled to the nearest window opening and climbed through.

I looked around in the darkness. Light from the street and surrounding buildings was coming through the square holes that would eventually become windows. There was enough light for my eyes to see into the shadows around the floor. About thirty feet away I saw movement next to a support pillar.

"Give it up Kane!" I shouted at the outline next to a square cement column. "It's over!"

"That thing out there wants me dead, and it'll kill you to get to me!" Kane's voice reverberated off the concrete surroundings.

I pulled the pistol from my waistband and started walking toward Kane.

"Let me worry about that. I'm your only chance of living through this night. I suggest you come with me."

"I don't like my odds with you much better. Even if you can get me past that beast, what reason do you have to keep me alive?"

"I want Lisa. You tell me where she is, and I won't kill you."

I could sense Kane's fear turning into arrogance as I saw him draw a knife. "I think you want more than Lisa. Now let's see just what could that be?"

Kane moved quietly to another column deeper in the shadows. I tried to not be betray just how good my eyes were. I kept moving toward his previous location.

After a period of silence Kane rattled on. "You want me. You want me alive so that you can turn me over the police and clear your name. But that can't happen. I'll tell them whatever I want, and they'll let me go.

That can mean only one thing. You intend to give me to the Sisterhood. They'll betray you, Fury! You can't trust them!"

"And I can trust you?"

"Yes. You can trust the Company. We keep our word. That's the only way an organization functions."

"I'm not buying it. The Company will take my memories and toss me aside. They don't need me. But I do need you. You come with me, and I'll get you out of here alive."

Kane quietly moved closer to me in the shadows. I walked on pretending I was going to pass him, but turned suddenly to my right and pointed the pistol at him standing less than five feet away.

"Drop the knife, Kane. Didn't they teach you to never bring a knife to a gun fight?"

"I'm not going with you. I'll die first."

"I won't let that happen."

Kane gasped and pointed toward the window opening I had come through. A dark shape was coming through the opening. Kane lunged forward and slashed at me with his knife. I jumped back and all Kane struck was empty air.

"Kane! Stop and stay quiet, if you want to live!"

I walked cautiously toward the figure, holding the pistol tightly and pointing it in front of me. As the distance closed between us, I could make out the features more clearly. The face looked both feline and human. But the eyes were all human, there was no mistaking that. I knew those eyes, I had seen them before. As the creature passed into a shaft of light, the gray tones took on color, and I saw a red mane.

"Dwayne! No! Is that you, Dwayne?"

The creature made a low growl. My ears heard a growl, but my mind filled in words.

"Yes. Dwayne."

"Oh my God! Dwayne. I'm so sorry. I tried to keep this from happening to you. Just stop. I'll take you to the Sisterhood. We'll get this fixed."

Dwayne growled and snarled. "No stop. No fix. Only kill. Kill Abomination."

"No Dwayne, You can't kill him."

The growl came back. "Must."

"Dwayne…"

Kane's voice interrupted from behind.

"What do you think you're doing, Fury? Can you really understand that thing?"

"Shut up, Kane! I'm trying to have an intelligent conversation!"

"Just kill the thing. Shoot the thing in the head and get it over with!"

"No! I don't need to. Now Shut Up!"

I addressed what used to be Dwayne.

"It's me. Chad. I'm a friend."

The creature sniffed the air, "Chad. Not friend, not abomination. Kill abomination."

I realized then there was no getting through. I raised the gun toward his head, and a huge paw slapped the back of my right hand. The gun went flying across the room. I could hear Kane moving toward it.

I ran for the gun, and the creature leapt upon me. We traded blows, his claws and mine. We fell to the floor, the creature on top of me with his paws and claws trying to rip through my flesh. I slashed back at every open surface. I managed to roll free, and found myself on top, slashing at him.

Neither of us were getting anywhere. The creature managed to get his legs under me and threw me across the room like a rag doll. My back crashed into a concrete pillar.

I was momentarily stunned. As I stood to my feet I saw Kane moving toward the gun and the creature getting ready to pounce on Kane. I ran toward the creature and leapt, landing on his back, with my legs wrapped around his rib cage. I placed my right hand under his chin, and my left across the top of his head. Kane retreated and waited for another opportunity.

"Dwayne, Stop. Don't make me do this!"

"No stop. Kill."

I took a deep breath.

"Forgive me, my friend. I'm truly sorry."

I pulled my arms apart sharply. Dwayne's head snapped to the right and over toward the left with a loud crack. His body shuddered. He fell face first, never to breathe again.

I let out a growl, before reaching over to get the gun lying just inches from Dwayne's lion head. I picked up the gun and scanned the area for Kane.

"It's you and me now, Kane! Come quietly or not, I don't care. I coming to get you!"

Kane was deep in the shadows against the opposite wall. He was moving through the shadows, headed slowly toward the elevator. I aimed the gun a few feet ahead of him and fired.

"Kane! Don't move!"

"You won't kill me, Fury! You want me alive!"

"True, but there's nothing to say I won't take off a hand or foot."

Kane kept moving. I put the gun under my waistband next to my spine and ran toward him. As I approached he pulled his knife with his right hand.

I took his right hand in my hand, and forced his elbow to bend by pushing his hand toward his right shoulder. I put my thumb on the back of his hand, and forced his wrist to bend downward. I added pressure slowly until the pain caused his knees to bend. Soon Kane was on kneeling on the concrete floor. I added just a little more pressure and his knife fell with a familiar chink. I took Kane by the shirt collar and threw him to the center of the room before I grabbed the knife.

I walked to the elevator. Near the elevator was a spool of heavy duty electrical wire. I used the knife cut two pieces, each about five feet long. Then I started looking for Kane again.

Kane was cowering in the shadows behind a pillar not far from where he had landed. He wasn't running. Kane was nursing his right knee which must have hit the cement when I threw him.

When I got to Kane, I forced his hands behind his back and tied them with a piece of electrical wire, then I tied his feet together. Kane wasn't putting up much of a fight; he kept silent.

I drug Kane by the shirt collar into the elevator. As we rode down, I searched him for his car keys, which I discovered in his right pants pocket.

Back on the ground again, I put Kane over my shoulder in a fireman's carry and walked toward the parking lot. I pressed the door lock button on the key fob. In the distance the lights on a black sedan flashed and the horn sounded. I walked another thirty feet to the car, hit the trunk button on the key fob and the trunk lid opened. I dropped Kane into the trunk. Kane complained, but I let it pass and slammed the trunk lid closed.

Inside the car, I started the engine before adjusting the seat and mirrors. I sat there a few seconds and hesitated putting the car in gear; I didn't know where I was and I needed to get home.

I pulled out of the lot and turned right onto the street.

It felt like I was heading north, but I couldn't be sure. I drove a few blocks until I saw a convenience store. I pulled in and asked for directions.

As soon as I walked into the store, the clerk behind the counter eyed me with a suspicious look.

"Hey buddy, you OK? You look like you've been in a hell of a fight."

I hadn't looked myself over, but I imagined that I probably looked pretty rough. My shirt was shredded from Dwayne's claws. My pants were ripped. I couldn't imagine what he thought about the broken handcuffs still on my wrists.

"You don't know the half of it. I need directions."

I gave him Uncle Allan's address, and he looked at me funny.

"That doesn't sound familiar. That wouldn't happen to be in Oklahoma City, would it?"

"It is."

"Well, you ain't there yet. You're in Mustang."

I asked for directions to the interstate highway, and then headed out the door. As I walked out, I saw a pay phone and started wishing I could call Uncle Allan.

I went back to the car and looked around; there was seventy-eight cents in the center cup holder. I took it and made a call home.

Uncle Allan answered on the sixth ring.

"Hello."

"Uncle Allan, it's me, Chad."

"Chad, son, how are you? Where are you? What's happened?"

"I'm OK. I'm in Mustang and I'll tell you all about it when I get there, in about an hour. Just pull your car out of the garage. I can't leave the car I'm driving parked on the street. Oh, and get on the message boards; post something for the Sisterhood."

"OK. What should I say?"

"Samuel is dead. I have Kane. You need his memories;

the Abomination knows where all of the books are except for two; one of them is yours."

"I got it. But you are OK, right?"

"I'm good. I can't wait to get back home."

CHAPTER THIRTY-SIX

It was a little past three AM when I pulled into the garage. I shut off the engine, got out of the car, and decided to not open the trunk. I figured it wouldn't hurt to let Kane stay there for a while, after all, turnabout's fair play. I hit the button on the wall to lower the garage door and went inside the house.

Uncle Allan was sitting in the den with my laptop sitting on the coffee table in front of him.

"Chad. You look awful. But at least you seem to be OK. Tell me all about it. Can I get you anything?"

"Actually I am thirsty, and hungry."

"Let's go the kitchen; you can tell me about everything while I pull out some leftovers. You can change clothes and clean-up after you eat, if that's OK?"

I nodded and followed Uncle Allan into the kitchen where he started producing food from the refrigerator. He loaded a plate with cold fried chicken and mashed potatoes and gravy and put it in the microwave oven. I pulled out a glass and filled it with water from the tap.

A few minutes later my plate was warm and we were seated in the dining room.

In between mouthfuls of chicken and potatoes I related

everything that had happened. Uncle Allan looked concerned as I told him the story. When I got to the part about killing Samuel, he interrupted.

"Chad, are you alright? I mean, do you need to talk more about that?"

I knew what he meant. This was the first time I ever killed anyone. And it was disturbing, but until that moment I hadn't had time to process the fact that I deliberately took another life.

"I'll be OK. I'll probably want to talk more, later. I don't even know how I feel about it right now. Killing Samuel didn't bother me as much as killing Dwayne?"

"Dwayne? Who's Dwayne?"

"You remember, Dwayne, who I tied up and kept on the third floor of the abandoned building? The guy with the lion tattoo?"

"What about him?"

"I killed him…just a…couple of hours ago."

I started weeping, and it turned into sobs.

"I…killed…Dwayne. My, God! I killed…he didn't deserve…"

Uncle Allan came over to my chair, and put hand on my shoulder. It's OK, Chad."

His gentle touch on my shoulder lifted me up out of my chair. Uncle Allan put his arms around me. I sobbed on his shoulder.

After a few minutes, I regained my composure.

"I'm sorry, Uncle. I don't know what came over me."

I wiped my face with a paper napkin and blew my nose.

"It's alright. In fact, I'm glad. I was worried that you wouldn't break down."

"What do you mean?"

"It means you have a heart. You're not a coldblooded killer. If you weren't bothered by all of this I was going to be very worried. Now, I know that whatever happens, you'll be fine…inside."

Uncle Allan touched a finger to my forehead. "In here"

and then placed his palm over my heart, "and in here."

I finished my story and Uncle Allan assured me that I hadn't killed Dwayne. That to him, it sounded like there wasn't much of Dwayne left, and I may have done the merciful thing. After that, he started talking about the Sisterhood and the Abomination.

"Chad, it sounds to me like there's not much difference between the Sisterhood and the Abomination. The Sisterhood uses people toward their own ends, and the Abomination is using the Sisterhood. The only real difference is their goals."

"I agree that they're both users, but I've met three of the Abomination, and there's a big difference. There was no kindness in any of them. If they are any indication of the rest, then there's nothing good in any of them."

"Speaking of…where's Kane? Shouldn't you get him out of the trunk and see if he's OK?"

"No. He stays put. He's dangerous. All he'd have to do is speak to you and you'd do whatever he says. We can't risk it."

"At least go open the trunk and take him a bottle of water. Even if he's no good, that doesn't excuse you from doing the right thing."

Arguing seemed pointless. I took a bottle of water from the refrigerator and headed out to the garage. When I opened the trunk I was greeted with a string of profanity. I offered Kane the water, and he refused, so I threw the bottle inside, slammed the trunk lid and left. When I reported the transaction to Uncle Allan, he just shook his head and walked away.

I was about to tell Uncle Allan that I was going clean up and go to bed when the doorbell rang. We both went to the door. Uncle Allan opened it slowly. On the other side were two women and one man in hand cuffs. I recognized one woman and the man. The woman I did not recognize was short, thin, and dark skinned. I would have said she was African American, except she had the same sweet cinnamon scent as the Sisterhood."

Uncle Allan spoke.

"May I help you?"

"Mr. Fury, I'm Fran. This is Carlee and Eric. May we come in?"

Uncle Allan gestured and the trio came through the door.

Fran looked at me and then at Uncle Allan. "Mr. Fury, Mr. Fury."

She smiled as though saying 'Mr. Fury' twice was somehow amusing.

"We're here for Kane, and to leave you this." She pointed to Eric.

Carlee spoke up in a surprisingly British accent.

"Beg your pardon. But I do believe that we need to have a talk. Would it be alright if we sat down?"

Uncle Allan replied, "Certainly. Please follow me."

He led the party to the den where the five of us seated ourselves.

I started the conversation.

"Excuse me, but how did you know where to find us?"

Fran deferred to Carlee with her eyes.

"Your Uncle gave us the address in his last post."

I looked at Uncle Allan; he cleared his throat.

"I thought it would save some time. But more to the point what did you mean by saying you were leaving this man with us?"

"Yeah", I chimed in. "What are we supposed to do with him?"

Fran grinned, "You shouldn't have to ask me. Put him in stasis…beam him into space…Open the pod bay doors and shove him out! I honestly don't care what you do with him. But if I were in your shoes…"

"OK", I said. "I deserved that."

Carlee continued, "I have something here."

Carlee pulled a large yellow envelope from her oversized purse.

"This is a confession, signed and notarized. It is Eric's confession to killing Emily Smith. There are several copies in the envelope."

I looked at Eric. He was silent and his head hung so low I thought it might fall off his shoulders.

I took the envelope and had to ask, "But what good is all of this? He'll say a few words to the police, and he'll be free."

Carlee grinned, "He can't do that anymore. He's had throat surgery. He only has one set of vocal chords now."

Uncle Allan spoke.

"I'm afraid we can't take him. This is my home, not a prison. I can't keep him here."

Fran looked at him with steel eyes.

"We're not asking. We're leaving him. Do with him what you want. But, this fulfills part of our bargain with Chad to get his life back. This will clear him of Emily's murder."

"Yes", I interrupted, "it clears me of murder, but what about all of the rest?"

Carlee looked at me and her tone changed to something a little more harsh.

"We're not responsible for any of that. It wasn't our fault that you took a gun onto the campus. You broke out of jail. You've been on the run. All of that has nothing to do with us. You'll have to figure that out for yourself. Now where is Kane? We're ready to leave."

I pulled the car keys from my pocket and tossed them to Carlee.

"He's in his car, in the trunk, in the garage."

Carlee looked at me.

"Thank you, Chad. What I said was a little harsh, but just try to understand. We can't fix your life. That's your responsibility. You have all the tools you need to clear your name.

You can make any kind of bargain you wish with any agency. Eric's not enough by himself, but you have a lot more than him to bargain with.

Oh, and we'll post on the message boards when we know where Lisa is being held."

I looked at Fran and Carlee.

"Let me ask you one thing. Dwayne. Do you feel any responsibility for what you did to him? I had to kill him. He's left a family behind. What are you going to do about that?"

Fran's face turned hard, and her eyes blazed.

"Mr. Fury! That is insolent! How dare you! One life is insignificant compared to what's at stake here. You have no right to pass judgment on us!"

"And you're not even human! What gives you the right to count any human life as insignificant? I'd better stop with that."

"I think you had", Carlee responded. "It appears we've overstayed our welcome. But before we leave there's something you should understand, and hear this well.

None of us care whether you approve of us, of our goals, or our methods. We have aided you because your interests have run in concert with ours. That will change, and when our interests no longer serve each other, our assistance will end. If your interests should ever run counter to ours, we will be an enemy to you."

With that, the ladies left without saying goodbye, and Uncle Allan showed them to the garage. I remained in the room with Eric while I heard the car start and the garage door close.

When Uncle Allan returned he sat down next to Eric.

"Eric, nobody's even spoken to you tonight. Is there anything you need to say? Is there anything Chad or I can do for you?"

Eric raised his head for the first time and looked us in the face. His eyes were cold; it was as if the soul behind them was void of compassion. Contempt crossed his face.

"There's nothing that can be done for me. I'm a dead man. My sentence was passed when I was handed over to those witches."

I looked at him a little puzzled.

"Not that I want to dispute you, but I don't understand?"

Eric swallowed, and it looked as though it caused him some pain.

"The Company doesn't accept failure. They will find me and kill me very slowly and painfully. The memories of my torture will be spread across the Company to help maintain order and control.

If for some reason the Company does not kill me, then your justice system will. I much prefer your death row to what the Company will do to me."

"Uncle, what do we do? Our new friend here will be highly motivated to leave, and I don't think he should be left alone."

Uncle Allan looked at me, "I agree. Suicide's not even out of the question."

I pulled the pistol from my waistband and handed it to Uncle Allan.

"This is the gun I took from Samuel. You should keep it with you. We'll need to take turns watching Eric."

Uncle Allan took it and held it uneasily in his right hand.

"Chad, I think we need to move quickly on this. It's almost seven AM; I'm going to start making some phone calls. I have an attorney friend and we need his advice."

I nodded and Uncle Allan left the room. I stayed and watched Eric. As cold and evil as I believed him to be, I still felt sorry for him. His arms had been cut countless times. There was no telling what the experience had been like for him. I was still pondering what had been happening to him, when Uncle Allan came back.

"Chad, you'd better get cleaned up. Henry Pearson will be coming over shortly. He's a criminal attorney that my friend recommended. I'm going to write out his retainer check, and you're going to reimburse me from the

Sisterhood's account."

I agreed and left to change. I used the lock pick set to finally remove the broken handcuffs from my wrists. I threw the clothes I was wearing in the trash; they were too far gone to be used for anything. I had no sooner showered and dressed when I heard Uncle Allan calling for me.

I hurried into the den to find Uncle Allan, Eric, and a new face. The new face belonged to a man wearing blue jeans, a tan sport coat and light blue shirt. He stood about six feet four inches and carried at least an extra sixty pounds he didn't need. His receding blonde hair was cut short and his blue eyes were almost hidden behind his cheekbones.

Uncle Allan did the introductions.

"Chad, I'd like you to meet Henry Pearson. He's your attorney. Mr. Pearson, this is your new client, Chad Fury."

Henry Pearson held out his right hand, and I shook it.

"I'm very glad to meet you, Chad. I hear that you have some trouble. Why don't you start from the beginning?"

"Before I do, is everything I say here attorney-client privileged? And if so, would you please assure me of what that means?'

Henry Pearson smiled.

"Yes. Your uncle paid the retainer. Anything you say to me is confidential, and will not be disclosed."

"OK. Uncle Allan, where do I start so that he'll believe all of this?"

Mr. Pearson interrupted, "Chad, I've heard it all before. There's not much you could say that would surprise me."

Uncle Allan spoke before I could, "You'd better have a seat while Chad talks. Chad, why don't you start with him the way you did with me; he's going to need a lot of convincing."

"Ok. I apologize for what I'm about to do to your coffee table."

I walked over to the table, raised my right hand with

my fingers curled, and swiftly brought my hand down onto the table. As expected, I was displaying the red scaly digits and claws. Henry Pearson let out some very salty words. I was amused to hear a lawyer cuss and swear.

"Dwayne would be proud of your choice of words."

Henry Pearson took his attention off of my hand, and looked at my face.

"What?"

"Oh, never mind. Someone I knew was very adept at swearing."

"Let me see that again."

I demonstrated several times. I even took off my shoes and socks, stamped my feet, and let him see them transform too.

After Henry was satisfied that this was not some kind of hoax, I began my story. It took some time to tell; I left nothing out.

While I was relating the story Uncle Allan was playing host, bringing water and coffee, and even serving up some scrambled eggs and toast.

After the story had been fully related and Henry had asked his questions, he pulled out a cell phone and made a call.

"Hello, Jim. I have job for you. I'm sitting here with a captured murder....No, I'm not answering any questions. I need you to come here and get him, and hold him until we're ready for him...No. I'm not crazy...Yes we will turn him over to the police, but not yet...I don't know how long you need to hold him, it could be a couple of days, maybe more."

Henry gave the man on the phone our address and hung up.

"That was Jim Garrison. He's a private investigator and has a private security company. He's going to keep Eric until we're ready for him.

Next, Chad, you and I are going to have a talk about how and what to trade with the FBI to clear your name."

CHAPTER THIRTY-SEVEN

Tuesday had been pretty intense just telling my attorney everything that had happened and getting his advice on what I should do about my situation. I wasn't real comfortable with what I had been told, but Uncle Allan agreed that it sounded like my best option, so I went along with it.

That's basically how I found myself sitting in Vitaly Dimitrievich's office on a Wednesday afternoon, with Vitaly staring over his desk at me.

"Mr. Fenton, I did not think I would be seeing you again."

"Mr. Dimitrievich, sir, thank you for seeing me. Let me first start by saying that you won't be dealing with Kane ever again."

Vitaly nodded slightly.

"I take that to mean that you killed him."

"No. I just removed him from the equation. I gave him to the group of women that he's been hunting. I assure you that he will never see the light of day again, but I don't know what their plans for him are."

"So, why are you here? You could have told me this over the phone."

"Because I want to be honest with you and correct some mistakes I've made."

"And that would be?"

"My name is not Charlie Fenton, it's Chad Fury."

Vitaly tilted his head slightly to the right and momentarily squinted his eyes at me.

"That's the name of the man who escaped from jail and is on the run. I heard on the news last night that he's in New Orleans. They think he's trying to get on a boat to get out of the country. But now that I look at you closely, you do look like the pictures of this Chad Fury. Why are you telling me this?"

"I've lied to you, and I want to correct that. I've also stolen from you, and I want to return what I took."

I used my right hand to lift the black leather briefcase I had brought with me and I laid it on Vitaly's desk. I paused before releasing the latches.

"With your permission, sir."

Vitally nodded, and I opened the briefcase. I turned it toward him.

"Mr. Dimitrievich, inside is every photograph I took and the data I copied from your computer. It's yours, and I'm returning it to you."

Vitaly frowned.

"And unless I do as you request the information is going to the FBI, correct?"

"No sir. It's yours, and I assure you there are no copies. You have not injured me. I backed you into a corner and I made you turn me over to Kane. I apologize for my behavior, and I want to make amends."

"No, you want more than that. I've learned to be suspicious of gifts. If someone wants to give me something, I usually can't afford it. What is the price behind this?"

"You are right. I do want something. I want to clear my name. I have one of the three men who murdered the woman I'm accused of killing. I have his signed confession. I intend to turn him over to the police, but that's not enough to clear me of everything. I need more that I can bargain with.

The women who have Kane sent me this address. It's where Lisa is being held. I want her back."

I held out a slip of paper. Vitaly took the slip from my hand and squinted at it.

"I know this address. It's one of the Hub locations. It used to be one of mine."

"What do you mean it used to be one of yours?"

Vitaly shifted in his seat and looked a little uncomfortable.

"The Company takes what it wants. They…acquired…that place, and they use some of my resources…"

"Without compensation", I continued for him.

Vitally didn't acknowledge my statement, so I took it to mean that I was correct.

"Mr. Dimitrievich, I might be able to help you with that."

"What do you have in mind?"

"I looked up the address on the internet. It's a warehouse and offices,"

"True."

"How much has the Company taken it out of your control? Do you still have access, can you still use it or do they own it completely?"

"I can still use it, but it is difficult for two businesses to share the same resources; they know it. I haven't used the location for several months."

What if you were to use it one more time, or rather, you were to let me use it?"

Vitaly folded his hands and laid his arms on his desk.

"What do you propose?"

"If I could set up a meeting at that place…with someone that the FBI would like to have. I could trade that person and whatever is in that place for my freedom."

"Interesting. And what kind of a meeting would you arrange?"

"A man in your position has enemies. You know people that you'd rather not deal with."

"I'm looking one right now."

Vitaly didn't smile, so I wasn't sure how much of a joke that was. I thought it was best to treat it like it was meant to be funny.

"I understand, but seriously, you know somebody that your organization would be better off without. Let me use that person to trade for my freedom. We both win. I get my life back, and you get rid of a nuisance."

Vitaly leaned back in his chair and stroked his chin with his right hand. He maintained that posture for almost a full minute before leaning forward across his desk.

"Mr. Fury. Do you know the name, Sirhan Jadiddian?"

"I do not."

"I assure you, that the FBI does. Sirhan fancies himself to be an arms dealer. He has screwed over my clients twice. His goods are second rate. The last time I dealt with him, he shorted my client on his order. He also has connections with certain terrorist organizations and keeps boasting that he can provide my clients with fissionable material. I could put you in contact with him, but the deal you make would be entirely yours."

"I understand."

Vitally opened the center drawer of his desk and removed a thin, red, leather bound notebook. He flipped through the pages until he found what he was looking for. He used his desk phone to make a call.

"Sirhan, my friend…Yes, it is good to hear from you too…I trust you're doing well…Fine, everyone is fine…Why I am calling you…I have a client, his associate is in my office right now. He is looking for some assault rifles, grenades, land mines, and rocket launchers. I was hoping you could help him out."

Vitaly pulled out a pen and a piece of paper while he

listened to the voice on the other end of the phone ramble on. He rolled his eyes once for the amusement of everyone in the room. I was the only one who smiled.

When it was finally Vitaly's turn to speak, he wrote down notes as he talked. "Yes. He would like one hundred of the FN Herstal, F2000, can you do that? …Yes, the one with the grenade launcher…Good. He would like one hundred grenades…"

Vitaly stayed on the phone for several minutes listing arms, munitions and quantities before the subject of nuclear material came up.

"…Yes. I do believe he would be interested in fissionable material…Do you have sixteen Kilos?" There was a long pause. "Good, sixteen Kilos. And, he will need a sample to verify the purity before the purchase…Yes, he can bring fifty thousand in cash today…Fine he will meet you at your shop at seven tonight…It was a pleasure talking to you."

Vitaly hung up the phone and said one word. "Moshennik"

"Mr. Fury. You are to bring fifty thousand dollars, in cash, to Sirhan's second hand furniture store tonight at seven PM. You will negotiate prices. Once you have settled on a price, you will be given a five gram sample of enriched uranium. It will be in a lead-lined container. I suggest you do not open it or inspect it. You will also be given a list of the items you have agreed to purchase. This entire affair is now yours, and I have no part in it. I wish you luck."

Vitaly handed me the paper he had used to take his notes. At the bottom was the address for Sirhan's store, 'Sir Hans Used Furniture'.

"I want to thank you for what you are doing for me."

"Do not thank me. One day you will return the favor. I will find you one day, and you will repay me for what I'm doing for you now."

Vitaly's comment made me shudder inside; I tried not

to show it. I didn't want to imagine what it might mean, so I put it to the back of my mind and stood up. Vitaly stood and extended his hand across the desk. I took his hand, and we exchange a very firm handshake.

"Chad, I wish you well."

"Thank you."

I turned and went. I wasted no time in getting to the car and driving to the bank. It was a short trip, mostly because my mind was churning over what was coming. I think any sane man would have been scared and would have run from the whole situation, but I had been through so much already that I didn't know how to feel about meeting an arms dealer.

I soon found myself in the bank lobby, standing in front of a teller. I first asked for my balance, I was told that there was exactly three hundred-thousand dollars in the account. It appeared that the Sisterhood was keeping the account funded. I passed the girl behind the counter my check for fifty thousand dollars made out for cash along with my fake driver's license.

"Mr. Fenton, I'll have to get approval for this. Please wait here."

I waited several minutes and the bank manager finally arrived. We had a long conversation in the managers' office about how unusual it is to withdraw that much cash, and he asked me a number of questions about why I wanted it. I refused to answer his questions, and it appeared to make him nervous.

The bank manager finally put a form in front of me to sign. I was told that by signing the form I was acknowledging that I had been told that the IRS would be notified about my withdrawal. I signed the paper, and the manager ordered the cash to be brought to me.

I returned to the teller window and the teller put five stacks of one hundred dollar bills on the counter. Each stack was wrapped with a brown and mustard colored paper strap, and the strap had "$10,000" printed across the center. The strap also had some kind of ink-stamp on it with someone's initials and a date.

The teller asked me if I wanted her to count it, and I told her no, I was betting that it had been counted multiple times before. The teller placed the stacks in a large manila envelope. I thanked her, took the envelope, and left.

When I got in the car and looked at my watch; it was five twenty-five. Across the street was a drive-in restaurant. I pulled into the restaurant, ordered a hotdog, fries and a drink, and then picked up my cell phone to report the day's events to my attorney.

Henry Pearson answered the call on the third ring.

"Hello, Henry Pearson speaking."

"Mr. Pearson. This is Chad. I've seen Vitaly, and now I'm sitting in my car. There's fifty thousand dollars in cash sitting in the seat next to me."

"What are you doing with that much money?"

I related the conversation with Vitaly, how I withdrew the money, and that I was going to meet Sirhan Jadiddian at seven.

"Chad, I, uh…I'm not entirely sure what to tell you. Did I hear you say 'nuclear material' somewhere in there?"

"Yeah. Vitaly kept calling it 'fissionable' material. He said it will be enriched uranium."

"OK. Here's what you do. Get to an office supply store. You need to look the part you're playing. You need to look like you're representing the buyer of this stuff. Get a briefcase, some pens, a notepad, a day planner… I wish there was time to have business cards made up; something with just your name on it and a fake business…"

"Hold on. I may have some. The Sisterhood made some cards for Charlie Fenton. I put a few in the glove box."

As I sat the phone in the car seat, a young girl came to the window with my food. I gave her the money plus a tip in exchange for the paper bag and drink she was holding.

Following the brief economic exchange, I looked in the

glove box. There was a small stack of my cards wrapped with a rubber band.

I picked up the phone.

"I found them. They read, 'Fenton Investment Services, Charles L. Fenton, CFP'; they're blank on the back. Nothing else on them."

"That's good; put a few in your shirt pocket. You need to leave one with Sirhan. Let him watch you put your phone number on it before you hand it to him. Now about how you conduct yourself, here's what I think needs to happen…"

I spent several minutes listening to Henry tell me everything from what to say, to how to stand. After a while we said goodbye, and I ate my food.

I went to the office supply store and got the briefcase and other items. I took the cash out of the envelope and placed it in the briefcase.

It was six fifty-five PM when I parked the car in front of Sirhan's used furniture store. I took a couple of deep breaths and reassured myself, "You can do this. Compared to what you've been through, Chad, this's a piece of cake."

I took the briefcase in my right hand and exited the car. It was a short walk to the front door, and it seemed to go in slow motion. "Get ahold of yourself, Fury", I muttered.

The lights were mostly off in the store, and the front door was locked. I rapped on the door, and in less than a minute a short, pudgy man came to the front. He turned the bolt on the door and cracked it open just enough to talk.

"We're closed." The voice was coarse, and the words were quick.

"Mr. Jadiddian is expecting me. I'm Charlie Fenton."

The man opened the door and motioned me through. I waited as he closed the door and turned the bolt. He looked at me and said, "Follow me."

I followed the man's balding head through the showroom as he waddled past rows of beds, dressers, dining tables, and sofas to a doorway in the back wall.

Past the doorway, we took a right turn and were facing an office door. The man opened the door and waited for me to enter. I stepped inside.

There was a tall, very thin woman with short black hair and too much makeup standing to my left. She was chewing a piece of gum. Ahead of me was a thin man with short brown hair, brown eyes, and a pencil thin mustache. The man was sitting on the desk instead of sitting behind it. He looked like something from an old gangster movie, minus the pinstriped suit. He wore black slacks, a black shirt, and too many gold chains around his neck.

I spoke first. "Mr. Jadiddian? I'm Charlie Fenton."

I moved the briefcase to my left hand, and extended my right to shake his hand.

"Yes, Mr. Fenton. Very good to meet you."

The man did not move or make any gesture that he would shake my hand. I waited with my hand extended.

"Relax your arm, Mr. Fenton. I don't shake hands until after we have a deal. This is my wife, Katrina."

Sirhan nodded toward the woman who was using her right thumbnail to dig something from underneath the nail of her forefinger on her left hand. She never looked at me.

"Hi." Her voice was nasal with a deep southern twang. "Nice to meet you."

"You've already met Sherman, my assistant."

I nodded toward the fat little man.

"Mr. Fenton. Let me begin by saying that I normally don't meet anyone without performing a thorough background check. If Mr. Dimitrievich had not called me personally, you would not be here now."

"I appreciate your seeing me."

Sirhan stood up and walked behind his large wooden desk and took a seat. Katrina and Sherman left the room, closing the door behind them. I sat down in a chair across from Sirhan.

"Mr. Fenton. I like to know who I'm dealing with. Who

do you represent?"

"I've not been told that I can disclose that."

Sirhan studied my face.

"Tell me, what will the goods be used for?"

"That's none of my concern, Mr. Jadiddian. I just make purchases and arrange deliveries."

Sirhan leaned back in his chair.

"I'm not comfortable dealing with people I don't know."

"Very well. If this is a waste of my time, I'll leave now."

I tightened my grip on the brief case and started to stand.

"Now, now. Hold on. I'm not saying I won't sell to you."

"Which is it? You want to sell me the weapons, or you don't?"

"Mr. Fenton. Just how well do you now Vitaly Dimitrievich?"

"We've done some business together."

"You're not very talkative. How do you propose gaining my trust?"

I picked up the briefcase and pulled out the stacks of hundreds and placed them on the desk slowly; one stack at a time.

I gave Sirhan my coldest gaze, "Trust that."

I had said it with as flat of a voice as possible. I closed the briefcase and placed it back on the floor next to my chair.

Sirhan grinned. He made his right hand into the shape of a gun, pointed his index finger at me, flicked his wrist and made a clicking sound with his tongue.

"You, I like. No extra words. All business. I trust that."

I kept my expression flat and didn't change my demeanor.

"Mr. Jadiddian. About the merchandise…"

"Yes. The goods. I have a list here."

Sirhan read the list. It was similar to what Vitaly wrote

down during the phone call, but it was different. I opened my briefcase and retrieved the list Vitaly had written down.

"Mr. Jadiddian. That's not exactly what was agreed to over the phone. There are several things missing. First, the FN Herstals…I asked for one hundred."

"That would clean me out. I can sell you fifty."

"I need one hundred."

"I'll sell you fifty."

"Let me understand; you have more, but won't sell them to me."

"Seventy-five is all I have in stock."

"I'll take seventy-five now and twenty-five when you have them."

"You'll pay for one hundred?"

"No. I'll pay for seventy-five."

"You'll pay for one hundred."

"I'll pay for seventy-five, and I'll give you a deposit for the other twenty-five, say ten percent."

"No…twenty-five percent."

I pretended to think it over.

"No. Twenty percent."

"Very well. Twenty percent, due now."

"No. I brought fifty thousand. You're looking at all of the cash I have with me. I'll bring the deposit when you deliver the seventy-five."

Sirhan agreed. This went on item by item through the entire list. The quantities and prices kept changing.

I could see why Vitaly didn't like the man. Sirhan made the entire process much longer than it needed to be. The more he talked, the more I felt like I was talking to a sleazy con man who wanted to wheel and deal with me over a piece of swamp land.

We finally came to the end of the list, and the sample of 'fissionable material'. Sirhan reached into the right hand drawer of his desk and took out a metal cylinder.

The shiny metal cylinder was about two inches in diameter and five inches long. There was a metal cap on the end that appeared to screw on.

"Here, Mr. Fenton, is the sample. Inside the tube is five grams of highly enriched uranium. It is a sufficient quantity for you to have tested."

I must have looked uneasy, because he made the effort to reassure me.

"There's no need for concern. The container is lined with zinc and lead."

I gave Sirhan an understanding nod.

"If this tests out to be weapons grade, we want sixteen Kilos."

"I am prepared to sell sixteen Kilos, but as to the price..."

"How much?"

"I was thinking five million."

"Keep thinking. I don't know how you got the uranium, and I don't really care. But I do know you didn't mine it or process it yourself. Let's be reasonable. It's only worth what you can get for it. I'm going to assume you've had it in your possession for quite some time. The longer you have something for sale, the less it's worth; that's pure economics."

Sirhan grinned and did the finger gesture again.

"I knew I liked you. You're sharp. I could use a man like you acquiring stock for me. How does two point five million sound?"

"It sounds like one point five million too much."

"Mr. Fenton, that's an insult."

"No, that's business."

"I can't go that low."

"Can't, or won't?"

"It doesn't matter. I'm assuming your employer has some deep pockets."

I waited. All of the sudden I realized I had gotten into the role I was playing and I was enjoying dickering over the price.

"Let's stop playing games, Mr. Jadiddian. I'm not going

to go above one point seven five. What are you going to do?"

Sirhan sat silent and looked contemplative.

"On one condition. I don't want cash for the sale, at least not all of it in cash. I want part of it in gold. Gold rounds, gold coins, gold bars…I don't care. Just gold."

"How much gold?"

"Gold for the uranium, one point seven five million. Can you do that?"

"I can make a call later, but I believe it can be done."

"You can make the call now. I'll give you some privacy."

Sirhan got up from his desk and left the room. I didn't know if anyone would be listening, so I put on a show. I pulled out my cell phone and dialed Henry Pearson.

Henry answered on the second ring.

"Hello, Henry Pearson speaking."

"Hey boss, it's Fenton."

"Chad? What's up? Are you OK?"

"Yeah, everything's fine. I know I wasn't supposed to call tonight, but there's one item I need your input on."

"OK, I'll play along. I assume you think someone's listening."

"That's right, I do. Anyway, we're about to close the deal. He wants to trade the uranium for gold, one point seven five million in gold. I know the price is OK, but can you get that much gold together, and how quickly?"

"I understand. You need to set a date for all this to go down, and you don't know what sounds reasonable. Well, neither do I.

Let's assume it takes a while to get all this together. Our friends are going to need some time too, for the other deal we're working on. Let's make this deal go down next Tuesday. That should give everyone enough time."

"OK. Thank you. I'll let him know we have a deal."

I was right, Sirhan had been listening. I had no sooner put my phone away before Sirhan came back into the room, grinning.

"I assume we have a deal?"

"We do. I have some conditions."

Sirhan looked concerned as he walked around his desk.

"What would those conditions be?"

"When and where. We will have your payment ready on Tuesday afternoon. As to where, I'm completing some business with Vitaly at his warehouse on Tuesday. If you could bring the merchandise there, we could transfer it from your trucks to ours pretty easily."

"I prefer to pick the location. That way I can control security. But, you said this is Vitaly's place?"

"Yes. I pulled a business card from my shirt pocket, wrote the address on the back and my phone number, and handed it to Sirhan."

Sirhan laughed when he saw the address.

"This is a Hub location, why didn't you say you were using the underground highway for transport? That's fine. I'll bring merchandise to the Hub."

"Good. I want something in writing, a list to give to my boss…"

"No problem."

Sirhan slid the laptop computer from the corner of his desk so it was directly facing him. He began typing.

"Come around so you can see."

I got up and went around the desk.

I watched Sirhan type the list of merchandise, quantities, and prices into a document. At the bottom of the document he put the location of the sale.

"Mr. Fenton, what time Tuesday do you want to conclude our business?"

"Let's say two PM."

Sirhan typed in the time and saved the document.

"Now, as to how you get your copy of this. I have a web site, you can download the invoice from there. Are you familiar with the TOR network?"

"I am."

"I'm going to create a user ID for you. What do you want?"

"How about Dragon Boy."

I remembered Lisa calling me Dragon Boy and it was the only thing that had come to mind.

Sirhan gave me a condescending look. "That's kind of nerdy. How about Dragon Master?"

"Whatever you think."

Sirhan typed and then spoke, "Dragon Master is taken." He continued typing he tried several things, and finally spoke again. "You win. Your user ID is Dragon Boy."

Sirhan took out a business card. On one side was a series of letters and numbers ending with '.onion'. He turned the card over and wrote my user ID and a password before handing me the card.

"Don't lose that card. The name of the website is 'Dark Realms'."

My heart skipped a beat. I tried not to show my excitement as he continued talking.

"Give the ID and password to your boss. Most of my merchandise is listed there. I'm sure we can do business again.'

"I'm sure we can."

I walked back around the desk, laid my briefcase on the desk, opened it, and put the cylinder with the uranium sample inside the briefcase.

Sirhan extended his hand, and we shook.

"Thank you Mr. Fenton."

"Thank you, sir. I will see you on Tuesday."

Sherman escorted me to the front door. He turned the bolt, and I exited giving him a friendly nod.

I was in my car and driving off the parking lot in almost no time. As soon as the rear wheels left the lot, I let out a shout. I couldn't believe this was working!

I drove a couple of miles before I thought to pick up my phone and call Henry. I started to tell him everything, but he stopped me and told me to come to his office, that we needed to talk and plan for the morning.

CHAPTER THIRTY-EIGHT

Nine AM, Thursday morning I was at 3301 West Memorial in Oklahoma City. Henry Pearson was standing in front of me with his right hand on the door handle and a briefcase in his left. He had worn a dark charcoal suit and looked very professional. I felt very underdressed in my khaki slacks and button down shirt.

"Well, Chad, are you ready for this?"

"I honestly don't know."

"It's OK to be nervous. Everything's going to be fine. Just stick to the script. I do the talking. You just sit back and relax as much as possible. This is going to work."

Henry opened the door, and I went in ahead of him. Inside light was pouring in through the curved glass behind us. Directly ahead of us was a large mahogany reception desk. On the wall behind the desk hung the FBI seal. A man in a dark suit sitting at the desk greeted us as we approached.

"May I help you?"

Henry spoke, "My name is Henry Pearson."

He handed a business card to the man.

"My client, Chad Fury is voluntarily turning himself in."

"Just a minute."

The man picked up a telephone. I probably should have paid attention to what that man was saying, but I was too nervous and anxious to listen. Instead, my eyes were taking in my surroundings. I noted the picture of the President of the United States to one side of the FBI seal, and the picture of FBI director on the other. There were several potted plants scattered around the area, and a large fichus tree close to the glass entrance.

As soon as the man at the desk hung up the telephone, another man and a woman, both sporting shoulder holsters, took up positions behind Henry and me. About thirty seconds later I saw a face I recognized coming toward us, out of a hallway.

The man approached Henry. "I'm Special Agent August Milton."

"Henry Pearson. It's a pleasure to meet you, sir."

"Likewise."

The two shook hands and then Agent Milton looked my direction.

"Mr. Fury. I'm surprised to see here today."

I nodded, but did not speak.

Agent Milton looked at Henry and back at me.

"What can I do for you gentlemen?"

Henry took out a business card and handed it to Agent Milton.

"Mr. Fury is my client; I will be his legal counsel, representing him in all matters pertaining to his current situation and speaking for him."

There was a momentary look of frustration on Agent Milton's face, but it passed as quickly as it came.

"Is there anything either of you would like to say before I read Mr. Fury his rights?"

Henry cleared his throat.

"Yes. I want everyone here to know that Mr. Fury came in of his own free will, and should be shown the respect and courtesy accorded to any individual who is cooperating with law enforcement.

Also we are here because my client is in possession of certain knowledge that would be of great interest to the FBI and other agencies. He would like to supply that knowledge to you for certain considerations."

Agent Milton grimaced.

"You mean he wants to cut a deal."

"That's not the wording I would choose, but it is essentially accurate."

Agent Milton asked me to extend my arms. I looked at Henry, who nodded back to me. I put my arms out and silver shackles snapped around my wrists. I took comfort in the fact that at least my hands were in front of me instead of behind me.

Agent Milton recited the Miranda rights, and then took hold of my left arm just above the elbow and guided me down a hallway and into a conference room.

Inside the room Agent Milton gestured toward the chairs on the far side of the oval, oak table. I sat in one of the red cloth chairs, and Henry sat on my left. Henry placed the briefcase between us.

I must have looked uncomfortable, because Henry looked at me and said, "Remember Chad, we talked about this. Everything's going to be just fine."

I nodded and I saw Agent Milton taking a seat.

Agent Milton reached into his shirt pocket and pulled out a digital recorder.

Henry sat his briefcase on the table, opened it and placed his digital recorder on the table. Both men turned their recorders on at the same time.

Agent Milton spoke first.

"This is Special Agent August Milton. I am in a conference room at the Oklahoma City FBI office, 3301 West Memorial. With me are Chadwick Fenton Fury and Mr. Henry Pearson, legal counsel for Chad Fury. Refer to this recording's metadata timestamp for the date and time."

Henry spoke.

"This is Henry Pearson, attorney for Chad Fury. Ditto."

Special agent Milton leaned forward.

"Mr. Fury. Why are you here today?"

I looked at Henry, and I kept quiet.

"Mr. Fury is here to turn himself in. He is in possession of knowledge that would be of great interest to the FBI and other agencies. He would like to supply that knowledge to you for certain considerations."

Special Agent Milton looked at Henry with what appeared to be contempt.

"Mr. Pearson. I would like to hear Mr. Fury answer my questions for himself."

Henry nodded at me, and I said what we had rehearsed.

"I have retained Henry Pearson as my counsel and authorized him to speak on my behalf regarding all matters pertaining to me. I will remain mute."

Special agent Milton placed both palms on the table top and pushed himself deep into the chair. He looked at Henry.

"Well, I guess this is between you and me, Mr. Pearson. So, one more time, why are you here? You could have gone to any law enforcement agency; sheriff, police, anything. Why choose the FBI?"

"My client is in possession of knowledge that must be acted upon quickly by the authorities that have the ability to use the information."

"Perhaps you had better describe the information."

Henry reached into his briefcase and pulled out a piece of paper. He handed it to agent Milton.

"This is a signed and notarized confession. This confession was made by Eric Schwartz. The confession states that he and two other men named in the document killed Emily Smith. He also states that Chad Fury had no connection to him, and was in no part responsible for Emily Smith's death."

Agent Milton looked over the paper. "That's fine, but you could have presented that directly to the District Attorney. You didn't need to bring it here. Plus, there's nothing here to bargain with."

"True. This is not the information that your agency should be concerned with. It is ancillary, and I wanted it in your hands along with the people that need to see it. Mr. Schwartz will be turned over to the authorities today, along with the original signed confession."

"That's well and good, but what is this other information?"

"Let's start with Mr. Fury's request. My client is asking for full immunity from prosecution for any and all matters related to any event up through today. He is also requesting that none of his family members or friends can be charged with any crime, for any reason, related to any of his activities."

"You don't want much."

"I am aware of the magnitude of the request. Mr. Fury is in possession of an address where two adult women and several children are being held for the purposes of human trafficking."

Agent Milton frowned.

"We do not take kindly to bargaining with the lives of women and children."

"My client is not bargaining with anyone's lives. He wants to see these people rescued. As a result of other information my client possesses, these people will be rescued."

"You need to explain."

"Do you know the name Sirhan Jadiddian?"

"I do."

"Yesterday evening, Mr. Jadiddian agreed to sell certain goods to my client."

Henry pulled another sheet of paper from the briefcase.

"This is a list of the goods that Mr. Jadiddian agreed to sell to Mr. Fury, my client. The list includes assault rifles, ammunition, grenades, land mines, and sixteen kilograms of weapons grade uranium."

"Is this real?"

"I assure you, this is very real. My client gave Mr. Jadiddian a deposit of fifty thousand dollars cash toward this sale."

"Do you have any proof of all of this besides this piece of paper?"

Mr. Pearson pulled a latex surgical glove from his coat pocket and placed it on his right hand. He then carefully removed the metal cylinder from the briefcase.

"According to Mr. Jadiddian, this cylinder contains five grams of enriched uranium. I cannot testify to the contents of the cylinder, but I can tell you that the outside of the cylinder has fingerprints belonging to two individuals, Sirhan Jadiddian and Chad Fury."

Agent Milton stared silently at the metal cylinder for several seconds.

"Who else knows about this?"

"Funny you should ask. Now is as good of a time as any to tell you about this."

Henry reached into his shirt pocket and removed his cell phone. He placed it on the table.

"My cell phone is on. I have it muted. I am on a call right now. The State Attorney General's office is on the other end of this call. I'm assuming they've conferenced several other people in by now."

Henry took the phone off of mute, put it on speaker, and placed it back on the table in front of him.

"Good morning ladies gentlemen. My phone is no longer on mute; I've placed it on speaker. Would you like to introduce yourselves to Agent Milton?"

Several voices on the other end of the line introduced themselves while Agent Milton quietly ground his teeth.

At the end of the introductions, Henry made his speech.

"Let me sum this up for you, ladies and gentlemen. On

Tuesday at two PM, Sirhan Jadiddian will be bringing illegal arms and sixteen kilograms of weapons grade uranium to a location known to my client.

Mr. Jadiddian expects to sell the items to my client for two million in cash and one point seven five million in gold. This deal will be happening at the same location where two women and several children are being held for the purposes of human trafficking."

Agent Milton picked up his recorder and turned it off.

"There's a man and a woman standing outside this room. If you need something, ask one of them."

Agent Milton stood and exited the room.

Henry told the voices on the call the Mr. Melton had departed, and the parties on the call made a few comments before hanging up.

I looked at Henry.

"Well, what do you think?"

"I think we've won, and they're going to figure that out shortly."

Henry and I sat there for about an hour and finally a new face came into the room. The woman was wearing blue surgical gloves and carrying a small brown paper bag. She didn't say a word or even acknowledge us when we spoke. She picked up the metal cylinder, put it in the bag, and left.

Henry and I talked for a while, mostly about nothing, and finally we troubled our guards for water, which they brought to us with great efficiency.

Just as I was telling Henry that I was getting tired of this, another new face came into the room. This time it was a dark skinned, African-American woman, about five and one-half feet tall. Her hair was pulled back tightly behind her head, forcing her cheekbones and chin to look sharp and imposing. Her eyes looked very intelligent. I got the feeling that she could size up just about any situation in a matter of seconds.

She adjusted her navy blue suit before sitting down

across from us.

"Gentlemen. I am Agent Saysha Givens. I am in charge of this office.

The two of you have successfully turned a normally busy day into a firestorm. I have been on the phone most of the time since you arrived here this morning. I've been fielding calls from everyone from the Oklahoma State Attorney General to directors of agencies that most people don't even know exist."

I just couldn't keep my mouth shut.

"I'm so sorry for your inconvenience."

The sarcasm was so thick you could spread it with a trowel.

Henry almost laughed and then gently scolded me.

"Chad. You need to let me do the talking."

Henry laid his right hand on the table and turned his palm up.

"Agent Givens, ma'am. The ball is in your court. How do intend to proceed?"

"Mr. Fury will be our guest for a while at the Federal Transfer Facility on McArthur Boulevard. He will wait there while we work with you on collecting and processing your evidence. You will be informed of our plans on a need to know basis."

Henry leaned forward.

"I will have unrestricted access to my client at all times."

"I can't guarantee that request."

"That wasn't a request."

Agent Givens leaned back in her chair. She folded her hands and let them rest in her lap. She was silent for several seconds.

"Mr. Pearson. Do you have your demands for a deal written out?"

Henry reached into the briefcase and pulled out a multi-page document stapled in the upper left corner. He placed the document in front of me and turned to the last page.

"Chad you need to sign this, just above my name."

Henry handed me a pen, I signed, and he slid the paper to Agent Givens.

Henry spoke up.

"Take his handcuffs off. We've demonstrated that he's not running. There's no need for the restraints."

Agent Givens called to the man standing outside the door, and in a few seconds, my hands were free.

"Mr. Pearson. Mr. Fury will be held at the Federal Transfer Facility. We need to know where he is at all times while this situation is discussed.

You may ride with him, or you may follow him over. You can stay in the same cell if you like; and you may come and go as you please. If you gentlemen will follow me."

Henry held up a hand.

"Not so fast. I need to make a phone call."

Henry dialed a number.

"Jim. It's Henry. How's Eric doing...That's good...We're ready for him. Bring him to the Federal Transfer Facility...It's on McArthur Boulevard...just look up the address...They'll be expecting you."

We were escorted out of the building, and I was placed in a black SUV. Henry decided to follow in his car.

It was a short trip to the facility, and I was placed in an ordinary cell. Henry followed me inside. Very soon we found ourselves alone and I felt like we could talk freely.

"Henry, do you still have your cell phone? No pun intended."

Henry laughed.

"Sure."

"I think it's time I called my mother...she deserves an explanation."

Henry retreated to a corner of the cell in a pretense of giving me some privacy.

CHAPTER THIRTY-NINE

By Tuesday morning I had decided that my stay at the Federal Transfer Facility wasn't too bad.

Uncle Allan had been to see me twice, and brought me a few changes of clothes and some books to read. Mom came down from Tulsa and had seen me three times. She was pretty upset that I had lied to her; she even slapped me for that. I can't say I blame her one bit. But mothers can be pretty forgiving and I think she understands now.

Mom has a pretty bizarre sense of humor. She made cookies and brought them on Sunday; she made them in the shape of files. She gave a few to the guards, and soon Doris Fury was their best friend.

But, back to Tuesday. It was about nine AM when agents of the FBI and the OSBI where standing in my cell helping me get dressed. I needed help because I was being wired up.

The FBI had placed a microphone in my shirt collar. The buttons on my shirt had been replaced to match a special button near the top of my shirt. The button was a camera. The batteries were small, and had been sewn into the shirt. The reception of the camera and microphone were tested, and everything seemed to be in working order.

Agent Givens made an appearance after I was dressed and the equipment had been tested. She seemed tense.

"Mr. Fury. It looks like you may be getting everything you want. I know you will if we can get Sirhan."

"Yes, ma'am. I will do what I can."

"You will do exactly what you're told!"

I was shocked by her sudden outburst, but then there was a lot riding on this for her too. She continued.

"You are to make the deal. When the deal's complete, I want you to say 'It was a pleasure doing business with you.' That's when the swat team will come in. Your job at that moment will be to take cover. Get out of the way. Once bullets start flying, I can't guarantee your safety."

"I understand."

"If something should go wrong before the deal is closed, just yell 'help.'"

"I thought you'd give me some kind of distress word."

"I just did. This isn't the movies. If you're in trouble, no fancy code word's going to do you any good. This is a dangerous situation, Mr. Fury. I don't like the fact that you've forced me to put you in it."

I had never considered that anyone at the FBI had that much concern for my wellbeing. I guess that's why they're called the good guys.

Agent Givens went on to explain the plan. I was to ride over to the warehouse in the cab of a semi. Inside the trailer would be some crates and large boxes at the far end. Behind the crates and boxes would be armed agents with vests and guns. They would come pouring out of the truck when the deal was complete. At the front of the trailer was a large duffle bag full of cash, and a small trunk with gold coins and gold rounds.

We arrived at the warehouse at one PM.

Thanks to a phone call Henry had made to Vitaly, the warehouse foreman was expecting us. We backed up to a dock and opened the trailer doors. The warehouse foreman brought over a palate jack for our use. Five men dressed in blue jeans and tee shirts walked over and introduced themselves.

"Hello, Chad. My name is Carl. Givens sent us. We're your crew to help load and unload. This is Tim, Brad, Phil, and Randy. We're each armed."

Carl turned around to show me the pistol visibly protruding from his waistband.

"Most of the people in this building are armed. We'd all look out of place if your crew was unarmed. By the way, you're not the only one wearing a wire. One of us will always be close enough to record what's going on. If you need something, yell for me first. I'll be the top man in your crew. You shouldn't need to talk to anyone else. Good luck, Chad."

With that, the men set about looking busy. Two of the men took the palate jack and shifted a few boxes around in the truck. The man who had been speaking to me had a brief conversation with the dock foreman about something, and a couple of others stood around and looked useless.

It was one-fifty when a blue semi pulled up to the dock next to us. A familiar figure strolled across the warehouse floor toward me and called out, "Mr. Fenton. How good to see you."

"Hello, Mr. Jadiddian. A pleasure as always."

As he approached we each put out an arm and shook hands.

"I assume you have the payment in full?"

"I do, and I assume you have my entire order…including the uranium?"

Sirhan turned and called out for Sherman. Sherman motioned to another man who opened the trailer doors. The two men entered the truck and came out each holding one end of a metal trunk.

"I would open the trunk, but that would not be too healthy for any of us. Here's a Geiger counter."

Sirhan took a device from a third man and moved it

around the case. The device clicked and popped.

I turned toward my crew.

"Carl. The payment."

Carl took two men with him into the truck. Carl exited with the duffle bag and placed it at my feet. The two other men carried the trunk to me and sat it by the bag. Carl unzipped the bag and opened the trunk.

"Very good, Mr. Fenton. I like doing business with a professional."

"Likewise. May I see the rest?"

"Of course."

I was nervous. I couldn't help it. As Sirhan's men were pulling pallets and crates into the open area of the warehouse. I looked at my watch several times. Sirhan noticed.

"Is there something wrong, Mr. Fenton?"

"No. Just a lot on my mind. This is going to be a very busy day for me."

Sirhan passed it off, and I tried to relax.

As the last box came off of the truck Sirhan started to grab the duffle bag.

"Not so fast. I haven't looked over my merchandise."

I turned toward my crew.

"Carl. Take a look at what we're buying."

Carl called to the rest of his men; they went to the crates and started opening them with pry bars they had borrowed from the warehouse foreman.

After a bit, Carl called back to me, "It's all here. It looks good Mr. Fenton."

I faced Sirhan and extended my arm.

"It's been a pleasure doing business with you."

With that men with pistols in bullet proof vests started pouring out of my truck amidst yells of 'Stop! FBI!'

Sirhan's men pulled their weapons, and someone fired a shot. Sirhan was near me; he grabbed the duffle bag and started running.

I hesitated. I had expected Sirhan to run out of the

warehouse, but instead, he ran into the shadows between rows of pallets, boxes, and shelving.

I bolted after him. I jumped to the top of the crates and ran along the top scanning for Sirhan. I spotted him heading toward the far wall, and a metal door.

I followed Sirhan by leaping across the tops of crates. Sirhan reached the door and went inside the dark hole. I had expected it to be an exit, but instead it was some kind of room. I waited. I didn't know whether to follow him in or not. Just as I was about to jump down and follow, Sirhan exited. The duffle bag was on one shoulder and he was dragging a woman, by an arm. She was gagged and her wrists were tied.

By the time I had recognized that the woman was Lisa, Sirhan was moving past me toward the open area of the warehouse. I ran a couple of steps across the top of the crates and leapt off head first, arms extended. My hands hit the back of Sirhan's shoulders and he went sprawling to the ground. Sirhan tried to get up, but I pushed him back down with a foot.

Lisa ran to me, and I removed her gag. I hit the cement floor with my fingertips and produced my claws. I used a claw to cut her wrists free.

"Chad! I never thought I would see you again! How did you find me?"

Sirhan tried again to get up, and again I pushed him back to the cement floor with my foot.

Lisa threw her arms around me. We kissed a little too long, and then she buried her head in my shoulder and sobbed.

CHAPTER FORTY

Well, Mr. Moon, that's pretty much the whole story, and I can tell that you're getting tired by the way that you're sinking in the west. It won't be long until you're replaced by the garish sun. But before you go, there's a few other things you ought to know.

First, I got the deal I was after. Henry Pearson did a great job seeing my deal through to the end. But it took a while. I had to spend several more nights at the Federal Transfer Facility.

On Thursday, two days after Sirhan's arrest I had a visit from Agent Givens. She escorted me from my cell to a conference room of sorts. There were four other agents in the room, three men and one woman. The introductions were brief, but the visit was lengthy. Agent Givens did most of the talking.

"Before we begin, Mr. Fury, I thought you would like to know that we rescued fourteen children at the warehouse, ten girls and four boys all ranging from ages five through twelve."

"I'm glad to hear it."

"Also, there was Lisa who you know and another woman named Alice. The women were admitted to the hospital for evaluation and care. They had been cut many times over their entire bodies."

I tried to look surprised.

"Really. Are they OK?"

"I'm told they're fine. But, that brings me to something else. Mr. Fury, Sirhan and the people at the warehouse are starting to name names. We're hearing a few people mention a group they call the Company. I'm more than a little concerned because I've never heard about the Company before. What can you tell me about it?"

"Honestly, I don't know that much. You probably know more than I do."

"I doubt that, Chad. I get the feeling you know a lot more. Any information you can give us might help us to bring down what appears to be a very vicious and powerful organization."

"If I could tell you anything, I would."

"Alright. This is not an interrogation, so I won't press you for any information. We are here to help you with your new identity."

I showed genuine surprise at that.

"What new identity? I've gone through a whole lot just to get my life back, not to become someone else."

"Believe it or not, I do know how you feel. I've helped several people get into the Witness Security Program. You know it better as the Witness Protection Program."

"Witness Protection?"

"Don't be naïve. This organization, the Company, appears to be powerful and ruthless. Then there's all of the other groups that were using the warehouse where the sting was conducted. There's a lot of people that have a lot of reasons to be angry with you. Your testimony is going to put a lot of people away for a very long time."

"What if I don't want to testify?"

"Really. You mean to sit there and tell me that after all you went through to get Sirhan and to get that place shut down, you're suddenly going to let all those people go free?"

"All I really wanted was my life back. Witness Protection isn't getting my life back."

"Face it Chad, your life's gone. Yes, every charge against you has been dropped, but just what do you think you're life's going to be like from now on? The people using that warehouse lost a lot because of you. There's a price on your head. There's at least two domestic terror groups that were implicated in that warehouse, not to mention the human traffickers and drug dealers. For your own safety and the safety of your friends and family, you need to disappear."

I knew she was right. Even without having a price on my head, my life couldn't be the same after all of this. There was no going back.

"OK. You win. I need your help. What do I have to do?"

"Ed, Bill, Glenn, and Sarah are with the US Marshals Service, which oversees the Witness Security Program. They are here to talk to you about your new identity and how the program works."

Agent Givens left the room while those four people showed me files, folders, and documents. They had me sign a bunch of papers using my old name and the new name they gave me, Drake Edward Manning. They also told me I would be living in Las Vegas.

After all of that was done, Agent Givens returned and we sat alone in the room. She said we needed to talk in private.

"Fury. I want to know something."

"What can I tell you?"

"Hmm. What indeed. You can tell me the truth."

"I don't know what you're talking about."

"I'm talking about you. Just what are you?"

"I don't know what mean? What am I?"

"Cut the crap. Or, maybe you really don't know what I'm talking about? Did you forget that you were wired for audio and video when you went chasing after Sirhan?"

"Oh, my, G…"

"So you did forget."

"Well, yeah. I did."

"I've spent a lot of hours looking over that video, and I don't have an explanation for what I saw. I've been keeping it out of other people's hands until I've talked to you. I'm hoping talking to you will help me decide what to do with it."

"I'd appreciate it if no one else ever saw that video. Why have you kept it quiet?"

"Just what am I supposed to say if I show it to someone? 'And this was shot while Chad Fury jumped straight up seventeen feet in the air to land on top of a stack crates?

This was taken as he jumped across the isles from crate top to crate top?

And this is him leaping head first onto Sirhan Jadiddian, knocking him to the ground?

Or how about this is where Chad's hand suddenly changed into something like a lizard and he used his claws to cut through the ropes on that woman's wrists?'

You tell me. I need a rational explanation and I don't have one."

"Truthfully, I don't have an explanation either, at least not one that anybody's going to believe."

"Try me."

"I'd rather not. It's best if I keep my secrets."

"I work for the F…B…I. I know a little something about secrets, Fury. People pay a huge price for keeping them. From the looks of this, I'd bet that keeping your secret will cost you a lot."

"What will it cost for me to let people know?"

Saysha didn't answer. She frowned and folded her arms.

"Fury! You're going to make my annual polygraph review hell!"

She escorted me back to my cell in silence.

The thought of that video being out there bothered me, and quite frankly it still does. It may come back to haunt me.

All in all, the rest of my stay there wasn't too bad. I had regular visits from Uncle Allan, mom, and Lisa.

On Friday, I had a visit from mom. I told her about the witness protection program, and a little about why I was being given a new identity.

Mom cried. She said that now that she finally had her son back that she couldn't bear losing him again. I agreed with her, and I could tell that both of us knew that there was no way I could ever go back to being Chad Fury. This was as permanent as death.

There's some other things still hanging out there that concern me. Like Vitaly's idea that I owe him a favor. I could lose a lot of sleep over that one, if I choose to think too much about it.

Then, there's Sirhan. When he grabbed the bag of cash, he ran straight for where Lisa was being held. He took Lisa. Why did he take Lisa? The only thing I can imagine is that he's tied up very closely with the Company.

Sirhan also ran that Dark Realms website. There's a whole lot more to that man than I know, and I'm concerned that I'm not done with him.

And there's the Sisterhood. The Matron came to see me yesterday. She told me that the Grand Council, whatever that is, was very impressed with how I delivered Kane to them. They had decided that they should maintain a relationship with me, regardless of my impertinence.

The Grand Council felt I could be useful to them. They also were very grateful for the knowledge they were gaining from Kane and as a reward, Lisa would continue to be my handler, and they would continue to fund a bank account for me to use whenever I was assisting them.

The Matron also gave me a transresinator. She taught me how to use it to contact the Sisterhood in case of an emergency.

The Matron also informed me that the Sisterhood had influenced the FBI and the US Marshals in regards to my going into the witness protection program.

It seems the Matron was responsible for choosing Las Vegas as the place I was going to live. According to the her, that's where the Sisterhood wants me.

Lisa was grateful too. She did two things for me. First, she was the one that selected my new name in the witness protection program. She wanted me to have a cool sounding name; Drake is an old Celtic name meaning dragon.

Lisa also saw to it that the Sisterhood got my car back. That's it parked in the street below; the black Ford Interceptor. The Sisterhood replaced the upholstery and performed some upgrades. I don't know what 'upgrades' means, but Lisa just laughs and tells me to try to keep the wheels on the ground.

And then there's me. Chad Fury's gone and he'll never be back. Drake is leaving for Las Vegas in just a few hours with his car packed with a few personal things that used to belong to Chad.

I can't guarantee what lies ahead, but whatever happens, it could turn out to be a hell of a ride.

ABOUT THE AUTHOR

Doug Gorden grew up in southern Missouri, and moved to Oklahoma over thirty years ago. Since migrating to Oklahoma he's tried his hand at several different careers including retail store manager, public school teacher, computer programmer, and licensed private investigator. In his most recent career he is a security analyst and performs computer forensics for a major corporation.

Doug takes every opportunity to be a public speaker on the subjects of computer crime, computer investigations, and human trafficking.

In his free time, Doug his enjoys the company of his family which currently includes one wife, two dogs, and four cats.

He also writes.

Made in the USA
San Bernardino, CA
14 August 2014